Virulent Winds

By:
Jim Clonts

PublishAmerica
Baltimore

First printing

ISBN: 1-59286-917-3
PUBLISHED BY PUBLISHAMERICA, LLLP
www.publishamerica.com
Baltimore

Printed in the United States of America

Dedication:

This book is dedicated to the men and women who wear the uniforms of the United States Armed Forces. These professional warriors, acting with discipline, honor and commitment, bear the burden of vigilance so we might enjoy the fruits of liberty. To the men and women who guard our skies, sail the oceans above and below and trade steel with enemies on the battlefield I thank you for your service and sacrifice. This book is for you.

Acknowledgments:

I want to thank Bill Parker, my friend and Webmaster from Parker Information Resources, who had confidence from the start that this book would go to press. I want to thank PublishAmerica, for believing in my potential. Finally, I want to thank my wife, Cindy, for her infinite patience and enduring love.

SOUTH OF THE DMZ, REPUBLIC OF KOREA
1400 HRS LOCAL TIME

"Olympus, Vapor Flight, say picture."

"Vapor Flight, bogey dope, two bandits, bearing Shasta 330 at 85, southbound, 440 knots."

Two North Korean MiGs were entering the DMZ about 85 miles northwest of the bulls-eye point, code-named Shasta. Two patrolling USAF F-15C Eagles were being vectored for the intercept. The North Koreans often flew patrols along the border, but they rarely entered the DMZ and when they did they were generally looking for trouble. This constituted a treaty violation, but lately the North Koreans seemed less concerned with treaties and more concerned with testing the military waters. Their economy was in shambles and their people were starving. There was a general feeling that if war was ever to come with the South it would happen sooner rather than later. Tensions were high and standing orders said shoot down anything that comes across the border. Vapor Lead knew this and he was sure the MiG pilots knew it as well.

"Olympus, Vapor Flight requests vector for bandits."

"Roger, Vapor, take heading 300, base plus 20, vector for bandits." The base altitude for the day was 10,000 feet. Base numbers were used as an added level of security, above and beyond their secure voice radios.

"Coming left, Thump," he called to his wingman. Captain David Olmstead, call sign Hawkeye, whipped his sleek F-15 Eagle up onto its left wing and pulled hard until the heading 300 was at the top of his heads-up display. Glancing back over his right shoulder he could see his wingman, Lieutenant Pete Fletcher, call sign Thumper, was still in position, after the violent 5G turn.

"Okay, Thump, lets blow and go," he called. "Vapor Flight is buster."

He nodded briefly at the gray helmeted figure in the other plane and smoothly pushed the throttles forward into afterburner. The twin General Electric F-100 turbofans produced a fiery orange glow and a tongue of blue flame forty feet long as raw fuel dumped into the exhaust stream. Diamond shockwaves formed in the blue glow. The combined 50,000 lbs of thrust propelled the two Eagles to over 600 knots, just under the speed of sound. Olmstead eased back on the stick until the nose of the sleek fighter was forty degrees above the horizon. The hands of the altimeter wound up madly as the Eagles rocketed to thirty thousand feet in less than a minute. Lt Pete Fletcher, eight years younger than his flight lead and fresh out of F-15 RTU, was finally starting to get the hang of flying the F-15.

Switching his radar display to Supplemental Remote Targeting Mode, Olmstead soon located the two MiGs off the nose at 70 miles via a data link between himself and the E3 AWACS' radar 100 miles to the south. Initially they'd run with their own onboard radar in standby so the MiGs would not detect their radar emissions, giving their position away. They were using the AWACS' radar through the data link and would turn on their own radars when ready to fire missiles.

"North Korean fighter aircraft on heading 180, Flight Level 330, this is Olympus on Guard," the AWACS plane announced. "You are in violation of the Demilitarized Zone at this time. Turn heading 360 and reduce airspeed immediately or you will be engaged." Silence.

The North Koreans were radar silent as well, obviously running their standard ground controlled intercept. The controller on the ground uses his radar to set up the engagement, even going so far as telling the MiGs when to shoot. The MiG-29s had their own data link and could use remote targeting as well. They were also equipped with radars that gave their pilots the capability of locating, targeting and engaging with no help from a ground controller, a concept becoming standard for the Russians, but still foreign to the North Koreans.

The MiGs' vector was directly towards them, head-to-head with closure of better than a thousand miles an hour. The NKs were playing chicken. Fine. *We'll see who the chicken is soon enough,* Olmstead thought, snugging his parachute straps tight. He had no time to notice the still snowy and quite beautiful mountains rushing under them on this cold, clear day in March. A half-century ago those snowy mountains ran red with blood as United Nations forces repelled the North Koreans, pushing them back above the 38th parallel. Now that snow was about to get stained once again.

"Olympus, Vapor Flight, remote tied on two bandits 50 miles. Parrot check," Olmstead said.

"Confirmed bandits, Vapor, cleared to engage, cleared hot."

A parrot check referred to the IFF. This system, Identification Friend or Foe, is a transponder in each allied aircraft that is set to a specific code of the day. Like the AWACS plane the F-15's radar can interrogate those transponders. If it gets back the right code, it's a "friendly", if not, it's a "bandit". In this case the AWACS interrogated the MiGs for the Eagles, whose radars were still in standby. The answer was silence, not a friendly.

"Roger, Vapor is hungry. Thump, go active, and engage. I'll take left, you take right. Let's put on our game face," Olmstead told his wingman, ordering him to turn on his radar as well. Both men went to radiate on their radars. Immediately their powerful Hughes APG-70 radars locked up the MiGs.

"Two's ray-gun, engaging, locked on 40 miles," Fletcher said, while clicking his oxygen mask securely into place. It had been casually dangling from the left side bayonet clip, but in the high G maneuvering of combat the loose bayonet clip can turn into a knife, slashing the face open.

Olmstead was locked onto the MiG on the left and Fletcher the one on the right. The MiGs looked to be in a loose deuce formation, a mirror image of Olmstead and Fletcher's formation. The 'loose deuce' formation consisted of two aircraft abeam each other and separated by a few hundred feet. This formation ensured that the two aircraft would be clear of each other when they fired their missiles. It also ensured that either fighter could become the 'engaged' fighter with his partner covering his tail throughout a close-in dogfight. In today's modern age of air combat the first shots were beyond visual range, or BVR, and both fighters stayed clear of each other until the missiles were on the way.

Olmstead smiled grimly beneath his gray oxygen mask. He had expected the NKs to be in a welded-wing formation, the wingman very close and covering his leader's tail at all times. *Apparently they've learned a few new tricks. Well, loose deuce won't matter to the AMRAAM II. In fact a loose deuce combat spread will make target discrimination all the easier*, he thought. A valid AIM-130, Advanced Medium Range Air to Air Missile, shot was as close to a guaranteed kill as you could come.

Olmstead pressed a sequence of buttons on his HOTAS, hands on throttle and stick system, and selected an AIM-130 AMRAAM II for launch. In the cockpit a thousand feet to the right, Fletcher selected the same. They were each armed with four AIM-130 AMRAAM II and four AIM-9X2 Sidewinders. The AMRAAM II was an active homing missile, guided by its own onboard radar. The Sidewinder was a heat seeker. Closing beak to beak the optimum range of the AMRAAM II was around 25-30 miles. The Sidewinder seeker head could see out almost 10 miles on a clear day, but that range diminished dramatically in haze or clouds. Once fired, both missiles home on their targets independently of the F-15, leaving the fighter free to maneuver away from the oncoming MiGs and their missiles.

At better than a thousand knots closure I'll have a shot in a few seconds, Olmstead thought. The two Eagles were abeam each other and well-separated ensuring clearance from each other's missile launches. The MiGs were still running radar silent. They passed 30 miles and still no radar activity from the MiGs. A small box on the bottom left of his HUD indicated the AIM-130 was in range. Olmstead decided to wait until 25 miles, if the MiGs stayed radar silent. He knew they would have to bring their radars up in order to lock on and take a shot. This gave him the chance to get in a little closer and ensure a good shot, making sure he was well within range and giving the MiGs minimum chance to outmaneuver his missiles.

At that moment his radar-warning receiver (RWR) suddenly came to life in an array of flashing lights. The MiGs up till now were running radar off. They had gone active on their radar and had the F-15s locked up. After only three seconds of active radar the warning receiver produced a high pitch tone indicating the enemy radar mode had switched to continuous wave mode, a missile guidance mode. Just as Olmstead was about to squeeze his own trigger he saw something out of the corner of his eye that distracted him.

He looked up from his radar and saw two corkscrewing smoke trails off the nose. *What the hell! Where did they come from?* The smoke trails were not moving in his windscreen, meaning they were homing on his flight. *That's not possible! Holy shit, we're under attack*, Olmstead said to himself. In a beyond visual range missile environment it is imperative to get the first shot. They'd already lost the advantage.

"Thumper, missile launch, break right, chaff, ECM to active," he called to his wingman, who was already in the hard breaking turn to put the missile on his left beam.

Missiles guided by pulse-Doppler radar require differential velocities to lock onto and track a target. They can be made to lose lock if the fighter's flight path is perpendicular to the missile's, thereby reducing the relative velocities to zero. The pulse Doppler radar filters out everything that isn't moving relative to the missile, such as a mountain. This perpendicular position is called the Doppler-notch. By flying in the "notch", the radar believes the aircraft to be ground clutter and the missile loses its lock. Olmstead and Fletcher were desperately trying to put their fighters in that notch position.

With a radar homing missile inbound all thoughts go on the defense. Defeat the most current threat then move to the offense. With the missile systems of today that pull 50 Gs a fighter pilot, no matter how good, just can't ignore the inbound missiles. The hard part was keeping situational awareness so an attack can instantly be prosecuted after evading the missile.

Damn, thought Olmstead, as he put his fighter in the notch and punched out chaff, bundles of aluminum strips that decoy radar missiles. *They must have long-burn AA-10s or possibly the new long-burn version of the AA-12.*

AA-10s can have either semi-active radar or infrared guidance. The AA-12 was the AMRAAMski, the Soviet copy of the AIM-130. The newest versions were rumored to have greater range than the American AIM-130. Long range and lethal described both missiles. They could reach out and touch you.

Olmstead's RWR gear showed the enemy radar at his nine o'clock. If the missiles were AA-10s then the MiG had to keep his radar on and pointed at the Eagle for his missile to guide. The AA-12 had no such restriction since, like the AMRAAM II, it carried its own onboard radar. The pilot could maneuver and press home a new attack while the first missile was in flight. At this moment it didn't matter which missile was homing on him. He just had to defeat it.

Craning his neck to the right he could see the long white smoke trail tracking toward him in irregular turns left and right. He rolled inverted and pulled hard on the stick in a desperate split S maneuver to avoid the tracking missile, punching chaff as he dove. The missile must have liked the chaff because it sensed passing a chaff cloud and detonated by proximity fuse several hundred feet above and behind the diving Eagle. He continued to pull the stick until he was level again, having lost 12000 feet in the process.

Turning towards the attacking MiGs, he lit the blowers and lifted the nose. He locked them up again on his radar at 15 miles. Out of the corner of his eye he saw a flash and a lone cloud of black smoke.

"Vapor Flight, check," he called to Fletcher. No answer. He didn't hear an ELT (Emergency Locator Transmitter) on the Guard frequency.

"Olympus, Vapor Flight, is defensive. One man down, negative ELT," he called to the AWACS.

"Roger, Vapor, Saber 23 Flight is inbound, ETA 5 minutes," AWACS called, indicating two more Eagles were being vectored to the scene.

His left side AMRAAM II was still selected. Locking up the bandit at fifteen miles, he fired. "Fox three, Vapor," he called out to nobody in particular.

The AMRAAM II ran straight and true to the madly maneuvering MiG, that now found itself suddenly on the defensive. The fight was no longer between two men, but man against missile, flesh and blood against gyros and microelectronics. Olmstead couldn't see the MiG at fifteen miles, but the tiny flash and cloud of smoke said it all.

The second MiG was still coming on strong on an attack vector. Inside of ten miles Olmstead switched to Sidewinders. Once again he was beaten to the punch as a missile leapt off the rails of the MiG in long plume of white smoke and raced toward him in a desperate face shot. He threw his fighter into a hard descending left turn, pulled his throttles to idle to lessen his heat signature and began ejecting flares, hot burning chunks of magnesium. The AA-8 Aphid heat seeker went for the flares and flashed by not more than twenty feet behind.

Pulling hard into the North Korean Olmstead found himself in a rolling scissors maneuver with the MiG, each turning into each other and crossing paths trying to bleed off speed and get in behind the other. It didn't take long before Olmstead realized he wasn't dealing with an amateur here. Intelligence on North Korean pilots indicated they were not trained in Air Combat Maneuver and would not engage in close-in dog fighting. He was supposed to fire his missiles at long range then scoot back over the border and run for home. *This guy must have missed that day of class*, Olmstead thought, his face red with exertion, straining against the G forces.

After several course reversals Olmstead tried the unexpected. He pulled back on the stick, slammed it left, and executed a perfect barrel roll leveling out to the left and abeam the MiG. Olmstead notice the swollen dorsal spine on this MiG and realized this was no ordinary MiG-29, but an advanced variant of the model, a MiG-29SMT. The MiG driver pulled up into a high yo-yo maneuver designed to trade speed for altitude, falling back slightly. He could clearly see the black helmeted figure in the MiG looking directly at him.

Then the unexpected happened: another missile came off the rails of the MiG. *Who the hell is this guy shooting at*, Olmstead wondered? *I'm over ninety degrees off his nose*. That was when the impossible happened: the missile flew ahead about a hundred feet, pivoted in space, in an impossibly tight turn, and headed straight for him. *Holy shit*, Olmstead said aloud as he rolled the F-15 left and pulled hard to avoid the missile, pumping flares as he went. *That was no AA-8! Only an Archer can move like that, an Archer with a helmet-mounted sighting system.*

The AA-11 Archer's engagement envelope was enormous, with an over the shoulder capability when mated with the helmet-mounted sight. The sight allowed the pilot to simply look at his enemy and the missile seeker would slave to that spot in space. This meant the missile could see beyond its normal field of view. The missile would leave the rail in terminal guidance mode, turning immediately in the direction it knew the enemy was located. With its large forward control surfaces and vectored thrust rocket motor, the Vympel R-73, NATO code-named AA-11 Archer, had the ability to pull almost 50 Gs. With a proximity fuse and flare rejection countermeasure programming, the AA-11 was the world's best heat seeking missile bar none.

It was lucky for Olmstead he rolled and loaded on the Gs when he did. The missile had been locked on the hot avionics compartment just behind the cockpit. Instead it struck the right engine's burner can, blowing the burner segment clean off the aircraft and shelling out the right side engine with the fragments. Engine firelights illuminated and Olmstead ran through the engine shut down procedure from memory, all the while diving and turning away in an attempt to disengage from the murderous MiG.

The MiG driver, satisfied with a probable "kill" that was trailing smoke and running for home, obviously decided flying further into South Korea was foolhardy and disengaged the fleeing, wounded Eagle. More likely his low fuel light was flashing at him and he had to RTB or perhaps he scanned his radar and saw two more F-15s at 50 miles on an intercept course. Whatever the reason, the battle was over as he turned and headed North across the DMZ.

The results were shocking: one F-15 damaged, one destroyed and an impressive demonstration of state of the art Russian missile technology. It also gave the US Air Force a lot to think about. This was the turning point everyone had predicted would come eventually. In over 100 air engagements to date no F-15 had ever been lost in aerial combat. This was the first and against a lowly MiG-29, no less. The technological edge the Americans enjoyed for forty years was in jeopardy. The playing field was level...at least for the time being. The F-22, the stealthy, new super- fighter, was still three years away from squadron service. A lot could happen in three years.

PUTINGRAD AIRBASE
SOUTHWEST RUSSIA

It was a cold, rainy and overcast morning in what used to be a far corner of the old Soviet Union. Dr. Charles David Michaels stamped his numbing feet, clouds of his own breath hovering about his face. He wondered at the events that had transpired to bring him to this broad expanse of concrete this far from home.

The cold, gray tarmac was more of an aviation archeological dig than an operational airfield. Ancient, rotting aircraft, their tires flat, pools of oil and hydraulic fluid under their weathered wings sat in quiet disarray around the field. Parked almost as if they had literally died in place, grass was growing up through the spider web of cracks in the concrete. One length of ivy came up through the concrete only to snake its way up the nose-gear of an old MiG-23 and disappear into its corroded innards. This expanse of concrete was an operational air defense base just a decade ago and already nature was overtaking one of Man's monuments to the war that never was.

Michaels shook his head as he inspected the aerodrome. He had spent the better part of his government service preoccupied with the threat this country and this base represented to the United States. He had spent many a troubled night pouring over satellite photos and intelligence estimates of the might of this country. Our great bombers and missiles had sat 24 hour alert for years waiting for the "bolt out of the blue" that never came. Now with the collapse of the Soviet Union he was able to first hand see the damage they had done. Without firing a shot the United States had decimated the military forces of the Soviet Union. The great build-up of the 80s had wrought such economic destruction that it reduced the old USSR to a loosely held commonwealth of individual states all vying for the remaining resources of a depleted and defeated nation.

During the breakup there was much infighting over how the weapon systems were to be split up between Russia, Ukraine, Belarus and the rest. What they should have worried about was the economic drain on those new countries that maintaining and operating those systems involved. As a result there were nuclear subs sitting in port rusting away, their corroding nuclear reactors now a danger to themselves rather than a foreign power. There were Mach 2 fighters sitting idle on flat tires with seized engines, bleeding oil staining their flanks.

The Cold War ended well over a decade earlier but this was the first chance Michaels had to visit his old enemy's homeland. He thought he would feel different when the day came. Now he stood amongst the ruins of the once proud Soviet Air Force and he felt...sad? *How can this be,* he asked himself? He'd spent his life's work leading up to this day and now he felt sorry for the bastards? *Would I have felt different if we'd shot down these planes in combat? If we had fought the war and soundly defeated the enemy?*

Yes, he had to admit. *That would have been better. They were a proud people and would have died heroes' deaths for Mother Russia. Now Russian soldiers pick potatoes so their people won't starve.* He also realized Americans would have died at the hands of these people and their weapons of war. And of course any conflict might have gone nuclear. Maybe it was for the best. Still it was sad.

"You will follow me, yes?" the young Russian captain asked Michaels, stirring him out of his reverie.

He blinked and jerked in surprise. "Oh---da," he said simply.

The young captain led him to a large darkened hangar in the very center of the flight line. The paint was peeling off the concrete block building and ivy was clawing its way up its north face. A side door to the large hangar opened and a bearded, heavyset man wearing a long flowing black trench coat walked out to greet Michaels. His steely blue eyes stood in marked contrast with his beard, streaked with gray. With a wide smile he extended his hands in greeting, Michaels own right hand disappearing into the massive hands of the Russian.

"Dr. Michaels, it is truly a pleasure to meet you," he said, pumping Michaels arm for all it was worth. "It is not often you get to meet an old nemesis under such conditions. Later when this is over we must have a drink and talk of old times, yes?"

Michaels knew this man by reputation only. He'd been briefed on his past and current roles within the Russian government. Victor Komiskov could be considered Michaels' counterpart. A security advisor to the Russian president, he too came from an intelligence background, no doubt spending long nights in KGB field offices pouring over photos and reports of the imminent US military threat.

Once upon a time it would have been unthinkable for the two to ever meet in person, although by their natures they would have studied each other's dossier very carefully. Once upon a time they were two key players in the game that was the Cold War. Now Michaels was just another customer and Komiskov reduced to a "used car" salesman.

"I think several drinks would be in order, Comrade Komiskov," Michaels said amicably.

Komiskov smiled broadly. "You can drop the 'comrade'. That went out with Gorbachev, yes? It is odd circumstances that bring us together. It is a very different world that we now live in, but we can discuss that over vodka later. Now you wish to see aircraft."

He led them to the door at the end of the hangar and held it open for Michaels. The young captain took up post outside the door. It was dark inside the hangar and all Michaels could see were eerie aerodynamic shapes in the gloom. Komiskov found the light switch and it sparked as he through the massive two-pronged switch closed. The overhead track lighting flickered and hummed then sprung to life with a blaze as the sodium arc lights ignited. Parked three deep with wing tips overlapping were four rows of gray, but gleaming, fighter jets. MiG-41s.

Komiskov gestured grandly at the fighters with a wave of his arm.

"Dr. Michaels, I give you the MiG-41," he said with drama. "This aircraft is an advanced production variant of the MiG 1.44 prototype, the first Fifth Generation jet fighter. We adopted the moniker MiG- 41 more for marketing reasons than any other. The number denotes an advanced model, but the aerodynamics and obviously stealthy attributes are, as I'm sure you will agree, a whole new look for modern Russian jet fighters. We took the best features of the MiG-29 and added speed, vectored thrust, advanced technology radars, range and stealth."

The first row of four aircraft all had full weapons loads on their nine pylon mounts. Michaels could make out AA-8s, AA-10s, AA-11, and AA-12 air to air missiles as well as an assortment of air to ground missiles, bombs, cluster bombs, rocket pods, and what appeared to be electronic countermeasure pods. There was no mention of weapons in the deal, but it was clear the Russians were trying to impress. They did look formidable. He had been skeptical about his mission, not anymore.

Michaels began his government service thirty years earlier as an intelligence analyst and eventually an operative for the Central Intelligence Agency. He had progressed up the career "ladder" and made the lateral transition to the Defense Intelligence Agency, where he rose to the level of Director. Now as a member of the President's National Security Council when someone whispered in the President's ear that someone was usually him. Michaels knew the real deal when he saw it and in his signature was the bargaining and buying power of the United States Government. These MiGs were the real deal.

"You are impressed, yes?" the grinning Russian asked with a slap on Michaels' back.

Michaels only smiled. He knew enough about sales not to appear too impressed. He walked over to the nearest aircraft and ran his hand along its shiny, smooth radome. The paint looked as if it were still wet. Walking around the aircraft he noted the brand new tires, unusual for a Russian aircraft, the polished afterburner cans and the general attention to detail. There was a maintenance stand in place so he could see into the cockpit. He climbed the stand and peered over into the cockpit, looking through the crystal clear Plexiglas of the huge "greenhouse" canopy. The avionics were indeed advanced for a Russian fighter, every bit as advanced in appearance as the latest generation F-15s and F-16s back home. Whether they worked as well was another matter. It was believed they would, however, as the new MiG radar was supposedly an equal to any Western radar and actually used a lot of exported Western electronics.

"Is that a Zhuk Phazotron?" he asked over his shoulder to the Russian.

"Phazotron RP-45," he answered proudly. "Capable of tracking 24 targets at 150 km and engaging six simultaneously. Coupled with the old version of the AA-12, this radar gives a standoff capability of greater than 45 KM. The newest AA-12B that we employ here in Russia has considerably more range, but I'm afraid that is classified and the missile not for export." The sound of pride swelled in his voice.

"Something you are not exporting?" Michaels snorted. "Imagine that."

Komiskov frowned as Michaels turned back to his inspection of the MiG. He was sure the American would seem more impressed. Perhaps he was impressed but didn't want to show it. Yes, that was it. *A most worthy adversary, indeed*, Komiskov thought.

Komiskov was right. Michaels had acted nonchalant about the MiG and the new AA-12 for a reason. The MiG scared the hell out of him. If what Komiskov said was true this aircraft could be quite a formidable threat to Western aircraft. It also scared him that the Russians were selling planes just like this one to radical Islamic Middle Eastern nations. In fact they were already flying aircraft just like this. The MiG-35 and MiG-41 had been on the export market for two years now and many countries already had entire squadrons of the aircraft. The next conflict the US flew in would no doubt see an F-15 and a MiG-41 head to head. The F-22 was coming on line slowly and supposedly the incredible stealthiness of that aircraft might give it the advantage, but in the short-run this MiG was a real problem.

Though the MiG-41 was a superior warplane the Russians didn't have any in their own inventory. This plane was for export only. After the breakup of the USSR the Sukoi design bureau gained significant political advantage and displaced the Mikoyan Industrial Group, as Mikoyan-Gurevich was now called, as the prime builder of Russian Air Force and Naval aircraft. The

Russians were going with the new series of Sukoi aircraft. All derivatives of the SU-27 Flanker, they were much larger, somewhat faster and could carry more weapons than the MiGs. They also used thrust vectoring for super-maneuvering and had 14 weapons pylons. They were flying battleships and designed to overcome their stealthy counterparts by sheer speed, powerful radars and very long-ranged missiles. Whereas the original Su-27 did have a weapon load and range advantage over the original MiG-29, the latest variants of the two were more evenly matched and the radars, electronic countermeasures and sensors were identical. These MiG-41s were a step above even the most advanced MiG-29. Michaels noted the full "glass" cockpits and fly by light flight control systems, very advanced indeed. Michaels climbed down off the stand. The Russian was standing there all smiles, arms crossed.

"What do you think, Doctor?" he asked simply.

Michaels ran his fingers through his wavy hair and took a deep breath. "I think you are insane for selling these to any country in the Middle East. That is what I think," he said, his eyes locked on the Russian. The Russian shrugged his shoulders as if that was explanation enough.

"Cash on the barrel-head, Doctor," he finally said. "We are *capitalist* now. We need capital. Simple economics I'm sure you can understand."

"I understand your country's economic problems, but you should consider your own security as well. These Muslim countries are run by terrorists and have no love for your country. They never liked your Communism and they don't care much for your Capitalism, either," Michaels said. "When you were the USSR you sold weapons to these countries. Did any one of them ever convert to Communism? Did they ever do anything you wanted of them? They took your weapons and thumbed their noses at you in the process. Did it accomplish anything?"

"The goal at that time was to keep you out of the Middle East and that was very successful. You were never a real military presence there until the war a decade ago, but that is ancient history and the region has little love for you now," the Russian said. "We need the capital and we have a force at home that can defend against anything a Third World country can throw at us, including these MiGs. You know the old saying, 'Keep your friends close, but keep your enemies closer still, so close they cannot move against you.' "

Michaels shook his head in disgust and looked back up at the MiG.

"Doctor Michaels, if you are not happy with the current situation you can only blame yourselves. These Middle East countries only have money because of all the oil your country buys so you can run your lawn mowers, jet skis and sport utility vehicles. Your country accounts for 60 percent of the world's oil consumption with only 5% of the world's population. You use that oil to attain your great wealth," Komiskov said defensively. "And now you stand here and complain that we are only interested in money. Well---Doctor Michaels, this is just capitalism at its finest, a lesson we learned from you. The price of these aircraft is based on simple supply and demand. The sticker price is $400 million dollars for these twelve aircraft. Now what can I do to put you in a MiG today, Doctor?"

Michaels nodded, but said nothing as he stared at the nearest MiG's gleaming canopy.

"Excellent," Komiskov said with a broad smile. "By the way, not that it's any of our concern, but exactly why do you want twelve MiG-41s?"

Michaels paused for just a moment then turned to Komiskov. "I think we need that drink now."

THE SEGRATOV HOTEL, SOUTHWEST RUSSIA 1900 HOURS LOCAL

The meal was extravagant by Russian standards. It was as close to a State dinner as could be expected on this desolate far corner of Russia. The dinner was served in a local hotel of some distinction (The distinction being it was the only hotel within 200 miles.), and there were an appropriate number of government officials with long titles and modest powers commiserate to the importance of Michaels' visit.

There was a modest attempt at steak, a grisly, twisted piece of bloody beef, more or less. The wine was a French Bordeaux as dry as last year's bird's nest, but Michael's found the more of it he drank the better the meal seemed. The courses came one at a time and the whole thing, which started with escargot, ended an interminable hour and a half later with an apéritif of a sweet Italian wine. The conversation was sparse and filled with nothing but trite courtesies, trivialities and hollow praise about one aspect or another of Russia or America. After the meal Komiskov waived off the others adjourned with Michaels to a suite complete with snifters of scotch and fine Cuban cigars.

"Single malt Scotch whiskey and cigars?" Michaels said, raising an eyebrow. "Now that is a capitalist's drink, Doctor," he chided the big Russian.

Komiskov laughed. "This is something else we learned from you," he said holding up the glass. "However, we have been enjoying the fine craftsmanship of our comrades in Cuba for generations, a pleasure illegal in your own country, but one you indulge in every time you go overseas, yes? And please call me Victor."

Michael's nodded and raised his glass in a mock toast. "And you may call me Charles."

"Ah. Now that is the name of a capitalist. Not Chuck?" Komiskov asked with a sly smile.

"My father called me Chuck…" Michaels said, taking a drink of scotch.

"Ah…well, there you are," Komiskov started.

"…but he was a drunk who chased whores and I never really cared what he called me," Michaels finished.

Komiskov's eyes lit up. "Speaking of whores, I believe that dancer in Prague called you Chuck, didn't she?"

Michaels frowned. "I don't know what you are talking about, Victor."

"It has been many years, but I would not think you would forget this girl," the large Russian beamed. "I will refresh your memory. "Prague. 1979. The Beaver's Lair. A red head with, shall we say, large tracts of land. I believe you knew her, in more ways than one. Greta Schultz."

Michaels' mouth fell open. It was all coming back to him now. Prague. Yes, there was a girl whom he'd met there. Greta was his contact in Prague and passed him valuable information concerning Soviet troop movements and IRBM basing. He had slept with her, but how did Komiskov know this?

"Do not look so surprised, Charles," he said hastily. "I slept with her, too. Greta had a thing for agents, on both sides. I think nearly every operative in the theatre had her at one time or another. I understand she's married to a small town mayor and has five children now. Must have played hell on her figure, although I doubt any of the babies went hungry, yes?"

Michaels was speechless. His mouth was open as if to reply, but no words would come. He stammered for a moment and turned beet red. After several moments trying to formulate words, all at the delight of his Russian host he finally blurted out, "But she was on our side?" It was more of a question than a statement of fact.

"Yes, she was…" Komiskov said. "…and ours as well. You paid her for information, yes? So did we. We ran across her during a surveillance of a British agent working in Prague. We knew she was passing information to NATO. In the old days standard practice dictated that she should disappear one evening, but we thought she'd be more useful to us if we could turn her.

There were three of us, all KGB, working in the city. We approached her one evening with our proposal, one 'she could not refuse' as you Americans say in the movies. We did not have the authority to make the offer, nor did we inform Moscow. We subcontracted her, so to speak. We matched what you were paying out of our miscellaneous expense funds and it kept her in jewelry and fine clothes, all she really wanted. Of course we received special favors of the more sensual nature as well. She was remarkably cooperative with us. We thought we might have to play the heavy hand on her, but she knew how the game was played."

"I don't believe this," Michaels said. "She passed us valuable information. I don't believe she ever led us astray. All her intelligence checked out. She was our most valuable source in the theatre."

Komiskov smiled that irritating smile, clearly pleased by Michael's discomfort. One last Cold War victory, if only a small one.

"We knew this and you are most correct. She would pass you very accurate data then call us and tell us exactly what she told you. She passed us information that was very useful. All around she was a very good source. In retrospect I don't believe she lied to any of us. She had a remarkable work ethic, so to speak," Komiskov paused, scratching his beard. He sighed wistfully.

"The only problem we had with her was of our own doing. It is true she was incredibly accurate in all her reports to us, but at the time we put little stock in her. We knew she was a double agent. We assumed anything we got from her could very well be tainted, so we didn't always use her intelligence to the fullest. We were also sleeping with her and she got to be more of a sex toy to us than a valuable intel source. She was a great lay."

Michaels was astonished by the Russian's admission. "You mean you didn't trust her? If we'd known she was a double we wouldn't have trusted her either. You're saying you were at a disadvantage because you knew she was a double? That is irony at its finest, Victor," Michaels said holding up his scotch in a mock toast. "The question I have is what drew your attention to me?"

The Russian took a large drink of Scotch and savored the malt whiskey as it burned its way down his throat. He felt the familiar warming sensation. It was not vodka, but it would do this evening. He returned the drink to its coaster on the antique coffee table and returned the big Cohiba to its rightful place, the left corner of his mouth.

"I first heard your name in bed, oddly enough," he said. "We had made love and were laying in bed smoking cigarettes, very bad Yugoslavian cigarettes, as I remember. She wanted to cuddle, a big cuddler, as I am sure you are aware. We were talking about her contacts for your side when she mentioned your name and told me I reminded her of you. Well, that intrigued me to no end, so I made you a study. It was only later that I realized how valuable that study was. You were quite the worthy adversary, Charles," he said, blowing a smoke ring as if in punctuation.

Michaels sat in silence for a moment. He wasn't sure what to think of this. He sipped his scotch, took a long drag off his cigar and looked down his nose at Komiskov before he spoke, "I had no idea I was such a topic of interest. I appreciate your compliment, but are you sure we are not still adversaries?" *Let him put that in his pipe and smoke it*, Michaels thought.

Komiskov paused in mid sip and coughed, an eyebrow raised ever so slightly. He smiled that patient smile at Michaels and took another long drink of the scotch, his second glass, now. Then he nodded.

"We are not worried."

"You are telling me you do not fear a nation that in a matter of minutes can target nukes at your heartland?" Michaels insisted. "Come now, Victor, surely this must make you just a bit nervous."

The big Russian smiled the patient smile again. "We are always nervous, Charles, about everything. We are a nervous people. Throughout our history we have faced many struggles with our neighbors, Napoleon, Hitler. After the carnage of World War II we as a nation vowed never to let one square meter of our soil fall to a foreign aggressor. It was this burning anger that carried us through the Cold War. Today, however, things are very different. War is not the same. War is waged with stocks and bonds, rather than arms. Resources such as oil and land are bought and sold, not conquered. My greatest fear is that within ten years your country will have bought up half of mine."

"Not likely," Michaels said, sipping his scotch.

"Perhaps not," Komiskov agreed. "I would still like to know why you want twelve MiG-41s."

"I'm not sure this is the place," Michaels said, gesturing to his ear. Komiskov nodded. *It was likely the place was bugged*, he thought.

The Russian's expression became stern. "Perhaps we should take a drive."

A WINDING, COUNTRY ROAD
2200 HOURS LOCAL

It was nearly dark and the driving rain that had been punctuated by the crash of thunder a mere hour ago was now just a light drizzle. The old ZIL, once a staff car in the service of the KGB, droned on, its engine surging as it struggled up some of the less modest inclines. Komiskov popped the headlights on and the two wide beams lit up the narrow lane they now found themselves on. The bottle of scotch sat between the two men on the bench seat.

After nearly thirty minutes they finally pulled up to a small dacha nestled among the trees of this desolate part of Russia. The cabin was not elaborate, nor was it merely a shack. *It is the perfect getaway for the man who needs to get away*, Michaels thought.

"Is this yours?" Michaels asked as they both got out of the car rather clumsily, thanks to their rapidly rising blood alcohol levels.

"Nyet," Komiskov said. "It is my brother's. He is a better capitalist than I. Ran a good portion of the Russian black market for years. Never got caught. Of course he had a brother in the KGB to watch over his interests. He is openly wealthy now. You don't make this kind of money as an undersecretary of anything, my friend."

"I heard that," Michaels agreed. "The curse of the civil servant. A lifetime of service for modest means."

"Some more modest than others," Komiskov snorted as he tilted the scotch bottle back and drank deeply.

Once inside the cabin Komiskov flipped a switch and the gas fireplace came to life. Michaels slung off the wet overcoat, hung it on a coat rack near the door and moved quickly to bask in the warmth of the orange-blue flames. He shivered involuntarily as his body absorbed the welcome heat.

"What weather your having here," he muttered. "I'd almost prefer snow than this cold rain."

The Russian plopped down on the couch near the fire and kicked off his shoes, stretching his socked feet towards the warmth. "Believe me, my friend, you don't want the snow, either, not the snow we get here," he said shaking his head. "Or the sub-zero temperatures that go with it. I'll take the rain any day."

Michaels sunk into the folds of the high back leather recliner opposite the couch and spread his feet out as well, though he left his shoes on. It was as if the chair melded to his body and the warmth of the fire was welcome.

The Russian produced a beautiful antique humidor full of more Cuban cigars and passed a fresh stogie to his American friend who rolled the length of it across his nostrils appreciatively. The Russian handed him a guillotine cutter and he clipped the end of the fifteen-dollar cigar.

There is a fine art to the lighting and smoking of a well-bred cigar. It should only be lit from a wooden match. One must be careful to allow all the sulfur to burn away prior to applying the flame. The cigar should be held at a 45-degree angle to the flame and rolled across the fingertips to distribute the heat evenly. After several seconds of gently kissing the tip with the flame the actual ignition may begin. The cigar comes to the lips and the first puff should actually be an exhalation, to prevent any residual sulfur on the match from entering the cigar. Finally when the flame begins its magic the puffing can begin. Short gentle puffs in and out while rolling the cigar slightly to ensure an even burn. This is critical. Michaels was a master of this art. The Russian on the other hand flipped open his Zippo lighter which he bought at the newsstand across from the United Nations Headquarters in New York and applied the flame, puffed deeply twice and the cigar was lit, albeit less artfully so.

Komiskov reached over the side of the couch and poured two brandies from the crystal bottle on a silver tray. He passed one to Michaels. Fine cigars, fine liquor, a cold night and a warm fire, everything was in its place. Michaels never thought such luxuries were available in Russia.

"Now, Charles, exactly why do you want twelve MiG-41s?"

Michaels nodded. It was decided from the inception of this plan that the Russians would be required as active partners. After exhaustive observation of the new Russian bureaucracy it was determined that Komiskov was the right man to approach with this proposal. He had the intelligence service background, the security clearance and the discretion the approach required. He also had the ear of the Russian President. Now he had to hook the big Russian bear.

"Victor, we are looking for a partner in the war on terrorism, an active partner. We have had our differences in the past, but we always knew we could count on Russia to act rationally. That was the whole basis of stability during the Cold War. You are not a country of religious zealots. You were not willing to commit nuclear suicide in the name of God by attacking the United States."

"The Party was our god, Charles," the big Russian said sarcastically, then his brow furrowed in seriousness. "And today there are those who would light that fuse---if they had access to it, yes?"

Michaels nodded. "We don't pretend for one second that these Islamic radicals wouldn't use a nuke if they had it. And bio-weapons...that scares us even more. You have had your issues with these factions, right?"

Komiskov took a deep breath and let it out slowly. "Da. We have our problems with the Muslims in the South."

"Victor, these terrorists have always been state sponsored," Michaels went on. "You know this as well as I. Some have been in the open, like Sandor and Kumar, others have been under the table. Now they have a coalition that not only controls oil production, but even terrorist activities."

"All true, my friend," the Russian admitted. "They sell you their oil in daylight and blow up your buildings by night. So what are you really proposing?"

Michaels knew he had to be careful here. You never really could be sure of Russian motivations.

"These Islamic countries historically have hated each other for centuries, fought wars against each other, like Kumar and Sandor," Michaels said. "The different sects of the Muslim faith even hate each other."

"Yes. Your point?"

"When these countries were fighting each other, they weren't killing us," Michaels said.

"True. Their resources were pitted against each other," Komiskov agreed. "What do you suggest, Charles, start a war between Sandor and Kumar?" he said with a sly smile.

Michaels held up his hands in protest. "The United States is not interested in ever starting a war between anybody, but if we could knock out their weapons of mass destruction programs and get them pointing the finger at each other---well, that could only help our position."

"You mean you want to break up their coalition, their unification against the West?"

"And against Russia," Michaels interjected.

"When you say 'weapons of mass destruction', what do you mean? Surely nuclear, but chemical and biological as well?"

Michaels nodded. "Whatever intelligence can verify they are doing."

"Hmmm. You do realize my country is currently building a nuclear power plant for Sandor?" Komiskov asked.

"Yes, we do realize this. It can in fact be used for producing plutonium, right?"

Komiskov ignored the question. "Would you consider that plant part of a 'nuclear program'?"

"Yes."

"And what do you plan to do about it?"

"Victor, you are getting paid well to build them a power plant, correct?"

"Yes."

"If the plant were destroyed do you suppose they would contract you to build another?"

Komiskov nodded. "Not an elegant solution, my friend, but practical, I suppose."

"And they would never suspect Russia had anything to do with destroying the plant," Michaels concluded.

"So who did blow it up---hypothetically?"

"A flight of Kumari MiG-41s attacked and destroyed the plant."

Komiskov nodded. This American was ambitious. "How very aggressive of them. So this is your plan? We attack our own nuclear plant and make it look like the Kumaris did it? You ask a lot of us, Charles."

"No. We blow it up, a joint covert strike team---US and Russian pilots working together. This is just one example of what we could do throughout the Middle East."

"What happens when we rebuild the plant for them?" Komiskov asked.

"The Kumaris will never allow that plant to come on line. I can guarantee this."

"I assume the Sandoris would become rather irate with the Kumaris, yes?"

"And there would have to be retribution," Michaels added.

"This is all well and good, Charles," Komiskov said. "However---wouldn't this dangerously destabilize the world oil markets? Isn't that always your primary concern, your whole reason for being in the Middle East?"

"Victor, those two countries fought a war for eight years and we still got cheap oil out of the Persian Gulf. Besides my president has pledged $10 billion to your country to build an infra-structure for oil production in Siberia," Michaels said. "That is a partnership that will pay huge dividends over time, my friend."

"Yes, I have heard rumors of this," Komiskov said.

"Take away the oil money from the US and Russia and you take a lot of capital out of the Middle East," Michaels said.

"The markets would adjust, my friend," Komiskov said. "The Arabs will drop prices to match."

"With Russian support we're willing to boycott," Michaels said.

"So this is a two prong attack? Break up their coalition and then boycott their oil," Komiskov said. "What about the rest of the world?"

"Some will still buy from the Arabs, but a boycott by the US and Russia would rob them of trillions," Michaels said. "And it takes capital to finance weapons of mass destruction."

Komiskov sat in silence for a moment as he rolled the Hoyo de Monterrey Double Corona across his lower lip. He was in deep thought, pondering the unprecedented proposal before him.

"If we were to agree to this covert team, where would they be based? Who would be in charge? I need details, Charles," he finally said.

Michaels shook his head. "The details can come later, Victor. This is a preliminary visit to see if we have a viable concept. Take this to whomever you need to. If you are still interested we can hammer out the details later. Can you arrange to come to the US in the two weeks?"

"Yes, that will not be a problem," Komiskov said, then he added, "if we are interested. I assume the MiG sale is dependent on the answer, yes?"

Michaels just smiled and blew smoke.

ROOM 312, THE SEGRETOV HOTEL
0200 HOURS

"So what do you think, Yuri?" Komiskov asked his deputy, Yuri Kamorova, a thin, balding ex-KGB man. The entire conversation with Michaels had been recorded, as procedure demanded of any conversation with a foreign diplomat.

"An interesting proposal. Surprisingly pro-active for Americans," the man said, a cigarette dangling from his lip.

"Do you think the Americans' motivations are what he claims?" Komiskov asked.

"Da. The Americans are focused almost exclusively on terrorism. Covertly destroying both country's weapons programs while disrupting their anti-American coalition sounds plausible," Kamorova said. "I believe he means what he says."

"So they do not wish to start a war between Sandor and Kumar?"

"I don't know about that. That is the sort of thing the Americans would always deny."

"It would be in their best interests if Sandor and Kumar were occupied with each other," Komiskov said.

"When you have two rabid dogs to deal with, you let one kill the other then you kill the remaining one which is weakened from the struggle," Kamorova said, blowing smoke through his nose.

"Da," the big Russian said. "What do you think about his comments on the Sandori reactor?"

"Like you said, my friend, practical if not elegant," Kamorova said. "Many in our own military worry about that reactor, especially with the terrorist attacks of late. It was foolish to offer that technology at any price; of course those contracts were let years ago, before we knew Sandor sponsored the terrorism in Chechnya. I spoke with General Kurgen just last week about that reactor. He has shared his concern with the President."

"And what was the President's reaction?"

"He didn't say," Kamorova said, blowing smoke. "I would imagine the President would lose no sleep over its destruction."

Komiskov got up out of his high-backed chair and moved to the window, looking out over a rainy blackness, lightning on the horizon.

"You did hear the threat, yes?" Komiskov asked.

"Threat?" Kamorova replied with an upturned eyebrow.

"Implied, but it was there, my friend," Komiskov said, turning away from the window. "More than the sale of the MiGs depends on this."

"The $10 billion for Siberian oil," Kamorova said with a nod. "They would withhold that funding?"

"Possibly not, but they'd like us to think they might," Komiskov said. "The President will not want to take the chance. However, there are opportunities here, Yuri," he said. "You do see that, yes?"

The other man nodded. "Da. If hostilities were to break out between Sandor and Kumar it would generate a huge demand for weapons, weapons we have sitting in warehouses right now."

"It is true we could profit by weapons sales, but I was thinking along more grander lines. The outcome of such a war might prove beneficial in another sense," Komiskov said with a smile.

"How?" Kamorova asked.

"Sandor."

"What about Sandor?"

"Sandor has both access to the Persian Gulf and huge oil reserves."

Kamorova laughed. “You are ambitious, my friend. I think the Scotch is working its magic. Sandor? We could not defeat Afghanistan with our whole army and you want to conquer Sandor?”

“The Americans and Europeans opposed us then,” he said. “Do you think they would oppose it now?”

The man shrugged. “I see your point, but we cannot invade and defeat Sandor. I do not believe it can be done, my friend.”

“You forget it will be a war by proxy, Yuri,” Komiskov said with a smile. “Kumar will do the fighting, the killing and the dying. Every country in the region hates the Sandoris. No one will come to their defense.”

“And when Kumar defeats Sandor how do we get those oil fields from Kumar?”

“You forget Kumar is a rogue nation, prone to using chemical and biological weapons.”

“So?”

“After Achmed has killed off his enemies we will march into Sandor with a UN mandate to ‘liberate’ the country from the hands of the Kumari criminal. Probably with the Americans at our side.”

“And why would we get that mandate?”

“Because Kumar used weapons of mass destruction in their victory, chemical and biological weapons.”

“And how do you know they will use these weapons?” Kamorova asked, skeptical.

Komiskov said nothing, but a thin smile creased his lips.

KIMPO AIRBASE, REPUBLIC OF KOREA

Captain David Olmstead managed to nurse his wounded F-15C home on one engine. The fire that had been caused by the missile blowing off his right burner can blew out as soon as the fuel shutoff T-handle was pulled. He had suffered damage to the hydraulic systems as well, but the standby system worked as advertised giving him the control necessary to return to base, however, he landed with virtually no brakes. The emergency crews rigged the arresting cables at the end of the runway and the Eagle’s arresting gear engaged the cables perfectly stopping him on the pavement.

After the Eagle came to a stop Olmstead opened the canopy and climbed down out of the cockpit. The damaged engine was still smoking and he knew a fire could erupt at any moment. The rule of thumb in this scenario said to run until either the aircraft explodes or you start to feel silly. Olmstead ran off about a hundred yards as the fire trucks moved in. They hit the aft end of the damaged fighter with a blast from their water cannon and the smoke turned to wispy tendrils of steam.

Olmstead tore off his helmet and flung it to the ground. He sat down on the pavement, out of breath and in mild state of shock. He cupped his palms to his face and ran his fingers through his jet-black hair, tears forming in the corners of his eyes. He took a deep breath and looked up. The sky was blue and the sun shone brightly. It was a beautiful day and the world went on, blindly unaware of the young fighter pilot's loss. Olmstead sobbed. Pete was gone. Blown out of the sky while on my wing.

He suddenly felt his stomach turning and he barely had time to roll over on all fours when the vomit came up, stinging his throat with stomach acid and bile. After a few seconds it was over, but the stomach contractions continued, dry heaving. He stayed down on all fours and hung his head, trying to breathe. Finally it subsided and he rolled back over to the seated position as the first emergency vehicle pulled up.

"You okay, sir?" the young medic asked as he rushed up. He noted the vomit along side the disheveled and pale captain, the corner of his lip rising in a grimace of disgust.

Olmstead nodded weakly. "Yeah, I'm just fine," he said. "Just fine."

Later that day at the flight surgeon's office Olmstead was getting a routine post incident physical when the door burst open and in strode the wing commander, flanked by a half dozen aids and PR types, waving cameras. Olmstead, still in his hospital gown, was astonished and simply stood there open-mouthed.

"Captain, it is a privilege to shake the hand of a fellow MiG-killer," the bald general said, his face all smiles and bad teeth. He grasped Olmstead's right hand, but did not shake. This was a photo-op handshake, contrived for the front page of a newspaper. He turned to the camera. It flashed and he continued his congratulations.

"I remember my MiG-23 kill over the Gulf a dozen years ago," he said. "It's something you'll always remember, son. Damn, good work out there. I'd love to cut loose some R&R for you right now, but you know the deal. We're gonna have to debrief this thing pretty thoroughly, but after that, son, I'll see to it you get some time off. I'm personally putting you in for the Silver Star for this one."

"Sir, an AIM-130 killed the MiG," Olmstead said through clenched teeth. "I just pulled the trigger."

Although this was clearly not the response he'd expected the general's broad grin did not waver, not in front of the Press. He slapped Olmstead on the back.

"Well, whatever you did, son," he said with a smile. "...there's one less Commie out there to threaten the vital interests of the United States and her allies. You get some rest, son, and good job," he said, already making for the door, his entourage in tow. Olmstead closed his eyes and shook his head slowly. A dull throb was starting to form behind his left eye and he had a feeling there would be many more headaches in the days to come.

Olmstead had expected a bit more somber reception; after all he had lost a wingman and received severe damage to his own aircraft. Still he had shot down a MiG and that made him a MiG-killer and a local base hero. Anytime a fighter pilot gets a kill it makes the news. If one listened to the local base media one would think he had personally driven off the Red Menace from the North. The Wing Commander's comments made it all the worse.

As the Wing Commander predicted he was awarded the Silver Star two weeks later, a phenomenally short time to process an award of that magnitude. Pete had been awarded a DFC (Posthumous). The base and local media were all over Olmstead. Several national publications wanted his story and it seemed his picture was in every magazine and every newspaper. Olmstead hated the attention. He felt personally responsible for Pete's loss, but for some reason they were treating him like a hero. This went on for several weeks.

Out of the public eye the Air Force still conducted a rigorous investigation. The Defense Intelligence Agency gathered all the data they could from the AWACS, a nearby RC-135 Electronic Surveillance plane and Olmstead's F-15 itself. It began to piece together the puzzle of how the US lost its first F-15 in air-to-air combat. Aside from the RWR gear, radar and electronic data sources, the best source of information was Olmstead himself. Olmstead knew this was coming and now found himself in a room with two DIA agents and a lot of questions.

They were seated at a single round table, Olmstead on one side, an older, silver-haired man to his right, a younger, very tall black man to his left. He wondered if either of them had ever been fighter pilots. Both wore the standard impeccable, yet utilitarian suit of a government agent. Olmstead imagined they had mirrored sunglasses in their vest pockets. He was not wrong.

"Captain Olmstead, let me start by saying this is an inquiry, not a trial," Special Agent Ben Maxwell said, trying to put the nervous young officer at ease. "Your testimony here is not permissible in a military court of law, even if you were to be prosecuted. We are not here to get you. We simply want to find out how we could lose an F-15 with AWACS support in a 2 v 2 fight. Nothing you say here can ever be used against you. That is why we expect complete cooperation. Is that clear?"

Olmstead nodded. He was still apprehensive. He'd heard this song and dance before from safety boards that went on to crucify some buddies of his who testified about their accidents. He would be truthful, but also very careful not to say something he'd regret later.

"Now, Captain," Special Agent Silas Greer started. Maxwell's assistant was a tall black man with a smattering of gray in his even beard. "You were on a routine air combat patrol, flying along the south side of the DMZ. This was your third flight that week, correct?" Olmstead said it was.

"You were armed with four AIM-130s and two AIM-9X2s, correct?"

"That's right," Olmstead said. "As well as a full magazine of 20 mike mike."

The black man nodded. "You had full connectivity with the AWACS and were vectored by them toward the MiGs?"

"That's right."

"Did you or your wingman have your radar on, Captain?" Maxwell asked.

"Negative," Olmstead said. "We were ordered to use emission control to the maximum extent possible. We were using a data link from the AWACS to provide us with targeting information. It is standard procedure to stay radar silent. This prevents the enemy from seeing a radar strobe on their RWR gear. They have to radiate to find us and we see their strobe. It's a matter of not giving yourself away unless you have to. If the AWACS wasn't there we would've been radiating the whole time."

Maxwell nodded and wrote in his notebook. " I see," he said. "As long as you were inside AWACS coverage and had the data link the established standard procedure says not to radiate. Correct?"

"That's right, unless you are about to fire your missile. You have to bring your radar up in order to fire an AIM-130."

"I see. It does say in your written statement that you did go to radiate with the intent of firing a missile. Is there any additional information or advantage you would have gained by using your own onboard radar earlier in the engagement?" Greer asked.

"No," Olmstead said confidently. "We get no more information from our onboard system than we do from the data link from the AWACS. In fact we give more away by using our own system. Our emissions alert the enemy of our presence."

"Well, can't the enemy see you on his radar?" Maxwell asked.

"The MiGs were running radar silent as well. We had no RWR indications from their radars. If they had been radiating they would have seen us and we would have turned ours on as well, as the surprise would have been over at that point."

Greer looked puzzled. "You said the MiGs were not radiating. How about the radar on the ground directing them?"

"We did get indications that a ground search radar was up," Olmstead admitted. "We couldn't be sure it wasn't a SAM radar or AAA radar, though. There's always a lot of radar activity from both sides of the DMZ. It was a Golf-band radar, very common to a lot of systems. It might have been a GCI. We weren't sure. The signal seemed weak and we couldn't verify they had seen us yet so we didn't go to radiate. We didn't feel like we needed to. Even if they saw us we had AWACS data link so we saw them as well."

"So that ground radar might have been sending the MiGs targeting information on you?" Greer asked.

"That is possible. Most of the Russian Fourth Generation aircraft have data link capability, though we were briefed the Russians never exported that system to the North Koreans."

Maxwell appeared pensive. "I see."

"Captain Olmstead, we've read the reports, but tell us in your own words how the engagement went down," Greer said.

Olmstead took a deep breath.

"We closed to 40 nautical miles before we went to radiate. The AIM-130 needs a radar lock for initial guidance. The radar scan of the missile is very narrow, so it uses the F-15 radar to lock on to the target before firing. Once enroute to the target the missile turns on its own radar and begins homing autonomously. We went to radiate and locked them up on our radar at 40 nautical miles, about a thousand knots closure. We were waiting for the in-range indication for the AIM-130. The missile won't even launch unless the computer says it's in range. In a max range face shot the computer assumes the target is not going to maneuver and will continue at his present speed towards the missile. It's using the enemy's velocity to increase the range of the missile. There are other factors the computer takes into account as well, temperature, altitude, etc.

"At 30 NM we got the indication we were in range. Since the MiGs were not radiating I knew they were not configured to take a shot. When they did come up it would take a few seconds to acquire and lock us up and a few more seconds to launch their missiles. Because of this I waited until I got further in range. I knew as soon as the missile was airborne they'd detect its radar and I didn't want them to maneuver and defeat a max range shot. If I was further in range it gave them less of a chance to defeat it.

"When we got to 25 miles they lit us up with their radar and locked on. I was preparing to fire my own missiles when out of the corner of my eye I saw the smoke trails of incoming missiles closing on us. I ordered a right break and turned my jammers to active and punched out chaff. Lieutenant Fletcher followed my break, but was hit by the missile while in the turn."

Maxwell raised his hand. "Just a moment Captain, if you don't mind. Let's stop right there for a moment and talk about those smoke trails." He paused and scratched his balding head. "How much time was there from the radar lock until you saw the smoke trails?"

"That was the part that didn't make sense," Olmstead said exasperated. "The RWR gear went off when they locked us up and when I looked up the missiles were right there. I couldn't believe how close they were. No missile moves that fast. From the time they went to radiate to impact had to be less than five seconds. No missile can cover twenty five miles in five seconds."

"Any chance those missiles came from the ground?" Greer asked.

"Those smoke trails were horizontal. They didn't come from the ground," Olmstead said certain of this fact.

"So you believe the missiles came from the MiGs, but you don't know how they could have covered so much ground so quickly," Maxwell asked.

"That's right."

"Do you think it possible they could have launched those missiles without a radar lock and then went to radiate just for the end game?" Greer asked. "Just shoot them ballistically in your general direction then give'em guidance at the last second?"

"I know that is a tactic for SAMs, but usually air to air missiles have a very low probability of a hit like that. Their flight times are too short and closure speeds too fast for last second guidance. I've never heard of a successful air-to-air engagement using that tactic. They could have gotten lucky I guess," Olmstead surmised.

"Yes---lucky," Maxwell said. Olmstead looked at him expectantly.

Maxwell looked at Greer with questioning eyes. Greer shrugged and nodded.

"We'd like to run something by you, Captain," Maxwell said. "Now this is just theory, but it is very privileged information. It doesn't leave this room. Can you live with that?"

Olmstead shrugged. He had no real choice. If he said no it would haunt him for the rest of his life. "Sure."

Maxwell nodded. "We are going under the assumption they shot radar guided missiles at you and that is exactly what they want us to think. We can't explain how the missiles covered the ground so fast or got enough last second radar guidance to complete the intercept. What if they had guidance all they way from launch?"

Olmstead shook his head. "I told you they didn't have radars up until about five seconds before impact. They would have been almost thirty miles away at launch. No IR seeker head can see that far, definitely not a face shot."

"The seeker doesn't have to see that far. The AA-10E Alamo is an IR seeking derivative of the AA-10 long-burn. Its range is estimated in the mid-thirties and its IR seeker can see in laser frequencies as well as its normal IR frequencies. We've seen reports that say the IR seeker can detect an IR signature over twenty miles and can see a laser reflection over thirty miles away, even with a face shot," Maxwell said.

"Sure, but how did it target us? They would have to be locked on to put the laser on us."

"It is possible the Korean MiGs are being retrofitted with a new long range Infrared Search and Track System. It would have to track a fighter-sized target at 35 miles in all aspects, but if it was bore sighted to a laser range finder then they could track you. Your track and position data could be fed into the AA-10E and it could be launched at maximum range. If it could guide on the reflected laser energy of the rangefinder until the IR seeker was able to lock onto you then we have an answer. The coup de grace was when they activated their continuous wave mode on the radar just before impact. Made you think a radar missile was guiding inbound so you turned and dumped chaff, right? The turn would actually increase your IR signature and the chaff had no effect on the IR seeker. Flares might have helped, but you assumed they were not in IR range so flares were never considered. Right?" Olmstead nodded.

"They turned on their radars at the last second to do two things: one, they wanted to get the radar lock for the next shot, which were probably AA-12s or more AA-10s, and two, they didn't want us to discover this little tactic of theirs," Maxwell said.

"That would explain how the missile covered the ground so fast," Greer agreed. "It didn't have to move fast. They just made you think it did."

"Look, I've never received any intel on any super long range Infra-red Search and Track or a laser seeker head in any air to air missile," Olmstead said, shaking his head. "If we knew the Russians had developed this stuff, why weren't the pilots in the field told about it?"

Greer looked at Maxwell and shrugged. "Well, Captain, this is all theory."

"Theory?" Olmstead said with an upturned eyebrow.

"We really only had rumors of something like this," Maxwell confessed. "The Russians were talking up some new IRST system at the last Paris Air Show, but there is always a lot of talk going on in Paris. I mean the Paris Air Show is where everybody's trying to dredge up sales and Russia tends to exaggerate about their capabilities in order to make sales."

"You mean the Russians themselves said 'Look what we've invented!' and we didn't pay any attention to them?" Olmstead said in disbelief.

"You have to understand, Captain, if it were a real breakthrough they wouldn't have said anything and they wouldn't be exporting it, either," Greer said.

"Unless they needed cash," Olmstead said angrily. "Does Russia need cash?"

"Captain, we haven't seen enough evidence to support this as anything more than theory," Greer said deadpan. "I'm not fully convinced this is what happened. There are other possibilities that don't include the NKs getting their hands on some super-state-of-the-art targeting system."

"What other possibilities?" Olmstead said angrily. Then he realized where they were going. "What? That I fucked up somehow? Is that it? I fell asleep at the wheel or something."

"We have to consider all possibilities," Maxwell said gently.

"Captain, look at it from our point of view," Greer said. "What is more likely: some super high-tech Russian targeting system gets deployed in North Korea with no detection by our intel sources in Russia or in North Korea, or maybe you or Lieutenant Fletcher got caught in the "fog of war" and missed something?"

Olmstead's eyes grew wide. Now he understood. "I get it," he said evenly. "You bastards and your intel sources missed the boat on this one and you need a scapegoat. You can't go reporting it was something you let slip through the cracks so you blame the pilots, more convenient when one is dead."

"Captain, you evaded the first missile and shot down a MiG," Greer said. "Fletcher got blown out of the sky. Is it possible he froze up and didn't react as quickly as you?"

"Maybe if he had he'd be alive right now and both MiG's would have been shot down," Maxwell finished.

Olmstead shook his head in wonder. He couldn't believe the audacity of these two.

"So that's what your report will say?" Olmstead said through clenched teeth. "Captain Fletcher is dead because he was stupid? You aren't going to mention the possibilities of a new long range IR targeting system?"

"Not until we get more data, Captain," Greer said in a level voice. "We will investigate this fully and if it merits a warning we will release it immediately."

"But I'd bet that investigation might take awhile, huh?" Olmstead said accusingly. "Maybe until the heat is off in this theatre and we get Pete in the ground, right?"

Maxwell nodded at Greer. They gathered their notes and stood up leaving Olmstead still seated and visibly showing his disgust. "I think we're finished here, Captain."

"Thank you for your cooperation, Captain Olmstead," Greer said. "Remember what we have discussed in this room is classified information, need to know only. You can't tell anyone. If you do you lose all immunity and your testimony could be used against you. Got it?"

Olmstead nodded absently. He couldn't believe his ears. He had to keep his mouth shut. The implications were clear. Shut up or you'll become our scapegoat. They hadn't said it in those words, but there was no doubt as to their meaning.

As Greer followed Maxwell out of the room he turned for a moment. "Oh---Captain, congratulations on your Silver Star," he said with a grim smile. Then he was gone.

Olmstead sat silently in his chair for several minutes, replaying in his mind the dual in the sky. It struck him just how different combat in the sky was from combat on the ground. Up there it in the blue of space it was deadly, but somehow pure, honest. Down here it might not be as deadly, but it was definitely far dirtier.

Olmstead was returned to flying duty and began patrolling the skies of

Korea again. Over the next few weeks he started to notice his squadron mates acting strangely around him. He would enter a room and the conversation would halt. It would begin again as soon as he left. It seemed no one wanted to be caught talking to him. They were complete professionals when they were flying with him, but on the ground he felt he was being ostracized, and the only thing that could mean is that they were fed up with all the attention and glory he was getting. He was fed up with it as well. He went to his flight commander, Major Rick Hudson, for advice.

"Come on in, Dave," Hudson said from behind his desk. "Close the door behind you."

Olmstead closed the door and sat down across from the burly, mustached major.

"What can I do for you?" Hudson asked with a smile.

Olmstead shrugged. "I don't know, Rick. I don't seem to know anything these days," he said. "What the hell is going on around here?"

"About what?"

"About me, Rick," Olmstead sighed.

"What about you?" he asked, holding his palms up.

"Come on," Olmstead complained. "What's with the cold shoulder I'm getting from everyone? Are they all just pissed with the damn Silver Star thing and all the attention I've been getting? Or is it something else?"

The major took a deep breath and sighed. "Well, Dave, now that you mention it I do think they are a trifle tired of seeing you on the cover of Air Force Times every other day. These guys fly the same patrols you fly. That's mostly what they're upset about."

"You said mostly," Olmstead said. "What else?"

Hudson rolled his eyes. "Dave, I don't want to go into that."

"Come on, Rick, give it to me."

Hudson looked at him for a few seconds, lips pursed. "Alright," he said finally. "It's not just the attention you're getting. A few of the guys think you blew it out there and by giving you the Silver Star it's the Air Force's way of putting a positive spin on the whole thing."

"What do you mean spin?"

"Dave, we lost an F-15 and a pilot, and your ship was a smoking wreck when you landed. Yeah, you killed one of the MiGs, but it was not a victory. They shouldn't even have gotten a shot off on you. The Air Force knows this, but perception is everything. If we build this up as a great victory, and you a great hero, then we get positive spin and nobody gets it trouble."

"That's why I'm getting all the attention?" Olmstead asked.

"The wing commander was worried he'd get fired over this, but he spun it right away to make you a hero. Hell, you single-handedly drove the Red Menace back across the DMZ. Sounds a lot better than what really happened, doesn't it?"

Olmstead was shaking his head. "So all this attention I've been getting, the awards, the interviews, all that crap has been a big propaganda game to protect some general's ass?"

"Not just his ass," Hudson snorted, "a trail of asses all the way back to the Pentagon. So naturally the guys here are gonna resent you. They broke the code weeks ago. I expected you would too."

"You think I fucked up?" Olmstead asked levelly.

The major sighed and looked Olmstead direct in the eyes. "The scuttlebutt floating around the squadron is that you froze up at a critical moment and it cost Pete his life. I'm not in a position to say one way or another. I've known you for a couple years, Dave. You're one of the best pilots in this squadron. I wasn't out there and I wasn't in the DIA debrief. You tell me you didn't fuck up I believe you, but from where I'm standing I can't say one way or another."

Olmstead looked away from the major's intense stare.

"I don't know, Rick. I played it by the book and Pete's dead. Maybe I am to blame, but I don't know what I could've done differently knowing what I did at the time. I feel trapped."

"How so?"

"Let's just say there are some things about the engagement I'm not at liberty to discuss," Olmstead said. "I feel responsible for Pete's death, the guys all think I'm responsible for Pete's death. The DIA says I'm not responsible, but that doesn't make me feel any better. It's bad enough to lose a wingman, but then they throw all these awards and glory on me. Then I find out they're only doing that to cover their own asses. And I have to go along with it."

"I know how you feel," Hudson sympathized. "Believe it or not I lost a wingman once."

"No shit?" Olmstead asked.

"No shit."

"Do you mind talking about it?" Olmstead asked.

Hudson shook his head. "We were flying in an exercise with the Navy out near China Lake about ten years ago. The weather was clear above ten thousand and a solid undercast below that. We were suppose to be flying a medium to high fight that day due to the weather, the hard deck was 12,000. A pair of Tomcats jumped us and I executed a Split S. It was a good solid maneuver tactically and we shook the Tomcats, but as we rolled out of the dive inverted we scraped the top of the undercast, the clouds were suppose to be at 10,000. They were higher than that, although I couldn't swear to you how high they were. Bottom line is I broke the hard deck by five hundred feet according to the HUD video, which still should have been clear of clouds. It wasn't. We entered the clouds inverted, while rolling back upright. I continued the move on instruments, but my wingman, a young kid from Tulsa with about 200 hours in the jet, got spatially disoriented. We later found out he rolled right through vertical and back upside down again then pulled up, or what he thought was up. He hit an 8300-foot ridgeline trying to recover. The accident board absolved me of any blame for his death although they said I did contribute to the spatial disorientation by breaking the hard deck. They said he should have been able to execute that maneuver on instruments and ruled the accident 'pilot error'."

"But you felt guilty about his death?" Olmstead asked.

"Yeah, for a while," Hudson said. "The guys in the squadron did blame me, though not to my face. I had a problem similar to yours, but without all the attention you're getting to make it worse."

"How'd you fix it with the guys?" Olmstead asked.

"It's called PCS, Permanent Change of Station. I left," he said. "I had to. It wasn't healthy staying around there. That's one of the benefits of the military moving us around, to clear our slate, so to speak."

Olmstead sighed. "So I need to just leave town? Is that it?"

"Couldn't hurt, Dave," the major confided. "It's only six months until your tour's up, anyway. You want me to put you in for a transfer? Get the ball rolling?"

Olmstead slumped in the chair and rubbed his temple with both hands. "Yeah, my work here is done," he said sarcastically.

THE RUSSIAN EMBASSY
WASHINGTON, D.C.

"We want them to train in the States...Nevada to be more precise," Michaels said. "I have a commander in mind, General George Tanner, an old friend I can count on. We would take six MiGs to Nevada and leave the other six in Russia for operational missions. We want as few players in this game as possible. We were thinking six pilots and an intel officer. You supply the weapons, fuel and maintenance for operational missions. You do have access to an abandoned airbase in Tangistan, right?"

Komiskov nodded. He knew the one Michaels was referring to, just a scant fifty miles from the Sandori border.

"One other thing," Michaels added. "Of the six pilots we want no more than two of them to be Russians."

Komiskov frowned. "And why is that?"

Michaels had to play this one carefully. "We are paying for all the training, most of the intelligence assets and the aircraft themselves. We have to have an American commander and we think four Americans and two Russians are the right combination. Two highly experienced Russians."

Komiskov nodded, but the frown did not disappear. "I suppose I could sell that as long as we had operational control of real world missions."

"Two commanders?" Michaels asked. He knew enough about the military to know that was a bad idea.

"Not exactly," Komiskov said. "When in training in the US your commander will be the only commander, but when deployed for real world operations you will have far more Russian personnel involved: maintenance, weapons loaders, intelligence, etc. For real-world operations we insist on operational command. Your general will handle your men, mine will handle everything else."

"I don't know if I can sell that, Victor," Michaels said with skepticism.

"It is a matter of trust, yes?" Komiskov said. "Your president is trusting us to supply oil as a hedge against the Arabs. You bring this proposal to us and then don't trust us?"

Michaels sighed. "Victor, our pilots are volunteers and what we may ask them to do borders on illegal, something their code of ethics may not support. If they receive a flagrantly illegal order they may not carry it out, even if it is the right thing to do. It is their prerogative as American officers. This may fly in the face of Russian officer tradition. "

"What defines legal and illegal, Charles?" Komiskov said with an upturn eyebrow.

"My point is that General Tanner must be in agreement with your commander for all operational decisions. The minutia of logistics, weapons and intelligence and the like is no problem, but he must be agree with the targets and the methods of attack, as must I."

"You?"

"Come now, Victor, surely you and I must be in loop," Michaels said. "not on a daily basis, but we must know what, when and where the team strikes."

The discussion continued for another two hours as the details were ironed out. Slowly but surely the points of contention were overcome and by the end of the meeting a timetable was confirmed for delivery of the MiGs, training, and eventual operational readiness. Both Komiskov and Michaels left the meeting satisfied with the results, but both believing they compromised too much. *Now I have to actually get Tanner on board*, Michaels thought, as he slid into the back seat of his limousine.

OFFICE OF THE NATIONAL SECURITY ADVISOR WEST WING, WHITE HOUSE, WASHINGTON DC

The big man waiting in Michaels's outer office paced impatiently. At over six feet tall with a pencil thin mustache and hair graying at the temples the big man was an imposing figure. His fierce blue eyes could burn with passion if you crossed him or grow cold, gray and dispassionate if it went beyond mere ire. Michaels knew the man intimately, having roomed with him in college at the University of Michigan. A trusted confidant, a fierce warrior, a true leader of men and a patriot all described Brigadier General George "Maddog" Tanner. He was also a man with an axe to grind against what he called "pencil-necked geeks trying to destroy my air force". He was a special man and Michaels needed a special man for a very special job.

Born and bred on the harsh, icy plains of North Dakota, this warrior tasted and savored combat for the first time behind the stick of an F-111 fighter/bomber, logging more than forty combat sorties as operations officer of a tactical fighter squadron. Decorated with the Silver Star for heroism he emerged from the war a hero and a combat tested leader. Assigned command of his own squadron he led his men to the highest ever score on the last Operational Readiness Inspection for the F-111F before its retirement. With his trusty steed off to the boneyard it seemed his career was only beginning. It was off to Headquarters Air Combat Command for a year followed by promotion and a year of Air War College.

Upon graduation he returned for a two-year stint as operations group commander of a squadron of F-15E fighter/bombers at RAF Lakenheath. He returned to the US with a star on his shoulder and was given his own wing. As commander of the 55th Fighter Wing he directed wing operations in the Balkan Conflict, his unit winning the Presidential Unit Citation for their contributions. His wing redeployed to the Middle East where they patrolled the borders of Kumar for a year. Finally his wing was diverted from the Kumari mission to fly cover for strikes on terrorist camps in Afghanistan.

Things were going wonderfully for the general and a second star seemed a sure thing. Then tragedy struck. A pair of his F-15Cs collided in the airspace over Afghanistan during a night sortie. Both pilots were lost in the accident and the further investigation showed one of the pilots had not completed LANTIRN (Low Altitude Night Tactical Infra-red Navigation) recurrency training in the previous six months. This was deemed a contributing factor to the accident and since he had ultimate responsibility as commander he became the chosen scapegoat.

He left the 55th Fighter Wing and landed rather heavily in an obscure office deep inside the cold walls of the Pentagon. The assignment he'd been dreading had arrived and the nearest jet fighter was over twenty miles away.

It was hard for Tanner to finally realize he was no longer on the fast track to the upper levels of Air Force leadership. Up until this assignment he'd been on that fast track and looked like he could go all the way, at least three stars, maybe a fourth. Now this low visibility assignment, coupled with the accident report, a copy of which now resided in his personnel file, meant he was no longer a player. He'd been relegated to the status of an also ran. He was a general officer, but a minor one with limited responsibilities and no real way to realize his true potential.

All assignments were supposed to have a bright side; this one was just a bit dimmer than usual. He was now working in the Pentagon in the nation's capital. It was true he didn't fly any more, he was never less than elbow deep in paper work, and he spent most of his time making viewgraphs that illustrated how well things were going or explaining the view graphs to a visiting three star who wanted to impress the Chairman of the Senate Armed Services Committee. They say an assignment is what you make of it. He was making himself miserable. He wanted out. He wanted to get back out there and make a difference and Michaels knew it.

"George, come on in and have a seat," Michaels said, waving the tall blue-suiter into his office. "How long has it been? Five years?"

"Eight, actually," Tanner said, reaching across the broad expanse of

Michaels' desk to shake his hand. "I think it was at that reception for the Soviet Rocket Forces Commander."

"It sure was," Michaels agreed. "My, God, how time flies. Seems like yesterday we were tapping a keg at the old Delta House, doesn't it?"

"Times have been good to you," Tanner said, gesturing about the office. "National Security Council---advisor to the President---I'm impressed."

"All I had to do was kiss the right ass. You're the war hero, George."

"That is ancient history and now I think we've sucked each others' dicks long enough. Talk to me. Why did you call me here? I assumed it wasn't to discuss the old frat house, otherwise we'd be into our third martini by now."

Michaels laughed. He'd forgotten just how forward Tanner could be. He wasn't dealing with any bureaucrat here; this was George Tanner, an old drinking buddy. It was this no nonsense side of Tanner he loved and it only reminded him of what a perfect choice he'd be for this assignment.

"You know, George, profanity is the crutch of the inarticulate motherfucker."

Tanner stared hard into Michaels' eyes, then suddenly the corners of the eyes wrinkled ever so slightly and he burst out laughing. "Touché."

"You are right about this being business, though. I have a job opening that may interest you. At least I hope you so."

Tanner shook his head. "Chuck, you know I don't get off on this political bull shit," he protested. "Besides they haven't put me out to pasture completely. I'm not ready to leave the service. I appreciate the thought, but..."

"You won't be leaving the service. I have an Air Force position in need of a motivated, dedicated, combat proven general officer," Michaels said.

"Maybe so---but I just got the job in the Pentagon and I..."

"You what? Can't leave it because you love it so much? Is that it?" Michaels interrupted. "Don't tell me you hate political bullshit and then try to feed me some. If you'd played better politics you wouldn't be in this predicament. You hate your job at the Pentagon. Don't look at me like that. I know you, George; you will dry up and die in that Puzzle Palace. Now I'm offering you a parole from that purgatory and the least you can do is hear me out."

Tanner turned red clamped his lips together tightly and shook his head in disgust. As much as he would like to tell Michaels off, he knew he was right. He did hate the job. He just didn't need an old buddy from college telling him he's screwed his career, especially a successful old buddy. Now here comes Chuck to the rescue. Tanner wanted to resent his interference, but the opportunistic side of him thought better to listen to what he had to say first.

"Go ahead. I'm listening."

Michaels smiled a tight-lipped smile. He knew Tanner better than Tanner knew himself. At least he hoped he did. The ballgame was riding on it.

"George, recently we've acquired twelve MiG-41 fighters from Russia. We're looking to train some our guys to fly them. Shall I go on?"

"Sure," Tanner said gesturing impatiently. He was leaning forward now, eyes widened. His body English said everything. Michaels had set the hook, now he just couldn't let this big fella break the line.

"What I'm looking for is a commander for a detachment established as a separate command outside the auspices of the Air Force. You'll answer to the NSC, namely to myself. In other words you'll be on your own with essentially unlimited resources…at least for the short term.

"You will assemble a team of four pilots and an intelligence officer. You are free to pick whomever you'd like. You'll be based out at Tonopah and most of the training will occur in the RED FLAG ranges surrounding Nellis. I hope you are interested, George. If not I've probably already told you more than I should have."

"You know damn well I'm interested, Chuck, but what is this all about? Why are we training in MiG-41s and why the NSC control? Shouldn't the Air Force be heading this up?"

"This project is incredibly black, George," Michaels said. "I can't go into the details with you until you agree to come on board. Let's just say we may have need for MiG-trained pilots to work alongside our new Russian allies."

Russian allies! Bullshit, Tanner thought. *That's an oxymoron if I ever heard one. What could we possibly be doing working alongside the Russians?* Apparently there is only one way to find out, he conceded.

"How do I get out of the Pentagon job, or have you already cleared that path for me?"

"Don't worry about that, I'll take care of it with a single phone call."

Tanner eyed him skeptically. Michaels could read his mind.

"George, I know I haven't given you much, but what do you really have to lose? You have everything to gain here, and I promise a few surprises along the way that will make it all worth while."

This caused Tanner to raise an eyebrow. The big general appeared pensive for only a moment then nodded, more to himself than Michaels. "When do I start?"

"Excellent," said Michaels reaching over his huge desk to shake Tanners hand enthusiastically. "You won't be sorry."

Phase one complete, thought Michaels. He leaned over and buzzed his secretary, who answered the call promptly.

"Jean, have my car brought around," Michaels said into the black box at his elbow. "I won't need a driver."

"Yes, Dr. Michaels."

Tanner raised his eyebrows. "You going somewhere?"

"*We* are, George," he said. "Now that you've accepted the position, there are some things we need to discuss, but not here…over lunch, my treat."

Why don't I like the look in his eyes, Tanner asked himself as they left the office?

Michaels pulled the big Lincoln out onto the Beltway and accelerated smoothly, blending seamlessly into the flow of noon traffic. With no particular destination in mind they rode in silence for several minutes while he planned his attack.

Michaels finally spoke. "George, we need to talk about this job you'll be taking," he paused, and then added. "I am taking you to lunch, but we need to talk first."

"Okay, so what's the deal," the general asked. "I'm curious as to what is so sensitive you couldn't tell me in your office."

"There are facets of your new job which have confidentiality a little too high for my office."

"But the front seat of a Lincoln is a more secure environment?"

"In this case, yes," Michaels said, looking briefly away from the road and into his friend's steel-blue eyes. The seriousness in Michaels' own eyes spoke volumes to Tanner.

"Okay, let's have it."

Michaels let him have it. When it was over Tanner only had one comment.

"Holy shit," he said, sitting back in his the seat.

"Still in?" Michaels asked.

"Sure."

THE KREMLIN

COMMONWEALTH OF INDEPENDENT STATES

"So the President gave approval for the operation?" Kamorova asked.

"Da. The President agrees with the Americans that this warrants special attention," Komiskov said.

"Did you give him your whole plan or just what the Americans promised?"

Komiskov chuckled. "The President is a smart man. If he does not see the opportunities in Sandor now he will as the situation develops. Of this I have no doubt."

"What about the Americans?"

"What about them?"

"They are in operational control of this new strike team. They have stated they do not wish to start a war. How do you get them to go along with you?" the lanky Russian asked.

"They *share* operational control, but they rely on our intelligence and targeting," Komiskov said. "General Kavinsky is a chess grand master. He will be able to move them when and where he wants, believe me."

"What about Michaels? Can he be bought if need be?" Kamorova asked.

"I'm not sure...possibly," Komiskov said, scratching his beard. "Or he may be susceptible to black-mail. Either way we should be able to count on him. If not we could eliminate him, I suppose."

"And this general of his? This Mad Cow?"

"Mad Dog," Komiskov corrected. "General Tanner is a soldier. He will do what he is ordered to do. Remember Tanner is the team leader in the US, but when deployed he shares command."

Kamorova nodded. He had been in the Red Army as a young man and knew what being a soldier meant.

"When is the first operation scheduled?" he asked.

"Six of the MiGs are already in Tonopah. Their training begins in one week. We anticipate three months until they are combat ready."

"According to the last schedule we saw before abandoning the project the Sandori reactor at Habruk will be fueling about that time frame," Kamorova said.

"Da."

TONAPAH AUXILLARY AIRFIELD, NEVADA

0730 LOCAL

As he took the podium he scanned his small audience. The men were braced at attention, the four pilots on the front row, the lone intelligence officer behind them. Their flight suits appeared cleaned and pressed, their unit and command patches bright and colorful. Tanner allowed himself a moment, if only a short one, to reflect on the men he'd chosen for this duty. These men were some of the best men his nation had to offer and he knew that. They were the instruments of national policy, the tip of the spear.

Tanner had scoured the Air Force to find these men. They alone, among hundreds of their peers, possessed all the qualities Tanner had been looking for. They were all instructor fighter pilots; all were Fighter Weapons School graduates, all with exemplary flying skills. Also they were all single with no family ties to bind them. Often for 'special' programs that was preferred. These traits alone could describe half of the fighter pilots in the Unites States Air Force, but each of these men had something else Tanner was looking for, they each had something to prove. Each could be called a maverick, although each for a different reason.

Captain David Olmstead, call sign "Hawkeye", was born and raised on a farm just outside Waterloo, Iowa. He spent his youth working long, hot summers in the cornfields for his old man. Backbreaking days that started before the sun came up and ended well after it disappeared over the horizon taught him valuable lessons of perseverance, hard work, and responsibility. He watched as the farm slowly killed his father little by little every day. Eventually his father lost the farm after a couple bad drought years and just a year later died of a heart attack in a rusty mobile home outside Cedar Rapids just as his son was graduating from high school. His mother was still in that trailer and a portion of his monthly pay went directly to her bank account.

Olmstead won an Air Force ROTC scholarship to the University of Iowa, where he studied mechanical engineering. He received his F-15 by finishing number two in his pilot training class. He went on to graduate at the top of his RTU class and was stationed at Luke AFB, Arizona. After three years in the Arizona desert he went on to Eglin AFB, Florida for three more years. During that time his unit deployed to Turkmenistan, a former Soviet republic, and flew fifty combat air patrols over Afghanistan in support of the war on terrorism, though he never saw any air-to-air action. Upon returning to the US he won a slot to the Fighter Weapons School at Nellis. Upon graduating he was assigned to the 4th Fighter Wing, Kimpo AB, Korea to defend the DMZ against an increasingly hostile North Korea. A superb F-15 pilot and flight instructor, he drew Tanner's attention when he downed a MiG-29 over the DMZ. Shot up and on fire, he returned to base on one engine and brought back excellent intelligence on the MiG, the AA-11 and AA-10.

The shootdown drew Tanner's attention, but what really sealed the deal was when he learned the full circumstances of the engagement. He knew the emotional baggage Olmstead was carrying and he knew his squadron mates were ostracizing him. That was when Tanner swooped in. It took about thirty seconds to get Olmstead to agree to leave his squadron for a special 'hazardous duty'. He felt the need to redeem himself as well as escape his past. Maybe Tanner could give him both.

Captain Francis Romano, call sign "Bear", was an anomaly. He graduated dead last from his Air Force Academy class, 991 out of a possible 991. If he'd gone to the Naval Academy he'd have been called the "Anchor", but in the Air Force he was simply called Lieutenant, as he liked to remind people who brought up his class standing. His call sign "Bear" reflected his physical stature. He was short, but broad shouldered and rock solid though and through.

Redeeming himself at pilot training he graduated number one and went on to fly the F-16. A hard-drinking, profanity-spewing Second Generation Italian from the Bronx, he didn't seem like the fighter pilot type. Being short and squat he had a tremendous G-tolerance, which he exercised regularly. Known for over-G-ing his AT-38 all through Fighter Lead In Training, in a furball he'd pull 7 G reversals until his opponent simply wore out or G-locked and passed out. The gun was his weapon of choice for close in combat.

His first assignment was the 21st Fighter Squadron at Hill AFB, Utah. His records indicated he'd deployed to the Middle East and flew three covert strike missions, all of which were classified Top Secret, Need to Know. Romano was decorated with the Distinguished Flying Cross for those missions and subsequently won a slot at the Fighter Weapons School, where he graduated at the top once again. His reward was assignment to the 57th Wing at Nellis, where he flew an adversary F-16 during RED FLAG exercises. When Tanner called the RED FLAG squadron commander to ask who he'd like to recommend for a special assignment away from RED FLAG, the response was immediate: Romano.

Romano was probably the best close-in dogfighting pilot in his squadron, but the commander was glad to get rid of him due to a few run-ins he'd had with the wing leadership. The young Italian had a habit of calling it like he saw it and never mind the consequences. If a formation was sloppy it didn't matter to Romano if he was debriefing a lieutenant of a lieutenant general. He'd berate anyone who didn't perform to his expectations. He was not exactly diplomatic and more than one field grader left a debriefing hot under the collar. The squadron commander did respect Romano's honesty, but smoothing things over with the wing leadership was getting old. He was happy to see Romano disappear for a few months.

Captain Johnny "Cowboy" Cahill grew up waste deep in tumbleweed in a small town in the Texas panhandle. Growing up poor in a trailer park, his old man died while driving drunk when he was four, leaving him, his older brother Josh and their mother to fend for themselves. His mother worked as a waitress at a local greasy spoon and was barely able to keep clothes on her growing boys. Johnny was a bright lad, however, and a hard worker, just like his brother Josh before him. When the time came for college Josh's thoughts were on other things. The money wasn't there and he wanted out of West Texas and didn't want to wait four more years, anyway. When Josh graduated high school he immediately enlisted in the Army, and ironically was stationed at Fort Hood, Texas. Johnny gave Josh a hard time about that but soon the Army moved Josh overseas and on to bigger things.

The Army was Josh's way out of the little trailer park and Johnny, not to be out done, would follow a similar route. Johnny graduated at the top of his high school class and received an ROTC scholarship to Texas A&M, the school all Texans held in reverence. He got his degree in Aerospace Engineering, his tearful mother pinning on his shiny butter bars at the commissioning ceremony. The tall, lanky Texan, who couldn't keep the swagger out of his step or the drawl from his voice, graduated number two from pilot training, number one in his F-15E training unit, and was a distinguished graduate of Fighter Weapons School. Having risen from a trailer park in West Texas to flying a sixty five million dollar fighter, Cahill considered himself the living personification of the American Dream. Deep down inside he wanted to make a difference in the world, a difference his daddy never made. If he could make that difference, then maybe siring a worthy offspring was the one thing his drunken father had done right.

Just after the last Gulf war, Sergeant Josh Cahill was killed during a chemical weapons attack by Achmed Al Faisal on a Hadishi village. He had been in the village with a UN team acting as military advisors to the Hadish. They were trying to build a faction with which to revolt against the regime of Achmed Al Faisal. Infiltrators managed to learn of the proposed revolt and

Achmed authorized an attack against that village. The little encampment was bombarded for two hours with chemical mortar fire. A combination of nerve and mustard gas mortar shells rained down of the village and hundreds were killed.

Sergeant Josh Cahill was medically evacuated after the attack and appeared to have survived the ordeal with a minor throat irritation. Three hours later blisters began to form in his throat and esophagus. Obviously exposed to a choking agent of some sort the doctors could only stand by and watch as his lungs filled with fluid and he died a slow, agonizing death. Tanner knew Cahill would jump at the chance for a little payback for his brother's death, especially if the mission were against Kumar.

Captain Michael "Fletch" Fletcher, graduated at the top of his Air Force Academy class. He went on to pilot training and graduated number one from there as well. He was a distinguished graduate from F-15 RTU and Squadron Officer School. Clearly on the fast track to command he was looking for something like this program to further distinguish himself. A stern, intense young man, with rigid military bearing, he expected nothing but excellence from himself, as well as those around him. He accepted no foolishness or failures either from himself or others. This did not endear him to many other fighter pilot types, but he was respected and they knew he was a man they could trust. Fiercely loyal to his sparse group of friends he had been a poster child for the Air Force and what it stood for. Tanner discovered Fletcher during a visit to Nellis where he was stationed as an instructor with the Fighter Weapons School. A steely-eyed, disciplined fighter pilot, he'd also seen combat in the Middle East, patrolling the No-Fly Zone over Kumar. Though he never saw any air-to-air action, he did have the distinction of having survived an SA-6 missile salvo fired at his flight. The SAM site was later destroyed by HARM missiles fired from an F-16CJ, vectored into the target area by Fletcher himself.

Tanner also knew Fletcher's little brother had been Olmstead's wingman and had been shot down over Korea. Fletcher blamed Olmstead for the incident, but equally blamed the Air Force for making Olmstead a hero afterward. The whole incident left Fletcher jaded toward the service and toward Olmstead. Tanner knew the Olmstead issue might be trouble, but also thought they would push each other to perform. It was a gamble bringing the two together, but a gamble Tanner felt had good odds of success. Conflict breeds creativity. Fletcher had some aggression to release and Tanner had just the place to release it.

"Seats," Tanner ordered. The men sat down. "Gentlemen, welcome to the desert. To start off, a few ground rules. There is a great deal of very Top Secret work going on out here. You've all heard about Dreamland, I assume. Well this isn't exactly Dreamland, but Tonopah is an emergency airfield for aircraft flying out of that facility. During the course of your stay you may from time to time see things you should not. This can't be helped, so the first rule is: for everything you say, see or do here you are sworn to secrecy. That means forever. By accepting this assignment you've already agreed to that.

"Second rule: no outside telephone calls from this point on, unless cleared by me personally. Third rule: no mail, faxes, or E-mail will be sent out from this location. No logging onto the Internet for stock quotes or dirty pictures, either. See Lt. Sutherland or me for anything you need. Bottom line is no communication with the outside world at all. This base is your world for the next twelve weeks."

There were visible frowns on the pilots' faces at this prospect and a murmur of discontent, the loudest coming from the irate Italian. *They wouldn't be fighter pilots if that didn't piss them off*, Tanner thought.

"Sir, does that mean the lieutenant can get us porn?" Romano asked, with a grin.

Tanner smiled. "Romano, you just give him your tastes and I'm sure he'll be able to come up with something." The men laughed. Lieutenant Sutherland, not getting the humor, studiously wrote on his notepad "Get porn". Later Romano would be surprised, but pleased.

"You have been selected for a very special, very unique program. You haven't been briefed on the exact nature of this program because it is constantly evolving in scope. As you know there has been a lull in terrorist ops over the last year. We believe these countries are taking a break from Jihad to re-arm. Our friends the Russians have up until recently been selling advanced MiGs to Sandor, Kumar and a few others...anybody with cash or oil. They finally started getting stung by terrorism and have wised up---or so they say.

"Unfortunately, unlike the good old days, this time the Russians sold them some very good hardware, utilizing Western technology and parts. They had the cash to produce the good stuff since they were funded by oil rich states that thought they needed an air force to compete with us.

"This proliferation of some very advanced hardware, such as the AA-11 and AA-12 air to air missiles makes for some dangerous ragheads in the Middle East who might not be so intimidated by the West if they have equal or superior weaponry. We get our ass kicked just once in the Gulf and the door will swing wide open to other anti-American attacks. It's our perceived invincibility that gives us an edge. We get a couple Vipers, or God forbid, Eagles splashed out there and that will open a lot of eyes. We need to know now how to prevent this," he looked at Olmstead, pausing for a moment, then continued. "That's where you guys come in. Gentlemen, follow me."

Tanner led them out of the classroom and down several corridors and flights of stairs until finally he stopped at the doorway to a massive, darkened hangar. He stopped outside the door and held it open for the five officers to enter. They stepped into total darkness. None of the buildings or hangars in the complex had any windows. The hangar doors were hermetically sealed, and the temperature and humidity kept constant for the more temperamental aircraft usually stored here. Tanner, always one for drama, let them stand in the darkness for a moment, wishing for a drum roll.

"Here is our hedge against the ragheads, gentlemen," he said, flicking the switch for the massive arc-lighting tracks overhead.

The sudden brightness made every man squint and shield his eyes for a moment. When they adjusted and opened their eyes they saw the "solution". Every mouth fell wide open. Lined up in echelon across the giant hangar were six, pristine, gleaming, MiG-41 fighters. The gray Russian-built aircraft seemed to glow in the bright overhead light, their canopies polished, throwing small rainbows. Under each wing was a full complement of state of the art, AA-10 Alamo, AA-11 Archer, and AA-12 Adder air-to-air missiles. The only markings on the aircraft were black, block numbers painted on their sleek noses.

"Holy shit," someone said.

Tanner smiled. As a fighter pilot himself he could appreciate their reaction to this unexpected surprise.

"Gentlemen, I present to you the only MiG-41s to ever touch US soil. This is why you are here," he said.

The four pilots and the intel officer rushed over to the first two birds of prey and began their first ever hands-on inspection of a state of the art Russian fighter. They walked around the warplanes touching them and commenting to each other on this and that. Though relations with Russia were much improved the same could not be said for the rest of the Third World. Every one of them knew that if they were to meet another plane in combat it would be one of these or something very similar.

Olmstead stood alone near the left wing of the second plane. The others were pointing out something on the infrared search and track, but he was just standing there, staring at the AA-10E slung under the wing. He reached out and touched it then pulled his hand back as if bit, remembering what a missile like this had done to Pete. Then he gazed at the AA-11 on the next pylon, and remembered what one like it did to his own F-15, how it had turned the impossible corner and came after him.

Tanner stood aside while his men got familiar with their new steeds. With the exception of Olmstead, they were like kids in a candy shop, hands all over the shiny new MiGs. Cahill actually kicked a nose wheel tire on one of the aircraft, as though he were buying a new Buick. The intel officer, Sutherland was also a focus of attention. Questions about the MiG were endless. He was a machine, though, spitting out facts and figures, turn rates, radar ranges, like a human encyclopedia. Sutherland had in fact seen the MiG-1.44 prototype before, but never a MiG-41. He was able to study the modern fighter up close at the Paris Air Show. After that brief exposure he went on to write an article for Air Power Journal about the future of Russian fighter design and it's impact on world security. That was why Tanner tagged him for this assignment.

First Lieutenant Todd Sutherland was young, only two years out of Purdue, but he knew his stuff. He was also extremely professional in his manner as well as his work. Dedicated and motivated weren't strong enough words to describe him. Tanner also knew he would be very, very loyal. A lieutenant looks upon a brigadier general the way a priest looks at the Pope.

"General, are you saying we're gonna get to fly these fuckers?" asked Romano. Then he turned red at his reversion to Bronx-verbiage. "Excuse me, sir."

"That's exactly what I'm saying, Captain," Tanner said, ignoring the language. "Each of you will learn to fly and fight in these "fuckers", as you so eloquently say. You will fly every day the MiGs are available. Over the next twelve weeks you will log roughly 100 hours in these birds. You will learn air-to-air as well as air-to-ground tactics, using actual CIS weapons."

"Where in the world did we get these airplanes, sir?" asked Cahill. "I thought the MiG-41 never went into production. Didn't Russia shut down the line after just a few prototypes?"

"They built about 150 of these before shutting it down. They were built and sold for export. These six, plus six others were in production when Russia clamped down on the exports. These airframes were completed and sat in mothballs for a year until we bought them.

"You will fly air to air missions both against each other and against our own aircraft. We will also conduct air to surface attacks using these aircraft in the strike role, with a defensive air-to-air secondary role, similar to the F-15E. At the end of three months you will be combat ready in the MiG-41."

"Are we expecting combat, General?" Romano asked.

"Well, gentlemen, you're not learning all this to go on the air show circuit," he said. "We are even now forging new alliances with the Russians for security, oil, trade, etc. The NSC feels we need some MiG-trained killers who could work with the Russians if necessary. I can't go into any more detail than that. A lot of those details are still being ironed out.

"This is an unprecedented and historical opportunity you are getting. That's the good news. Now here is the bad news. This program is black world, Top Secret, Need to Know. All of the civilians and military personnel you see in this complex are flown in every day in three shifts. There are no living quarters on this base. You on the other hand will be staying here. You will live in a Quonset hut behind this hangar. It is air-conditioned, but it's basically a left over from World War II. You will have a community shower and toilet. You were only going to have cots, but I managed to scrounge up some single beds from Nellis billeting. You will have an office in this building. Each of you will have your own desk. There is one computer in the office. I know the conditions are a bit Spartan, but unfortunately we have to do this on the cheap. Your schedule will be far too busy to spend hours on a transport plane every day. Also we don't want any security leaks or other such distractions.

"There is a chow hall and an O'club annex on base. There is also a gymnasium with a well-equipped weight room. Since this place works three shifts all facilities are opened 24 hours a day. We also expect you to stay in excellent condition, and even improve your G-tolerance, so you will hit the gym daily for weight training.

"You'll spend today getting your quarters squared away and your office set up. There will be four copies of the MiG-41 Flight Manual in your office. You can take them to your quarters for study, but that's as far as they go. We don't want anybody in the O'club buffet line seeing a MiG-41 Flight Manual. They are also to be locked up in the safe in the office at night. There is a cipher lock on the door so you can get in 24 hours a day.

"That's about it, gentlemen," Tanner said. "Tomorrow you will start your first MiG-41 systems class at 0800 in the small classroom. It would help if you looked over the manual tonight after you settle in. Are there any questions?"

Fletcher raised his hand. "Where is your office, sir?"

"I won't be out here with you on a day to day basis," Tanner said. "When I'm here I'll be in your office. There's not much need for a one star on this end. I'm going back to Langley for a couple of weeks and then stop by the Puzzle Palace before coming back here. By the time I get back you should be in the air-to-air phase. Any other questions?" There weren't any.

"Okay, gentlemen, lunch is in an hour. I suggest you guys get to know each other and move your stuff into the barracks. I'll meet you at the Club in an hour. They serve a wicked pepper steak on Mondays.

"I want to stress the importance of keeping the hangar doors closed. Remember no words about this program outside your quarters or the hangar. When we leave this building we close the hangar doors behind us. Got it?" The men nodded. "See you at lunch."

"Oh…by the way," he said over his shoulder as he left. "Don't even tell me you don't belong to the O'club."

"John Cahill, call sign Cowboy," Cahill said to Olmstead reaching out to shake his hand.

"Dave Olmstead, call me Hawkeye. Nice to meet you, Cowboy," Olmstead said. "I assume you're from Texas?"

"Good guess. You a college boy, ain't cha?" the Texan said in his best down home drawl. "Hey, you met ole Bear, over here?" he asked tapping Romano on the shoulder.

"Bear, this here's Hawkeye," Cahill said introducing the two pilots. "Hawkeye, Francis Romano."

The squat New Yorker grimaced at the tall Texan. "Just call me Bear. No one calls me Francis, except my mother and Private Pyle here," he said hooking a thumb at the grinning Texan.

The two men shook hands. "So where you from, Hawk?" Romano asked.

"Iowa," he replied. "You must be from Jersey."

"Don't start by getting on my bad side, Hawk," Romano warned. "I wouldn't be caught fucking dead in fucking Jersey." Olmstead laughed.

"So you finally crawled out from the rock you were hiding under, Olmstead," Fletcher said, staring directly into the young captain's eyes.

Olmstead had been dreading this moment since he walked into the classroom. Luckily there was an empty seat next to Cahill. Seeing Pete's brother was a real shocker for him, especially since he knew how Mike Fletcher felt about him. He blamed him for his brother's death. This was very bad.

"You two know each other?" asked Cahill. Olmstead nodded.

"Oh, sure everybody knows the Hawkeye," Fletcher said. "Hell, he was on the cover of Air Force Times two months ago."

"I didn't expect to see you here," Olmstead evenly, ignoring the goading.

"No, I didn't think you would, " Fletcher said, his voice venom. "Probably wouldn't have come, huh?"

"Uhhh…do I sense a little tension here?" Romano asked.

"Oh no," Fletcher assured him. "It's not a *little* tension."

"Alright, what's the deal?" Cahill asked, suddenly very serious.

"Why don't you ask him about his Silver Star," Fletcher said.

Olmstead stared at him for a moment. He saw the hatred in Fletcher's eyes.

"Mike is Pete Fletcher's older brother. Pete was my wingman back in Korea. He was shot down when we were engaged by two MiG-29s over the DMZ," he said. "Took an AA-12 in the mid-body fuel tank. The plane exploded and he had no time to get out. I took the guy out who got him with a Slammer," Olmstead cringed inwardly. He hated that he still had to lie about the incident.

"Oh yeah, you got him all right," Fletcher spat. "They pin a fucking medal on your chest and call you a 'hero'. Pete got a pine box for his dental work, which was all they recovered of him, and a posthumous DFC. Nice touch."

"Your brother knew the risks, just like you know it."

"Yeah, well you were his flight lead. You were responsible for him. He counted on you to keep him alive and you let him down."

"I did everything by the book, Mike," Olmstead insisted. "Believe me I would have taken the missile myself to save him. He was like a brother to me." Immediately Olmstead knew he'd said the wrong thing. The loathing that burned in Fletcher's eyes flared bright then turned ice cold, dispassionate.

"He *was* my brother. Tell me; were your jamming pods on? Was your radar in radiate?"

"Yeah, we were radiating," Olmstead said, intentionally not elaborating on the issue.

"You were radiating the whole time? I heard you didn't go to radiate until you were in Slammer range," Fletcher said.

"Initially we were running radar silent. We didn't want to give away our position with a radar strobe," Olmstead insisted. "It's standard operating procedure in that theatre when operating with an AWACS. If you'd ever served in Korea you'd know that."

"Give away your position? The bad guys were doing a GCI. And with their data link capability they knew where you were!" Fletcher said exasperated. "Why do you think they went to radiate when they did? They knew you were inside the AA-12 envelope for a face shot. I bet it took them less than five seconds to lock you up, right?"

"Yeah, about five seconds, " Olmstead said, again bending the truth.

"And you had an almost immediate missile launch indication?"

"Well---yes---but…"

"They fired the missile boresighted to their IRST, then let the missile radiate for the terminal portion of the intercept. That missile was airborne before you ever got the radar indication. That wasn't the MiG radar that locked you up it was the AA-12s active radar. If you'd had your pods on it might not have been able to lock you up. Then you could have gotten off the Slammer in time to get the first shot," Fletcher shouted. "They suckered you in too close. Then you froze up. Besides if you'd been radiating from the start they would have known you were F-15s and not some little wimpy Korean F-5. They might've lost their nerve and turned tail."

That's a big 'if'," Olmstead shouted back. He did not want to get into this argument with Fletcher, who was already too close to the truth. "You can't know any of that for sure. We followed the doctrine. We did it by the book and they got lucky."

"Were they lucky when they got you too?" Fletcher said.

"They didn't get me," Olmstead said. "I brought the plane back. Besides he fired that AA-11 damn near over the shoulder."

"Excuses," Fletcher said vehemently. "Now you are blaming the missile. That's combat! You fight with what you bring. You should've splashed the bandit before you ever got into heater range. If you would just admit that you screwed up maybe I'd cut you some slack, but you never admit anything." Olmstead just shook his head and sighed. It was an old argument and this was going nowhere.

"Well that was an icebreaker," Romano said sarcastically.

"Look, if you guys cain't work together then you best tell Tanner or we will," Cowboy said. "We gotta be a team and if you two don't trust each other you ain't worth a damn to the team. I get real mad when someone lets the team down. Now can you fellers put this aside for now and play nice together? Or are you gonna let me down?" Cowboy asked menacingly. Both Olmstead and Fletcher understood the tone in that voice.

"Hey, I'm too good to let my personal problems interfere. It doesn't matter what I think of this sorry son of a bitch. I'll save his neck when the time comes," Fletcher said. "I expect I'll have to. That way he'll learn how to protect a wingman. But, listen close, Mr. Silver Star, I'll be watching you and I'll make damn sure next time you don't wind up with an Air Force Cross and me in the pine box."

The two men glared at each other. Romano and Cahill looked at each other with grim expressions. This was a potential powder keg.

"Well, that gave me a warm fuzzy feeling inside. I think I'm misting up over here," Romano said, wiping away an imaginary tear. "Is it lunch time yet?"

They spent the next hour moving their gear over to their "new" home. New was not the proper adjective. The old, decrepit Quonset hut had protruded from the desert floor for over sixty years. The desert is a low humidity environment, but even here the age showed and the sinks and toilets were rust-stained remnants of the days of Winston Churchill and P-51 Mustangs. The beds were little more than army cots with a mattress thrown on top, mattresses that looked a little older than the plumbing. No doubt they had come from Nellis billeting. They were probably being thrown out. Large wool blankets bearing the insignia US were folded at the foot of the beds and pillows that once could have been called white were at the head.

The one bright point was the ancient air conditioner, obviously a heavy-duty industrial model. It looked and sounded like a caged tornado and dripped water in a continuously fed puddle, which drained through the cracks in the wooden floor. But it was ice cold inside, shielding them from the intense 115-degree heat outdoors. It was something.

There was a 70's yellow refrigerator and a small electric stove in a corner kitchenette. In the cabinets over the single sink were four plates, four chipped plastic cups, and four sets of utensils. A lone black and white TV with bent rabbit ear antennas sat on a small stand in the other corner of the room, facing two torn naugahyde recliners flanking a stained couch with the left armrest ripped open and the stuffing exposed. These were the "Spartan" conditions Tanner had glossed over, all the comforts of home.

The four pilots each chose a bunk and stowed their gear under them. They wandered around with mouths open in disbelief as they looked for the silver lining in this dirty cloud. They could find none.

"Can you believe this shit?" Romano said finally.

Olmstead couldn't believe it either and could only shake his head. Cowboy plopped down on one of the old beds and it shook and squeaked in protest.

He stood up quickly before it collapsed entirely.

"This sucks," Cowboy said. "I haven't lived this way since college." He disappeared into the bathroom.

Fletcher, snorted, muttered something under his breath that could have been a curse, and left, slamming the torn screen door behind him.

"I take it he wasn't thrilled with the accommodations," Romano said.

"I don't think he's thrilled about anything right now," Olmstead said with a sigh.

"Well the water pressure in the urinal is just a little high," Cowboy said, emerging from the bathroom, the front of his flight-suit soaking wet.

Olmstead and Romano looked at the drenched pilot, glanced at each other and burst into laughter.

"Hey, man, this ain't nothin to laugh about," Cowboy insisted, annoyed. "This is my only clean uniform. We're supposed to meet the General at the club in ten minutes and I smell like piss!"

Olmstead and Romano wiped the tears from their eyes and nodded in sympathy, then burst into laughter again.

Romano stopped laughing for a moment and said, "Don't sweat it, man. The General knows you're from Texas. He'll expect you to smell like piss." With that he fell back into hysterical laughter, leaving the soaked Cahill glaring.

"Oh, man, I wish I hadn't eaten that pepper steak," Romano groaned, as they walked down the long dark corridor toward their new office. "Cowboy, you got any Tums on you?"

"Yeah, sure, like I carry antacids in my flight suit," Cahill replied sarcastically, "besides the General said it was a "wicked" pepper steak. You shoulda gotten the clue when he ordered the meatloaf."

"Yeah, well I assumed all Texans carried antacids with the road kill you guys grill and call bar-b-que," Romano said, getting his licks in. The burly Texan just grunted.

They came to the end of the corridor and found the inconspicuous office with a simple 117 on the door. Romano thought the number was strange since there were only about five doors in the whole building. Cowboy tried the door and it swung open freely.

The lights were on inside and Fletcher was already behind one of the government-issue desks. He was leaning back in his swivel chair; his feet perched at the top left side of the desk, absorbed in a very thick aircraft manual. He paused and looked up for a moment, saw Olmstead with the other two, grunted, and went back to his reading.

The room was nearly as Spartan as their barracks. Six desks all in a row facing toward the door, at one end of the room a lone computer sat atop a rickety computer stand, at the other end stood a single massive steel safe with a cipher lock near the handle. This was where the secrets were kept and the thing must have weighed two thousand pounds. There was a single giant air-conditioning duct on the ceiling in the very center of the room, an arctic blast coming down on the center two desks, while the two outside desks were a good twenty degrees hotter. There were no windows.

"Nice," Romano said. "Well, Cowboy, stake your claim. You want next to the wall?"

"I'll take the end desk," Olmstead said, clearly putting as much distance between himself and Fletcher as possible. Fletcher didn't look up, but smiled to himself.

Olmstead slid behind his desk and opened the center drawer. It contained three paperclips and a single red rubber band that was slowly disintegrating. His side drawers netted him a legal pad and a phone book from 1963. "Outstanding," he muttered under his breath.

Cowboy was clearly not pleased by what he found in his desk, a bag of what at one time was moldy French fries and a flying schedule from Nellis Air Force Base. He couldn't make out the date, but the schedule showed a three ship of P-80 Shooting Stars departing at 0700.

"Jesus H. Christ," Cowboy muttered. "I'm starting to lose faith in the program, boys. Does this look like some kinda critical national defense program to any of you?"

Olmstead shook his head. "God help this country if it is."

"Well at least they're being consistent," Romano sighed.

Fletcher slammed his book down hard enough to get their attention.

"Damnit, I'm trying to study here," he said, annoyed. "You don't like the facilities? Either do something about it or shut the fuck up. I'm not happy with this either, but try to remember we volunteered for this."

"I volunteered for a highly critical, top secret program. I assumed there would be *some* funding, that we'd be given the tools we need to do the job right," Romano said. "Hell, I'll bet we have to pump our own gas into the jets. And that rats nest they call our 'quarters'? Hell, I've been in brothels with a higher level of sanitation. Does Tanner really expect us to live and work in these conditions for three months?"

"That's exactly what I expect."

Every body spun around and there in the doorway stood Brigadier General George "Maddog" Tanner in all his one star glory. He was only six feet tall, but still managed to look down on the pilots with eyes of fire. Romano wished he were back in the relative safety of the New York City subway system, actually any place but here and now would do.

"As I have said," he started, his voice booming. "I am aware of the working and living conditions. I am trying to fix some of the problems, but you are going to have to be patient and also realize that you are no longer regular Air Force officers. Don't even think about the Air Force and it's cushy billeting, forty cable channels and extravagant TDY pay to exotic locations where civilians vacation. Think of yourselves in the Army, or better yet the Marine Corps. You are on an operational mission and right now you are in the trenches getting ready to lob hand grenades over the top. This will not be a cushy assignment. There will not be a mint on your pillow every morning. I expect discipline, dedication and professionalism at all times. You are in my Air Force now and it doesn't come with a maid or 126 cable channels. Is that understood?"

The men simply nodded their heads, mouths open, speechless.

"I don't want to have this conversation again, gents. Understood?" With that he was gone, slamming the door behind him.

"Thanks, Bear," Fletcher said sarcastically. "I really needed that."

The squat New Yorker was silent, except for a long sigh, his shoulders slumped, the fire in him gone.

"Welcome to Tanner's Air Force," Olmstead said.

ROOM 7A, TONAPAH AUXILLARY AIRFIELD, NEVADA
0730 LOCAL

"Gentlemen, this is Major Gunter Dreschler of the German Luftwaffe, formerly of the East German Air Force," Tanner said, introducing the lanky, blond pilot. "He is a MiG instructor pilot and the leading authority, this side of Russia, on the MiG-41. Gunter has over 2500 hours in MiG-29s, MiG-35s and MiG-41s. He has served with the Luftwaffe Tactics School as an adversary and tactics instructor and spent two years as a MiG instructor pilot on exchange with the Russian Republic at the MiG factory in Lukhovitsky. Major

Dreschler played an essential part in the MiG-41s development. There is no better man alive to teach adversary combat in the MiG than this man. He was the adversary for a few years. Now he's one of us and we're damned lucky to have him on our side of the pipper.

"You will listen to him, learn from him. He will evaluate your performance and report directly to me," Tanner paused for a moment then continued with a stern warning. " Gentlemen, the Cold War has been over for ten years. I expect nothing from you but complete cooperation and total respect for his rank and experience. What you learn from this man may just keep you alive someday."

Cahill snorted and Tanner glowered at him, a silent warning to the lanky Texan. Cahill got the message.

"Gentlemen, I will leave you in Major Dreschler's capable hands. I'm headed back to the Puzzle Palace and won't be back for another two weeks. I'll expect to see some progress when I return. By the way, Major Dreschler will secure fax me a report of your performances every morning. So the cat's not quite away, understood? Good."

Before leaving Tanner shook hands with Dreschler, whispered something in his ear, at which the tall, blond German chuckled.

Cahill turned to Olmstead and whispered. "Ole Maddog's pretty tight with the Nazi, huh?"

Olmstead raised an eyebrow and said nothing.

Dreschler, standing tall over the lectern, looked at faces of the four pilots, each in turn, with steely blue eyes, the eyes of a hunter.

"Gentlemen," he said in a thick German accent. "I'm Major Gunter Dreschler, call sign "Hammer". You may call me Major Dreschler or Hammer. You will find out why I am called Hammer as we progress." He smiled a tight smile and continued. "Herr General expects you to be flying when he returns. We shall see about that. If I am satisfied with your performance you will fly. Not a moment before. This is where the Hammer comes down, so to speak. These MiGs are a valuable resource and you must convince me you are worthy to fly them.

"All Fourth and Fifth Generation MiGs are easy to fly, especially the MiG-41, so I expect no problems from US fighter pilots," he said. *Was that sarcasm*, wondered Olmstead?

"It is an easy aircraft to fly, but not so easy to take into combat. US pilots are very accustomed to how you say 'user friendly' aircraft. The MiG, like all Russian hardware is not as 'user friendly' as the F-16 or F-15. This is a small handicap we must overcome. Once you get used to the MiG you will find it is just as deadly as any Western fighter aircraft, with some advantages. Most of the problems with Fourth Generation aircraft, such as the MiG-29, dealt with the radar, computer capacity and the short range of the aircraft. The MiG-41's avionics are state of the art and utilize Western microprocessors. It has almost three times the range as the MiG-29 and its computer threat prioritization is on par with comparable Western Fighters. While not a true stealth aircraft it's shape and radar absorbent coatings give it a significantly decreased radar cross-section. It has a fully digital fly by light flight control system and thrust vectored engines with a thrust to weight ratio of 1.4:1. Do not be fooled. The flight characteristics and super-maneuverability of the MiG-41 are better than either the F-16 or the F-15."

Superior to the F-15, thought Olmstead? *Maybe Cahill's right. The guy is a Nazi.*

"It is very easy to lose situational awareness in this aircraft. That is why I want you to have these aircraft specifications, procedures, and systems absolutely committed to memory. This will be essential to your success in the program, as well as your safety," Dreschler continued.

He had been pacing back and forth as he spoke. Now he returned to the lectern and consulted his notes. He turned his back on the pilots and turned on the PowerPoint slide system behind the lectern. The first slide came up and said: Basic Configuration: MAPO-MiG-41. He turned back to the group.

"Gentlemen, we'll start with basic aircraft configuration. Over the next two weeks we will cover flight characteristic, electrics, hydraulics, fly by light, pneumatics, radar, and flight instruments. Are there any questions what the objectives are? Good. There will be a test each morning on the previous day's systems."

"What happens if we fail a test?" Romano asked.

"Trust me, Captain, it is best for you not to dwell on such things. You will not fail any tests. Is that understood?" he said in a calm, cool, very menacing voice.

When Dreschler looked back down at his notes Cahill leaned over to Romano and whispered in his best German accent, "You fail za test, thirty days in za kooler." Romano shook his head and chuckled under his breath. It was enough to get Dreschler's attention.

"Captain, you have something amusing to share with us, yes?" he asked, glaring down at an innocent looking Romano. Romano simply shook his head and raised his hands in protest.

"I thought not," Dreschler said. "Gentlemen, I know you are concerned with your performance. You have to start thinking like a German. We never worry about failing. We assume success."

Maybe that's why you lost two world wars in the last hundred years, Cahill thought. Cahill glanced over at Olmstead who had a grin on his face, as if he had read the Texan's mind.

The tall German flicked a switch and a new slide appeared. This slide compared the relative sizes of the MiG-41 to the F-16, F-18 and F-15.

"The MiG- 41 airframe is a hybrid design. It incorporates some characteristics of the MiG-29 Fulcrum, but it has many improvements over the original Fulcrum. The engineers at MAPO listened to the criticism of the users and most of the Fulcrum's weaknesses have been eliminated in the Fastback. As you can see the MiG-41 is roughly the same size as the F-18 Hornet, but its flight characteristics are closer to the F-16. That is when it is at combat gross weights. The engineers at Mikoyan had to address the relatively short range of the previous MiGs if the MiG-41 was to be a success. As you can see the dorsal spine is much larger than previous designs. This provided room for more internal fuel and a more powerful onboard active jammer. The total internal fuel of the MiG-41 is almost 10,000 lbs, over twice the MiG-29 fuel load.

"Although the dorsal spine gives a swollen appearance to the fuselage and it tapers back to a rather unattractively flat beaver tail between the engines, the new design can actually attain higher AOA than previous MiGs at light weight. The MiG-41 is really two distinctly different aircraft when at maximum gross weight versus combat weight. The extra fuel is meant to get you to the fight, not to be carried during the fight. After burning 4000 lbs of fuel getting to the target, the airframe has slightly better aerodynamics than its predecessor, and far better maneuverability with its vectored thrust RD-333K engines. The MiG does have the advantage of two engines and a higher overall thrust to weight ratio than the F-16. It's G limits and instantaneous turn rates are slightly better than the F-16, although in a high-G furball the F-16 pilot might have better G tolerance due to the Combat Edge G-suit. However, whereas the F-16 flight control computer will not allow the pilot to pull more than 9 Gs, the MiG-41 does not have a G limiter and it is possible to pull greater than 9 Gs in a turning fight, assuming the pilot can stay conscious.

"The fuselage itself is a lifting body design, not unlike the F-14. It employs leading edge wing root extensions, similar to the F-18's. The nose contour now resembles the flatter nose of the F-16 and the twin tails are angled in a fashion similar to the new F-22. These angled stabilizers reduce the radar cross section of the MiG. The aircraft is not a true stealth design, but it does have half the radar cross-section of the MiG-29. It's wings are swept to 35 degrees and do not stall until 56 degrees angle of attack, giving the MiG the ability to really move its nose around in a close-in dogfight, especially with the vectored thrust."

He changed slides again. This showed a table of statistical data.

"The MiG-41 has two advanced RD-333K afterburning turbofans, each rated at 30,000 lbs thrust, with two dimensional thrust vectoring. It is capable of Mach 2.3 in level flight with afterburners and Mach 1.3 at full dry thrust. The basic weight of the aircraft is 24,000 lbs. Maximum gross weight is 38,000 lbs, giving the MiG a thrust to weight ratio of 1.4:1 with full fuel and weapons. The aircraft can roll at better than 300 degrees per second and pull in excess of 10 Gs positive sustained and 4.0 Gs negative. The MiG-41 flight control system utilizes a state of the art four-channel, doubly redundant fly-by-light control system. It incorporates a unique fiber optic cable design used by all primary flight control systems. It uses less power, has faster data transfer rates, and is less susceptible to battle damage than a conventional fly-by-wire system.

"The weapons of choice for the MiG-41 include: AA-10 Alamo, AA-11 Archer, and AA-12 Adder, and nearly any other Russian air to air missile. We will discuss in detail weapons employment and tactics in another briefing later.

"The MiG also carries one GSU-123 30 MM electric cannon with 100 rounds of ammo. Do not be fooled by the lack of ammo. The gun is radar guided and only requires five hits to kill a fighter-sized target. It is a very large projectile. The air-to-air radar is an advanced version of the Zhuk Phazotron RP-45, code-named Slotback IV. It can search out to 100 miles, track 24 targets and engage 6 simultaneously. The radar automatically prioritizes the targets and engages the closest six, a much-needed improvement over the Fourth Generation avionics.

"The MiG-41 also has the improved Infrared Search and Track (IRST) which utilizes a laser range-finder. It can detect and track a fighter at 35 miles and slew the radar to the target. It can track a fighter and fire on it without ever radiating. The MiG also has data link capability with other airborne interceptors, AWACs planes, or ground-based GCI. They can use the data link to find the target, then lock it up with IRST and shoot it in the face with the long-burn infrared version of the AA-10. The newest AA-10s and some older retro-fitted models have laser seeker heads as well as their standard IR seekers, so they can guide off the reflected laser energy of the built in range-finder."

Fletcher's mouth fell open in disbelief. Here was a piece of intelligence he'd never heard before. Why hadn't they been briefing this back in the squadron, for God's sake? This made him wonder again just how his brother had died. Fletcher read the official report that said his brother had been hit by an active radar-guided missile, probably an AA-12. Olmstead had said nothing to indicate otherwise. Did he not know or was he covering something up? Maybe it had been a long burn AA-10 with this laser seeker-head. If it had been, why didn't the official report indicate that? Olmstead's own testimony had not indicated what type missile had been employed. *Did they give this asshole a medal for his silence*, he wondered? Could Olmstead have been bought that easily? He didn't know, but he'd find out.

Olmstead was just relieved that somebody was passing on the intelligence he was forbidden to discuss. He knew that Dreschler would be aware of these tactics. He probably helped develop them. He also knew that if it were being discussed here it would eventually get out, hopefully before somebody got killed.

"The AA-10 Alamo comes in five versions: two semi-active radar homing, and three infrared versions. The AA-10A is a normal semi-active radar homing missile with a range of approximately 22 NM for a beak-to-beak aspect angle. The AA-10B is the heat seeking version with the same kinematic range, but it's IR seeker can only see out to about 12 miles. Obviously tail shots will cut the ranges in half. The real problem is the long-burns, the AA-10C and AA-10D. The Charlie is radar guided and has a range of 35 NM, while the Delta is the infrared version of the same range. The E model is another long-burn and has the laser seeker as well as an improved IR seeker.

"Each missile has its unique weaknesses. Both radar versions have semi-active guidance, so you must keep the nose pointed at the target until impact. The –D model long burn IR seeker head cannot detect a target at the missile's maximum kinematic range. Typically they will launch it boresighted to the radar, the IRST or along a vector the GCI provides. It will fly a simple unguided, ballistic profile until its seeker head detects the target heat signature, then it tracks. If the target maneuvers outside the field of view of the seeker it will stay stupid and never acquire the target. Unless it's fired at night and the rocket flash is visible, the target will never see it coming. In VMC conditions the E models can guide off their laser seeker heads until the IR seekers can detect and lock onto you at about 20 miles with their new and improved seeker head. There is contact fusing with proximity back up for all versions. Our exploitation tests in Germany indicate the long-burn range of this missile is equal or greater than the AIM-130 AMRAAM. Of course the missile requires VMC. Neither its IR nor laser seeker can penetrate clouds or fog.

"As deadly as the AA-10 is, the AA-11 is even better at short range. The latest AA-11, called R-73M, is a cooled seeker head IR missile with devastating accuracy. It has flare rejection, proportional guidance and is the best short-range missile in the world today. It has a kinematic range of 10 nautical miles, nearly medium range, but its new seeker head also has a new super sensitive element allowing lock on of an approaching fighter at almost 20 nautical miles in VMC.

"If one must merge with a MiG-41, he is at an extreme disadvantage. Like the MiG-29 and MiG-35, the MiG-41 with the helmet-mounted sight can designate a target from more than 90 degrees off boresight. The AA-11B version of the Archer is actually a rearward firing missile and can be fired at a target 180 degrees off the nose. If you are carrying both versions the weapon system will actually select the correct missile for the situation.

"If there is sufficient lateral distance between aircraft the forward firing version of the missile can be launched "over the shoulder" if you will. This capability is lacking in the current AIM-9X2, of which I am sure you are all familiar. The US Air Force decided the "over the shoulder" capability was not necessary, so to save money that feature was eliminated. This means in the merge the MiG-41 will have a much wider engagement envelope than a Western fighter. Close in it has a 360-degree weapons detection and launch capability. Using the helmet mounted sighting system the pilot can keep the trigger squeezed and the computer will automatically launch a missile when a target gets within range. If he can see it, he can kill it.

"During German dissimilar air combat exercises we find the MiG-35 and MiG-41 with the AA-11 to be more than a match for F-15s and F-16s. Inside 10 nautical miles the MiGs are nearly unbeatable. The MiG can also perform the Cobra Maneuver, utilizing his extreme AOA capability, in the horizontal as well as vertical plane to move his nose and therefore the missile seeker head into the firing envelope. The Cobra is also augmented by the thrust vectoring system. This maneuver can also be used defensively to break missile lock and we will discuss this in a later class.

"As if the AA-10 and 11 weren't bad enough, there is more bad news for the unlucky pilot who must fight a MiG-41. Russia is now exporting to several Middle Eastern countries the latest long-burn version of the R-77D NATO code-named AA-12D Adder. This missile is a very long range, active radar homing missile capable of pulling over 50 Gs in the terminal mode of the intercept. It's range is over 40 nm and the missile travels at approximately Mach 3. It is launched in semi-active mode using the MiG's radar for the first 10 seconds or so of flight. Then its onboard radar goes active and it homes on the target autonomously. The missile does have a home on jam feature that prohibits noise jamming. If you try to jam the missile its onboard radar will sense when the noise level gets too high and it will go into home on jam mode. If it detects too many targets it will assume it is being deception jammed and will employ a very sophisticated algorithm that causes the radar to frequency hop at a rate most ECM suites cannot keep up with. If noise jamming stops it will start radiating on its own and go back to active homing. It may be susceptible to chaff, at least in a proximity fuse busting role. The AA-12 is basically a longer ranged AMRAAM. In an engagement against an F-15 or F16 the unlucky pilot could expect at least one missile in the face before he ever gets in AIM-130 range."

"He won't get a lock on an F-22 at that range," Romano snorted.

Dreschler smiled patiently "The stealthiness of the F-22 means the MiG's radar won't detect it until much closer, eliminating the range advantage of the AA-12. Now, Captain Romano, how many F-22s are there in service at the moment?"

"None at the moment," Romano admitted sheepishly.

"How many will there be next year?" Dreschler pushed the point.

"None," Romano said, deflated.

"So the point is moot for the time being," Dreschler said, with a dismissive wave. He continued.

"We've only discussed air to air weapons so far, but the MiG-41 is capable of carrying a vast array of Russian general purpose gravity bombs, cluster bombs, TV guided and laser guided bombs and missiles, and anti-radiation missiles. We will cover all of these in another weapons class later.

"Now we will discuss some of the unique flying characteristics of this aircraft," he said. He flipped a switch on the wall behind him and a large projection screen lowered from the ceiling. He flipped on another switch and a VCR hummed to life behind the podium. The lights went down and he hit play.

The screen remained black for a moment then the slightly blurred image of a Russian MiG-41 came into focus flying a very high angle of attack, its nose well above the horizon, seeming to stand on it's engines' burner flames.

"As you can see the low speed handling of this aircraft is superb," he said, "the wing can reach 56 degrees AOA and while the lateral responsiveness is sluggish it is still very stable."

The aircraft on the screen executed a series of Dutch rolls right and left to show the responsiveness of the ailerons and rudders at such low speed. Suddenly the aircraft pitched up beyond 90 degrees nose high, seemed to hang for a moment, then the nose came forward again into level flight in a seemingly impossible maneuver.

"This is the Cobra Maneuver," Dreschler said with respect in his voice. "The aircraft nose pitches up to over 100 degrees, well pass vertical, and the aircraft has enough elevator authority to push it back down into level flight. It can be performed with vectored thrust augmentation or without. During this maneuver the nose can point over 90 degrees from the direction of flight and the forward airspeed drops to nearly zero. With the exception of a VerTOL aircraft, like the AV-8B Harrier, there is no aircraft in the world that can stay behind a MiG or a SU-27 variant when they perform this maneuver. The bad news for any potential enemy is that the AA-11 Archer is a point and shoot missile and the MiG can perform this maneuver either in the vertical or horizontal plane, putting the missile into its launch envelope briefly and getting a shot off.

"The MiG-41 is also capable of the Bell Maneuver, a full translation, essentially a 360 degree pivot in space where the nose goes all the way around," he said. The screen showed an SU-37 performing what started out to be a Cobra, but instead of the nose coming back forward it continued backward and came all the way back to level flight from a reverse pivot in space, again a seemingly impossible maneuver.

"The MiG-41 can perform this same maneuver utilizing its thrust vectoring engines for pitch authority. In this instance it might be possible for the MiG to execute a move like this and fire an IR missile while the nose is pointing aft, like during a merge before the initial turn. A word of caution here---when executing this maneuver the forward airspeed literally drops to zero. You must go to full burner to get back your energy. The MiG wing will stall, but the aircraft is amazingly spin-resistant."

The American pilots were sitting in rapt attention, hanging on the German's every word after seeing the Cobra and Bell Maneuver video. They were clearly impressed and also concerned that fighters like the F-15 and F-16, aircraft they considered state of the art, were incapable of these maneuvers. The US Air Force leadership long ago declared these maneuvers as tricks and not useful in combat, but it was hard to swallow that dogma sitting here now. Useful or not it concerned them all that Russian fighters had a level of maneuverability that went beyond the US fighters' capabilities.

They could just see an F-16 tail-chasing this bird when it pulls the Bell Maneuver. The hapless Viper driver would wonder what the hell just happened---and that would be his last thought. This aircraft's maneuverability, coupled with the AA-11 Archer's wide envelope, lethality and helmet-mounted sight, make it a deadly weapon that was not to be trifled with. Furthermore this MiG was not the only plane the Russians had that could perform these maneuvers or fire these weapons. They had several and were selling them to the highest bidder.

The US Air Force leadership decided that the era of close-in dogfighting was coming to an end and rather than compete with the Russians inside 10 miles, it was much better to kill them at 30 miles and go home. The services' reliance on the AIM –130 AMRAAM II to win the day from medium range was a gamble. The AIM-130 fired from a stealthy F-22 Raptor would take out the bad guys before they could ever get off a shot. The stealthiness of the Raptor prevented the enemy from getting a radar lock and firing that AA-12 at long range. The MiGs would have to press in close to lock up the Raptor and the F-22 would kill it before it ever got close. Great idea.

The down side was that the F-22 was still three years from deployment, and four years from deployment in meaningful numbers. In the meantime the trusty Eagle was still the mainstay of US air-superiority. The fact that the Eagles were almost thirty years old and not significantly upgraded for the last eight years was not considered. The Eagles had the best air to air kill ratio in the history of aerial warfare, but if war broke out in the next two years with a well-trained, well equipped enemy, those same twenty five year old Eagles would meet brand new, state of the art MiGs and Sukois, and that did worry some in the Pentagon. The hope was that a real war, with a real enemy, would not come until the F-22s were ready. It was a gamble.

Over the next week all four pilots survived their initial familiarization sorties. The only loss was a nose gear strut that Cahill swore was ready to fail anyway. Dreschler was pleased with the flying, less so with the pop quizzes he gave every morning. Of course the Americans argued he always chose the most obscure system possible to quiz them on. His philosophy was if they knew the obscure, they'd know the important stuff as well. Now it was time to begin the tactical training. Air-to-Air Phase would start tomorrow. It would prove to be an eye-opener for the pilots, who would now realize the real power of the MiG-41.

TONAPAH AUXILIARY AIRFIELD, NEVADA
0830 LOCAL

Tanner entered the classroom just as Dreschler was beginning the day's lessons and dropped a bombshell. *He had with him two flight-suited figures with odd rank insignia on their shoulders and something about their flight suits just didn't look right*, Olmstead thought. He'd seen that kind of flight suit and insignia before, but where? Then it struck him like a lightning bolt. Russians. *They were Russians*.

"Gentlemen, congratulations on completing Basic Flight," the General said with a broad smile. "You've proven you can fly this airplane without killing yourself. Now we will teach you how to kill others with it." He paused for a moment and the smile faded somewhat while he pondered how to proceed. "Men, the scope of this program being what it is we have been receiving considerable support from our Russian allies. That support until now has concerned mostly logistics support for our MiGs. Now that cooperation reaches a new plateau. Gentleman, I'd like to introduce and formally welcome Major Sergei Gurevich and Captain Michel Dobrinsky of the Russian Air Force. These officers will be joining our team as tactical instructor pilots, to pass on to us the same tactics many of our potential adversaries will be employing. "

Gurevich was tall, blond and had cold blue eyes that scanned the room quickly, coming to rest locked onto the equally cold, blue-eyed gaze of Olmstead. Dobrinsky looked like a Russian version of Romano, short, heavy set with curly black hair, a bushy mustache and a wide smile.

"We are extremely lucky to have these two gentlemen with us on this program," the general said, uneasily. "They are a wealth of combat information concerning the MiG-41. They will also be joining us in the literal sense as well. They are to be integrated into our flight program and will fly with you whenever possible."

Romano leaned over and whispered into Olmstead's ear. "Great. First it's the Nazi, now we gotta kiss up to the fucking Commies. Don't we have any real enemies anymore?"

Olmstead's eyes never left Gurevich's gaze, but he nodded slightly in response. Finally Gurevich broke the eye contact quickly, appearing uneasy.

There was something familiar about this man, Olmstead thought. He was sure he'd never met a Russian before, but still something in this man's gaze made him wonder. The man stared back at Olmstead with knowing eyes as well. What was the connection here? *This Gurevich acts like he recognizes me*, Olmstead thought. *Gurevich? Mikoyan-Gurevich? Could this guy be a grandson or great-grandson of the original Gurevich of Mikoyan-Gurevich, the very origin of the word MiG?*

"Well I won't keep you from your studies any longer," Tanner said. "I'll be on base for the rest of the morning, but I have to run down to Nellis for a few days to get you some F-15 support from the Weapons School boys. Needless to say you must do well against them. I expect only the best from you guys. Sorry again for the interruption, Major. I'll leave these gentlemen with you, " he said gesturing to the Russians. "Major Dreschler here will see to your needs in getting settled. Welcome aboard," he said, shaking their hands and making his way toward the door. "Keep your seats, gentlemen."

Dreschler was clearly uneasy as to where to go with the load Tanner just dropped on him. He was as surprised to see the two Russians as his students were. He also dreaded their presence. He'd worked with Russians before and knew the attitudes they took with foreigners. In this environment Dreschler was set up to be the resident expert, now these two walk through the door. *I'll be damned*, he thought. *If they walk over me like they did in Moscow I won't put up with it here, he thought.*

"Gentlemen, welcome to Tonopah," Dreschler said with as much courtesy as he could muster. "I am Major Gunter Dreschler of the Unified German Air Force," he stressed the word 'unified'. "I spent two years as an instructor at MAPO-MiG during the initial flight testing of the MiG 35 and MiG-41 a few years ago. At the time Germany was evaluating the possibility of trading our old MiG-29s for new MiG-35s. We eventually decided to go another direction, however," he said taking an opening shot.

Dobrinsky smiled and took Dreschler's hand and shook it vigorously. "It is a pleasure, Major," he said simply. Dreschler, surprised by the cordiality, had almost expected to be called 'comrade'.

Gurevich took Dreschler's hand and shook with a grip that was just a bit too firm to be called friendly. "I have comrades back home who speak of you, Herr Dreschler," he said, his eyes still cold. "I look forward to flying with a hero of the People's Democratic Republic," he said, using the name of the former East Germany.

Dreschler was not amused. The PDR was dead over ten years now, and he didn't like to discuss his Communist past. He knew the Russian was feeling him out, probing for weaknesses. He would not let him find any.

"On the contrary, I was no hero, just a humble patriot in the service of the Party, as were we all, yes?" he said, with contempt in his voice. "And I of course have heard of you. It helps one's position to have a name favorable with the Party, yes?"

Gurevich smiled through tight lips and said nothing. Clearly the return volley fired by Dreschler hit a sore spot. Dreschler made note of it for future use, as did his students who were watching the exchange with rapt attention. He then in turn introduced each of the Americans, giving brief backgrounds on each. Olmstead and Gurevich once again made eye contact, the icy stares still intense and puzzlingly familiar.

Dreschler turned to the waiting Americans, sitting patiently and enjoying the verbal thrusts and parries of their foreign colleagues. He beckoned Lt. Sutherland to the podium and whispered in his ear, to which the young lieutenant nodded.

"I will leave you with Lieutenant Sutherland," he told the pilots. "who will teach the electronic warfare block. It's a three-hour lesson plan. Meanwhile I'll help our Russian friends get settled in and I'll see you back here after lunch." He led the Russians out of the conference room.

The room grew dark as Sutherland turned down the lights. He turned on the slide projector at the back of the class and advanced to the first slide. It read: "Electronic Warfare in Modern Air Combat".

"Gentlemen, the next three hours will probably be the most important three hours of this entire course. The good major may disagree with that. He may talk about engines, G-forces, turn radius, cornering velocity, but this is the course that will mean life or death. You can't get that kill if you are dead."

He advanced to the next slide that showed an Israeli F-4 going down in flames after being hit by and surface to air missile. The next slide showed an F-18 breaking up after an AA-6 Acrid missile launched from a Kumari MiG-25 intercepted it over the skies of Kumar. The point was clear: missiles kill aircraft, and sometimes their pilots.

"The F-4 was hit by a Syrian SA-6 during the 1973 war over the Bekka Valley. The F-18 you saw was the only recorded Kumari air-to-air kill of the last war in the region. The MiG-25 launched his AA-6 at extreme range and the missile guided. Simple engagement. The result was a dead F-18, of course the MiG pilot didn't live long enough to celebrate. He was shot down minutes later by an F-15," Sutherland said matter-of-factly. "The point here is that there are missile systems out there, both ground and air-launched, that specialize in one thing: killing airplanes. In some cases there's a lot a pilot can do to defeat the threat, in other cases he can try a lot of things, but all they will do is make him feel good about the way he's about to die."

"The MiG-41 has an excellent state of the art electronic combat suite. It has an Advanced Sirena 360 degree passive detection system, including detection of both radar and IR missiles. It can also detect laser energy, meaning it can tell if a laser rangefinder is locked on to the aircraft. The detection antennae and sensors are located at the extreme edges of the aircraft, both wingtips, horizontal stab tips, vertical stab tip, and under the nose," Sutherland said, pointing to those areas with his laser pointer, a glowing red dot darting across the screen.

"It has the capability of triangulating radar bearings relative to the MiGs speed and direction of flight and calculate an approximate range to the threat radar. This feature can only be used against SAMs and AAA radars since it assumes the threat radar is stationary." He hit the advance button and the new slide showed an aircraft and a SAM and had distances and bearings drawn as an example. "This gives the pilot the ability to skirt the edge of a missile engagement zone and stay just out of range, a valuable capability.

"Its passive and active jamming systems are fully integrated and can operate in the automatic mode. In this mode the passive detection system will detect and identify the radar threat and the Gardenyia programmable jammer will jam automatically utilizing a preset mode," Sutherland said. "The pilot can select noise/barrage, continuous wave, modulated deception and range gate pull-off modes."

The next slide showed the frequency ranges covered by the detectors and jammers of the MiG.

"As you can see the passive detection system can see virtually anything out there that can threaten you. While it can see anything looking at you, it cannot counter everything shooting at you. It can jam in the Delta, Golf, Hotel and India Bands, the most common threat radar bands."

Sutherland hit the switch for the next slide and it showed the standard jamming patterns around the aircraft as well as a sample radarscope showing the effects of the jamming. It showed noise jamming, the screen blanked out in places by white static. The jamming patterns were concentrated off the nose and tail, but also covered the areas off the wings, although the jamming intensity was not as great. This was due to the antennae size, shape and placement on the aircraft.

"The Gardenyia-4 active jammer is located on the dorsal spine, here," he said pointing at the swollen spine on the aircraft diagram with his laser pointer. "Its antennae are integrated into the leading edge wing root extensions on both side of the aircraft."

He advanced the slide showing the affects of deception and range gate pull off.

"The best bet is to deception jam or utilize the range gate pull off mode if you are trying to avoid a radar lock. The deception mode floods an enemy's screen with false targets. It's basically a form of modulated jamming where incoming signals are analyzed and re-transmitted back at the source slightly off his radar timing so he shows many targets on the scope and he can't tell which one is you.

"The range gate pull off is similar, but instead of showing many false targets he will get only one. He may not even know he's being jammed. The system sends a modulated signal based on his PRF and frequency back, which induces a velocity error in your position. You have two modes to choose from in range gate pull off, near and far. If you select near the false return will appear closer to him than you actually are, the far mode means the return will be farther from him than you. This mode is very useful as it can make him take an out of the envelope missile shot and waste a missile.

Sutherland advanced the slide to show the expendables inventory. "Your aircraft carries two racks of 30 flares each and 60 bundles of chaff. These can be preprogrammed or utilized in a manual mode by a button on your HOTAS or in automatic mode when the passive detection system picks up a threat. In automatic the system has a bad habit of releasing flares and chaff if it detects your wingman behind you. The chaff and flares are dispensed from ports built into the fuselage just above the wing root. "

The next slide showed a highlighted stinger located between the engines. "This stinger you see between the engines has a rearward facing single glass lens from which a laser is directed to the area specified by the IR passive detection systems on the tips of the tail surfaces. The laser fires a beam at the area the missile must past through and hopefully will blind the IR seeker in the missile, by burning out the sensitive cooled-seeker. In auto mode it can mistake an aircraft behind you for a missile and fire its laser and blind the pilot. Your wingman might not like that. This is a very advanced feature not found on previous MiGs and is usually not installed on MiGs for export."

The briefing continued for a full hour describing the various systems. It was clear that the Russians definitely did their homework on this one. The capabilities described were awesome, but like the sales pitch of a used car salesman, the Americans remained skeptical. They wanted to see the system in action. No matter what the capability the Russians touted, it only counts where the rubber meets the road.

ROOM 7A, TONAPAH AUXILLARY AIRFIELD, NEVADA
1300 LOCAL

"Gentlemen," Major Gunter Dreschler said, looking out over the class with a grim smile, "this is how you say in America---where the tire meets the pavement? Unlike your previous block of instruction, which taught you how to stay alive, this block teaches you how to kill. The MiG-41 is a tremendous weapons platform with amazing abilities, but in order for you to use this aircraft, as it was intended you must become its master. Here I will teach you how to use the radar to find the enemy, how to use the IRST to target your enemy, how to use the helmet-mounted sight to widen your firing envelop and how to use the missiles to get the kill.

"To kill the enemy you must find him, target him, move into an advantageous firing position, and take a shot within the weapons launch parameters. These things must be done quickly, with precision, any stumble along the way, any gaff with a switch or radar mode and you may lose the shot. In today's engagements if you lose the shot you won't get a second one.

Dreschler flipped a switch on his remote and the first slide appeared on the screen behind him. It said: MiG-41 Sensor and Targeting systems, An Overview.

"The MiG-41 is equipped with the Zhuk Phazotron RP-45 pulse Doppler look-down, shoot-down radar, NATO code-named Slotback IV. It has four distinct operating modes: air-to-air, ground mapping, terrain following and continuous wave illumination. It transmits and receives in the India Band portion of the spectrum, very close to the frequency ranges used by the F-15 and F-16. It has a search range of 120 nautical miles and can track twenty-four targets and engage 6 simultaneously thanks to the new generation weapon control computer. The older Slotbacks were capable radars, but processing of data was not nearly so advanced. The new Slotback IV prioritizes the threats based on aspect angle, speed and range.

"In the air to air mode it has the typical pulse Doppler characteristics you are familiar with. It is a true lookdown, shoot-down system and pulse Doppler radar filters out the terrain and all objects not moving with respect to your aircraft. The radar must sense a velocity differential of at least 90 knots or it will drop the object off the screen. This means like any other pulse-Doppler system it is susceptible to a maneuver into the Doppler's dead zone, or roughly perpendicular to your line of flight. If the enemy puts you on his wing your relative velocity will drop low enough to beat your Doppler threshold. In this position he will drop off your screen. If you have fired an AA-12 at him, its onboard radar is pulse Doppler also and it will lose lock if he enters the beam position. Of course his odds of beating your missile kinematically improve greatly on the beam.

"The radar also has as an excellent jamming filter system, with some very complex algorithms shifting frequencies in such a way as to cut out a majority of false targets in a jamming environment. There are several modes to choose from when you are jammed and each uses a more complex algorithm to determine the frequency jumps than the one before it. The more complex the algorithm, however, the greater the degradation to your radar presentation.

"If jamming becomes too heavy you can set up the IRST in boresight mode or slave it to the radar cross-hairs. The IRST can be selected as the primary targeting system and two lines will appear on your HUD giving you a reference for the field of view of the IRST. With IRST selected it will automatically slave the AA-11 seeker heads to whatever it locks onto. If you select Helmet as primary targeting control the same applies to your helmet-mounted sight. The helmet has a series of sensors that determine where you are looking and it slaves the IR seekers to that part of the sky. The HMS allows the missile seeker heads to lock onto objects not normally within their field of view. You can launch a missile over 90 degrees off boresight so long as the HMS is locked onto the enemy and there is enough lateral distance for the AA-11 to make the turn, or you can fire a rearward firing AA-11 if you are so equipped."

Olmstead sat up and took note of that. The AA-11 is what almost got him back in Korea.

"The HMS is a bit bulky and takes some getting used to, but it is a valuable asset you must learn to use. It provides you with such an advantage you cannot ignore it. It allows you to take missile shots simply unheard of in any fighter you've ever flown before. It will take some getting used to simply recognizing that you are in the launch envelope. Some Russian pilots actually fly with the AA-11 selected and the trigger depressed. The missile won't launch unless it's locked onto something. If the IRST locks onto a target or the HMS locks something up momentarily the missile will launch automatically. This way the pilot can concentrate on just getting the "snapshot" if you will. If he can just get the right picture for a short moment the missile computers will do the rest. This is where the Cobra and Bell Maneuvers can become important. If you can just get the nose swung far enough around for you to lock him up with the HMS you can take a shot even when you are defensive.

"The IRST can be used for targeting and launching medium range missiles as well," Dreschler continued. "Once the IRST is locked on the laser range finder will give you range to target and this data is fed into the missile computer which calculates a safe and in range point and allows you to fire an AA-10D, IR version, at medium range, about 34 nautical miles. The AA-10D has a new supersensitive seeker head that can see out to nearly 20 nm. The missile flies under inertial guidance for the first 10 miles or so then starts looking for a heat signature to lock onto. The danger here is that it can be decoyed by anything flying in or near its path. It can also be defeated if the enemy turns away before it gains IR lock-on. It is a low probability of kill shot, but the enemy cannot detect its launch, giving you the advantage of surprise. The new AA-10E, however, can actually guide using the reflected laser energy from your rangefinder in VFR conditions, until the IR seeker locks on. This shot has a higher PK than strictly inertial guidance. If you have AA-12 onboard it does not make sense to use the AA-10 first, save the IR version until you can guarantee lock on. Are there any questions so far?"

Romano scratched his chin thoughtfully. "You mentioned the AA-10D can be launched at 34 miles in the blind, but its seeker head can detect and lock on to a fighter at 20 nm. Does that mean at 20 nm it will lock-on while still on the pylon?"

"Yes, that is correct."

"So even if the radar is down, and the IRST inop, the AA-10 will still get an IR lock at 20 NM?" Romano asked.

"Yes, assuming the target is in the 45 degree field of view," Dreschler answered. "Of course you cannot tell who it is locked onto without the IRST. If you fired it into a furball there is no telling who it will go after."

"How good is the telescopic camera?" Fletcher asked. "At what range is the resolution good enough to tell one fighter from another?"

"At 34 nautical miles, you can tell a MiG-29 from an Su-27," Dreschler answered. *Apparently the resolution is very, very good,* Fletcher thought.

Dreschler continued. "The doctrine of Russian air to air capability differs significantly from American doctrine. Both rely heavily on new technologies, but where the US put it's money into stealth and the ability to go undetected, the Russians put their money into new sensors and long range missiles. The typical Russian Su-27 variant in service has fourteen weapons pylons, a flying battleship. The radars are big and powerful, the missiles long range, and the IRST technology state of the art. The general feeling in the CIS was they would not be able to develop stealth technology and weapons for the 21st century at the same time. The Russians knew the United States was unlikely to export stealth technology. In the meantime this would set the Russians up to supply the rest of the world with arms. They knew the developing nations, especially the oil rich ones, would be looking for aircraft, and they intended to be the supplier. And just to hedge their bets against a possible encounter with the US, they developed advanced infra-red sensors, as well as more powerful radars, in hopes of defeating some of that stealthiness. It is all a matter of detection. Detect the target as far out as possible and make sure your club is longer than his. Simple."

They spent the next three days going pouring over technical manuals for the MiG-41 sensor systems, answering endless questions from Dreschler and enduring the patronizing comments of the Russian officers who were now being integrated into their training. The squat one, Dobrinsky, seemed genuinely helpful, but the tall thin one, Gurevich, less so. He did not speak often and seemed arrogant and aloof. When he did speak he used few words, made his point quickly and often with a tinge of sarcasm. It was beginning to grate on the four American's nerves. Even Olmstead and Fletcher seemed to get along a little better around Gurevich. A really strong hate has to be focused and they couldn't hate each other with Gurevich in the room. He was like a control rod in a nuclear reactor. When the chain reaction began to get out of control, drop in Gurevich and he absorbed the hate. It did not take long for the Americans to form a healthy dislike for the man. He also confused them. They could see he was an arrogant bastard, but they had never encountered anyone who seemed to relish in it the way he did.

A week later they began the first air-to-air practice engagements. At first they teamed Olmstead and Fletcher as one team and Romano and Cahill as another, both taking turns against the two Russians in the skies over RED FLAG Range. At first the Russians were unbeatable, but with each sortie the Americans got better and better, learned some new tactic or discovered some new nuance of the Russian fighter that helped their efforts. By the end of the month they were beginning to win against the Russians. They were approaching combat readiness in the MiGs and gaining personal familiarity with their new steeds. More importantly they were becoming comfortable with controlling the high performance jet, able to decipher sensor inputs instantly, change radar search patterns quickly and employ weapons with both accuracy and precision. By the end of the six weeks of practice sorties they were beating the Russians 50% of the time. That was good enough for Tanner. Now they needed a new challenge.

TONOPAH
1300 LOCAL

"Chet, you have to be bullshitting me," General George Armstrong Tanner said in disbelief. "Are you really telling me the Weapons School refuses to fly against us? I mean I'd think you'd have to beat them off with a stick!"

"You'd think so, George, but it all goes much deeper than that," Colonel Chet Sommers, Chief of Curriculum of the Fighter Weapons School, said into the telephone. "You know the politics of Nellis and especially Weapons School. Sure the pilots would love to take on your MiGs, but Colonel Schmidt won't let it happen, and he's got the backing of Colonel Davenport, the Squadron Commander. They can't take the heat if their boys lose. They're supposed to be the best of the best. They aren't taking the chance."

"I know all that, Chet, but that's the whole point," Tanner insisted. "The question is how will our best do against this new Russian hardware? What your telling me is they don't have the balls to face my MiGs cause we might wax a few tails? Come on! This is a matter of national security. We have to know how we'll do against this stuff. If they don't find out right now, they'll find out next month or next year in the Gulf or over the Balkans or North Korea. Jesus!"

"You don't have to sell me, George. I agree with you," the Colonel said. "I'd love to send my boys up against yours. It'd be a great fight and we'd learn a lot from it, but there are careers on the line here."

"Screw the careers," the general said disgustedly. "This is bigger than any one career. Besides--- that's just bullshit, anyway. "

"Tell that to Colonel Davenport, George," Sommers said. "As commander it's his call who his boys play with."

Tanner was dumbfounded. "I know all about career politics, believe me, Chet, I do," Tanner assured him. "I just can't believe these guys won't cooperate."

"Hey, George, this program may be secret, but it's not that secret. Sure the results will be kept secret, but everyone will still know the outcome," Sommers said. " If your boys kick some ass Davenport believes it will reflect negatively on him."

"I could up the ante," Tanner mused. "Go over his head."

Sommers snorted in reply. "Sure you could, George, but who you got working for you? Any big guns?"

"I have somebody at NSA that can make things happen," Tanner replied, referring to Michaels.

There was an awkward silence for a moment. "Chet, you still there?" Tanner asked.

"Yeah, I'm here, George," Sommers said with a sigh. "Look you can try your NSA guy but I gotta be straight with you. Most of the big Air Force brass is against this whole program, some very big brass. They feel this is money best spent buying new hardware. They will stonewall you at every corner and by the time you force their cooperation it won't even matter. The feeling behind the closed doors is that we can't afford to look bad right now and they are afraid that's exactly what you are going to do, make them look bad with a bunch of Russian "junk". It's a lot easier for them to simply dismiss these MiGs as cheap knock-offs of our stuff, than let you prove them otherwise. That's why it ain't gonna happen."

Tanner sighed. To come this far and hit a brick wall from his own service! It was almost laughable. For thirty years we spied on Russia and tried like hell to get every scrap of intelligence we could on the capabilities of their aircraft. Now we actually own six of them and we don't want to find out how good they might be. Now those answers are too scary. They weren't too scary with global nuclear war hanging over our heads, but they are scary today when it could mean a career or lucrative contract may be affected.

"So that's it?" he asked Sommers. "Is that the best advice you have, Chet? Just forget it? I need to make this happen. The country needs this to happen. Tell me how I can make it happen."

Sommers paused for a moment before speaking. "There is one way, George," he said at last.

"I'm listening."

"What you need is to find equivalent talent who never for a moment thinks they can be beaten," Sommers said. "You need Weapons School pilots for whom the concept of losing a dogfight never enters their thick skulls. You need to talk to the Naval Fighter Weapons School."

That was the answer. The Navy. *Why hadn't it occurred to me before*, wondered Tanner? The Navy would never back down from a fight, especially one they knew their Air Force counterparts had already backed down from. And the results would not make the Navy look bad even if the MiGs did well. The Navy could always argue that comparing land based versus carrier-based aircraft was like comparing apples to oranges. The carrier-based planes were much heavier and penalized by the excess strength required to land on a carrier day in and day out. They couldn't pull the 9G turns of the MiG-41. They did carry the modern avionics, radars and missiles, which Tanner wanted to simulate in his mock engagements. And no self-respecting Navy fighter jock would ever back down from this challenge. That was how the proposal had to be made to the Naval Fighter Weapons School at China Lake, and that was how two weeks later six gleaming F-18Es touched down on the runway of Tonopah. The Navy was here to play.

The Naval Fighter Weapons School, traditionally known as Top Gun, had its roots over the skies of Viet Nam. It was over the jungles and rice paddies that Russian-built MiG 17 and MiG 21s tangled with the mighty McDonnell-Douglas F-4 Phantom. The problem was the mighty Phantom wasn't so mighty. In fact the F-4 was doing extraordinarily poorly early on in the war. The kill ratio of MiGs to F-4s before the advent of Top Gun was a dismal 2 to 1. Granted we were killing 2 MiGs for every F-4 lost, but with the MiG 21 costing only a million bucks or so and the F-4 costing $9 million each, the economics were unacceptable. Since the F-4 had two crew members lost for every plane shot down and the MiGs only one, the personnel ratio was one to one, the low point in the history of American combat aviation.

The real problem with the F-4 began on the engineers' drawing boards. Conceived as an 'interceptor' for the Navy it was built for high speed, long range, and the ability to launch radar-guided medium range missiles at bombers and relatively slow maneuvering fighter-bombers who were threatening the fleet. The F-4 was big, bulky, and not aerodynamically efficient. At high altitudes where the air is thin the Phantom did not want to turn worth a damn. It did have two JP-4 gulping monster motors that spat flame forty feet in burner and propelled the Phantom to over 800 knots on the deck and Mach 2.0 at high altitude. The Phantom could carry the AIM-7 Sparrow, the then-new medium range semi-active radar guided missile, and the early versions of the AIM-9 Sidewinder.

The F-4 was designed and brought on line in the early days of air-to-air missiles. The assumption back then was that these "wonder weapons" were going to do the fighting for the Phantom. The pilot would just get the plane into firing position and the missiles would do the rest. The new missiles were expected to be a one weapon-one kill system. No enemy plane would be able to defeat them and as long as we got the first shot the F-4 would come out the victor. That thinking was premature by over 30 years.

The early missiles were not the one missile-one kill weapons they expected them to be. In fact the Sparrow had a dismal track record throughout its 30 years of service, averaging only a 30 percent kill rate. The Sidewinder was much better, almost 80 percent reliable and later versions even better. The problem was the pilot had to get into position to fire the Sidewinder at short range and this involved a little thing the Navy and Air Force stopped teaching: dogfighting. The tactics of the day said the F-4 would take the missile shot head-on with the attacker at maximum range and that the missile would kill him.

When the rules of engagement in Viet Nam said the F-4 crew had to visually identify the enemy that negated the range advantage of the F-4's Sparrow missiles and now you had a giant with a shotgun fighting a midget with knife inside a phone booth. Now the F-4 had to perform Air Combat Maneuvering with the MiG to get into firing position, again something the fleet no longer trained for. The missile mindset was so prevalent in those days that the F-4 was brought into service without guns, a flaw that would be remedied with later models. Many times an F-4 found himself on his opponents six and no missiles left. He could only wave his fist in anger and try to disengage without giving the MiG a shot. The MiG had guns, big guns.

The MiG 17, a lightweight but much less sophisticated aircraft with a large swept wing, was more nimble than the F-4 and could turn inside the big Phantom and often would get the tailshot and a victory. The MiG 21 could outturn the F-4 at high altitude, but if the Phantom lured him down to 15,000 feet or so he could turn with the MiG provided he stayed fast. The MiGs engine and wings were optimized for the higher altitudes and the '21 would bleed energy faster than the F-4 at the lower altitudes. The MiG couldn't get that energy back as fast as the F-4 with its massive engines and the Phantom would gain the advantage quickly. The trick was picking your battles and making the enemy come to your battleground, where you could use your strengths and capitalize on his weaknesses.

Top Gun was formed at Miramar in 1969 to address all these problems, the poor Sparrow performance, the F-4 aerodynamic weaknesses, and the lack of dogfighting skills. The school had a rough beginning and faced many hard days when the rest of the Navy opposed 'what they were doing out there on the West Coast'. The school was deemed graduate level, so the curriculum was no walk in the park. The classes were tough and chocked full of details concerning very detailed energy management diagrams for the F-4 and tactics to employ against the enemy MiGs. The MiGs capabilities were studied and memorized. The maneuverability of the enemy and the F-4 across a broad range of altitudes and speeds had to be considered in any engagement and would often determine how to fight the enemy.

In the air the foundation of the training was dissimilar air combat, in this case F-4s versus A-4's simulating the MiG-17 and F-5s simulating the MiG –21. The F-4s found their smaller adversaries quicker and more maneuverable, although lacking the sheer power of the Phantom. The goal of course was to exploit the F-4's advantages of speed and power. The nature of dissimilar air combat was a new concept for many pilots who hassled with like aircraft and the battle was merely man against man. When the machines were different the men could fight differently and the outcomes were not as easy to predict. It caused the US pilots to learn to adapt to the enemy they were fighting. One thing was certain they would never fight a war F-4 against F-4. Each plane had its strengths and weaknesses and like Sun Szu said centuries ago: to win you must know your enemy and know yourself.

Tanner was sure with that the Navy would jump at the chance to play with his MiGs. He could appeal to their since of history, since they practically founded dissimilar air combat. The old pioneer spirit was still alive and kicking at Top Gun. It was just the challenge they were looking for. The Navy still believed in dissimilar air combat. They used F-16s to simulate MiG-29s at Top Gun and routinely fought F-18s and F-14s in simulated combat. The chance to engage real MiGs was a gift from heaven to the squids. And the Navy would benefit from the experience since they, stationed out around the world in unfriendly regions, would more than likely be the first to encounter a hostile MiG-41. It was a win-win situation.

TONAPAH AUXILLARY AIRFIELD
GAME DAY

0600 HOURS LOCAL

"Gentlemen, good morning," Tanner said addressing the small group of aviators, clustered around the conference room table. The Navy pilots were on one side of the big table, their Air Force counterparts facing them, along with the two Russians. Their eyes were clear, their jaws set. They had their game faces on.

"Today you will come as close to actual combat as perhaps you ever will in peacetime," Tanner said. "The rules are simple, there really are none. This is war. And of course as we all know there is no second place in combat. In this exercise there will be no restriction to aircraft maneuvering, speed or altitudes. There will be no restriction on your aircraft's electronic combat capability. This means radar and comm jamming is authorized."

He clicked the pointer device in his palm and the PowerPoint presentation lit up the screen. On it was displayed the status of the aircraft. All of the MiGs and five of the Super Hornets were mission ready. The sixth F-18 was getting a flap position switch replaced and would be ready before the crews arrived at the jets. All jets had full fuel loads. The next slide showed the weapons loads, which of course were simulated weapons. The F-18s showed a load-out of four AIM-130s and two AIM-9X2, as well as 750 rounds of 20mm shells.

The MiGs were loaded out with two AA-12 Adders, two AA-10 Alamos and two AA-11 Archers, as well as a 100 rounds of 30 mm shells. In actuality each airplane had an ACMI pod on the right wing, an AA-11 Archer simulator on the left and an AA-12 simulator on the right wing. The Super Hornets carried AIM –120 and AIM-9X2 simulators as well. These training rounds had the full sensor suite of the missiles they simulated. The heat seeking missile simulators carried cooled seeker heads, which behaved just like the real thing, and the radar missile simulators would duplicate the radar signals of the real thing. Together they made the training as close as possible to the real thing, short of firing real missiles.

The next slide showed the Restricted Areas that would be used for the exercise. They covered most of the great expanse of desert north of Nellis. The entire RED FLAG Range was theirs, free of all military and commercial traffic, surface to 60,000 feet. The frequencies for launch, strike and recovery, as well as the daily mode 1,2,3 and 4 transponder codes for the Navy jets were printed up on comm cards and passed out to the crews. The MiGs had their own set of codes that were not compatible with the F-18's codes. Once established in the range, all modes, except mode 4 would be turned off. This was the friend or foe code, IFF, which allowed an aircraft to interrogate a potential enemy to see if his code was friendly.

The last slide showed the "actual" rules. Though few in numbers these were set up for safety sake and were mostly common sense. The weather was expected to be clear and a million miles visibility so most of the weather rules weren't applicable. Unlike RED FLAG, head-on passes were allowed during this exercise, with one safety constraint thrown in, the MiGs would fly at odd altitudes the F-18s at even altitudes during the pass. That meant they could be as close as one hundred feet, but still be separated. Once past each other the fight was on and it was a gut wrenching, turning battle to get position for a shot. Simple.

"Gentlemen, there are very few rules out there today," Tanner said, "but one cardinal rule is that if we call you dead---you are dead. The kill removal is a direct vector back to the orbit you started from. Once dead you will stay dead until the next set up, there is no kill regeneration.

"You will monitor RED FLAG Control and follow their instructions at all times. There won't be many. Each flight will be given three set-up orbits. You will go to a new one each time we reset. You will also go to standby on your radars after your formation has joined up and is headed to your orbit. This ensures that you will not know where your adversary will be coming from, nor will he know where you are. There will be no vectors from AWACS or GCI to help you out there today. You are on your own and in the immortal words of Manfred Von Richtoften, 'you must rove in the area allotted to you, find the enemy and shoot him down. Anything else is rubbish.' We are planning three engagements per hop, but if anybody gets short of gas, don't be a hero out there. We want you and your plane back to fight real bad guys. Get your bird back on the ground. Are there any questions?" There were none.

The men rose from the table and shook hands. The mood was more somber than the night before, the wisecracks and ribbing would come tonight. This was game day and they were all here to win.

The war was going to be split into AM launches at 1000, 1100 and 1200 and a PM launch at 1500. The AM pushes would all be 2 v 2 engagements while the PM push would be a classic gorilla package. The breakdown would be Fletcher and Olmstead at 1000, Romano and Dobrinsky at 1100 and Cahill and Gurevich at high noon. The PM push would have Olmstead leading the six-ship.

The pilots were quiet as they donned their G-suits in Life Support and pre-flighted their helmets and parachutes. There was an aura of seriousness not unlike that experienced just before actual combat. The Navy pilots' gear was stowed in a different building and their planes were parked across the ramp from the MiGs, just now being towed out of the protective hangars. The engine starts and take-offs were scheduled ten minutes apart, the F-18s taking off first. The next time they would see each other would be over the high desert of Nevada and after the announcement "fights on, fights on".

Olmstead and Fletcher were on the first "push" of the day and the tension between them was as taut as ever. Few words were spoken and then the responses terse and to the point. Romano and Cahill noticed the terse exchanges and both glanced at each other simultaneously as if asking "are you thinking what I'm thinking?".

"How can these guys fight as a team? They can't even stand to be around each other," Romano whispered to Cahill. The Texan just shook his head, a glum expression across his long face.

All six of the pilots got their gear at the same time, even though the last AM launch wasn't until two hours later. As a team they rode out on the blue Air Force bus together to drop off Olmstead and Fletcher, their two MiGs gleaming in the morning sun, dew running off the fiberglass noses in little trickles. The other four MiGs were parked nearby, but these two were the current objects of attention. Once these jets left the chocks the ground crew would turn their attention to the next two MiGs to fly. All had been through a thorough pre-flight the night before, but they would still get one last minute systems check, pitot covers would be pulled, safety pins removed from the ejection seats, and one last check of fuel quantity and a check for hydraulic leaks, an ever present problem whether an F-18 or a MiG-41.

Olmstead and Fletcher dropped their gear off in front of their airplanes and began a cursory walk- around of the jets. The pilot's walk-around checks for very simple things, fuel and hydraulic leaks, missing rivets, cracks in the skin, insufficient tread on the tires, etc. If something doesn't look right, it probably isn't right. A crew chief can be very conscientious, but in the final analysis is only human and can always miss something big, while concentrating on something small. The elephants sometimes get missed while trying to kill the ants.

The age-old sign of complete trust between a crew chief and his pilot was the pilot who simply climbed the ladder and got into the cockpit, but those days were nearly gone. The crew chiefs were some of the best enlisted men in the Air Force, but the jets were too expensive, too complex and the consequences too high should something go wrong. Once upon a time the crew chief and the pilot would serve together for a long time and develop a working trust. Today the crew chief works on the plane that's by his name on the schedule board and pilots rarely flew the planes with their names on the side. These crew chiefs, chosen from the very best in the Air Force, were just assigned to the new MiG detachment and the pilots would be seeing plenty of them in the future. They were probably the best maintenance team in either the US or Russian Air Forces. They were also becoming fiercely possessive of these beautiful MiGs as most crew chiefs do for the aircraft they tend. They sensed these planes were something special and they were special for keeping them flying.

Olmstead and Fletcher finished their walk-arounds and found no discrepancies. They glanced over the aircraft forms and signed them off, noting the full fuel load, chaff, flares, and the missile simulators on the left wing and an ACMI pod under the right one.

They climbed up their ladders and lowered themselves into the cockpits. Within two seconds the crew chiefs were at the top of the ladder assisting them in strapping into their ejection seats. They connected oxygen hoses, secured lap belts, and clipped the gold-key of the automatic parachute-opening device to the ejection seat snaps.

This gold key ensured the parachute would open instantly if the pilot had to eject at low altitude, such as just after take-off and that it would open at 14,500 feet altitude if the pilot left the plane at high altitude. Of course the pilot could always pull the D-ring and the chute would open instantly, a very bad thing if you were very high. If the chute opens at 35,000 feet it takes roughly 30-45 minutes to float all the way down. The air is too thin and the temperature too cold at those altitudes to survive that long. A pilot opening his chute at 35,000 feet will die of hypoxia and frostbite before he ever hits the ground. That's why the automatic features of the chute wait to 14,500 feet before opening. A small barometric sensing device triggers the chute when it gets below 14,500 feet, that way the pilot can be unconscious and his chute would still open.

Once strapped in and helmet donned the real pre-flight could begin. Olmstead clicked his throttle mic switch, "You there, chief?" he asked.

"Roger, sir," he heard through his helmet ear-cups speakers. The crew chief could now talk with him through the ground cord plugged into the comm box in the nose gear wheel well.

"Batteries- on," Olmstead said, flipping a series of switches on the side electrical panel. The cockpit indicator lights flickered to life and he could hear the whine of a gyro spinning up on battery power. "Going to external power," he said. "Clear?"

"Clear, sir," the chief responded, telling him the power cart was connected and ready.

Olmstead flipped another series of switches and new hum began to build as several gyros began spinning up under external power. The battery discharge light extinguished. He reached over to his left and flipped a series of switches on the hydraulic panel and the standby hydraulic pump engaged, the needles on the gauges moving up into their normal operating ranges.

"I've got power and hydraulics, chief," he announced.

"Roger, standing by for engine start" he responded. "Fire guard is posted and clear."

"Starting both engines," he called, as he flipped the engine starter switches on.

A blast of compressed air from an onboard tank now flowed through the two RD-333K engines with a loud hiss, through the exhaust ports. The huge turbines began to spin and a low whine began to replace the hiss. The whine built until the needles on the RPM gauges reached 15 percent of maximum RPM, the normal RPM for engine start. He advanced the twin throttles up and out of their detent. The needles of his fuel flow gauges swung to life as JP-8 poured into the swirling airstream moving through the heart of the engine core. As the air-fuel mixture hit the combustion chamber electric spark igniters flashed the vapors into red and yellow fire which poured from the rear turbine blades for a couple of seconds before they disappeared in the high speed exhaust stream, with the RPMs settling at 65 percent. Both engines were started and oil pressure, fuel flow, and exhaust gas temperature needles all settled into the green bands on the gauges, nominal.

Olmstead turned his attention to the electrical panel and brought both engine driven generators to life. With a blink the generators took over the electrical loads from the power cart, which the crew chief promptly disconnected. The air conditioning system was activated and cooling air began to flow through the heat sensitive electronics and poured from the vents at the pilot's feet. The engine driven hydraulics were also selected and pressures were normal.

With aircraft power and cooling air Olmstead flipped on the inertial navigation system and entered the coordinates of his parking stub. The inertial navigator took about 3 minutes to align, so he took that time to enter the waypoints he'd need for this mission. At any time he could command his nav system to steer him to one of those points and the computer would present a flight command indicator or FCI on his front head's up display. He simply had to center the FCI and the system would fly him to the point. He loaded his departure routing, the edge of RED FLAG range and the daily bulls eye, a coded point designated daily that aircrew can use to relay information without giving away their position to the enemy.

The bulls eye itself usually has a name like Coke or Pepsi, or maybe Dodge or Chevy. A normal call might be, "Bandit, Coke 230 at 50" which meant bandit on a radial of 230 at fifty miles from the point Coke. Today's bull's eye was called Shasta. With his INS aligned and ready he was almost ready to taxi.

"Flight control check, chief," he called.

"Rog."

With that he began a series of control inputs that the crew chief would check, verifying the controls were operating normally. Left aileron, right aileron, checks. Up elevator, down elevator, checks, left rudder, right, rudder, checks. Before taxi the crew chief would check the final trim settings.

Special care was given to flight control checks after the F-15 accident in Germany some years back. Somehow a four-way hydraulic valve on an F-15 got installed 90 degrees out. When the stick moved to activate the right aileron, it raised the elevator instead, and moved to the left it lowered the elevator. The pilot never realized there was a mistake made because he performed an old check called 'stirring the pot'. This is where you move the stick around in a circular fashion and move each control surface in the sequence. The crew chief really couldn't verify if the stick was performing the right function, he just knew all the control surfaces were moving and he assumed all was well. During take-off the pilot attempted to raise the nose and rotate and instead rolled the aircraft to the right and dragged a wingtip. The pilot died instantly in the fireball just off the runway.

Olmstead completed his flight control check and looked over at Fletcher who was just finishing up his. He reached down and turned the radar mode control to warm-up and began turning on the various advanced systems of the MiG. The HUD came to life, the IRST began it's cool down cycle, the MFDs glowed green and came into focus and his helmet mounted sight passed it's BIT, built in test. He programmed his weapons panel for the simulated missiles he would be carrying and ran a self-test on both the ACMI and missile simulators under each wing. All systems were in the green.

"Okay, thanks, chief," he called. "You are cleared to disconnect and pull chocks, brakes are set. See you later."

"Good hunting, sir," the crew chief said, in the traditional blessing of the fighter pilot. He disconnected the interphone cord, pulled the chocks, ran them over to the side of the tarmac and stowed them with his gear. He reached into his tool box, grabbed a set of flashlights and moved in front of the gleaming, screaming fighter, preparing to marshal the bird clear of the parking area in front of the hangar and out onto the open tarmac of Tonopah.

Olmstead glanced at his watch, one minute to taxi time. He knew two F-18s were at this moment rolling down the runway behind the large hangar just out of his view. He'd see them soon enough. He looked over at Fletcher who gave him a thumbs up which Olmstead returned. This morning Fletcher was flight lead and Olmstead would follow him. Olmstead waited for Fletcher to break the silence of the radio.

"Tonopah Ground, Ivan 20 flight of two, taxi with Tango," Fletcher called.

"Roger, Ivan 20, taxi to runway 15, altimeter 29.99," Ground replied.

"Taxiing to 15, 29.99," Fletcher replied. Unlike normal flights where the ground controller reads the entire route of flight over the radio for the pilot to copy, the flights this morning were special and everyone at Tonopah knew where they were going. It didn't take a rocket scientist to figure out what was going on when two F-18s take-off, followed by two MiG-41s five minutes later.

The two aircraft taxied out of parking, Fletcher in the lead, both watching the marshallers carefully. No one wanted to hit a piece of ground equipment on the way to the war. As they swung clear of the obstructions and onto the main taxiway both crew chiefs came stiffly to attention and saluted the passing MiGs, whose pilots snapped a sharp salute in reply.

As the two crew chiefs walked back to the truck to get ready for the next launch, the senior man, a crusty old tech sergeant, turned to his partner. "Fifteen years in this man's Air Force and I never dreamt I'd be salutin' a MiG on the taxi out."

Fletcher taxied slowly and carefully, even deliberately, along the taxiway, at the standard brisk walk speed, uncharacteristic of fighter pilots. Fletcher always played by the rules and it was his staunch adherence to the rules that kept him at the top of his game.

Olmstead on the other hand played a bit looser with the rules, but made up for it with sheer God-given talent. Olmstead was the better stick and rudder man, but Fletcher was a tactical master, capable of thinking as fast as his jet could fly. He succeeded not by pilot prowess, but by thinking ahead of his opponent's jet as well as his own. His situational awareness was excellent and he could tell in the middle of a furball what his opponent's indicated airspeed was within ten knots. He had an uncanny gift of always knowing his opponent's energy state. That was what determined whether he could attack or defend and how he would do it. He rarely made a fantastically difficult move. He just always seemed to know what his opponent would do next and he'd be ready to exploit that knowledge and get the first shot. If was almost as though he could read minds.

They taxied into the hammerhead and ran their last minute systems checks. This took only a minute. "Two, you ready?" Fletcher asked.

"Two's in."

Fletcher called the tower and got clearance for the take-off. They taxied onto the runway and as they lined up Olmstead thought about the impending battle. This was it...the whole ball game. They had best make it a good fight.

The take-off went smoothly and climb out was uneventful, even peaceful, like the calm before the storm. It was a beautiful sunny day, calm winds and clear visibility. *It will be easy to spot the enemy visually today*, Olmstead thought, as he inched into a tight, right echelon position off Fletcher. *This was Fletcher's show, he reminded himself. Today I'm the wingman. My first duty is to protect my leader...unless I get the 'tally' first.*

The 'tally' meant visual contact. Whoever spots the enemy first in the loose deuce takes the lead and becomes the 'engaged' fighter. The other becomes the 'non-engaged' and moves to both protect his leader and be ready to take the shot his leader sets up for him. The idea was for the engaged fighter to 'push' the bandit to a point in space where either he or the non-engaged fighter can take the shot. It was a bullying tactic that worked well. This works well one versus two, but when there is a non-engaged bandit to deal with a classic furball can develop quickly. This is where the non-engaged fighter must press home an attack against the non-engaged bandit, either because he is threatening him or his wingman. Then it becomes two separate one-versus-one engagements and the better, or sometimes luckier, man will win.

Olmstead's thoughts turned to Dreschler's pre-takeoff briefing. The German had spoken slowly, his voice calm, his thoughts collected.

"Gentlemen, it is graduation day," he began. "I have taught you all you need to know to defeat any enemy. You have the talent and the necessary knowledge, but it is up to you to adapt to the dynamics of combat. I cannot give you any hard and fast rules. You must take what you know, observe the enemy, counter his attack while prosecuting your own. Remember there are no restrictions on this combat and the only simulations are the weapons themselves. You will get no help from AWACS or GCI. You can expect a full electronic combat environment. The jamming will be heavy, both radar and possibly communications. Be prepared to use both to your advantage. Fletcher, you are the flight lead. Olmstead, you will take his orders, your duty as a wingman. I speak the obvious because I know of the hard feelings between the two of you. Put them aside. They will not serve you in combat. Good hunting."

Fletcher's voice on the radio stirred Olmstead back to the present. "RED FLAG Control, Ivan 20 flight, checking in as fragged, Superman," Fletcher called, saying he was at the prescribed altitude and course and had the planned number of aircraft in his package. If he had been short his wingman he would have checked in as "Spiderman".

"Ivan 20 Flight, RED FLAG, cleared into Reveille, push Gold for strike," the controller said.

"Ivan, push Gold," Fletcher said.

"Two," Olmstead replied before twisting the knob on the radio to the preset channel.

"Ivan, check," Fletcher said, on Gold channel.

"Two."

"RED FLAG, Ivan is up Gold, ready to play, approaching Sandlot, base plus 12," Fletcher said, announcing he was on frequency, at 20,000 feet and approaching his predetermined marshalling point.

Both flights were given their three marshalling points in advance, where they would reset between engagements. Rules called for each aircraft to go radar standby at the "knock it off" call and fly at predetermined altitudes toward their new marshalling points. This way they could not use their radars to locate the other flight prior to the fight. At the "fight's on" call they could go back to radiate. RED FLAG control had both flights' ACMI telemetry monitored and could tell instantly if they were cheating.

"Roger, Ivan, this is your strike controller, acknowledge all calls and proceed to Little League upon hearing "knock it off"," the controller said. "You are cleared surface to Flight Level 600 for all sectors. Good hunting."

Fletcher reached the marshalling point and set up a holding pattern orbit about the point. He looked over his right shoulder and saw Olmstead's MiG in tight echelon. *Flies a pretty tight formation*, Fletcher thought with grudging approval. *Hope he doesn't hit me.*

At precisely 1020 local time the call came. "To all players, RED FLAG Control, time now 1720 Zulu, fight's on, fight's on."

At that moment Fletcher turned his jet toward the west and went to radiate on his radar. He selected a range while search mode that swept the sky ahead of him using a long pulse repetition frequency. This was the optimum mode for a long-range search. They had been orbiting on the north east corner of the range and knew the Navy fighters had to be somewhere west of them, possibly southwest.

He and Olmstead moved out thirty miles into the heart of the vast range and set up a grinder, a counter-rotating circular search pattern. The idea was to cover each other's backs and let the bad guys come to them. Olmstead would radiate and search toward the southeast while on the other side of the circle Fletcher would move northwest and search that direction. That way all directions were covered.

They knew they would either pick up the enemy on their active radars or receive a strobe indication from the passive receivers on the wing tips if the enemy was not radar silent. In this environment, with no GCI or AWACS, everyone would be radiating, Fletcher knew.

He also knew this tactic would draw the Navy boys in, as they were too impatient to set up a search pattern like this. Fletcher was a deer hunter and knew the patience required to let his prey walk into a trap. Whereas Olmstead would be more likely to seek out an enemy, Fletcher would let them give themselves away. He would be patient and give them just enough rope to hang themselves.

One advantage to using a "grinder" was that one of the fighters was always in a firing position. The only thing Fletcher didn't like about the tactic was that it required Olmstead to act semi-autonomously, and he hoped he was up to the task and wouldn't hot dog it.

Sure enough the Navy boys came looking for the fight. The two F-18s started abeam them in the northwest corner of the box and had been moving steadily east since the fight's on call. The leader recognized the tactic Fletcher was employing by the slight change in the PRFs every minute or so. The radar strobe would flicker out then return on a slightly different frequency. That suggested two aircraft in a grinder out front. Their RWR scopes showed the spikes of Fletcher and Olmstead's India-band Advanced Slot-Back radar clearly.

The Hornet driver paused for only a moment then committed. He really had no choice. The MiGs were radiating and would locate them any minute if they pushed closer. *The PRFs suggested they were still in a range while search (RWS) mode so they probably haven't seen us yet,* the young lieutenant commander thought. *They will very soon, though.*

"Okay, Slim, light'em up," he called to his wingman, who went to radiate at the same time. The Hughes APG-65 radar began pumping out the "trons", trying to paint the two MiGs off the nose. They turned to an intercept heading, putting them beak-to-beak, and accelerated to combat speed to give their missiles that extra shove of energy.

"I'm getting intermittent contacts at 12 o'clock, but I can't keep'em locked up," his wingman replied. The MiGs were rumored to be somewhat stealthy, covered with radar absorbent material.

In the MiGs sixty-five miles away the effect was more alarming. The RWR gear showed an AI threat in search to the northwest. Olmstead who was on the backside of the pattern, facing away from the threat immediately pulled a hard seven G turn, returning to Fletcher's wing. Once rolled out and a mile abeam Fletcher his radar showed a single faint blip at 60 miles off the nose. They were still too far away for either radars to lock the other up, and they were still far outside missile range.

"Back with you, Fletch," Olmstead called. "I'm spiked at 12 o'clock," he said, indicating an AI threat radar off the nose.

"Roger, spike," Fletcher replied. "Master arm is on. Lead's hot, cleared to engage. Let's give'em some music," he said, activating his deception jamming system. Olmstead did the same.

The effect on the Hornets' radarscopes was to say the least spectacular. The scopes filled with false targets, each of which could be the MiGs. Due to the low radar cross-section of the MiGs they were not close enough to get a valid radar "lock". Now they could not be sure when they locked on it would be the right blip. The Hornet pilots activated their own jammers at this point and the MiGs screen filled with clutter. Both flights activated their electronic counter-countermeasures, devices used to filter out the false targets by changing the radar's frequency through its entire operating spectrum based on a pre-programmed complex algorithm. If the frequency jumps were often enough and unpredictable the false targets would fall off the screen and only the solid target would remain.

The screens in the Hornets cleared briefly, but still at least half the false targets remained. The situation in the MiGs was comparable. The range between the flights was now down to 40 nautical miles and closing rapidly.

The radar would now indicate a valid lock on a selected blip, but the problem was knowing if it was the real target or not. There were only two choices, lock something up and shoot, hoping to get the kill, or move in close enough for the radar to 'burn through' the jamming. The Navy elected to take the shot. Fletcher had something else in mind.

As they approached missile launch range he ordered Olmstead to break off and drop low and run south ten miles, turning back in an attempt to catch them in a pincer, while they were still sorting out the jamming problem. Olmstead peeled off Fletcher's wing and buried the nose on a southerly heading. He hit the burners and accelerated to 630 knots in a move perpendicular to the oncoming Hornets. Normally the wingman stays with his leader, so the Hornets weren't expecting the move.

Fletcher turned toward the northwest, moving closer to the notch position but not quite reaching it. He gave Olmstead a couple minutes to moves south and get into position. He was the bait and Olmstead the shooter. If this worked the Hornets would come after him and Olmstead could move through the jamming unnoticed and get the tail shot while they're attention was on him. He knew he had to sweeten the bait somewhat.

"Two's ready," Olmstead called.

"Rog," Fletcher replied.

Olmstead moved south unnoticed, descended down to about 10,000 feet AGL and was now working back to the right. When he left Fletcher he left his radar on just long enough to get his IRST locked onto the oncoming Hornets out at 35 miles. Once they were locked up by the IRST he went to standby on the radar. The automatic features of the IRST stayed locked onto the hot thermal images of the F-18s as Olmstead worked to south, 10,000 feet below the prey he was now stalking. Olmstead smiled behind his oxygen mask as he saw the Hornets taking the bait.

When Fletcher heard Olmstead was in place he reached down and flipped his jamming systems off. Immediately the northern half of the Hornets' radarscopes cleared and the lone return that remained was now too tempting to resist. The Hornet pilots locked up Fletcher's MiG and pressed for the AIM-130 shot. They were at the extreme range of the AIM-130 for the speed and aspect angle, or angle off the nose. The lead Navy pilot didn't like taking a shot with this much angle, it would be too easy for the MiG to notch the missile and evade. The MiG was traveling northward now and the Hornets turned northeast to gain a better angle for the shot.

As they turned northeast Fletcher's RWR showed them locked at 8 o'clock and he slid farther left, luring them into a south to north tail chase. This is what Olmstead had been waiting for. When he saw the F-18s swing another forty degrees to the northeast he knew he was in the catbird seat. His radar had been off ever since he left Fletcher's wing. This way he gave off no emissions that would give his position away. The RWR gear in the Hornets showed only one MiG radar and it was off the nose. He was using the MiG's IRST to the maximum advantage and the F-18s had no idea they were being targeted. He banked up to the right and slid in behind them at about 10 miles in trail, still radar silent. He knew he was 10 nautical miles thanks to the laser rangefinder slewed to the IRST. He switched his display to telescopic camera, verified the target as Hornets, and then toggled the camera switch to get a few pictures of the Hornets locked up in his CRT. *That'll make a nice conversation piece in debrief*, he thought. He switched back to IRST. And was solidly locked on to the F-18s' twin exhaust plumes. It was a classic "blue sky" shot, looking up at the hot engines against a cold blue sky.

The lead F-18 was now almost happy with his shot. The angle on the MiG looked better and he seemed to be trying to disengage rather than fight, which seemed both strange and cowardly to the Navy pilot. Had he given it much more thought he might have realized a deception was in the works, but he was too focused on getting the shot. He was still at the extreme range for the AIM-130 tail shot so he lit the burners in an attempt to close a few more miles on the MiG before launching. His radar indicated the MiG was only traveling about 450 knots and he could accelerate and make up a couple of miles easily. He also knew the MiG was approaching the northern border of the area and would have to turn back to the south soon. *Come to papa*, he thought, with a wry smile under his oxygen mask.

Meanwhile, in the F-18 to his left, his wingman just wished he'd take the shot. *Something seems screwy here*, the lieutenant thought. *Why weren't they engaging?* He swung his head as if on a gimbal scanning the skies frantically looking for some hidden threat that would take his leader down. He didn't see anything visually; he had nothing on radar except the lone MiG off the nose. Where was the other MiG? There was still a lot of jamming coming from the south, but his RWR gear was silent in that direction. There was no MiG radar behind them. They weren't being targeted. *That MiG has to be south of us somewhere*, he thought. *If he is down there he's not radiating and hence he's not a threat...yet.* He wished his boss would stop waiting for the perfect shot and get on with it. He wanted to find that other MiG before it found them.

"C'mon, Rip, take the shot," he said impatiently.

"Just a few more seconds and I got'em," he replied.

"I'm engaging Fletch, break left," Olmstead called.

Fletcher reached down and reactivated his jamming systems, once again flooding the Hornets' screens with false targets. As he did he broke hard left. This time the Hornet's APG-65 stayed locked onto the turning MiG amidst the false targets.

"I got'em," Lt Commander Craig "Ripper" Breedlove said as he prepared to fire.

"Fox Two, Ivan 21, Fox Two, Ivan 21," Olmstead called to RED FLAG in a calm almost serene voice, the locked-on tone of the AA-11 steady in his ear cups.

"Sailor Flight, RED FLAG has you a double kill at this time," the range controller announced. "All players, knock it off, knock it off, cleared own navigation to Little League, gadgets to standby."

As the two flights separated and headed toward their new marshalling points there was much conversation between the Hornet pilots on their private frequency. What really pissed them off was they still didn't know how the other MiG got the shots off. He had to get in behind them somehow, but they still didn't know how. And they were facing a new fight starting in about 5 minutes.

"They must be using a split tactic, Slim," Breedlove said to his wingman. "One of them moved south on us through the jamming and came up on our six. That's the only explanation. You've got to check six."

"I was checking six and I didn't see anything back there," Lt Danny "Slim" Carlin insisted. "If he launched from back there he was beyond visual and just how did he target us? His radar was down. It had to be, my RWR gear showed only one spike and that was in front of us."

"Alright, we need a new game plan here," Breedlove said. "We get spiked you run toward the heavy jamming this time and be my eyeball. I'll take a shot up the center and you look to pinch'em from the flank. If they are running split you find that other guy and keep him busy. I'll deal with the leader."

"Roger that," Carlin said.

Both flights reached their second marshalling point, called Little League, and checked in with Red Flag. The two F-18s were in the Southwest corner of the range and the MiGs were in the North center region.

"Red Flag, Sailor Flight, Little League, ready to play," Breedlove reported.

"Red Flag, Ivan Flight, is Little League, ready to play," Fletcher echoed.

The Red Flag controller started the ACMI recorders once again and checked range status. He finally called, "To all players, Red Flag Control, cleared gadgets, fight's on, fight's on."

Both flights activated their radars, which had been off until this time to prevent cheating. The MiGs took up a southerly heading while the F-18s proceeded to the Northeast. Almost immediately both flights got RWR spikes indicating their relative positions. The F-18s turned Northward and began closing beak to beak with the MiGs, still over 100 miles away.

Olmstead examined his RWR gear and the bright strobe of the F-18s APG-65 radar pointing off the nose. He knew they were on an intercept course, now was the time to throw in the monkey wrench. Fletcher had been thinking the same thing.

"Ivan Flight, music," Fletcher called, activating his jamming system. Olmstead did the same.

Just as before the F-18s radar was flooded with false targets. Breedlove let out a curse as he activated his own jammers as his wingman did likewise a moment later. The radar spectrum was now flooded with India band radar jamming, false target blips filling their scopes. Without an AWACS with its high-powered radar and complex counter-countermeasure systems getting a valid radar lock in this jamming environment was hopeless. *We need more complex anti-jamming features on our air to air radars*, Breedlove thought with irritation. *The current algorithmic frequency jumps must be through too narrow a bandwidth.*

The new low probability of intercept (LPI) radar currently being developed for the F-22 was still a few years away. It would use a very low powered radar that frequency hops over such a large spectrum that it is both difficult to detect and very hard to jam over such a large bandwidth. An added benefit to this type radar is that it is so low powered and operates over such a large frequency range that it will not exceed the threshold of detection of most modern radar warning receivers. It was assumed that the F-18 Super Hornets in service would be retrofitted with a similar system. Today, however, Breedlove had to deal with a jammed spectrum and an enemy that somehow could target them without the use of the radar.

"I'm spiked off the nose and the centroid of the jamming seems to be at about 55 miles," Breedlove said. "Slim, you run due north cover high and I'll split about ten miles east and go low. I'm gonna assume the center of the jamming is where they are. If it looks like the jamming is moving east I'll be there to nail'em." With that the two Hornets separated, Breedlove descending and moving off to the east.

Fletcher smiled to himself, calmly in control. "Hawk, go to RGPO," he said, instructing Olmstead to switch his jamming system from false target mode to range gate pull off mode.

Immediately the screens in both F-18s cleared showing two neat blips in echelon formation, separated by about two miles. Breedlove turned back hard left to lock his radar onto the closing MiGs.

"Okay---Rip, the jamming's down, I got the one on the starboard locked, you take the port," he called.

"Rog, I'm on him," Carlin said elated by the turn of fortune. "In range, taking the shot. Sailor 02, Fox 3," he called.

"Sailor 01, Fox 3," Breedlove called, his radar locked onto the oncoming MiG.

The two MiGs did not even maneuver. They continued straight ahead into the simulated missiles now at 30 nautical miles. *This is gonna be easy*, Breedlove thought, as he waited patiently for the confirmed kill from RED FLAG. It never came.

"Ahhh---Sailor Flight, RED FLAG, no kill, no kill," came the response.

Breedlove couldn't believe it. As he looked back down at his scope the two blips disappeared again in a swarm of false targets, at least a dozen blips filled his screen between 25 and 35 nautical miles, any of which could be the MiGs. Last he saw they were still closing at better than a thousand knots.

Fletcher and Olmstead had switched to the range gate pull off deception to accomplish two objectives, 1) get the Hornets to waste a couple of missiles and 2) to get in closer where they could use the IRST to boresight their radar on the oncoming F-18s and get a radar shot through the heavy jamming. The range gate pull off deception jamming fooled the APG-65 radars of the F-18s into believing they were about ten miles closer than they actually were. They fired the simulated missiles outside the AIM-130 envelope.

In the ensuing confusion they reactivated the false target generator and set up their IRSTs to find the Hornets now bearing down on them. At about 22 miles Olmstead got an IRST lock on the first Hornet, Fletcher found his target a moment later. After a momentary bit of confusion as to who would shoot whom they got it sorted out. The jamming was still intense and the there were a least a dozen blips to choose from on the screen. The ambiguity was resolved by the IRST and laser range finder. With those two locked on they knew exactly where the Hornets were. They slaved their radars to these spots in space and sure enough two radar returns were located there, the real radar returns. They manually locked the radars to the IRSTs and fired two missiles each at 18 miles.

The radar warning receivers in the Hornets screamed their warning tones as the Slot Backs locked them up. The mode switched to high PRF and they knew two simulated missiles were inbound. Both Hornets broke hard right in an attempt to avoid the simulated AA-12s. At around 5 seconds into the simulated missile flight time the AA-12 was programmed to go active and would autonomously track and home on the F-18s with its onboard radar.

The Hornets pulled seven Gs in the turn, both men crushed into their seats; their G suits squeezing the very breath out of them. They punched out chaff and flares in the turn in an attempt to decoy the incoming missiles. The ACMI telemetry showed the hard turn and the chaff and flare ejection and the computer chugged for a moment and called one Hornet a kill.

"Sailor Flight, Sailor 02 is a kill at this time, 270 for kill removal," RED FLAG called.

Carlin slammed his fist on the dash as he whipped his jet up on its left wing and pulled out of the fight to the west. Breedlove was still alive and defensive. Having reached the coveted notch position in time to break the missile lock, he was defensive, turning out of the notch looking for a target and revenge.

It would have been better for him to stay defensive. Fletcher still had him locked on his IRST and waited until he got a slightly better angle on his wing leading edge then loosed an AA-11 at 8 miles.

"Ivan 01, Fox2," he called.

The AA-11 was well inside its maximum range and his simulator on the wing was locked onto the hot leading edge of the wing-root against the cold blue sky 8 miles away, a growling in his helmet. In real life it would have been no contest. Breedlove was low on energy after the hard turn out of the notch and did not have anywhere near the maneuverability to defeat the AA-11 inbound off the nose. To make matters worse he had his burners lit, trying to recover lost energy, and his IR signature was huge, even with the frontal profile.

"Sailor 01, Red Flag, you are a confirmed kill at this time," Red Flag announced. "Knock it off, knock it off. Gadgets to standby. Proceed own navigation to Big League."

How are they doing it? Infrared? He knew that the MiGs had IRST systems, but could they prosecute an attack with IRST only? From medium range? He didn't know and was afraid of what the answer might be.

"Slim, I think they're using their IRST to target us somehow. Apparently they can boresight a missile to the IRST and fire an IR missile at medium to long range. I know the AA-10D long burn has a range of around 35 miles, but I assumed they only used the IR seeker as a backup to the radar seeker," Breedlove told his wingman.

"The last missile that got me was radar guided, but that would explain the earlier tailshot and how he got past us," Carlin said. "We need some strategy here. The radar ain't gonna help us today, not unless we can get in close and burn through the jamming."

Breedlove shook his head. "I don't think we want to get in close with the AA-11," he said. "Remember what we teach, 'don't merge with an AA-11 armed MiG'. We need to get the AIM-130 shot."

"That isn't gonna happen, Rip...unless the jamming clears."

"What if we go in low?" he asked.

"How low we are talking?"

"Very, very low," Breedlove answered. "Maybe we can defeat their infra-red down in the dirt. That desert looks pretty hot down there. We have to try something. Maybe we can get close enough to burn through the jamming while defeating the infra-red."

Carlin was agreeable. At this point he'd agree to try just about anything different.

"Okay, let's get down before the fight's on call," Breedlove said, pushing his nose over. Carlin stayed on his wing in the quick descent as though he was welded into place.

"Will we hear the fight's on call in the dirt?" Carlin asked. "There's a lot of terrain out here to block the transmission if we're at TFR altitudes."

"It won't matter," Breedlove said, as they passed ten thousand feet in a spiraling descent. "When their radar comes back up we'll know the fight's on. We just gotta watch the RWR gear."

They leveled off at 300 feet above the rugged desert, ridgelines all around to hide them from the MiGs once the fight was on. They would stay down low in the dirt, hidden from the prying eyes of the Slotback radars, running radar silent themselves. They would wait for the RWR gear to give the enemy's position away. They would lie in wait for the MiGs that no doubt would come searching for them. Once the enemy RWR indications were sufficiently high in signal strength, they would spring out of their canyon, lock up the MiGs and get off an AIM-130 snapshot. The dirt around them should protect them from the super-cooled eyes of the IRST as well as the radar until the enemy got very close, then they would be close enough to burn through the jamming and get off the Fox-3.

Fifty miles away Fletcher was having his own problems. He was up and radiating in 100 km scope, but could find no targets. He glanced at the dark RWR panel and willed it to light up. Nothing. Wherever they were, they were running silent.

"I don't like this, Hawk," Fletch called to his wingman. "You got anything out there?"

"Negative," was the reply.

"I bet they've gone low," he said, more to himself than Olmstead.

"Roger that. Probably hiding behind some chunk of dirt out there waiting for us to wander by," Olmstead agreed.

They were on the extreme southeast corner of the area and Fletch knew they had to be northwest of them somewhere. The Navy pilots decided to try patience, rather than the head to head bullying tactic that had failed them twice so far today. Fletch turned to the northwest, Olmstead out about a half mile to his right. He looked at his fuel gauge and knew he could wait out the Hornets if he had to, but this would be a good test of the MiG's capability. Besides, not knowing where the bad guys are coming from is suppose to be the nature of the game. Sometimes in the confines of RED FLAG Range that was hard to exploit.

"Hawk, slow to 350 knots and be ready to go to a defensive Cobra," Fletch radioed.

"Roger."

They slowed down to a velocity that allowed minimum turn radius if they had to maneuver. Normally one had to get off the first shot in order to survive, but in this case he felt he might not get that first shot and he had to be ready. The MiGs had one advantage the Hornets didn't have, super-maneuverability. With the Cobra and Bell maneuvers the MiG could not only turn inside an enemy and defeat him in close-in dogfighting, he could also defeat the incoming missiles' radars by performing those same maneuvers.

The pulse Doppler radar of the AIM-130 would be locked onto the MiG until he performed a Cobra or Bell Maneuver. For a short period during each maneuver the relative velocity of the MiG would decrease to a point that the both the fighter and missile radars would lose lock. Indeed the forward velocity during both maneuvers actually reach nearly zero. For several, precious seconds the missile would lose lock and lose guidance, a perfect opportunity for the MiG to use his thrust vectoring to change direction and escape the missile, or punch out fuse-busting chaff. The missile would reacquire the target as the MiG driver hit his burners and accelerated back into normal flight, however the Mach 4 missile would probably not be able to pull the Gs required to guide back to target after running off course.

Fletcher decided to fly this intercept from a defensive standpoint, slow enough to be ready to maneuver quickly and fast enough to be able to get his energy back in a dive with burners. As they cruised to the Northwest, Fletcher and Olmstead kept their eyes bouncing back and forth between the radar and the RWR gear. For several minutes the RWR gear stayed dark and the radarscope was clear.

Then suddenly the RWR began to squeal as the Hornets popped out behind a ridgeline, acquired the MiGs and snapped off a couple of simulated AIM-130s. The two MiGs' automatic jammers kicked in, but too late to do any good. They were close enough, within ten miles, to burn through the jamming and lock on to the MiGs. The stealthiness of the MiGs worked well at medium range, but inside ten miles they showed clear as day.

The MiG radars locked up the Hornets, just as the missile guidance warning tone blared through their helmet earcups. No time to get a shot off at this short range, Fletcher said to himself as he pulled his throttles to idle, extended his speedbrakes and pulled hard to the notch position. Olmstead broke the opposite direction and was executing his own evasive maneuver.

Fletcher pulled hard until the stall warning began, then unloaded the aircraft briefly and pulled hard again to initiate the Cobra Maneuver in the horizontal plane. Olmstead, three miles to his right, was performing the maneuver in the vertical plane. Both planes seemed to stand still in the sky. The Hornet radars immediately lost lock and the AIM-130 shots were deemed invalid.

At the top of the maneuver Fletcher decided to transition into a Bell maneuver. He tapped his thrust-vectoring paddle and swung the ass-end of his fighter in space, the whole aircraft essentially somersaulting in space. As his nose rose back to the horizontal due to the momentum of the pivot, he hit his burners and a combined 50,000 lbs of thrust nudged him in the back as he accelerated back into level flight. His radar had lost lock as he pivoted in space, but now as the nose rose again it regained lock on the lead Hornet. He got a solid lock-on tone and squeezed the trigger. The simulated missile left the rails only five miles off the nose of the enemy Hornets, now climbing on burner to get some energy for the expected turning fight.

"Fox 3, Ivan Lead ," he radioed to the controller.

He didn't wait for the reply from the controller. He thumbed a button on his HOTAS and selected Archer for the weapon and Helmet for the targeting device. He was closing beak to beak with two angry Hornets and the dual was about to turn into a knife fight.

"Sailor Lead, you are a kill at this time, vector 270 for kill removal," the controller called. Then he added, "Ivan Two, you are a kill at this time, vector 180 for kill removal."

Damn it, Fletcher cursed. The number two Hornet must have got a valid shot or a second shot on Olmstead. Now it was one v one, Hornet versus MiG. His radar indicated the F-18 was at his 2 o'clock, range eight miles. The aspect angle as they circled each other was no good for a radar shot. The Hornet was closing to IR range and now looking for the angle on him. Fletcher pulled hard into the Hornet and finally got a tally off the nose at three miles, just in time to see a flash as the Hornet screamed by off his left wing. Even though the AIM-9X2 was an all aspect weapon, the probability of a face shot kill at this close range and high speed was small, even smaller in an exercise than in real life, as the controllers didn't like to award frontal IR kills.

The Hornet driver performed a climbing reversal, loading on the G forces, white vapor trails streaming from his wingtips. Fletcher had a tally on the F-18 and as he swung up over the top of his reversal, Fletcher once again performed a Bell maneuver, his eyes never leaving his target, and therefore his IR seeker heads never leaving it either. As he pivoted his aircraft in space the nose swung around and the blip of heat that was the F-18 swung into the IRST field of view. As it did, Fletcher squeezed the trigger and called out, "Fox 3, Ivan Lead."

The aspect angle was not perfect, but the F-18 was low on energy as it came over the top of its reversal and it only took the ground computer a microsecond to deem the shot valid. Actually it was no contest. The Archer was well inside it's parameters and could have guided under much more adverse conditions. In fact technically, Fletcher could have selected a rearward firing AA-11 and not even performed the Bell maneuver at all. As was briefed, the MiG was a real killer inside ten miles. In the three engagements the only success the Hornets had was a medium range, BVR shot on Olmstead. It was an eye-opener for all involved.

The rest of the day went pretty much as expected. Romano and Cowboy came away with two victories to the Hornet pilots' one and later in the day during the big furball the fog of war set in and the match was split evenly. Overall the MiGs had two more kills than the Hornets. By the end of the day it was clear they were not just a contender, but serious opposition.

That night the Hornet drivers bought the steak and the beer at the Nellis O'Club. All things considered the evening went well. It was fighter pilot heaven. Lot's of beer and a crud table to themselves. Tanner had reserved the small game room with the idea of limiting the Navy boys' access to real trouble, "real trouble" defined as the uncontrolled interaction between Navy and Air Force fighter pilots. They also wanted to keep their Russian colleagues from the general base population. No need to raise questions.

Cowboy was in charge of security a detail he was well suited for. His steel blue eyes, cold and menacing, caused all but the most bold to walk away. Those that didn't have the survival instinct to detect his intentions were made aware of them by his Texas drawl.

"This room is reserved, boys. You fellers, don't want to be playing in here tonight, right?" he would say in his low, guttural drawl. The unwelcome pilots would smile thinly and walk away. Hint taken.

They managed twenty-three rounds of crud with many bruises from the hard fought competition, but no real injuries. This time the Navy came out slightly ahead. Overall the whole exercise had been a great success, at least from the MiG Drivers point of view. The MiG-41 had proven itself and so had its pilots.

TONAPAH AUXILLARY AIRFIELD
0900 LOCAL

"Room, ten hut!" shouted Sutherland as he held the door open for the general. Everyone in the room sprang to their feet, braced at attention.

Tanner walked in grim-faced and moved to his customary seat at the head of the conference room table, the placard "Commander" marking his place. He carried a locked brief case, which he placed on the table.

"Seats," he ordered, sitting down heavily himself. The pilots, the intel officer and the two Russians all took their seats; the only noticeable absence was Dreschler, who was on his way back to Germany. "Lieutenant, secure the room please," he ordered Sutherland, who got back up to close and lock the door. He disconnected the telephone from its wall jack and turned off his own pocket pager.

"Room secure, sir," Sutherland said, taking his seat.

Tanner smiled a tight-lipped smile. "Gentlemen, when you came to this program three months ago you were told there may come a time when we needed MiG-trained pilots to fly alongside our Russian allies. That day is here, gentlemen. We have a special job for you… several special jobs," Tanner said.

"We have been fighting terrorism for years now, however the bad guys who back the terrorists, namely Kumar and Sandor, are changing strategy. They are no longer satisfied with blowing up an embassy or an airplane. These countries are now working feverishly to develop weapons of mass destruction, namely nuclear and biological weapons. They can get a much bigger bang for the buck and let's face it, it's hard to gather evidence after a tactical nuke lights off. Most of the major components and research going into these programs can be masked under the guise of legitimate nuclear and medical research. The equipment and materials required to create a genetically engineered virus are the same as those used in conventional gene therapy and other form of genetic research. Weapons grade materials for a nuclear device can be created in breeder reactors, commercial nuclear plants.

"Diplomacy has failed us here. We just can't get the United Nations to deal with these countries and we cannot unilaterally apply military forces against nuclear power plants or hospitals. However---if we were able to launch an attack covertly, making it appear another nation launched the attack, a nation likely to take such action, we might be able to knock out some of these potentially dangerous activities and turn back the clock on the enemy's weapons programs."

"And that's where the MiGs come in?" Olmstead asked.

"Yes. The MiG-41 was built for export only and is flown by both Sandor and Kumar. In fact these very aircraft were on their way to Sandor when Russia stopped the sale. Since these two countries historically harbor ill will towards each other it would be relatively easy for a flight of MiG-41s attacking one country to appear as though they came from the other. What we are talking about here is a force operating independently of normal military channels. A strike force used principally to destroy WMD facilities in Kumar and Sandor and possibly assassination of known terrorists figures in those countries.

"Our Russian friends here are partners in this endeavor. There are six more MiG-41s, mirror images to these aircraft, waiting for you in Southern Russia. The Russians will handle the logistics of basing, fueling, maintenance, and weapons, as well as some intelligence. We provide the aircrews, the training, and the satellite intelligence. Now we are going operational."

The general knew this would be a real shock for them, but now he had to sell them on the idea. Normally he could order them to fly, but since these missions would fall outside anyone's definition of legal, he had to win their hearts and minds.

"Gentlemen," he said slowly. "When I first recruited you, before you ever saw a MiG, I told you this was a very secret, very dangerous program which could profoundly affect the security of the United States, even the whole world. At that time you agreed to come on board even though you knew nothing about the project. Now you know. You are here. You are ready for combat.

"What I said about this profoundly affecting this country's security was absolutely true. We have a unique, precious opportunity here that we cannot waste. With these MiGs and the help of the Russians we can set these bastards back decades, make sure they don't get the bomb or develop some virus that will kill us all. We have to take the initiative and secure our future, because it's not secure right now."

"General are we talking about starting a war between Sandor and Kumar? Not that that's a bad idea, but..." Olmstead asked. "This isn't exactly legal is it? This seems more like espionage, even sabotage...and assassination?"

Tanner knew this question would come up. He had to play this very carefully.

"No, it is not exactly legal," he said with a sigh. "We will be executing missions outside the normal chain of command. The President has a vague idea that some things might happen soon, but he is intentionally being left in the dark on key issues so he can maintain 'plausible deniability'. The same is true for the Russian president. As I understand it Congress has no knowledge of this. Our point man with the President is his National Security Advisor, Dr. Charles Michaels, an old college buddy of mine. He will act as an intermediary between ourselves and the White House."

Fletcher shook his head. "General, are you out of your mind? In today's day and age you want us to try and pull off something like this? If we get caught we go to jail. If we get shot down we get executed as criminals. You can't order us to break the law. That violates our oath of office."

"You are absolutely right, Captain," Tanner said in a calming voice.

"Then how did you ever expect us to cooperate? Olmstead asked.

"It was our hope that if you knew the targets we were going to take out you would volunteer to go. Every warrior looks for a chance to really make a difference in his country's security. I can tell you this: if you fly these missions you will do more for national, not to mention world, security than you could ever do through the normal course of your careers. Here is your chance to make an impact, a big one, and help make the early 21st Century a safer place for your families. This is your chance to secure their future."

The four pilots and the intelligence officer looked at each other for a moment, eyes questioning. Several shrugs of the shoulders later, Fletcher spoke up. "Okay, General, we're still listening," he said simply. "No promises."

"Fair enough," Tanner said. He opened the brief case in front of him and extracted several sets of manila folders. He pushed them down the length of the table and they distributed them amongst each other. They opened the folders and began reading. *This was the deciding moment*, he thought. *If they don't buy this, it's all over*. Tanner smiled as he saw several mouths fall open and many eyebrows raise at what they were reading.

"Whew," someone said, with a low whistle.

"Is this some kinda joke?" Romano asked in disbelief. "I mean we would really go after this stuff?"

"Absolutely."

"This is a little preemptive, isn't it, sir?" Olmstead asked.

"Yes. It is," Tanner said simply.

Olmstead closed the folder and laid it back on the table in front of him. One hand rubbed his chin while the other was tucked under the opposite arm. He stared off into space, deep in thought. Cahill was the most animated, looking around for some reaction from the others and not getting any.

"Rules of engagement, General," Fletcher said. "I want to know the ROE on this stuff. Who are the players?"

Tanner nodded. "It's a very simple game with as few players as possible. We're looking at a minimal support staff. Lieutenant Sutherland will act as intel and mission planner, you four and our Russian friends are the pilots. General Kavinsky and I will share command once we deploy."

"Share command?" Romano said with upturned eyebrow.

Tanner shrugged. "A political necessity, Captain. We are working together. That does not mean we trust each other explicitly."

"Do we take orders from you, sir?" Olmstead asked warily.

"Yes, of course, Captain," Tanner assured him. "It's just that those orders will have to be agreed upon by both myself and General Kavinsky. You should feel lucky to have two sets of eyes watching out for you."

Olmstead didn't feel lucky.

"Ground crews?" Fletcher asked.

"The initial pre-flights, fuel and weapons loading will be done by Russian ground crews at a remote airstrip in Tangistan. You will launch from that airstrip, drop to low level and penetrate the Kumari or Sandori air defenses, covertly strike your targets, and then get the hell out and back to your recovery base. During the flights there will be opportunities to deceive the enemy into believing you are from the opposing country. That's really all there is to it. Simple."

"So besides the nine of us in this room, is there anybody else in this country who will know what we're doing?" Olmstead asked.

"Dr. Michaels will know and as I said the President will have an idea something is going on," Tanner replied. "In fact the President, acting through Dr. Michaels, will be the executing authority for the missions." *Not exactly true*, Tanner thought, *but close enough for government work.*

"What happens if we are killed or captured?" Olmstead asked.

Tanner shrugged. "If you are killed there is no problem. We will notify your next of kin that you died in the line of duty, full military honors, 21-gun salute, flag draped coffin, appropriate number of mourners, the works.

"If you are captured it is not so easy," he said grimly. "As far as we'll be concerned we never heard of you. That is the down side. Just like they used to say on Mission Impossible, 'the secretary will disavow any knowledge of your actions', and he will because he *won't* know who the hell you are. You'll be on your own, with a understandably pissed captor. You would probably we tried as a war criminal, hung or shot, then dragged through the streets for all to spit on. Any questions?"

"Oh, as long as we're dead when the drag us through the streets," Romano said, sarcastically.

"I know these are tough choices, but these are also tough times. You have a great opportunity and an awesome responsibility. Please don't waste this chance. The plans are simple, the logistics sound, the equipment the best available and the targets very worthwhile. If performed as planned you will come back to the States a couple months from now to a country with a whole new lease on life. What do you say?"

The four American pilots glanced around at each other, eyes questioning. Lieutenant Sutherland was already giving his 'thumbs up'. He was bright and extremely gifted, but also young, foolish and naïve. *Of course he's going along with it*, Fletcher thought. *Not much chance of him being dragged through the streets.* He wanted to speak with the other three pilots.

"General, we're going to need a few minutes to discuss this," Fletcher said.

"I understand," he motioned to the Russians to leave as he moved toward the door himself. "I'll be in the office. Let me know what you decide."

Once the general, the lieutenant and the Russians were gone, the debate moved into high gear. The discussion was heated, but resolution was forthcoming. Several nods and shoulder shrugs later they were in agreement.

"Are we fucking up, here?" Romano asked the group.

"Probably," Fletcher said, his face grim. "Did any of you know we'd be flying covert missions?"

"I thought it was possible," Olmstead said, "but nothing this pre-emptive in nature."

"Maybe it's time to get pre-emptive with these terrorists, instead of waiting for them to drop a nuke on Kansas City or Chicago or Austin," Cowboy said. Cahill was anxious for payback for his brother and here was the way to get it dropped right into his lap.

"Who gives a fuck about Austin?" Romano asked with furrowed brow. "How would you even know if a nuke went off there?" Cowboy punched him hard in the left bicep. Romano winced.

"Okay, okay, you care. Good enough," he said, smiling and rubbing his left arm.

"We're onboard, General," Olmstead said for the group, standing in the doorway of the little office. "Don't disappoint us, sir."

Thank God, Tanner thought to himself with relief. It was going to happen after all. Now if he could just keep the Russians doing their part. Tanner stood up and moved around the desk to shake their hands.

"You won't regret it, boys," he said. "If I were just ten years younger I'd be fighting you for a cockpit myself."

When he finished shaking their hands he turned to the others were also crowded into the office. "Gentlemen" he said. "Tonight the dinner is on me."

"Great," Romano groaned. "More pepper steak?"

The general laughed. "First of all, Captain, there is nothing wrong with the pepper steak, secondly there will be no pepper steak tonight. Tonight our dinner is waiting for us in Las Vegas. I have to get down to Nellis for a meeting tomorrow and you are going with me. My personal C-21 is waiting on the ramp. I've called billeting at Nellis and you all have rooms for three nights as well as vehicles reserved. You'll get $100 dollars a day per diem. Don't blow it all at the craps table. You have three days to recuperate from the last three months then Monday morning we fly back up here and get to work. I wish I could give you more time off, but time is now a factor. Hopefully when this is all over I can arrange 30 days off for each of you."

Olmstead shook his head, amazed by the general's actions. "You knew we'd go along with this, didn't you?"

Tanner smiled and shook the target folder at Olmstead. "Are you kidding? With these targets? How could you turn me down? Besides, I was gonna have you shot if you did," he said cheerily.

LAS VEGAS, NEVADA
2100 HOURS LOCAL

Nellis Air Force Base sits just to the north of downtown Las Vegas. They arrived at Nellis just as the sun was setting over the mountains to the west. It created a beautiful orange glow that saturated the brown desert floor with color. The sunrises and sunsets were arguably the most beautiful displays of nature you could witness. In the mornings at Nellis the sun peeks over the top of Sunrise Mountain to the east and once again the colors wash the normally dead desert with a life of their own, at least until the orange turns to yellow, the temperatures rise and the unforgiving sun bakes the cracked desert floor for another day.

Tonight it was a cool 75 with a 10-knot wind blowing in from the West. The skies were clear, but the stars were dim as they tried unsuccessfully to outshine the glitz and neon that is Las Vegas. The general led his troops out of the C-21 and across the cooling tarmac to base ops. A bus was waiting to carry the happy troops to the motor pool where three Air Force vans were reserved for them.

"This is great, Bear," Cowboy said to Romano. "I want a real steak, real Texas beef, a good soak in a hot tub with a cold margarita, and maybe a couple hours at the craps table and I'll be in heaven."

Romano snorted. "You think that's heaven? I got a place for you. I'll show you what heaven is, my friend. Besides I promised Dobie I'd show him a few special places I know about in town."

"Casinos?" Cowboy asked as he held the door to base ops open for Romano.

"Tits," Romano replied.

Ahhh..." said Cowboy knowingly, nodding his head as he followed his friend into base ops.

The general moved to the nearest phone and began dialing. A few minutes later he hung up and turned to his troops.

"Okay, I've got a vehicle outside waiting for me," he said. "The bus driver will take you guys to the motor pool where you'll get three vans. You divvy them up however you like. I have reservations for us at 2200 hours at Anthony's over in the Mirage. Take some time to find your rooms, clean up and get squared away and be at the Mirage at 2200. It's my treat tonight. That means you show up, eat and be grateful because it's more than you deserve," he said with a smile. "Oh, Romano..."

"Yes, sir?"

"I'd consider a personal insult if you blow me off to go to a titty bar," he said.

"Yes, sir," Romano said, ashamed that he'd been thinking just that.

As the general turned to leave he paused and turned back to Romano, leaned over and whispered something in his ear. Romano smiled and shook hands with him. The general slapped him on the back walked out the door.

After Tanner left Cowboy turned to Romano. "What'd he say?"

"He said Cheetahs is open til 4 AM and has free cover for military personnel," he replied, smiling broadly.

ANTHONY'S STEAK HOUSE
LAS VEGAS, NEVADA
2200 LOCAL

This is not typical Las Vegas, Romano thought, *not a neon tube in sight*. The decor of the restaurant was very posh and very pretentious. This was the kind of place Gurevich's communists teachers told him about back in the old Soviet Union, built on the backs of the Proletariat, they would say. Of course all of Las Vegas fit that description.

Tanner was dropping some bread here tonight, Romano decided. The chairs were stuffed leather and you more or less melted into them. Even the menus were bound in leather. The wine list was superb and the steaks reputed to be the best in Nevada, which of course meant nothing to Cowboy. The eight Air Force officers, seven of whom were not use to this level of sophistication, took their places around the big round table. Tanner had also warned them a collar was mandatory and after looking around, they were a little embarrassed that they met the minimum requirements. The wine captain presented the wine list to Tanner and he chose for the group, a fine Bordeaux from the lush vineyards of Southern France.

As the soup of the day was placed in front of the hungry warriors, they chose their steaks from a wheeled serving tray that displayed the choices cuts of the day. The wine finally came and was poured with much pomp and circumstance, after of course the ritual of presenting of the wine to Tanner for approval.

"Gentlemen," Tanner said, holding up his wine glass. "I want to remind you that in regards to the adventure we are about to embark on, the hangar doors are definitely closed. However, I'd like to present a toast. To duty, honor, and the country we defend and to the finest group of warriors I've had the pleasure of serving with."

"Here, here," came the reply in unison, all raising their glasses in toast, the Russian looking a bit uncomfortable with the lack of plurality in Tanner's toast.

"Whoa there, Lieutenant," Cowboy said, reaching out and grabbing his glass from Sutherland's hand before he could take a drink.

"What? What's the matter?" Sutherland asked, puzzled by the Texan's actions.

The expression on Cowboy's face was deathly serious. "You never toast the living with water. Toasting with water is reserved for 'heroes who have fallen in battle'," he lectured patiently.

"That's right, Lieutenant," Tanner said disapprovingly. "You almost jinxed the whole deal."

A look of embarrassment crossed the young lieutenant's face. There was silence at the table for a full twenty seconds, everyone staring at Sutherland's beet red face.

Then Romano leaned over, took pity, and let the poor kid off the hook. "The General's messing with you, Lieutenant."

Sutherland looked at Tanner questioningly and the general let out a chuckle.

"You're lucky, Lieutenant," Tanner said, nodding at Romano. "When I was a lieutenant they would have made me feel like crap for three days. Romano let you off the hook after twenty seconds. I had a colonel pull something a lot worse on me. The bastard that got me let me squirm for two months. I thought my career was over," Tanner said before popping a forkful of salad into his mouth.

"That sounds like a story, General," Olmstead said with a smile. "Come on, sir. This is the part of the evening where the silver-haired general tells the old war stories of yesteryear, so let's have it."

Tanner rolled his eyes as he swallowed. He took a drink of wine.

"Silver-haired, my ass," he muttered. "I had just been checked out in the F-15 and was brand new to my squadron," he began. "My first BFM flight in the unit was out over the Atlantic in a big Whiskey Area off Myrtle Beach. My squadron commander was my flight lead and he was giving me a no notice checkride. We took off together, flew out to the Whiskey Area and separated in preparation for some one-v-one dogfighting.

"The engagements went well and I even got one kill on the son of a bitch, however as we were returning to our push points I got a call from the airspace controller saying I was approaching the edge of the area and to turn south immediately. Well I didn't realize I was so close to the edge. The controller was right. I banked it up and stayed inside the area...at least I thought I did."

"You went outside?" Cowboy asked.

"No, in fact I didn't, I was inside with about two miles to spare," Tanner replied. "However, my boss out there hears the radio call, see. We finish the engagements, form up again and head for home. I'm thinking all is well. We land and he debriefs me on the checkride. He says he heard the radio call that I got close to the edge of the area and he tells me how happy he was that I didn't go out. He said if I did it would be an automatic bust on the checkride and I'd probably never make flight lead if I busted my initial check.

"Well I sweat that a little, but what the hell, a Qual Level One is a Qual Level one, no matter how ugly," he said. The others laughed knowingly. They'd all been there at one time or another.

"After the debrief that bastard went over to the FAA radar approach control on base and picked up some FAA stationary. He wrote me a letter with FAA letterhead saying that a violation had been filed against me deviating from my flight plan without proper clearance and that my squadron commander would be notified in due course. Obviously I freaked out when I read it. I didn't know what to do. Do I go fess up to him about the violation so he hears it from me first or do I just wait for him to find out? I decided to lay low and wait it out," he said, smiling and shaking his head at the memory.

"So what happened?" Fletcher asked.

"Nothing...nothing for almost two months," he replied. "I sweated it out every time I saw the man. Every time I walked by his office I expected to hear him yell at me. He even called me into his office several times to talk about other stuff, prolonging the torture; all the while he knew I was dying inside.

"Finally at the squadron Christmas party he announces a new tradition of giving gifts to the oldest and youngest flyer in the squadron. This old major was called up front and he got a nice desk nameplate with the squadron logo on it. Then he called me up. Right there in front of God and everybody. He told me my gift was quote 'a new lease on life', he even had it written up on a certificate. He told the whole story about the violation to the squadron and all the wives. It seems another old tradition that squadron had was playing a yearly practical joke on the youngest lieutenant and I was this year's entertainment.

"Well naturally you can't act too pissed in front of everybody at a Christmas party which was for the best, because I went on to really like that old bastard. He turned out to be a great commander and being the butt of such a successful joke seemed to endear me to him. I got a lot of good deals out of that practical joke," Tanner finished with a smile and a stare off into space and back twenty years in time.

"Well I guess I'm lucky, sir," Sutherland said.

His comment jolted Tanner from his reverie. He took another drink of wine and looked down the table at Sutherland through narrowed eyes.

"You're damn right you're lucky, Lieutenant," he said, taking another long drink. "You're lucky you didn't drink that toast with water."

The steaks, laced with butter-sautéed mushrooms and wrapped in bacon, were outstanding. Even Cowboy admitted you could find no better in Texas, although he argued that he was sure this was Texas beef. The desert of strawberry cheesecake and rich, strong Colombian coffee were the finishing touches on a perfect meal.

"That was great," said Olmstead, stirring his coffee absently. "I'm so stuffed I could just sleep for three days."

"No way, pal," Romano said. "That's what the coffee's for. You can sleep when you're dead."

"What's on the agenda?" Cowboy asked. "We got three days and time's a wasting."

"Well, I've got an early meeting over at Nellis in the morning so I'm heading back to base," Tanner said, stretching as he backed his chair away from the table. "Can I give somebody a ride?"

"Yes, General," Gurevich said quickly. "I believe I will be turning in as well. You are coming?" he asked Dobrinsky.

The curly-haired Russian seemed to hesitate for a moment. He stole a glance at Romano who was giving him the thumbs up, encouraging him.

"Nyet, Major," he told Gurevich. "I promised to accompany Captain Romano and keep him out of trouble and be his...how you say...designated driver? I will get my ride back to the base from these gentlemen."

"As you wish, Captain," he said simply.

"Lieutenant," Tanner said and both young officers looked up. "You have your own transportation, correct?"

"Yes, sir," Sutherland said. "I have a car. I've got an old college buddy in town. I'll probably crash at his place, sir."

Tanner smiled, getting up from the table. "Don't crash too hard, Lieutenant. Just make the flight on Monday morning and stay out of trouble. That goes for all of you. Have fun and be careful," he said. "I am not going to bail anybody out of jail tonight. Is that clear enough?"

It was clear enough and they all thanked the general for the dinner as he was leaving. Before he was out the door, though, Romano already had the game plan down for the night. The transportation dilemma was simple enough. They had one van between the five of them, so where one went so they all went. Neither Fletcher nor Olmstead seemed overly thrilled about the prospect, but if Romano wanted to drag them to a titty bar and relive their youth, well they would play the part of the horny fighter pilot. What the hell!

Romano, a frequent visitor to gentlemen's clubs throughout the world, much less Vegas, had the agenda all laid out for them. He picked out his three favorite clubs and made them the targets for the evening. They were three very different clubs by nature. One was very upscale, the girls beautiful, costumed in elaborate evening gowns, the decor very modern with long flowing curtains and an almost Roman motif. The second was more of a standard titty bar, average to beautiful women, bikinis that were discarded after the second song of the set and the standard acrobatics about a brass pole on the stage lit by strobes and black light. The last stop of the night was what one would call a dump, the girls average, but naughty, with a little fondling and groping during the $25 lap dances. The place was dark and smelled like a musty basement soaked in soured beer, which it more or less was. You couldn't find the tourist crowd here. The clientele consisted more of the local element, the biker element to be exact.

Things went great at the first club, with Dobrinsky and Cowboy sitting with mouths open and eyes wide. The Russian had seen strippers in his own homeland, but none like the beauties he saw now. The big Texan was equally impressed as the only club he'd ever been to was a border bar in El Paso and not nearly up to the standards of this place. Romano was amazed by Cowboy's lack of experience with these things. After all he was a fighter pilot and traveled all over the world, including Vegas many times before. If the truth were known Cowboy just always considered those places personally off-limits, because he felt no good could come from frequenting them. In fact he never even thought about them when deployed. Romano never looked for any good to come about either, but he didn't mind finding a little bad now and then.

The girls were friendly but kept their distance, per the rules of the house. There was no touching allowed and a large, burly man with side-burns and a cowboy hat ensured the purity of the hard working girls.

The second place was a bit more liberal with the touching rules. Romano showed them how it was done as a stripper pulled his face into her bare bosoms and proceeded to slap him silly with her breast. Once free he slipped the lone dollar bill into her g-string and sat back with a silly look on his face. After that Cowboy got noticeably nervous and got up from his stage side seat and moved back to Olmstead and Fletcher's table to escape the terrible titties of the stripper now attacking Dobrinsky. Once free the Russian sat back with a blissful look on his face as he surrendered the dollar bill.

Olmstead and Fletcher never moved from their back table. Olmstead watched the girls dancing but Fletcher seemed more interested in getting drunk than girl watching. Olmstead knew something was eating at him, but he felt he was the last one who should ask. They were still on fairly bad terms, although they were working better together. Outside of work Olmstead wasn't so sure. He was on unfamiliar turf here and didn't know how his colleague would react to him. The music was so loud that he didn't need to make conversation with Fletcher. Olmstead wasn't sure what was going through his mind and decided to play it safe. At one point he got up to get a beer and asked Fletcher if he wanted one. He said sure and thanked him for the beer, though slightly curt in response.

By the time they made it to the third bar it was nearly 2 AM and Fletcher was definitely three sheets to the wind. Olmstead seemed to be the only one who noticed just how drunk he really was. Olmstead elected to be designated driver and stayed sober for the evening in marked contrast to his wingman. It was decided after Dobrinsky almost got them killed in a head on with a delivery truck that making the Russian designated driver was a phenomenally bad idea.

As they pulled up a chair in the last and final bar of the night, Fletcher was beginning to reach the level of obnoxiously drunk. Romano grabbed

Cowboy and Dobie and ushered them off to one of the three darkened dance floors, where a glandularly enhanced young woman was working the varnish off the dance floor with her bare buttocks. This left Olmstead alone to deal with Fletcher.

"You wanna know why I'm drunk tonight," Fletcher slurred loudly, several heads turning to see what was going on.

Olmstead was clearly uncomfortable. "Look...Fletch, let's just keep it down a little, okay?" he whispered, glancing at the biker eyeing them from the edge of the bar, closest to Fletcher. "But... yeah, tell me why your drunk if it'll make you feel better."

"Oh, it won't make me feel better," he said loudly again, bobbing and weaving in his chair slightly. "It'll make you feel worse. That's why I'm a gonna tell ya."

"Tell me what?" Olmstead said, hoping to get whatever it was out in the open and over with before it drew more attention to them.

Fletcher took another shot of tequila, of which he had five lined up in front of him, swayed slightly from side to side for a moment then said, "It's been exactly six months to the day you killed my little brother, or had you forgotten?"

Actually Olmstead had forgotten, but it was not something he celebrated from month to month. He spent most of his time not dwelling on it, unlike Fletcher who seemed to relive the loss every day.

"Look, for the last time," Olmstead warned. "I didn't kill Pete. What the hell have you been doing for the last three months, anyway? Are you telling me you can't see how a MiG-29 got the jump on us? After all we've been through? You want to blame somebody you blame the bastard that pulled the trigger and go to North Korea and shit on his grave, but until you do I don't want to hear shit about this anymore," Olmstead said, his anger working up to the boiling point.

Fletcher seemed to come out of his drunken stupor for only a moment as his temper flared as well. He stood up suddenly, weaved drunkenly for a moment and waved a hooked finger at Olmstead. "You want a piece of me right now?"

He stumbled backwards and bumped into the biker at the edge of the bar who had been listening to the whole exchange. The impact managed to dump the biker's beer down the front of his leather jacket and riding chaps. The bearded, tattooed stranger was the kind of guy who enjoyed a good bar fight and looked for any excuse to start one. Here, to his great joy, was a reason to fight literally falling into his lap. *It was going to be especially good tonight*, the biker thought. He could tell by the way the two pilots dressed and the way they spoke they were college boys and military. The only thing he hated more than college boys was military types who thought they were hotshit, their egos a mile wide.

"Oh...sorry," Fletcher said realizing the mess he'd made, even through blurry eyes. "Let me buy you fresh drink."

"Another drink?" the biker said with a snort of indignation. "You hear that, boys?" he asked his cohorts at the bar. "He's gonna buy me fresh drink. Throw a little money at the white trash and he goes away, is that it, punk?" the biker said, spitting his words and pushing Fletcher, who fell over backwards and landed flat on his ass.

The combination of alcohol and the biker's actions created a surge of adrenaline in Fletcher, which for only a moment or so overpowered his blood alcohol level. Rather than do him any good, though, it only served to diminish his otherwise sound judgment just long enough to really get in trouble. Fletcher let loose a string of obscenities as he rose to his feet, his fists balling up at his sides. The biker had momentarily under-estimated Fletcher's level of intoxication and turned his back to make a comment to his buddies. He'd assumed since Fletcher went down so easy he wouldn't be coming back for more. Unfortunately that level of logic was not at work for Fletcher, who lunged at the biker, pushing him hard in the back and slamming him into the bar rail, knocking the breath out of him.

The biker, surprised and now gasping for air saw things were going awry and in a moment of fear pulled a four-inch knife from his boot and lunged toward Fletcher. Before the knife hit anything vital the biker sensed a blur of motion and the knife flew from his hand when Olmstead's foot hit his wrist. The knife, deflected from its intended target, flew from the man's hand, burying itself harmlessly in the ceiling. The impact managed to break the biker's wrist, which he held to his chest. Just when Olmstead thought the whole thing might be over, the biker pulled a small snub-nosed .38 from under his jacket. Once again Olmstead was a blur and before the gun even cleared the folds of his overcoat Olmstead delivered a crushing left cross to the man's chin. There was a crunch of broken jawbone and river of red from the man's mouth as his head swiveled at the impact and he slid to the ground unconscious, the gun falling at his feet. Olmstead kicked it under the bar.

Most people are used to seeing blows like that all the time in the movies. The hero hits the villain across the jaw and the bad guy passes out. The good guy rubs his hand and walks away smiling as though the only damage was a little scrape on the knuckles. In real life nothing is that clean. Aside from the audible evidence that Olmstead broke his jaw, the damage to Olmstead was nearly as severe. For every action there is an equal and opposite reaction. Olmstead might have knocked the man unconscious and broke his jaw, but Olmstead broke his hand simultaneously. At first he didn't realize the damage he'd endured, the only feeling in his hand a dull throb. It was only later, after they'd made their getaway, that he started to realize something was wrong.

Romano witnessed the whole incident across the room peering over the shoulder of a very enthusiastic young woman giving him the lap dance of a lifetime. Romano stood up so rapidly he almost sent the girl flying. He hastily apologized, slapped a twenty into her palm, grabbed Cowboy and Dobie and moved to his friends' aid. He took one look at the man on the floor, the knife in the ceiling, the still shaken Fletcher and Olmstead holding his left hand and wincing and knew just what to do. They were going to get the hell out of there. He herded Olmstead and Fletcher out of the now very busy little bar.

Once safely in their Air Force van and moving up Las Vegas Boulevard Olmstead relaxed and tried flexing his hand. He could tell right away it was broken. It was already beginning to swell and turn blue. Romano was at the wheel now. Although he'd had a few drinks he figured he was still legal. He had a rule about getting drunk in titty bars: it costs way too much, both in drinks and tips.

"You really fucked this one up, pal," he said to Fletcher, who hadn't said a word since they got in the van. "What in the hell did you say or do to that guy to make him pull the knife in the first place. Do you have a freakin death wish? Guys like you don't pick fights with guys like that. And you," he said looking over his shoulder at Olmstead, who was still cradling his broken hand, "we gotta get you to a doctor to look at that hand."

"No, no, no," Olmstead said fervently. "No way I'm gonna get grounded for this. We don't see a doctor. It's probably just sprained anyway."

"Look you dumb son of a bitch," Romano insisted. "You gotta at least have x-rays. If it's broken you can't fly and you know it."

"I can fly," Olmstead said. "Why do you think I hit him with my left hand? It just sits on throttles for God's sake."

"Bullshit," Romano said. "How you gonna work the radar on the HOTAS with a broken hand?"

"I can manage it," Olmstead insisted. "No doctors."

Cowboy was simply sitting there shaking his head throughout the whole exchange. "Yes, you will see a doctor, pardner," Cowboy said in that quiet menacing voice he used when he got serious. "You are gonna get that hand x-rayed so we'll know for sure what's wrong with it. Then we'll decide what to do."

"They'll ground me and I'll be through," Olmstead said, shaking his head. "You really want that?"

Cowboy was through fooling around.

"Bear, stop the van," he said quietly.

"What?" Romano asked looking over at his friend in confusion.

"Stop the van right now," Cowboy ordered. Romano pulled over to side of the road. Cowboy turned in his seat.

"Now you listen to me," he said looking directly at Olmstead and Fletcher. "I am tired of this crap between you two. Bear and I have been patient trying to let you guys work it out. Now I'm gonna work it out for you.

"You," he said pointing a finger at Fletcher. "This dumb bastard just risked his life in a bar fight saving your sorry drunken ass. I don't care what happened before between you two, obviously this man will come to your rescue if need be. He proved that tonight. Bear and I have been worried about that for three months. Frankly we were worried about going into combat with you two. Olmstead here just showed he'll put his life on the line for you. Will you do the same? If not the whole program ends right here and now. I'll stop it dead in its tracks if necessary and we'll all go home. Now what's it gonna be, Fletch?"

Cowboy looked hard into Fletcher's eyes. Fletcher knew he was serious and this was it one way or another. *Olmstead did save my neck*, he thought. *Maybe this whole thing has gone on long enough*. He'd tried hard to separate his flying with Olmstead from his personal feelings, but the stress of the dichotomy was too great. He either had to forgive him or keep on hating him. No two ways about it. It's hard to hate a man who just saved your life only moments after calling him a son of a bitch.

"I will," he said simply, nodding.

"Good," Cowboy bellowed. "Now shake hands."

"Isn't that kinda much?" Romano asked.

"Shut the fuck up, Bear!" Cowboy spat.

The two men looked at each other for about five seconds and Olmstead stretched out his hand. For a moment it looked as if Fletcher would not take it. Everyone held their breath. Finally he reached out to take Olmstead's hand and suddenly Olmstead pulled it back.

"Sorry, wrong one," he said extending his good hand before Fletcher could squeeze his already broken hand.

They shook hands and both looked at Cowboy to see if he was satisfied before letting go. He nodded in approval.

"Okay," he said, in his menacing voice again. "Now we're all friends. If I hear any more shit from you two I swear I'll break both of your thumbs…your other thumb too, Olmstead."

They agreed that it was clear, and neither doubted the big Texan's thumb breaking skills.

"Now we are going to get you some x-rays, but we'll go to a civilian hospital," he told Olmstead, as if there was no more debate about what to do. "Let's go," he said to Romano, gesturing to the road ahead.

"Where to?" Romano asked.

"That big hospital we saw on the way out to Hoover Dam. We'll hit the emergency room and get some pictures taken, then we'll decide how to handle it."

CLARK COUNTY GENERAL HOSPITAL

They arrived at the hospital at 0330 and immediately went to the emergency room. It must have been a sleepy night in Vegas because Olmstead and his band were the only ones in the big waiting room. Olmstead claimed not to have any insurance and produced a wad of hundred dollar bills that would more than cover the X-rays and a doctor's diagnosis. Since it was a county hospital they were more than happy to take cash, rather than deal with an HMO or insurance company. The nurse told Olmstead to take a seat and they'd be with him shortly.

"Well, I've got the munchies," Romano declared. "Is the cafeteria open?" he asked the nurse at the desk. She said it was open 24 hours and he and Cahill went down for a snack, leaving a sobering Fletcher and an injured Olmstead in the waiting room.

After they were gone Olmstead decided to take the opportunity to mend another wound. In the quiet, empty waiting room, Olmstead opened up.

"Hey, Mike, uh, I need to tell you something," he started, his voice wavering.

"What is it now?" Fletcher answered in a weary voice, his eyes closed as he stretched out on the waiting room couch.

"I want to tell you about your brother's death, what really happened," he said.

Fletcher's eyes snapped open; he sat up straight and looked hard at Olmstead.

"It's about fucking time," he said, tight-lipped. "Okay, let's have it."

"This is Top Secret stuff and I wasn't to divulge this to anyone," he said. "But you have a right to know. You've always had a right to know."

"Go on."

Olmstead recounted the air battle for Fletcher, the missiles coming out of nowhere, the conclusion about the laser guided AA-10 using IRST and laser targeting, everything.

"Since the intelligence boys at DIA dropped the ball the whole engagement was classified and the report falsified. It wasn't an AA-12 that killed your brother. It was a new long burn version of the AA-10 with laser and IR seeker heads. You already know about that technology now that we fly the MiG, but I thought you should know how your brother died. I swear, Fletch, I had no idea the Koreans had that capability or I wouldn't have put your brother in that position."

Fletcher sat and listened in stony silence. Olmstead tried to gauge his reaction as he spoke, but the man was a wall of stone. When he finished Olmstead simply waited for a response, good or bad. Finally after maybe a minute of uncomfortable silence Fletcher spoke.

"I figured it was something like that after Dreschler's briefing on the IRST/laser capability," he said wistfully. "Damn."

"I hesitate to ask this, but---uh---are we cool?" Olmstead asked.

Fletcher smiled thinly and rolled his eyes. "Yeah, we're cool. Apparently my problem isn't with you." He shook his head and rubbed his tired, bloodshot eyes. "It just made him look bad. Damn. No wonder they gave you a medal. You deserve a medal to put up with that line of crap." Olmstead breathed a sigh of relief. It was a full minute before Fletcher broke the silence.

"So why'd you save my skin tonight?" he asked with a grim smile. "Really."

Olmstead snorted. "You'd have done the same for me, Fletch."

Fletcher raised an eyebrow. "You think so, huh. How do you know I would? You really don't know me that well and I haven't exactly demonstrated my warm, cuddly side."

Olmstead turned in his chair. "No, Mike, I don't know you that well," he admitted. "but, I knew your brother. Pete wouldn't have let his worse enemy get stabbed in a bar. I just figured you were cut from the same stock." Fletcher smiled weakly, nodded, but said nothing.

Several hours later they knew the whole story. One meta-carpal on Olmstead's left hand was broken. It was not a bad break, really just a hairline fracture and couldn't be set. The only way to fix it was to immobilize the hand for four to six weeks. It would heal itself given enough time. Even the swelling wasn't too noticeable. Now came the hard part. What to do about it.

"I'm telling you guys I can still fly fine with this," Olmstead said. "It's a little painful if I stretch my hand too much or grip too hard, but I can still move the wrist, hand and fingers."

The correct answer was of course to see the flight surgeon and he would decide. In this case he would decide to ground him. Of that there was no doubt. There was no reason to put a pilot with a broken hand into a jet short of war. Of course the flight surgeon would not know about the upcoming missions, which would come pretty close to war. If he did know they were going into combat he would definitely ground him. You can't run the risk of losing a plane or the mission if an injured pilot somehow screws up or isn't up to snuff. A pilot has to be 100% going into combat, that is the law, unless you had very few pilots and were losing the war, neither of which was the case.

"You sure you can fly like that?" Romano asked.

Olmstead nodded enthusiastically.

Cowboy wasn't so sure. He argued against it until an unexpected voice was heard.

"Don't worry about it, Cowboy," Fletcher said, slapping Olmstead on the shoulder. "He'll be fine and I'll watch out for him." As Fletcher walked out the door towards the van four sets of wide eyes followed him and beneath them four mouths hung open in disbelief, Olmstead's the widest.

And with that it was settled. Olmstead would fly and they would conceal the broken hand from everyone who didn't already know, that included Sutherland, Gurevich and of course the general. It wouldn't be too hard to conceal. Olmstead was right handed anyway.

It also appeared that Olmstead now had a guardian angel watching out for him. Apparently the score had been settled in that dank, dark and dangerous bar. It seemed like a mistake at the time to have gone there, but later it was generally agreed, though not aloud, that it was the best decision they ever made.

NELLIS BASE OPERATIONS

0730 LOCAL, MONDAY MORNING

Monday morning the refreshed and rested troops showed up bright and early at Base Ops for the trip back home to Tonopah. Like most military operations they showed up early and now had to wait an hour for the ground crew to gas up the C-21. The crew chief didn't expect the general to show for another hour and he apologized profusely. Tanner told him it was all right and really his fault for changing the take off time and not telling the ground crew.

As they sat, drank coffee and discussed the weekend's adventures Tanner noticed a distinct difference in his people. Olmstead was sitting next to Fletcher and they actually appeared to be talking, even laughing about something! He knew there had been friction between the two over Pete Fletcher's death, but apparently they had settled their differences. That was good. It had been a point of concern for Tanner since the beginning, the only real unknown variable that could have wrecked the program. Hmmmm. Was Olmstead favoring his left hand?

HABRUK NUCLEAR POWER STATION NORTH CENTRAL SANDOR

"What progress have we made, Hakim," the tall, dark skinned director of the new Habruk Nuclear Power Station asked his chief engineer.

The burly, bearded man, shook his head and wiped sweat from his brow.

"The control rod extraction mechanism design is bulky and ungainly, but effective enough," he said, then added, "Like most things Russian."

The other man smiled patiently. *Hakim had too much humor*, Hassan-Mohammad thought.

"We've tested the mechanism three times this week and the last two have been successful," the engineer continued. "The mechanism jammed on a misaligned guide on the first test run. That was easy to fix."

"What about the pumps?" the Director asked.

"The primary coolant circulation pump tested at 150% pressure for twenty four hours. No problems. The secondary unit had a gasket leak on its pressure test. That has been corrected as well. Both pumps have been x-rayed for flaws and fractures. None were found."

"So we will be ready for fuel loading on schedule, yes?" Hassan-

Mohammad asked.

The engineer nodded, as he lit up a cigarette, his hands cupping his lighter to his face. He blew smoke away from his director.

"We will be ready two days earlier than expected, if Allah continues to bless," the man said.

"Two days? Very good, my friend," the Director said clapping him on the shoulder. "Since the fuel will be delivered a week early you may begin when ready. Excellent. So we could expect enough plutonium for a weapon within…what…six months?"

"Allah willing, those are the figures."

"Then six months more for manufacture," he said wistfully. "That will be a great day, my friend. Imagine…the infidel at the mercy of Islamic Jihad."

"They too have nuclear weapons," Hakim said. "Many more than we will ever hope to produce."

"Ahhh---but they have not the will to use them, my friend," Hassan-Mohammad said with a broad smile. "Besides we will not have to use them…once the balance of power has shifted."

"One question, though, Director," Hakim asked. "Can security be in place two days early?"

The older man shrugged. "Security is not an issue, my friend. We have army personnel, razor wire and concrete walls a meter thick. No one will get in here."

"What about the missiles?" the engineer asked.

The Director frowned. Yes. The damn missiles.

"The Hawks won't be available until the end of the month," he admitted, referring to the US made Hawk missile sold to Sandor during the 80's. "However, the local air defense commander assures me the SA-10s will be up and ready a week before the fueling is to begin. They will bring in two ZSU Triple-A guns at the same time. Are you expecting trouble, my friend."

The engineer shrugged. "I cannot help but think of the Kumari reactor destroyed by the Zionists just days before going operational."

"It is a different world now, my friend," he assured the man. "The Jews are too busy with Palestine. Besides we are far out of their reach."

"With aircraft," the engineer corrected him, as tactfully as he could.

The Director nodded absently. "With aircraft," he said.

TONOPAH
0700 HOURS

The next morning the pilots, including the Russians, met at 0700 deep in the bowels of the intelligence center, a dingy gray block of windowless concrete surrounded by a tall fence topped with concertina wire and motion detectors. The sign near the cipher lock entrance said simply, "Access only on authority of Base Commander. Use of deadly force is authorized." Several feet of concrete, electrical shielding, and sound deadening material separated the intelligence officers from the outside world. It was in places like these that combat mission plans were laid out, picked apart and put back together with real world data and even in some cases real time imagery and intelligence.

"Good morning, sirs," Sutherland said cheerfully as he entered the room with two boxes in his arms. He opened them both displaying two-dozen donuts of varying variety and plopped them down on the large mission-planning table.

"There is coffee in the cubby hole just out that door and to the left," he said, pointing the way. "Coffee fund is two dollars a month, or .25 cents a cup. Please don't spill coffee or jelly donut on the satellite photos. I have to give most of these back when we're done."

As everyone gathered to grab a donut and fill their coffee cups, Sutherland rolled out a large chart on the big table. The chart was Operational Navigation Chart of the Sandor-Kumar border and the surrounding areas. He opened his brief case and passed out a red strike folder to each pilot. Inside the folder were strip charts cut to cover only the route of flight and immediate area around the route. They were cut small enough and bound in a tight little booklet that allowed them fit on a kneeboard inside the cramped cockpit.

Both the smaller charts as well as the big full-size one depicted the route of flight of the aircraft, the target, and the take-off and landing bases. It also depicted every Kumari and Sandori airfield with fighters stationed there listed for reference. It showed the surface to air missile batteries and their associated threat rings, the ranges at which they were able to attack. Along the margins of each page of the charts were critical pieces of information that the pilot may need to access quickly in flight such as radio frequencies, fuel requirements, minimum safe altitudes, etc. Long-range radar warning lines for each country were also depicted for various altitudes. It also included a cheat sheet with SAM types, ranges and radar frequencies they operated on.

"Gentlemen, this is a notional strike on the Habruk Nuclear Power Station," Sutherland said, waving at the chart on the table in front of them. "Your point of departure will be a small, deserted airstrip in the extreme south of

Tangistan. The Soviet Air Force," he said, glancing up nervously at Gurevich and Dobrinsky, "used to use this base as a forward operating location for Middle Eastern operations. It is mostly deserted now, though the Russian Air Force still lands there occasionally to refuel during deployments around the Middle East. It has jet fuel, air and power carts, and other ground equipment required for operations, though the equipment is in storage and the base is normally unoccupied. The MiGs will fly in from Russia the day before the mission with weapons already uploaded. There are no weapons loaders at this forward location. There they will be refueled, hydraulics serviced and pre-flighted for the mission.

"Each plane will be armed with a maximum weapons load," Sutherland said. "You will each carry as much as possible. Every plane will also carry a centerline fuel tank. Two of the MiGs will be dedicated fighter sweep sorties armed with four AA-12s and four AA-11s each. Two aircraft will be dedicated air defense suppression sorties with two AS-23 anti-radiation missiles, a jammer pod and two AA-11s for self-defense. The last two will be the dedicated strikers with four AS-22 laser-guided missiles with penetrator warheads each and two AA-11s on the outboard pylons. All will have the full 100 rounds of 30 mm for the gun. Together as a package you've got a lot of firepower to deal with both the target and any threats that may pop up." Sutherland reached across the table with his pointer and indicated the take off base.

"You will take off from here at 0100 hours," he said. "You will stay at low level, under 200 feet, all modes and codes strangled, radar in standby, nav lights off. You will fly with NVGs for station keeping. You can also operate the radar altimeter. At altitudes below 200 feet the side lobes of the radar altimeter can be detected only at very short range. You will proceed on a southwesterly heading, cutting just to the West of Lake Ubana in Northern Sandor. You will cross into Kumar and turn south to parallel the border on the Kumari side. You will drive about 75 miles south then turn left suddenly to cross the border at a ninety-degree angle.

"Once on the Sandori side you will continue terrain following and transit the mountains to the southeast. You will cross this range through a saddle here---then turn south and fly down the length of this valley that funnels you into the target area. The terrain should mask your approach to the target until you get within about 15 miles.

"The target itself sits out in the open and is very isolated. Even though it is not yet in operation it has a huge thermal signature among the cool mountains behind it. Since this breeder reactor is going to be the primary producer of fissionable material for Sandor's nuclear program it is obviously well protected. You can expect a point defense of the facility with fixed and mobile radar guided AAA as well as a newly installed SA-10 battery for long-range defense. They could possibly have SA-6 batteries for anything that gets close in."

At the mention of the SA-10 Grumble, Cahill let out a long whistle and wiped his now sweating brow. The SA-10 was the baddest of the bad Russian-made surface to air missiles. A strategic and therefore mostly fixed system, it had very long range, an active onboard radar capable of targeting low flying cruise missiles, state of the art electronic counter-countermeasures and a home on jam capability. It was every flyer's worst nightmare. There was no known defense against the SA-10 other than to avoid it whenever possible. Very similar to the US Patriot missile, it flew an up and over profile, launching straight up then arcing over to come down on top of a low flying target at very high speed. Its warhead was large enough that the blast from a near miss could still down the average fighter-sized target.

"Whoa, whoa, whoa...hold it right there for a second, Hoss," Cowboy exclaimed, waving his arms. "Taking off at o'dark thirty and crossing the border low level...no problem, flying TFR through the mountains and into the valley...no sweat, but SA-10s? SA-6s? How we supposed to get by them?"

"By definition a point defense means they are dedicated to defending the target itself," Fletcher said. "We'll have to fly into its threat engagement zone to attack the target. There is no going around them."

Sutherland nodded in agreement. "That is true. You cannot avoid them. You will have to take them out. That's where your HARM shooters come in. The two aircraft with the AS-23s will have to lead the strikers into the target area and sweep the SAMs. The onboard jammers should be able to take down any functioning AAA radars, so they will probably be severely degraded and not a factor."

"What if the SAM radars aren't radiating when we turn inbound?" Olmstead asked. "If they come up when we're off target and we have our backs to them we're just sitting ducks for a tail shot."

"We're actually counting on them being down when you are inbound," Sutherland said. "The SA-10 and SA-6 radars both use a lot of juice and have a short mean time between failures. The Sandoris have positioned them there mostly as a deterrent against day attack. It would be suicide to try to attack this complex in the daytime with these SAMs operating. Since the

Sandoris know Kumar does not train for night ground attack that is when they do their repair work and shut down the radars to make them last longer between repairs. Our RC-135 intelligence reports show that 90 percent of the time those SAM radars are down between midnight and 0500."

"But if they are up?" Romano asked.

"If you are inbound you take them out," Sutherland said. "If you are off hot and they come up you probably won't have to worry about the SA-6 because he's very limited in range during a tail chase. You are also firing your AS-22s far enough out that you'll be out of his engagement zone before he can react. The SA-10 can still haul you down, but it might bite off on some chaff and detonate the proximity fuse during a tail chase. It's 15 nautical miles to the nearest ridgeline. If you fire the AS-22s at 6 miles then haul ass outbound, you can probably make it behind the ridgeline before he can acquire you and get off a shot. You can also jam the SA-10 acquisition radar, just not the missile radar itself. We believe the SA-10 operators will be asleep this time of night, anyway. For them to react fast enough to get you they'd have to be sitting at the radar controls with the system warmed up and in standby, not likely. "

The pilots looked at each other for reactions to this. Fletcher had a raised eyebrow. Cahill's lips were pursed and he squinted his eyes in thought. Olmstead only shrugged. Romano laughed nervously.

"Okay---continue," Olmstead said.

Sutherland continued. "The target is a nuclear materials processing facility. This is where the uranium is refined into bomb grade material. The Sandoris are using a modified Russian commercial reactor as a breeder to yield the PU-239 they need for bombs. The project was started by the Russians, but when they backed out the French took over. They are now working as consultants for the Sandoris. The goal is to take out the breeder reactor, located in the center of the main complex. The two strikers will employ four AS-22s each on the complex, launched at a range of about six miles. The special penetrating warheads will actually go through the walls of the complex before exploding inside."

Romano raised his hand. "Uh---I hate to be bleeding heart about this, but won't there be a lot of radiation released to the environment if we blow large holes in a nuclear reactor?" he asked. "I mean I don't mind blowing up concrete and steel, but I don't want to cause another Chernobyl."

"Not to worry," Sutherland said. "This facility is not online yet. In fact it is still under construction and is not expected to be complete for another six weeks. The fueling operation should not occur for another month, by which time you will have reduced it to a pile of expensive concrete. So there is no danger of radiation."

"Uh, huh," Romano said rubbing his chin absently, suddenly realizing what that time frame meant.

"You launch your missiles at six miles, pull a 9 G-turn and haul ass for the mountains behind you," Sutherland said. "The first sign that you are even there will probably be when the first warhead explodes. You should be well beyond those mountains by the time they bring up those point defenses."

"Okay, so we're outbound now," Olmstead said, pointing to the mountains. "Which way? Back the way we came?"

"No," said Sutherland with a grin. "Now is when the real game begins." He indicated the route of flight with his laser pointer. "You will continue to fly TFR through these mountains, this time on a westerly heading. About ten miles from the Kumari border you will climb to 2000 feet AGL. This will give Sandori radar a good hard look at you, something we hope they haven't been able to do yet. It will also give them a chance to see your radar strobes on their passive detection listening posts along the border. They will identify you as MiGs, either 29s, 35s or 41s, it doesn't matter, so long as they know you are a MiG."

Romano raised his hand and broke in. "Isn't that hanging it out just a bit?"

Sutherland shrugged. "Well, at this point you are close enough to the border that Sandor can't do much about you. We just want them to know that a flight of MiGs just attacked a very critical national asset and now is heading into Kumari airspace."

"Yeah, well, won't the Kumaris be a little interested in us?" Fletcher asked.

"Absolutely," Sutherland said, rubbing his hands together in excitement. "This is where we are counting on the Kumaris to act like Kumaris. As you cross the border into Kumar the leader will squawk the standard Kumari military IFF code. Undoubtedly they will attempt to contact you on Guard frequency. One of our Russian friends, Dobrinsky, is fluent in the Arabic dialects spoken in Kumar. He will tell them they are a special flight authorized by General Abdul Hassad, the Kumari air minister and ask for descent and landing instructions at Kirjil. The controller will obviously not have any flight plan for you, but at the mention of General Hassad, he will issue you vectors for Kirjil. The Kumaris have a very persuasive system of command

and control. It's called fear. It is not uncommon for a general to personally authorize operations and our intel suggests this Hassad fellow is one bad mother," he said, letting that sink in for a moment. "You must also fly a tight formation. If the Kumari thinks he's vectoring a pair of fighters it won't cause quite the alarm as a half-dozen warplanes suddenly appearing on his scope."

"Won't he also alert Kumari air defense?" Olmstead asked.

Sutherland nodded. "Sure, however as long as you follow his vectors and don't appear to be deviating he should let you proceed. They may scramble a few fighters, but the Kumari Air Force does not fly at night and even if they did they probably couldn't find you, much less intercept you. They know it would be a waste of time, especially if you appear to be cooperating.

"In any event it doesn't matter," Sutherland said. "We just want to make sure the Sandoris hear us contact Kumari air control and get vectored by them for landing. Once you have the vector, which should be to the northwest, you'll declare an emergency, say something about mid-air collision, dive to the deck and drop off their radarscopes. Their ATC radar coverage does not extend below 1000 feet, nor does their air defense radar. Once you are in the dive pickle off any remaining missiles and empty fuel tanks. The idea is to give them a fireball on the ground and some debris to investigate."

"Yeah, but they'll know the debris is not an airplane," Cahill said, confused.

"True," Sutherland agreed, "but it'll be the next day before they find that out and it'll look to Sandor like they lost their strike package and just didn't want to admit their own incompetence."

"So we're back at TFR--" Olmstead said impatiently, prompting Sutherland to continue.

"Yes," Sutherland said. "You will continue at TFR, 200 feet AGL, on a northerly heading. You will cross back into Sandor below their radar coverage then fly straight up the left side of the lake again and cross back over into Tangistan. You will land, hot-pit refuel, and take off again, this time landing at a small airstrip in Southern Russia before the sun even comes up. Well that's about it. What do you think?"

The pilots looked at each other as if for reassurance. There was none to be found. Cowboy was shaking his head and Sutherland noticed.

"Sir, what are you thinking?" he asked the Texan hunched over the map.

"Well...this whole deal really hinges on us gettin across Northern Sandor undetected, both coming and going," he started. "We sure the Sandori radar can't see us down at 200 feet? And what about mobile threats like those SA-

6s, or some AAA radars spread about? If they are up we might get detected, right? I mean the whole thing's shot to shit if they don't think we're Kumari, right? Do we have a contingency plan if we are detected?"

Sutherland shook his head. "No, if you are detected it is a mission abort."

"How we even know if we're detected?" Cahill asked.

"If you get locked up by any radar. That's a no-brainer," he said. "If you are swept by a search radar or ATC radar above a certain detection threshold we also have to assume you are on their scope."

"What about visual sightings?" Fletcher asked.

"It will be about 0200 in the morning on a moonless night," Sutherland said. "No one is gonna get a good look at you. If they do see you what will they say? They will not really know what you are and for all they know you could be friendly. Sandor flies these aircraft as well."

"That brings up a good point," Olmstead said. "I take it they don't fly night patrols?"

Sutherland shook his head. "No, they don't train for night intercepts, although their aircraft are capable of night BVR ops. They do maintain night instrument proficiency. Each pilot is required to fly two night sorties every six months, but those are pattern only sorties and the aircraft should not be armed with missiles, maybe bullets for the guns. Most of those night sorties are on the deck by midnight, however. They never fly as late as 0200 and if they have to scramble and launch you will be off target and over the border before they can become a threat to you."

"Besides the –41 what other aircraft do they fly?" Romano asked.

"They fly a mix of Soviet and US iron," the lieutenant said. "MiG-29s,-35s, -23s, 21s, and –25s, supplemented by a few F-14s and F-4s left over from the 70s. They do have the AIM-54 Phoenix, but they are all almost thirty years old and are probably no longer operational."

"Probably? What about SAMs? Besides the ones in the target area?" Olmstead asked, concern in his voice. "Are there any others we need to worry about out there?"

Sutherland nodded. "Yes, they do operate a fairly large number of SAMs, however they do not employ them in an area defense. They put all their heavy hitters in the point defense role around critical assets and Hanrah. The areas you are flying through are sparsely populated and the only item of real interest worth protecting is the nuclear plant. You will of course be inside the SA-5 engagement envelope almost the whole time, but at TFR with all that dirt out there that radar has line of sight problems at long range and it shouldn't be a problem. You get down around Hanrah and you'd see a lot more SA-10s and even the I-Hawks we sold them back in the mid-80s."

"We sold them I-HAWKs?" Romano asked incredulously.

"You must remember that Scandal," Sutherland said. "We sold the Sandoris I-HAWKs then funneled the funds to freedom fighters in Central America. It was a big scandal back then, still is if you run up against one of those I-HAWKs."

The I-HAWK was a surface to air missile system built in the United States for use by the US Army. HAWK stood for Homing All the Way Killer. The "I" stood for Improved. The HAWK was a devastatingly accurate SAM with excellent range and powerful radar that had the best in anti-jamming capability. A MiG-41 would be dead meat at the hands of a HAWK missile, unless the HARM shooters got it first, which was a difficult prospect given the short acquisition/engagement time required by the HAWK. The US-made radar could lock up an enemy and fire the missile in only a few short seconds. Once airborne the HAWK's active radar seeker homes in on the target with deadly precision. The US Army's motto for firing the HAWK was "if it flies, it dies".

"So we shouldn't have to worry about the HAWK, right?" Romano asked.

"No, you should not see it in the areas you are flying," Sutherland said with confidence.

"Any other SAMs?" Fletcher asked.

"Besides the HAWK they operate the SA-2, SA-3, SA-5, SA-6, SA-8 and SA-10," he said, "as well as the SA-7 and SA-14 MANPAD heat seekers. The MANPADS can turn up anywhere, but they'd really have to know you were coming and wait in just the right spot to get you...again highly unlikely. They also operate a lot of radar guided AAA, such as ZSU-23-4s and ZSU-57-2s. These have very short range and their radars will give them away, and they are jammable."

"Should you encounter any radar threat, such as a SAM, the rules are simple, 'save yourself and your aircraft'," Sutherland said. "Turn away from the threat, and go around it if possible. If that's not possible you can actively jam the radar and use chaff to decoy the missile. If the threat has you locked up prior to crossing over into Kumar the first time then it's a mission abort. After that it will look like they are jamming a Kumari aircraft attempting to penetrate their airspace. It will be your discretion at that point as to whether or not to continue, depending on the level of threat."

"We are completely cleared for self-defense, right?" Olmstead asked.

"Completely," Tanner said loudly, having slipped into the room unnoticed. "You are cleared to employ deadly force against any weapon system that poses a direct threat to you, any SAM, AAA or fighter.

"I suggest you become very familiar with this plan, though. This is basically the product of one evening of hectic planning by our lieutenant here," he said, gesturing at the intel officer. "As competent as he is, this is still a plan in the works. I want you all to go over every detail of this mission. I want you to chair fly it a hundred times if necessary and pick it apart, find every little glitch that could lead to failure. We don't want any surprises if we have to execute this. Is that clear?"

They all nodded with grim expressions on their faces.

After Tanner left the vault the room noticeably cooled down a few degrees. The pressure was on. Now they knew what lie ahead. As they gazed over the chart before them, marking their way into Sandor and back, they couldn't help feel apprehensive. This plan was not only harrowing from a purely military point of view; it also relied heavily on both stealth and deception. Without these two factors the game would be over, maybe permanently.

WASHINGTON BELTWAY
1400 HOURS

"The time is ripe, my friend," Komiskov said, sitting in the passenger seat of Michaels' Town car. "We have a very tight window of opportunity on this one, Charles. We must deploy now."

Michaels nodded absently. He was already thinking ahead, had been ever since he received the coded message to pick up Komiskov. The congested traffic of the Washington Beltway provided the best anonymity possible for the dealings.

"Charles, are you listening to me?" the Russian asked angrily, breaking Michaels out of his trance.

"Yes, sorry, Victor," he said. "I was just thinking. Yes, you are right. We have to move quickly on this Sandori reactor. I hope we are ready."

The Russian smiled grimly. "I hope so as well," he confided. "Will you tell your president directly?"

"I'm not sure---you?" Michaels asked.

"My president desires to know of these things," he said, "but yours has more media vulnerability."

"So you think I should keep it from him?"

"I did not say that," the Russian said with a wave of his hand. "You know him and his position better than I."

"Yes. I do," Michaels nodded.

LATER THE SAME DAY

Normally when a unit deploys overseas there is a formal deployment order written and passed down from headquarters. This starts a mad logistical scramble to find transportation, organize and pack the equipment, fuel and service the deploying aircraft, and move entire organizations within the deploying unit. The process usually takes a couple of days and a whole lot of hard work and suffering, but a lot sooner than you would think, C-5 Galaxies, C-17 Globemasters or C-141 Starlifters would be winging their way overseas, filled with troops, equipment and of course the staple of military life, paperwork. Fighters and tankers would be rolling down runways and off into the skies in large formations, the little fighters staying close to their tankers, like baby ducks to their mothers. Within three or four days the base would be a ghost town as the whole Wing moved lock stock and barrel to some base in England, or Saudi Arabia or some other exotic location.

This deployment was a bit less obvious. Basically four US fighter pilots, an intelligence officer and a one star general simply disappeared overnight.

"So what are we suppose to be, man, tourists?" Romano asked Cowboy, who was sitting next to him on TWA Flight 910, nonstop service from Chicago to Berlin. They'd flown into O'Hara to catch the international flight and had a two-hour layover there. The flight from Vegas had been five mind-numbing hours. Now they were seven hours into an eleven-hour flight to Berlin.

The tall Texan pulled his right knee up to his chest and grimaced, his long legs feeling as though they were filled with sand.

"I don't know, pard," he admitted. "All I know is I hate flying," he complained, trying to find a comfortable position in his tiny seat in the coach class cabin.

"Humph," Romano grunted. "I bet Tanner's sitting in First Class on his flight. I guess it wouldn't be proper protocol to have a general flying with a bunch of captains."

Suddenly Fletcher appeared over the seat from the row behind them. "You guys, what to shut the hell up," he said under his breath, clearly irritated. "We're suppose to be under cover here and you're talking about generals and captains. That's the kind of talk that draws attention. We're on an international flight and you might want to keep a low profile, got it?"

Romano just nodded absently and went back to reading his magazine. Cowboy was still fidgeting, trying to get comfortable. Olmstead was the only one of them that knew how to travel. He fell asleep about an hour after take-off and had slept for six straight hours. He still showed no signs of stirring. Several times throughout the flight Fletcher felt like he needed to borrow a mirror to see if his friend was still breathing.

In order to appear as inconspicuous as possible Tanner and Sutherland were booked on a different flight. Their tickets were purchased separately and they were not sitting near each other. The Russians themselves had taken a more direct flight, Aeroflot direct to Russia, then on to Tangistan by military transport. It was felt it was best if they traveled independently of their American colleagues.

The four pilots' voyage would take them to Berlin, then by Turkish Airways to Incirlik, then by Aeroflot to a small city in southwest Russia. From there they would be taken to their forward operating base in Tangistan by Russian military helicopter. The whole trip took three uncomfortable and sleepless days. Sleepless for everyone but Olmstead, that is. He managed to sleep the better part of two whole days.

"So you are alive," Fletch commented through half-closed eyes as he saw Olmstead stir back awake.

"How long was I out?" Olmstead asked, rubbing his eyes.

"About six hours this time," Fletch said. "Maybe not a record for you, but a good showing all the same."

"Maybe I can break that record before it's all over," Olmstead grunted. "How's Tweedle-dum and Tweedle-dee?" he asked, hooking a thumb in Romano and Cahill's direction.

"They've been bitching nonstop for four hours, but I think they're both asleep now," he answered.

Olmstead looked around, now fully awake.

"Why are the lights out?" he asked.

"It's the middle of the night for the rest of us," Fletcher said, checking the glowing hands of the Breitling on his wrist.

Olmstead sighed and stared straight ahead.

"Does this seem right to you?" he asked to nobody in particular.

Fletcher arched an eyebrow and opened an eye. "What seems right to me?" he asked.

"Oh…nothing. I'm just paranoid, I guess," Olmstead sighed. Then he asked, "Why'd you decide to join the Air Force, anyway?"

Fletcher shrugged his shoulders. "I don't know," he said. "Never really gave anything else any thought. I guess I wanted to fly. My old man flew in Nam."

Olmstead sat up straighter and turned in his seat. "Really? I didn't know that. Air Force?"

"Army," he said. "Warrant officer. Flew gunships."

"He retired?"

"I guess you could say that," Fletcher grunted. "The Viet Cong retired him in '69."

Olmstead couldn't help but think of Pete. Like father, like son. Damn, was it a curse? *Did it run in their family or what*, he wondered?

"I'm sorry, Mike," he said quietly. "Didn't mean to stir up bad memories."

"No memories good or bad," he said matter-of-factly. "I have no memories of my father. He died when I was two years old."

"Pete never mentioned him," Olmstead said.

"Pete, wasn't even born until a month after he was dead," Fletcher said.

"Your mother remarry?"

Fletcher nodded. "Yeah, she did alright," he yawned. "Found a nice stable insurance salesman. No one ever shot at him---though many probably wanted to."

"Yeah," was the only thing Olmstead could think of to say.

Three hours later they touched down in Berlin. They sat around the airport for three more hours waiting for their Turkish Airways flight, which was delayed for maintenance. They tried to be inconspicuous, but four clean-shaven, shorthaired Americans traveling together cannot be inconspicuous no matter how hard they try. Finally they were allowed to board the Turkish Airbus 320, where they spent an additional hour waiting for the baggage to be loaded. Apparently they could not start loading the baggage until the maintenance had finished. Just as they were collectively at wits end the plane taxied out and took the active runway. Soon they were airborne and headed for Incirlik.

The connecting flight to Russia had its problems as well. Aeroflot has never had an exactly stellar record of reliability or safety for that matter. They were allowed to board the plane immediately upon arrival at the gate. They were hopeful this meant things were going well. They were wrong.

The weather at the destination airport was closing down the runway there and they were not allowed to takeoff until the weather cleared. Rather than let the passengers disembark and wait in the terminal, Aeroflot policy called for them to remain in their seats on the aircraft, probably a policy left over from the days of the Iron Curtain when they were afraid the passengers would defect if allowed off the aircraft.

This time the delay was five excruciating hours of boredom, babies crying and stale air. The flight crew refused to run the air conditioning while sitting at the gate. Even though the temperature outside was a cool 55, the hundred and twenty bodies inside the Tupolev were radiating 98.6 degrees each and within the first hour the cabin temperature hit 90. Sweat poured off every brow and the smell of the hygienically challenged became nearly intolerable. Intolerable to the Americans, that is. The Europeans and Asians onboard did not even notice. They were accustomed to the stench and it was considered as much a part of air travel in that region as packages of pretzels on domestic US flights.

When they finally stepped down off the aircraft in Russia and met their contact they were relieved, but when he immediately ushered them to another aircraft, a dubious looking helicopter, they let out collective groans. Even Olmstead hadn't been able to sleep through this nightmare. The flight was loud and bumpy, the whine of the twin turbines deafening and the turbulence constant. When they stepped down off the landing skid at Stovacore AB, they didn't want to touch another aircraft for a very long time. Unknown to them, a very long time was going to be about twelve hours.

STOVACORE AIRBASE, TANGISTAN
0800 LOCAL

"Gentlemen, welcome to Tangistan," Tanner said as they stepped down off the ancient Russian transport helicopter. He noted the skepticism on their faces as they surveyed the bleak little airbase.

"I know it doesn't look like much," Tanner admitted, "but it will serve our needs nicely."

He wasn't exaggerating about the base not looking like much; indeed there was not much to the base. Romano shook his head as he took in his new "home base". A single cracked and broken runway, maybe 5000 feet long, Romano guessed, was the center of the base. There was a small ramp area that might hold a dozen aircraft, a single large and rusty fuel tank sitting next to the "hangar", which consisted of a large Quonset hut with both ends removed. The base operations building was a square cinder block building with an observation deck on top that must be the "control tower", Romano thought. The windows on the building were opaque with dirt and grime, except for the one that was missing entirely.

"Just how long is that runway, General?" Romano asked, the other pilots interested in that question as well.

"Just under 4500 feet," Tanner replied. Cahill let out a low whistle and rolled his eyes.

"It'll be plenty of runway when you return lightweight," Tanner assured them.

Just how lightweight would they be, Olmstead wondered? Fletcher and he exchanged glances, as if they were reading each other's thoughts. Fletcher shrugged.

"How about when we're heavy and taking off?" he asked Olmstead just over a whisper. This time Olmstead shrugged.

Three tents were erected behind the base ops building. One was the living quarters for the pilots, one was the intelligence tent, which doubled as Sutherland's quarters and the third belonged to Tanner and Kavinsky, the Russian detachment commander. The bathroom was inside the base ops building that reeked of long broken plumbing. There was running water in the bathroom, but the best one could do was maybe sponge off. Any chance at a shower was gone with the trickle of water pressure.

Sutherland had the intel shack all set up, having arrived hours earlier with Tanner on the aging Russian transport that brought in their equipment. The Quonset hut hangar was filled with six MiG-41 aircraft, all marked in Sandori livery, and not nearly as pristine as the birds back in the States. Stains lined their flanks from months of hydraulic fluid leaks and fuel spills during over the wing refueling. In actuality they were intentionally stained in this manner. Mechanically they were in excellent condition, but they looked used and abused, the way a Sandori MiG might look. The MiGs were fully armed and fueled, waiting for their pilots and the word to launch.

"Gentlemen, we've had a slight change in plans," Tanner told them. "I'm sorry you don't have more time to get settled in, but we need to brief you on something that's developing as we speak. Report to the Intel tent immediately. Lt Sutherland has a briefing for you. He has orders to start without me. I have a satellite conference in just a few minutes. I know you are tired, but this won't wait. You can get some rest after the briefing...if your nerves will let you, that is," he added, walking away.

"What do you think?" Cahill asked Romano.

Romano shrugged his shoulders. "Who knows? All I know is I'm tired, I'm hungry and the chances of finding a pizza joint around here that delivers is just about zero."

"There's your pizza joint," Cahill said, hooking a thumb at a crate of MREs. Romano winced.

The intel tent was set up like a briefing room with chairs in front of an easel from which Sutherland would brief. Next to the easel was a planning table with a large chart of the Middle East. There would be no PowerPoint slide show this time. The pilots took their seats. A few moments later Gurevich and Dobrinsky came in and sat down quietly at the end of the row. The Russians had arrived on a transport hours earlier with the aircraft mechanics. Romano shook hands with Dobrinksy and slapped him on the back.

Sutherland came into the tent and moved to the front, carrying reams of charts, photos and documents. He dropped the load of paperwork on the big table at the front. Sutherland picked up a pointer and took center stage. A large chart depicting the route of flight, threat rings and targets was spread across the table.

"Good morning, sirs. We've had a change of plan and some late breaking intelligence we have to act on immediately," he said, very seriously. "Originally we were planning to take out that reactor at Habruk, but due to some very late-breaking intelligence we have the opportunity to go after something much more time critical.

"For months the Russians have had an informant working within the Kumari Guard and in close proximity to Achmed Al Faisal's defense minister, his nephew, Abdul Al Faisal. Abdul is linked to no less than fourteen terrorists attacks around the globe. He has supplied Hammas, Islamic Jihad and Al Qaeda with arms and funding. Now we know when, where and how he is traveling tonight. He is your target."

"Tell us about this informant, Lieutenant," Olmstead asked. "He just in it for the money or does he have a gripe with Al Faisal?"

"He is a key player in the Guard and assigned to Abdul's personal security detail. He's given us details relating to whom Abdul has been meeting with and where he has gone, all very reliable, however," Sutherland grimaced. "Like most informants he's in it for the money. Unfortunately that's also what got him in trouble. During a random security check of personal it was discovered he had money in his bank account for which he could not account for. Achmed's tax laws make the IRS look like the Social Security Administration. Since he had money unaccounted for it was assumed he was embezzling from the government and evading taxes, both of which were probably true. He was arrested about four hours ago and executed shortly thereafter. If nothing else Achmed believes in quick justice," he said wryly.

"Before he was arrested, he sent us a message by courier," Sutherland continued. "Abdul will be traveling tonight from Kagned to Hanruk. His convoy will be leaving at midnight and should arrive in Hanruk by 0400 hours. During that time he will be traveling through some very remote desert and his convoy of cars and tracked vehicles will make an excellent IR target," Sutherland said, pausing to clear his throat. He continued, "Since our informant is explaining himself to Allah at the moment, we need to act as soon as possible. We may not get another chance at this for some time."

"So we're going after the Kumari Defense Minister? Assassination?" Olmstead asked.

"He is a confirmed terrorist, but essentially…yes," Sutherland said.

"Okay."

"Just how big a convoy is it?" Fletcher asked.

"That's the tricky part," Sutherland said, referring to a sketch on the easel. "The convoy will consist of 10 identical white limousines spaced out over a two mile stretch of road, interspersed with mobile AAA, SA-6 batteries, as well as troop trucks with MANPADS mixed in with them. Only Achmed himself has better security. The trick is hitting the right vehicle while the others are shooting at you."

"Shooting at us?" Romano said nervously.

"Mission survival shouldn't be your problem on this one," Sutherland said confidently. "Finding and hitting the right car will be the problem."

"And just how do we do that?" Cahill asked, very interested in how he could kill one of the men responsible for his brother's death.

"You don't," Sutherland said. "You take them all out, or at least as many as you can. We're getting ahead of ourselves, though. Let's start back at take-off and I'll take you through it step by step."

"Why doesn't this guy just fly to Hanruk?" Romano asked impatiently.

"Ever since the last war no one in the Kumari High Command ever flies. They feel if we know they're on a plane or helicopter we'll try to take them out, or the Sandoris will try, both of which are probably true," Sutherland said. "They are also afraid of sabotage, even a terrorist bomb."

"They're afraid of terrorists?" Fletcher asked, smiling at the irony of the situation.

"Achmed and his boys have made a lot of enemies over the years,"

Sutherland said matter-of-factly.

He beckoned them to join him around the big table where the route of flight was laid out. He spent the next ten minutes describing the late night, maximum gross weight take-off and climb out, the low level penetration of Sandori airspace, the crossing into Kumar and approach to the target area.

"This base is only about fifty miles from the Sandori border so there won't be much dead head time. About ten miles out of Sandor you should kill your nav lights and station keep by IRST only," he said. "You will each be in terrain following mode at an altitude of 200 feet, in line-astern formation. You want to cross over into Sandori airspace on the same track one right behind the other so as to minimize the area you cover and minimize your chances of detection. You will stay in this formation all the way through Sandor, keeping the HARM shooters out front. They should move to line abreast once inside Kumar. If you are detected inside Sandor they won't shoot for fear you are one of their own. They'll want to investigate first. They may launch interceptors but the chances of them reaching you before you cross into Kumar are nil.

"You will cross over here," he pointed to a saddle in some terrain. "Once into Kumari airspace you will only have about eighty miles to fly. You will remain at terrain following in formation until you reach ten miles out. The two SEAD aircraft, Olmstead and Gurevich, armed with AS-23 HARMS will break off the approach and split, one heading northeast the other southwest to cover the strikers from both directions. They will stay low until the four strikers call IP inbound at which time they will pop to 5000 feet, arm their anti-radiation missiles and turn inbound themselves, staying clear of the target area, though. Two of the four strikers, Romano and Dobrinsky, will be carrying 12 CBUs each on six pylons with AA-11s on the wingtips.

"The other two strikers, Fletcher and Cahill, will carry eight CBUs on four pylons, two AA-12s on the outboard pylon, and two AA-11s on the wingtips. They will deal with any AIs that might turn up. Each MiG will also carry a centerline fuel tank that is to be jettisoned when empty. Remember the fuel tank is both speed and G limited and must be jettisoned prior to speeding up for the ingress to the target area. It is planned that you feed first from your external tanks and jettison them when empty, well before the target area. Also remember your internal gun fire control is inhibited until the tank is jettisoned. So get rid of it as soon as it's empty.

"The timing of the mission will be such that by the time you reach the convoy, here," he pointed to the chart, "the vehicles will be on a stretch of road that runs through a narrow gap cut in the desert. There is little to no room for a vehicle to maneuver in there so they should be sitting ducks.

"You will get one pass, from the southwest to the northeast. The strikers will accelerate to 550 knots and climb to 1100 feet AGL. This altitude gives the best spread of the bomblets. The minimum altitude for canisters to open is 500 feet, but you get a very narrow spread like that. Minimum airspeed is 300 knots, but you should never be that slow. The four-ship should close it up tight in a V formation for the release, the two leads being wingtip to wingtip and the other two stacked up in tight echelon.

"You will each have different Desired Mean Points of Impact (DMPI), since we want to cover the whole convoy," Sutherland said. "The left lead will aim and release on the last vehicle, his bomb train spacing the CBUs out to cover an area one mile long. The right lead will aim 6000 feet down the train and release his bombs on the second mile of vehicles. Number three will aim about a half mile down the convoy, the number four plane will aim will aim a mile and a half down the convoy. Each CBU will cover an area the size of a football field, so we should be able to saturate the whole convoy.

"Stealth and surprise are our allies here," Sutherland cautioned. "We get one run at this. There won't be any racetracks. We can catch them with their pants down initially, but they'll have their AAA and SAMs up and ready if we try a second pass, assuming we don't destroy their air defenses on the first past. In any event you drive in at TFR, climb at the last second, bomb the hell out of the convoy, and make for Sandor like a bat out of hell."

"This is where the deception comes in," he continued. "You have to climb high enough that Kumari Mil radar can get a fix on you. We estimate 6000 feet should give them a solid plot of you making like bandits for home, in this case Sandor. Once your RWR gear says you've been tracked, go ahead and jam the Kumaris and dive back to 200 foot TFR.

"You will cross back into Sandor about here, and once ten miles inside turn north and parallel the border. Once back inside you should slow to best range airspeed to conserve fuel. You will be slower but your sonic footprint will be smaller. Your egress routing will be the same as your ingress routing inside Sandor. The route is designed to give you the best terrain masking and the least likelihood of detection. It may not seem sound to cover the same ground going out as going in, but we think it is very safe ground and if you get in safely, then coming out the same way is the best bet to avoid detection. Besides if anybody actually catches a visual of you on a moonless night they will assume you are friendly. The single file in trail formation minimizes your footprint. Once you are out of Sandori airspace you can form back up. You will want to stay below 2000 feet all the way home, though."

"When you recover back here you will be very light weight. The recovery fuel is planned at 800 lbs, and there is no alternate airfield. Do not use burners except for take-off or if you come under attack by an enemy fighter. You can't afford to use the gas. We wish you didn't have to use the burners for take-off, but with 4500 feet of runway we don't have a choice."

"What happens if we need to use burners?" Romano asked.

"If your close enough to home base you can log some glider time, if not...well, it's a long walk back to the barn," Sutherland said wryly.

"You're not exactly inspiring confidence in us, you know," Fletcher said grimly.

"I don't want to sugarcoat anything," Sutherland said. "Gas is gonna be short on this profile and that's just an operational constraint we have to deal with."

"What about threats?" Cahill asked in his slow Texas drawl.

The young lieutenant grabbed a pointer and began to run down the threat list.

"If all goes well you will not encounter any threats until you enter the target area," he said. "You will probably detect Sandori and Kumari long range acquisition radars, such as the Tall King, Spoon Rest and Flat Face, on your threat warning receivers. Do not attempt to jam them manually and do not leave your jammers in auto. That will only let them know you are coming. We estimate their early warning radars are useless below 1000 feet. At the ranges and altitudes you will be flying those ground-based radars will not be able to lock onto you and probably won't be able to get you through the ground clutter. If you try to jam them it will put a strobe on their screen that points right at you. Keep the jammers silent. Stealth is the name of the game," he paused for emphasis, then moved on to a threat ring near the border. "You will skirt several SA-2 and SA-3 sites, so you may see a Fansong or Low Blow radar. You will be at their extreme detection range and that's only if they are looking for you with data from an acquisition radar. Even if they find you, you will be outside missile engagement range.

"You will be inside Sandori SA-5 coverage for all of the time you are inside Sandor, ingressing and egressing. The SA-5 is very long range, however the Square Pair radar is line of sight and you will be below its radar horizon most of the time. Terrain will mask you for most of the flight through Sandor. The SA-5 deployment is not optimized for an attack coming from the north, obviously they would expect a Kumari attack from the west."

"What about the emissions from the terrain following radar?" Fletcher asked.

"At 200 feet the radar horizon is about 10 miles and any terrain out there will shortened that. Given your altitude, the terrain out there and the low power of your radar system they shouldn't be able to detect much less track you by your emissions," Sutherland said confidently.

"Until you enter the target area all your threats will be of the fixed strategic SAM variety. As you enter the target area your primary threats will be of a tactical nature. Mobile ZSU-23-4s, mobile SA-6 tracked vehicles and of course MANPADs, mostly SA-7s, maybe SA-14s, will be your primary threats. At the speed and direction you will be flying I wouldn't worry about the MANPADs. You'll be bombs away before they know you are there. If you punch out preemptive flares at night you'll only highlight yourself for every soldier with a rifle and of course the ZSUs. You can jam the Gun Dish fire-control radars and the SA-6 acquisition, but watch out for the SA-6 Straight Flush TTR. If you jam this you can easily cause the missile to home on jam. Also have your chaff dispensers programmed to dump chaff throughout the target run. Most radar missiles' proximity fuses will bite off on the chaff during a tail shot. Besides the chaff will clutter the target area for all the radars making their life more difficult. You should be in and out before they can resolve your location, get a fire-control solution and launch a missile."

"You're saying to just ignore the MANPADs?" Romano asked.

"Essentially, yes. No offense to our Russian friends here, but the SA-7 is not much of a threat at the speeds and altitudes you will be flying. It is not a user-friendly weapon and can really only get you in a tail shot. Even if he sees you he will wait for the tail shot and if you are dispensing CBUs as you fly over he won't be alive long enough to get his shot off," he said confidently.

"What about the SA-14?" Cowboy asked.

"Well..." he said with a frown. "It is all-aspect and does have flare rejection, but the odds of someone getting a shot off at you are pretty remote."

Cowboy leaned over to Romano and whispered, "So it can kill us, right?"

"It can kill us," Romano confirmed with a casual nod.

The briefed threats were cause for some concern and the pilots' faces betrayed their thoughts. Even Gurevich, normally cocky and confident, seemed nervous about the SA-6. He and Dobrinsky knew first hand how dangerous that missile was. The "three fingers of death" as the SA-6 was nicknamed, was designed for fast, low flying targets. Its radar was extremely powerful and consists of an acquisition, a target tracker and an illuminator. One of the first true "smart" missiles it could sense when it's being jammed and revert to a home on jam mode, where it homes in on the jamming strobe from the target aircraft. The SA-6 was mobile, but was best at point defense, where it could sit up above the target, preferably on a hill with an unobstructed radar view of the surrounding area. Deployed around high value assets, although mobile, it's stationary when employed. Not ideally suited for defending a moving convoy, it nevertheless was deadly and could be employed with minimal difficulty in this fashion. Usually the best way to defend against an SA-6 is to either avoid it or HARM it. Since it usually sits next to the intended target, avoiding it is not always an option. HARM missiles love the strong radar of the SA-6 and a kill on the radar ensures the missiles are out of action as well.

If the strikers keep the element of surprise on their side the SA-6 should not be a player, but the AAA was another story. The ZSU-23-4 also worried the pilots. Anti-aircraft artillery historically has killed far more aircraft than fighters or SAMs. The ZSU is a 23 mm, four-barreled, radar-guided gun, capable of spitting out almost 100 rounds a second. The hail of lead and copper produced by the ZSU can cut a fighter in half, sawing the wings clean off. The range is short, but they would definitely be in range when attacking the convoy. The jamming might help, but the ZSU can also be fired with other ZSUs to create a curtain of fire any enemy must fly through. This curtain fire is sometimes more likely to kill an attacker than direct fire. It can certainly cause the striker to take evasive action and possibly break off an attack.

"What about AIs?" Fletcher asked.

"Neither the Sandoris nor the Kumaris train for night intercepts," Sutherland said. "There may be somebody airborne carrying out night proficiency training, but at this time of the night it would be very unlikely. In any event they probably won't be armed. If you are engaged...splash the bandit, simple," he said shrugging his shoulders. Romano turned up an eyebrow at that and smiled.

"Okay, you briefed the SEAD guys will be breaking off to the northeast and southwest to make a covering HARM run," Olmstead said. "Do we want preemptive HARMS or just if we get locked up?"

The tactic of the preemptive HARM launch meant that you launched the missile dumb toward the target area during a critical time in the bomb run you are covering. If the radar came up during the HARM time of flight it would lock on and destroy that radar before it knew what hit them. This has the advantage of very rapid engagement time. Sometimes if the HARM shooter is far enough away and the target aircraft is only a few miles off, even the incredibly fast HARM missiles can't get there before the SAM hits the target. There is a point on any bomb run when you are so close to the SAM site that a HARM will not do you any good. The down side of the pre-emptive launch is that you might waste a HARM you might otherwise need a few minutes later. If you have HARMs to spare pre-emptive is the way to go. In this case there were few HARMs and they would have to be more selective.

"We do not want you to launch any pre-emptive HARMs," Sutherland answered. "By climbing and staying farther out than the strikers we're hoping the SEAD guys will present an attractive target. You're essentially a lethal diversion. If they try to lock you up---HARM'em. They will go for the obvious target and that will be the HARM shooters. The strikers, down low until the last second should skate right in while they are engaging the SEAD guys."

"You mentioned the SEAD package would turn inbound when the strikers called their Initial Point," Fletcher said. "How do we make that call? What kind of comm security do we have?"

"The MiGs have two radios each, one with secure voice," he said. "You will communicate only as necessary on the secure voice and in clear text. That will be your emergency interplane frequency. It will be scrambled by the secure voice so if you use it don't worry about lexicon or code words. The other radio will be the active interplane radio, completely unsecure. You will use this radio to make your IP call and you will use the lexicon we provide for you. This is going to require a little practice before the mission because the IP lexicon is in the language of Sandor. We're trying to use standard Sandori tactical lexicon for our IP inbound call. No doubt that transmission will be picked up by listening posts in Kumar and will add to the illusion that you are Sandori. The IP call is highlighted on the comm cheat sheet you will put on your kneeboards."

"Are there any more comm questions?" Sutherland asked.

"Do we ever talk to any ATC?" Cahill asked.

"Negative, you won't contact the tower for launch or recovery, nor any ATC facility while airborne."

They finished up the whole briefing almost an hour later and the pilots stayed to study the plan for two hours after that. Each man went over the mission from launch to recovery, chair flying the mission so to speak, jotting down notes that might help in flight. Olmstead and Gurevich went back over the AS-23 anti-radiation missile capabilities, programming and launch parameters, ensuring when the time came they could take out the SAMs if necessary.

The other four pilots studied in great detail the stretch of terrain that would be the target area if all went right. There was a little rise to the south that would mask their approach until they got about 2 miles out. Those two miles would be covered in a little over 14 seconds, not a lot of time to find the target, line up the bomb reticule, and maneuver the aircraft for release. Not a long time, but it should be long enough if they were where they thought they would be and if the IRST targeting system was working. Without the IRST they'd have to use the radar to line up on the target and the depression would hide the target from radar until the last second. If the convoy was not yet to the area specified the plan was to follow the road down to the southeast until they were spotted. If they weren't spotted prior to crossing the 32d parallel, they were to abort the mission and return to base due to fuel considerations.

Finally a little after 2 PM Tanner came in and ran his boys out. He gave them a direct order to eat dinner and get some sleep; easier said than done. The show time was midnight, launch at 0200. It would be a long night.

"I don't like this one bit, Igor," Tanner said to the Russian general, back in their shared quarters. "The plan was to take out the reactor first. That was really the critical target, you know."

"I understand your concern, George," General Igor Kavinsky replied. "All things being equal the Sandori reactor is more important that getting the Kumari defense minister."

Tanner shook his head and began to pace. "I know we have this rare opportunity that may never come again, but we're risking the Sandor mission. We kill this guy and make it look like Sandor did it the Sandoris will be looking for some move. We can't afford to lose the surprise factor. That's why we wanted to do the reactor first. It wouldn't carry the emotion of the assassination of a bureaucrat."

"You hide your concerns well, my friend," Kavinsky said with a sly smile.

"What do you mean?" Tanner replied, confused.

"You pretend to be concerned with the Sandor mission, but you are actually nervous about tonight, no?" the Russian said with a smile.

Tanner smiled a wry smile. "I guess I am nervous about tonight," he admitted. "Did we miss something? Are they ready?"

Kavinsky slapped him on the back as he got up from the edge of his cot.

"We got it right, my friend. Everything will be as you say...a pie walk."

"That's a cake walk, Igor," Tanner said and laughed, "and I hope you are right."

Olmstead came out of the makeshift mess hall and saw Fletcher sitting on the tailgate of a camouflaged Russian truck smoking a cigarette. He walked over and plopped down on the tailgate.

"When did you start smoking," Olmstead asked looking straight ahead.

"About an hour ago," Fletcher replied.

"When we came out of the briefing?" Olmstead asked.

"That's right," he said holding out the pack. "They're Russian. Want one? "

"Aren't they habit forming?" Olmstead asked.

Fletcher inhaled deeply and blew the smoke out in one long stream. "I think they'll kill you too fast to be habit forming."

Olmstead thought that over for a second and took a cigarette from the pack. Fletcher held out a Zippo and lit him up. Olmstead took a deep draw and choked.

"Boy, they are Russian, aren't they," he said, throwing the cigarette down in the sand after just one puff. Fletcher took another long toke, not seeming to mind the harsh tobacco.

"So what do you really think?" Olmstead asked.

"You mean what do I think now that we're alone and won't screw up anybody's head but yours with my thoughts?" he answered.

"Precisely."

Fletcher took a deep breath, looking straight ahead.

"I don't like it, Dave," he admitted. "Not one bit."

"The threats don't seem as heavy as the Sandori mission," Olmstead said casually.

"Yeah, but they're also unknown. The problem here is we really don't know what's gonna be there. They're all mobile tactical threats," he said. "Sure there's gonna be MANPADs, AAA, and SAMs. How many? Are they really gonna be surprised?

"The other thing that bothers me is we have no clear target, like the reactor," he complained. "We're striking a convoy that may be here or there at this or that time. The target is one of the vehicles and we don't know which one. We have to hit them all. Let me tell you, Dave, we won't kill every vehicle in that convoy, even if we do this right. Hell, if I were this Abdul guy I'd be riding in one of the tanks. Let the enemy think I'm in a limo."

"So you think it won't be as easy as Sutherland said?" Olmstead asked.

"Well, what do you think?" Fletcher asked, looking into Olmstead's eyes.

He shook his head. "I don't know," he admitted. "I think it's doable, but you're right, we might pull it off just as planned and not take out the target. Or we might fly out to the middle of nowhere and find nothing. Or they might be waiting for us."

Fletcher turned to face him, a look of amazement on his face. "Finally somebody who thinks like me! I was thinking the same thing but was scared to actually say it. We got this information from a traitor in Achmed's own Republican Guard. Just how reliable is this guy if he betrays his country for money?"

"So he might have been feeding us bad stuff all along?"

"Who knows? I might just be paranoid," Fletcher said. "I'm just glad somebody else is thinking along those lines. It means I'm not a total paranoid."

"Just because your paranoid doesn't mean they aren't out to get you," he said with a smile. "So why didn't you bring it up at the briefing or take it to Tanner?"

"Take what to him? My suspicions? Oh yeah, that will override months of Intelligence work. I mean there could be a trap waiting for us on every mission," he said. "I have no intel that says the informant was lying. That's a judgment call made above our pay grade, Dave."

"So what do we do?"

"Trust our intel, bomb the shit out of the convoy, avoid all the threats, and come back alive," he said, blowing out his last puff of smoke, then flipping the cigarette butt into the sand. "Simple."

As they got off the tailgate and began to walk back to their tent Fletcher grabbed Olmstead by the shoulder and spun him around.

"What?" Olmstead said, surprised.

Under his breath Fletcher whispered. "Keep close tabs on Gurevich tonight. I got a bad feeling about this guy."

Olmstead nodded. "He is a cocky bastard."

Fletcher shook his head. "That's what bothers me. Is he really as good as he thinks he is? That's the question."

"I hope like hell he is," Olmstead said.

It was still daylight outside when they hit the sack. Olmstead tossed and turned before finally nodding off at around 1800 hours. Finally a culmination of fatigue and jet lag took over and once asleep they slept soundly.

At 2330 promptly Lt Sutherland arrived for the wake up call, flashlights blinding them and eliciting some suggestions of what strange anatomical places he could stow it. Sutherland apologized but made sure they were all awake. Tanner had been explicit with his orders. The brief was at midnight and the clock was ticking.

They shaved and washed their faces in warm water poured from jugs sitting outside their tents. Toweling off they donned their flight suits, Sandori officers' rank on the collars. The flight suits were specially prepared for them, standard Sandori issue Nomex flyers coveralls. The boots were likewise Sandori. The planes had Sandori markings, so would they. Each man knew what this part of the deception really meant. Obviously if captured they would never pass for Sandori, but if their wrecked planes and dead bodies were examined they would appear Sandori. It was a cold reminder of the stakes they were playing for and the price of failure. It was also assumed that death would be preferable to capture, since the US would never acknowledge their identities. In one of their zippered pockets was a single cyanide capsule. It was an option they had insisted on, and Tanner hadn't argued with them.

If they elected not to take the cyanide, another pocket contained ground maps of the whole Sandor/Kumar region. If they had to walk out they would at least have a map to show the way. The maps themselves also had some Sandori written on them and a few airbases circled inside Sandor to give the Kumaris something to ponder should they search their dead bodies and find the maps.

The pilots entered the briefing tent at 2355. Sutherland was filling in some last minute intel updates on the big master chart. When he saw them come in, he waved them over to a corner of the tent where life support gear was stowed.

"Good evening, sirs, if you will step this way we have some life support stuff for you," Sutherland said. "Your helmets and parachutes are prepositioned in your aircraft. Your survival map is already in your left breast pocket. Most of what you'll need to survive and evade is in your ejection seat kit. It has been slightly modified from what you are used to. Every item is either Russian or Sandori, including your radio, compass, beacons, etc. You will each receive a shoulder holster and 9mm Russian pistol. You will have two full clips, including one in the weapon," he said passing out the holsters then opening a crate of pistols. Each man took one weapon and three clips. Fletcher chose not to load his having heard horror stories of downed fliers shot with their own weapons in previous wars.

"Please don't load your weapons until you get to your aircraft and try not to shoot anyone or blow a hole in your aircraft while you are loading it," Sutherland said, noticing Cowboy practicing his quick draw against and imaginary black-hatted foe on some imagined Western street.

They all gathered around the chart table as the two Russians entered the tent, already wearing their own sidearms. Olmstead nodded to Gurevich, who nodded back coolly. Dobrinsky and Romano exchanged good-natured ribbings. Fletcher was going over the comm sheet while Cowboy and Sutherland engaged in a sidebar discussion of IR missiles. Finally Tanner and Kavinsky entered the tent and all discussion came to an abrupt end as the room was called to attention. The two general officers moved to the chart table, the captains moving aside like Moses had parted the sea.

"Please, gentlemen, gather round," Kavinsky said, urging Cowboy and Fletcher back around the table. They resumed their places, all with a view of the "big picture".

"Let's get on with it, Lieutenant," Tanner said, signaling Sutherland to begin.

"The tactical situation has changed slightly since the briefing this afternoon," Sutherland said, pointing to an area of flat desert to the north of the original target area. "Both satellite and covert intelligence indicates the convoy left Kagned about an hour earlier than expected. By the time you intercept the convoy it will be about forty miles north of where we planned to attack, about here.

"As you can see the terrain is much flatter and there won't be much out there to mask your approach. If the convoy's SA-6s are radiating they will see you at a range of about 12 miles or about a minute and a ten seconds out from the target. Before the convoy was going to be in that slight depression and it would mask your approach right up to the bomb release point. Now they will get about a minute's warning time. We still feel this will be enough time. They can see you on radar while the convoy is moving, but have to stop to take a shot. It will take a few seconds to get a firing solution on you after the vehicle has come to a stop and few more seconds to actually initiate the launch sequence. This also assumes they are cleared to fire on any blip on the scope, which normally the operator has to defer to the convoy commander. That will give you even more time.

"The flatter terrain isn't all bad news, however," he said with a smile. "It also means the HARMs will get a clear shot at the radars and you should know well in advance if the SA-6 radar is up and radiating."

Fletcher glanced at Olmstead who returned the look of concern. Both glanced sideways across the table at Gurevich, whose face was solid granite. He looked up at the two of them for a second then back at the chart, not blinking.

"The good news," Sutherland said, "is since the target is farther north, you won't travel as far south and won't burn as much fuel. The bad news is that we underestimated the basic weight of your aircraft. These MiGs are about 600 pounds heavier than the MiGs back in the States. We re-ran the take-off data and discovered none of you can take-off fully loaded with gas and weapons on 4500 feet of runway without burners. So rather than take weapons off your planes, we had to de-fuel six hundred pounds of gas from your aircraft. At this new gross weight the take-off data says you can get by without burners."

"Why don't we just leave the gas onboard and use the burners?" Fletcher asked.

"Because the afterburner take-off will use more fuel than you would save," Gurevich snapped impatiently.

"We're taking off on a 4500 foot runway without burners?" Cowboy asked incredulously. "You sure of the take-off data?"

"The runway is 4500 feet, however there is an additional 250 feet of overrun on each end," Tanner said. "You'll have to back taxi onto the overrun and use it for takeoff."

"Isn't that gonna screw up our formation departure?" Romano asked.

"The runway is wide enough to fit two aircraft side by side, just barely," Tanner said. "The wingmen will follow lead onto the overrun and one at a time do a 180 and takeoff. Watch your wingtip clearance, though." Romano let out a whistle.

Wingtip clearance, Olmstead thought! My God, it's a moonless night, and we're supposed to do a tight 180 and watch our wingtip clearance when we go flying by on take-off roll!

"General, I'd like to have a wing-walker out there to watch our separation and direct the turn back to take-off roll," Fletcher asked.

Tanner nodded. "Yes, Mike, a good idea," he agreed. "We'll have somebody out there with flashlights directing you, might even be me."

"That'd be great, sir," Fletcher said. "Hate to kill this thing before it even gets started."

The briefing ended at 0100, not because it was over but because it had to be over. They were on a schedule and timing was critical. Besides at some point you just have to stop playing the "what ifs" and start flying the mission.

They walked out of the briefing tent, charts and mission essentials under their arms. The crew chiefs were using the lone truck and make-shift tow bar to pull each plane out of its shelter and into a single file on the taxi way. Once they started engines it would be a very short taxi straight ahead to the end of the runway. The planes were being positioned in order and in this fashion to use as little fuel as possible for the ground operations.

Each man went to his aircraft and began to go over its sleek lines. It was pitch black outside and the only light came from the truck's headlights, now turned around to wash over the six MiGs. The pilots walked around their steeds and hit the various critical pre-flight items with their flashlights. They would really have to trust the crew chiefs tonight as even with the flashlights and headlight the planes were still awash in darkness. One very noticeable feature that was not on the MiGs back in the states was the big Sandori flag on the twin vertical stabilizers.

Satisfied all was well one by one they climbed the ladders and climbed into the small cramped cockpits, sliding their legs into the rudder pedal tunnels and pulling their parachute harnesses on with the help of the crew chiefs at the top of the ladder. They ran their pre-flight checklist silently and efficiently, the beams of their red flashlights dancing about the instrument panels.

At exactly 0130 Olmstead keyed his radio and said a single word, "Check."

"Two."

"Three."

"Four."

"Five."

"Six," came the solitary monosyllabic responses.

At exactly 0145 each man advanced his throttles to idle and hit the starters. Seconds later the silence of the night was broken by the whine of twelve turbines spinning up. At 0155 Olmstead released his brakes and began moving to the end of the runway. One by one they pushed up their throttles and followed.

As they moved toward the runway each man was a blur of activity inside their respective cockpits, checking instruments, weapons status, flight controls, hydraulics and all the other critical systems while keeping an eye on the plane in front of them. Running into the back of your leader was not only a way to scrub the mission, but a pretty horrible way to die, based on where the MiG's designers chose to locate the pilot's seat.

Olmstead reached the end of the runway and turned left onto the overrun, Gurevich following close behind. As he reached the end he swung his aircraft back around to face down the runway, his fellow MiG drivers lined up dangerously close to his right wing. He could see Tanner out there with the flashlight, directing Cowboy to move a little to his left. The General was waving Cahill over then seemed satisfied as he turned to Olmstead and gave him a salute with the flashlight.

Olmstead looked down at his watch, thirty seconds to go. He checked his systems one last time. Fuel, hydraulic pressure, electrical load, engine RPM, fuel flow and EGTs all normal. He took a deep breath and advanced the throttles of the twin RD-333s to Military Rated Thrust, maximum thrust without burner. RPMs were stable; EGTs and fuel flow in the green. As the second hand swung past twelve he released his brakes and began to move. As he moved away Gurevich moved up and swung in place to follow him 15 seconds in trail and so on.

Olmstead knew his wingmen were already following him down the pitch-black runway, but they were the least of his concerns at the moment. Without burners and heavy with gas and four large 3000-pound missiles his MiG was accelerating slowly. There were no distance-remaining markers on the runway so he could really only tell by intuition how much runway was left. His landing lights only illuminated a few hundred feet of concrete in front of him. He strained to see into the blackness and waited for the end of the runway to come up. The airspeed in the HUD said 70, then 80, and so on, climbing slowly. Too slowly? He wasn't sure. All he could do was concentrate on the airspeed and wait for rotation speed. He took comfort in his airspeed indication, not that it was climbing slowly, but that it was a distraction from trying to see the end of the runway. That magic number was all that mattered now. He had to see that magic airspeed number, the airplane would not fly until it reached that speed.

The take-off roll seemed to last forever and he was sure he was about to leave the pavement and wind up in a fireball off the departure end....100 knots. He knew after he perished in the fireball they would go back and rerun the take-off data and someone would say, "Oh, yeah, I forgot they were carrying a 200 gallon external tank. Yep, they needed 5500 feet, alright."

He was tempted to hit the burners just for a moment...120knots...just to feel that kick in the pants, maybe give him just the extra ten knots he needed, but he did not...130. Just a quick twenty more knots and he'd be there. Damn, a five second burst of burner would give him that...140. Almost there, he began applying backpressure to the stick and he could feel the aircraft lighten as the weight was moving from wheels to wings. Don't over-rotate!! Let it come up gradually...you don't have any power to spare here...150...magic time. The MiG left the ground just as he saw the end of the runway flash beneath him.

He lowered the nose slightly and let the airspeed build and he sucked up his gear and retracted the lift giving flaps and slats. He breathed a sigh of relief, leveled his aircraft at 300 meters and turned on course for the first waypoint and pulled the power back to stabilize his airspeed at 300 knots to let his wingmen catch up. Already he could see Gurevich and Fletcher moving into echelon, their nav lights shown bright, then dimmed as they fell into formation. He waited until he saw the remaining aircraft in formation, when Cowboy's nav lights went to dim he pushed his throttles up and headed for the Sandori border, now only thirty miles away.

AIRBORNE
0208 LOCAL

Olmstead could barely make out the horizon off the nose in the clear dark night. It blended into the sky and only way to tell where the sky stopped and the ground began was a couple of blinking lights on the ground that clearly were not stars. He glanced down at his IRST display, now cooled down sufficiently to give him a near-daytime view of the terrain in front of the ground hugging MiG. *Sure could have used that IRST during take-off*, he thought. Unfortunately the cool-down period for the IRST seeker head was about twenty minutes and it required ram-cooling air so it could not be used on the ground.

As they killed their nav lights and prepared to penetrate the Sandori airspace each plane fell back into trail formation. This ensured that they all passed over the same real estate and their sonic footprint would be very small. Olmstead aimed his flight at the dark void ahead, a preplanned spot the map showed to be free of roads, houses or marine operations. The needle on the dial hovered at a stable 440 knots indicated airspeed and they were right on time.

An amber master caution light flashed to life on Olmstead's front panel, indicating his external tank was empty. The fuel panel showed that the engines were now feeding off internal fuel. He reached down and punched off the master caution and jettisoned the empty tank in one motion. He heard a hiss and a thump and felt a small jolt through the stick as his external tank was jettisoned by a small explosive charge. The indicator light for the external tank went out on the fuel panel. Olmstead knew his wingmen would be punching off their own tanks any moment. The status of each aircraft would be by exception only. If somebody had a problem they would speak up, if not the radios would stay silent. Olmstead waited patiently until he knew the Sandori border was sliding under his ground hugging MiG, now in terrain following mode. *Everybody's quiet, must be in the green*, he thought.

The border came and went at over 500 miles an hour. According to the flight data sheet they were right on the money as far as timing and fuel burn, two pieces of good news. Back in the number six position Cowboy was having problems with his radar sector scan in ground map, but felt it wasn't bad enough to warrant worrying anyone else in the formation. The aircraft had a write-up in the forms about the sector scan. The forms said it had been fixed and flown twice since. Cowboy wasn't overly worried, though. They'd encountered the same problem with one of the MiGs back in the States and the TFR continued to function perfectly, regardless of the display. The terrain following was working perfectly tonight and his only real problem seemed to be intermittent losses of video in the sector scan. Since he had a valid GPS lock-on, an excellent IRST, and he was in the number six position he wasn't worried. It would affect his aim point on the bomb run, however. He'd pretty much have to use the IRST only for aiming, and it was not as accurate as radar.

After twenty minutes of terrain following through one valley then the next the time came to turn west and head toward the border. Olmstead turned his plane to the westerly heading, the five wingman sliding around the turn in trail. The RWR gear had been relatively quiet up until this time, but now it showed a powerful early warning radar in search mode to the south. The radar was still in search and Olmstead was sure they were not being detected due to their altitude; still he was glad they were turning away from the threat. Their new vector put the search radar on their beam and getting about 5 miles farther away each minute of flight.

The ground rushed by unseen under the desert skimming MiGs. The TFR mode was set to maximum maneuvering, which meant the aircraft automatically started all climbs over terrain at the last possible second, minimizing the time they were higher than 200 feet, but also making for a jolting, rough, roller coaster-like ride.

After six short minutes on this heading Olmstead could see the saddle in the ridgeline that would funnel them down into Kumari airspace. Inside their cockpits each man was now arming his weapons for release. Olmstead and

Gurevich un-caged the seeker-heads of their anti-radiation missiles and got a reassuring tone in their helmets indicating properly operating radar seekers. Each man finally flipped his master arm switch, the last safety before release. They each took special care to avoid the top left button on their control sticks, which now had a whole new meaning with the master arm on. One press of a button and a stick of CBUs would fall away. Actually there was no danger of accidentally launching a missile. Both the AA-11 and AA-12 required a valid lock onto a target. They would not just simply blast off into the cold night air looking for a target at the push of a button. They were smarter than that. One thought raced through each man's mind, 'Now was not the time to screw up'. The hunt was on and the prey was nearby.

The Kumari border slid under them inconspicuously. The black, moonless night was a perfect setting for this blackest of black missions. The Sandori early warning radar behind them grew faint and the RWR gear went silent, though only momentarily. The RWR gear promptly lit up indicating some disturbing news off the nose. This time it was no early warning radar, the RWR gear showed an AI threat off the nose. The frequency and PRF indicated the Foxfire radar of a MiG-25. The signal was weak, but that could change rapidly with the great speed of the MiG-25. Although the huge AA-6 missiles it did carry were long ranged, the good news was that it's rudimentary look-down/ shoot-down radar was unlikely to pick the MiG-41s out of the ground clutter.

More than likely the MiG-25 was out for night proficiency training, Olmstead thought. He decided it did not present a threat to the mission, at least not at these low altitudes. He resisted the urge to bring up his air-to-air search radar and pinpoint the enemy MiG. This would only set off the Foxbat's primitive RWR gear and alert him he was being locked up. This would cause some consternation for the Foxbat pilot who would radio the Kumari controller and ask who else was airborne tonight. That would only serve to get more interceptors, maybe more capable interceptors, airborne. No, they would ignore the MiG-25 until it became a direct threat.

Ahead Olmstead could see a highway with traffic on it. He turned the formation so as to cross the road perpendicular to it. He also kept his head on a swivel as he went over the road in case any of the trucks carried soldiers with MANPADs. Of course he thought he was just being paranoid. After all the Kumaris didn't know they were coming. They were not at war and search radars hadn't yet detected them.

They reached the split point and Olmstead and Gurevich peeled off to the northeast and southwest respectively. The MiG-25 signal was coming from the north, Olmstead reminded himself. He knew in a few moments he and Gurevich would be climbing to 5000 feet, exposing more of themselves to the scrutiny of the MiG-25 radar as well as the SAM radars that might be in the target area. Olmstead began to worry the MiG would interfere with his HARM run.

The only air-to-air missile he was carrying was the AA-11, deadly, but too short-ranged for dealing with a MiG-25. The Foxbat would launch his radar-guided missiles from well beyond 20 miles, then run for home. This was standard tactics for the fast, but heavy and sluggish fighter. The MiG-25 was an interceptor, not a dog-fighter. It was capable of Mach 3 dashes of speed and had an ancient, but powerful, radar. However, its construction was mostly stainless steel and its gross weight was a runway-cracking 80,000 pounds, making it a poor performer in a turning fight.

With Olmstead and Gurevich out of the formation, Fletcher was now in the lead. He reached the assigned initial point and turned to the northwest. He called out the IP over the non-secure radio in excellent Sandori. If the intelligence boys were right, somewhere in the next thirty miles or so should be a convoy two miles long with a terrorist who didn't have long to live. The bomb run heading had them coming straight up the highway. The plan was to overtake the convoy from behind. Normally you wouldn't want to follow a road, but in this case the target would be on the road.

As soon as Olmstead heard the IP call he turned back to the west and began a climb to 5000 feet. Forty miles to the southwest he knew Gurevich would be doing the same. He set his throttles to give him the best maneuvering airspeed for the MiG-41. His RWR gear was active now. The MiG-25 was still up at his three O'clock, but now a Gun Dish AAA radar and a Straight Flush SA-6 radar were up and searching at his one O'clock. Damn, the SA-6 is up! He'd have to deal with it.

His HARM missile was already locked onto the Straight Flush and ready to fire. The RWR gear, using the strength of the signal, estimated the range to the radar as being within range of the missile and he got a solid tone indicating ready to fire. He checked once again making sure it was the SA-6 he was engaging, not the AAA radar. Everything looked good, he closed his eyes to avoid being blinded by the rocket flash pushed the little red button on his stick. The HARM lit off and raced away from the MiG with a whoosh. At almost the same time the RWR gear indicated the SA-6 had him locked up and the illuminator was up, indicating possible missile in flight.

With the HARM gone he was now cleared to maneuver. He rolled the MiG inverted and dove toward the ground in a left breaking, low altitude split S, rolling out perpendicular to the SA-6 and punching out clouds of fuse busting chaff. The SA-6 is a dangerous and deadly missile and even with these radical maneuvers the MiG was in deep trouble. The missile should have hit Olmstead's right wing and sent him plunging to his death, but the Gainful missile had one shortcoming...it was not as fast as the AS-23 that slammed into it's radar about six seconds into it's flight, disrupting its guidance a short four seconds before impact. It fell behind Olmstead as it lost guidance and exploded on the ground well behind him. Whew, he gasped!

There was no time to relax, though. He climbed back up to his SEAD patrolling altitude and began round two of the deadly cat and mouse game he had to play with the SAMs. The MiG-25 was still at his three O'clock...but the signal was now stronger, a fact he managed to overlook in the heat of his battle with the SA-6.

Meanwhile the strike aircraft were now on the bomb run heading racing up the highway, so low at times they were kicking up rooster tails of sand in the dark night. Romano was now in the lead aircraft and his wingmen were in tight formation with him. The V-shaped wedge of MiGs was in position to release their CBUs with maximum effectiveness while ensuring they didn't frag their buddies.

The night outside the cockpit was black as coal and it was useless to try to see anything with the naked eye. He knew the convoy would have some kind of headlights, but they were approaching from behind and they would be very dim. He probably wouldn't see them until he was on top of them. He split his time between the radarscope and the IRST display. He knew at this low altitude he would only get a scant 10 seconds or so to line up with the convoy and release and he was concentrating hard to see the first signs of a convoy on the radar. He knew he'd see them first on radar and then on the IRST, which he would use to aim, the IRST now being bore sighted to the line of flight and therefore the line of flight for the bombs as they dropped away.

Cowboy was having more radar problems now. The radar video wasn't just intermittent anymore; it was simply gone. He was also getting transmitter faults on the radar and the TFR was beginning to act erratic. He punched off the autopilot and took over manually, holding his MiG in the formation as it bounced along in the thermals rising off the now cooling desert floor. He finally decided he should tell the rest of the formation of his condition, since in the event of a fighter attack he would be radar out and virtually helpless.

"Lead, Six is gadget-bent," he said simply over secure voice.

"Rog," was the only reply from Romano.

He was too near the target area to think about much else at this moment. Cowboy probably could have said, "I'm on fire" and it wouldn't have mattered to Romano at this point. He was the very essence of concentration as he finally saw a little blip enter the edge of his scope about ten miles ahead.

This is it, he thought.

"Tally ho," he said over secure voice radio. This told the others in the formation he had acquired the target, or at least the tail end of it. He was lined up perfectly with the end of the convoy. The vehicles appeared to be stopped on the road, but it was difficult to tell closing with them so rapidly. Suddenly his RWR gear sounded an alarm. A AAA radar was up and searching off the nose.

"AAA, 12 o'clock, lead's jamming," he called, activating his onboard jammers and sending out a storm of electromagnetic energy for the hapless radar operators to deal with. His wingmen also activated their jammers at the same time, so he was confident the AAA radar screen was now a maze of crazy static and strobes.

He knew the jamming was effective for one very simple reason. The sky ahead erupted in AAA fire, ZSU-23-4s spitting out thousands of rounds of ammo in a barrage fire. It wasn't aimed at them, but they would have to fly through that mess if they wanted to hit the target. He momentarily considered aborting the mission. Obviously surprise was not on their side. He dismissed the idea as soon as it entered his mind. Here was a chance to take out a known terrorist and by God he'd take his chances with the AAA for a shot at him. They pressed on.

"Flight, lead, Mil power," he called pushing his throttles up to the stops, but not into burner. If he had to go through that mess he wanted to get through it as fast as possible. He'd worry about gas later.

The MiGs accelerated to 550 knots indicated airspeed, better than 600 miles an hour. Romano moved his radar x-hairs to the end of the convoy, his wingmen aiming at their predetermined spots along the long parade of limos and trucks. We're about to wipe out a week of Mercedes production, he mused.

The AAA was getting thick and panning the sky wildly, seeking out a target. He could also see small arms fire coming from the convoy. Even if they could see the MiGs in the dark getting a hit was virtually impossible.

Getting a lucky hit was easier. *There's way too much flak for this to be a surprise attack*, he thought suddenly. *They knew we were coming. Somehow they knew*. As he flew over the end of the convoy and his bombs began to fall away, his windscreen filled with the blinding light of flares fired by the soldiers below and the flashes of small and large caliber weapons he had a sudden paralyzing thought. If they knew we were coming...the target's not down there.

Meanwhile a few miles to the northeast Olmstead was battling another SA-6. He was also beginning to realize that surprise was not on their side and that pesky MiG-25 was still out there. He sent another HARM missile streaking away into the night. This time connecting before the SA-6 missile could leave the rails. He was now out of HARMs and knew the strike team would have to rely on Gurevich for SEAD cover.

He turned his MiG away and ran outside SA-6 range, climbing. He knew he could still be effective by simply providing himself as a target and by jamming any radars that came up. By jamming the radars he would throw off their range gate and they wouldn't know how far away he was. This might trick some worried SAM operator into taking a shot at him well out of range. He knew after killing two SA-6 radars the rest of the missile crews would be hesitant about even turning on their radars. In fact after his second SA-6 kill no radars remained operating. More than likely they were afraid to radiate. A HARM missile is a powerful deterrent once you see your buddies killed by one.

Olmstead heard Romano's off hot call and realized the strikers were bombs away and now outbound off the target. The plan was to rejoin twenty miles to the northeast of the target. Unfortunately that was the direction the RWR gear said the MiG-25 was. They might still have to deal with the lone Foxbat.

The strikers drove right down the center of the convoy after a last second climb to 400 meters, punching off their CBUs as they went. The carnage on the ground was spectacular as the CBUs release their bomblets in fiery bursts of steel fragments. The jagged, torn pieces of steel ripped through vehicles, fuel tanks, boxes of ammunition and people with abandon. The fuel tanks exploded in the shotgun like blasts of steel cubes. The CBU pattern covered about 85 percent of the convoy, destroying nearly every vehicle in the path. As the bombs detonated the AAA and small arms fire fell silent. Most of the convoy was either ripped apart or now on fire. If Abdul Al Faisal was in the convoy he was probably dead.

Romano had no time to reflect on the possibility of the terrorist's death.

He was in trouble. They'd made their bomb run and released their weapons on the target, now they had to get out of Dodge and the little array of amber warning lights at his left sleeve was taunting him. He knew he had taken some AAA. He could feel the hits as they ripped into his MiG. Now it was a question of just how much damage was done.

They were back in TFR at 100 meters above the desert floor heading off to rendezvous with Olmstead and Gurevich for the trip home. *Olmstead was somewhere off the nose and Gurevich should be coming up from behind,* Romano thought. Once they join up and were clear of the target area they would climb, wait to be detected by the Kumari search radars and head for Sandor.

Making it to Sandor might be wishful thinking, Romano mused as he checked his systems. He could tell by his gauges he was losing fuel from the port side outboard tank. He immediately set up his fuel system to transfer as much of the outboard fuel as possible to the inboards. He had been feeding from the inboards and knew they were nearly empty anyway. Hopefully he'd be able to fill them up from the outboards before he lost too much fuel. He could really only afford to lose a couple hundred kilograms at most, and that might get him within gliding distance of home plate.

The amber caution lights also indicated a loss of hydraulic pressure on the secondary system, no big deal unless the primary system failed. He also had one of his two generators offline and tried resetting the errant generator. As he hit the reset switch he heard a loud buzzing in his helmet and saw sparks from under the instrument panel. The cockpit lights dimmed for a moment and he could smell the acrid odor of ozone and burned insulation. Okay, we won't try that again, he said to himself. He could return on one generator, but he no longer had the power available to operate his onboard radar jammers. Hopefully I won't need to, he prayed. His IRST showed a contact at two o'clock swinging toward him on an intercept.

"Gotcha on the IRST, Hawkeye," he called out on secure voice to Olmstead.

"Rog, I've got you buddy-spiked," Olmstead said. "Almost there."

"Trails in," Gurevich suddenly called.

Cahill looked over his shoulder and saw the ghostly shape of Gurevich's MiG floating in formation about fifty feet away. Finally Olmstead dropped into the lead position, just ahead of Romano.

"Lead's in," he called. "Flight check."

"Two."

"Three."

"Four."

"Five."

"Six."

"Flight, ASC, now," Olmstead called over secure voice, asking for the Aircraft Systems Check. "Lead's in the green, Winchester," he said indicating he was out of HARM missiles.

"Two's got outboard fuel leak, one generator offline, and negative secondary hydraulic system," Romano called.

"Three's in the green," Dobrinsky called.

"Four took some ack-ack, but is in the green," Fletcher called.

"Five is gadget bent," Cahill called, indicating total loss of radar. He was holding his position manually by using the radar altimeter and the IRST/ laser range finder for position.

"Six is in the green," Gurevich called.

Olmstead mulled that over for a minute as they skimmed above the earth at better than 10 miles a minute. Romano would be in trouble before long. If he leaks more than 400 lbs he'll be landing dead stick, if more than that, he'd be taking the "nylon ILS".

The plan called for them to fly due east to cross over into Sandor, but with Romano in fuel trouble he considered the alternative. He could cut the corner by flying northeast and crossing over into Sandor farther north than planned. That would save some time and therefore some gas. It was a good plan except for three problems. First there was only one Sandori base to the north and they would have to convince the Kumaris they were heading towards it. Second the route was not planned and not on his strip chart on his kneeboard. He didn't know what threats lay in that direction. Finally, third, the vector to the northeast put them on an intercept course with that pesky MiG-25 that was out there. By now that MiG would know there were intruders in his airspace and if he was armed he would be looking for them. Olmstead turned his MiG to a heading of 030 degrees and decided to take the risks, come what may.

"Flight, we're taking vector 030 for gas," he announced. "This'll cut about 50 miles off our route. Fletch and Cowboy, take the lead. Possible Mike- 25 at 12 o'clock. We may have to splash the bandit. Flight, climb to 2000 meters, now."

"Rog, Hawk, moving up on the right, climbing to 2000," Fletch called. "Permission to spike'em and fire?" He was asking permission to lock the

Foxbat up on his radar.

"Negative," Olmstead said. "Cleared to sweep him, do not lock him up, do not fire unless we get a spike, understood?"

"Roger, he spikes us, he's dead," Fletcher said matter-of-factly, selecting his AA-12 Adder missiles for firing.

"Hey, Boss," Cowboy called to Olmstead. "I'm still gadget bent back here, but I'll tag along for moral support."

Damn, Olmstead cursed under his breath. He had forgotten Cowboy's radar was down. Fletch and Cowboy were the only two of the six that carried long-range missiles and now Cowboy's radar was down. Without that radar he couldn't fire the missiles. That meant Fletcher alone would have to take out the Foxbat if it proved hostile.

The MiG-25 was still out there and sweeping them with its powerful Foxfire radar. So far it had not locked onto them, but that could change in an instant. The Foxbat pilot could be looking at them right now.

Seventy-two miles off their nose the pilot of the MiG-25 was staring intently at the series of blips on the outermost portion of his screen. He queried Kumari Mil about their presence. Something strange was going on tonight. They had told him to standby, and although he advised them he was bingo fuel, he received direct orders to remain on station and to proceed toward the bogeys on his scope. He asked for permission to lock up the unknown aircraft and received only static on his radio. Damn, he cursed, slamming his fist down on the glare shield. He was being vectored into an intercept against an unknown threat and not given permission to at least get their radar data, heading, speed, altitude, etc.

The Kumari philosophy of an air-to-air intercept centered on complete GCI authority. The pilot had to follow the commands of his controller to the letter and could not even turn on his radar with out permission. The Kumari pilot, a veteran of fifteen years service, and one of the few pilots actually checked out for night intercepts, was clearly unhappy with his current dilemma. He was at forty four thousand feet, very high altitude for a MiG-41, but about half the ceiling of a MiG-25. He throttled back his speed to under 500 knots to lengthen the intercept and give the controllers more time to get their collective asses in gear. He knew if these were hostile aircraft that phones would be ringing off the hook all over the Kumari Air Defense Command, trying to find some one who would give the authority to shoot. Meanwhile he was closing at better that 20 miles a minute and was almost in range for a shot with the huge AA-6 Acrids that hung beneath his shoulder mounted wings.

Just then his RWR gear went off indicating an India-band radar off the nose, clearly coming from the bogeys. Just a standard scan pattern, they were not locked onto him yet, but the pucker factor became even greater and sweat broke out across his forehead. He lifted his visor and wiped his brow with the back of his gloved hand. The India-band radar was transmitting around 9.0 gigahertz, which meant it could be coming from just about any air interceptor in the world. The F-16 and F-15 radars fell near that frequency, but so did the MiG-29, Su-27 and most Russian made aircraft. If it was Russian made it was probably one of ours, but if it was Western, then he was facing an Israeli foe and was in deep trouble.

Why would an Israeli be this far west, he wondered? *Maybe an attack on Sandor? That would be fine with me*, he thought. *If only I could call and tell the Israeli, Go ahead bomb the bastard Shiites! But no, if it were an Israeli attack on Sandor I would soon become a kill mark on some Jew's aircraft. I would be in the way and the Jew never let anyone get in his way. If only the bastards down in GCI would get their act together I could light off these AA-6s and make for home at Mach 3, let them try to catch me.*

Suddenly his headphones inside his helmet came to life with a hiss of static. He had permission to lock onto the bogeys now closing with him. Thank Allah, he said to himself, switching radar modes and placing a pair of brackets around the first blip on his screen. He was now tracking the first blip, its speed 475 knots, altitude 2000 meters, bearing 003 degrees off the nose, range 42 nautical miles. With radar information now available to the missile he got a solid in range tone from the AA-6 Acrid on his right wing.

"Flight 234, Kumari Mil, confirm bandits, cleared to engage," an excited controller said. "How copy?"

"234 copies, engaging," he answered absently, concentrating on his task at hand. He was now cleared to splash the bandits. If they were Sandori he had little fear, he realized, but if they were Israeli...that was a different story.

The four AA-6 Acrid missiles he carried under his wings were semi-active radar guided. This meant he had to keep his radar locked onto the target all they way until impact. It also meant he could not launch them individually at individual targets. He counted a cluster of six aircraft, very closely spaced. He knew when he fired they would sense his illuminator and scatter like cockroaches. The missiles would sense the reflected energy off the targets and home on them, but he could not control which target they homed on. All four missiles, depending on luck, could hit the first target. He could set a right of left bias and he did so on his third and fourth missiles. If they saw two targets they would go to the right or left as programmed. It was the best he could do.

He pulled his throttles to idle to slow his closure and improve his turn radius. He squeezed the trigger four times, each time the squeeze accompanied by a loud whoosh and a blinding light as the solid rocket motors of the AA-6 lit up and raced away from the MiG. Once all missiles were gone he activated his continuous wave illuminator and turned sixty degrees to the right. This put the targets within the 180-degree radar cone, but close to the beam so he could go defensive the minute they hit or missed. With total disregard for his waning fuel state he lit the burners of the two massive Tumansky turbofans and began a shallow climb to 80,000 feet, where he could get Mach 3.0 if needed.

In the MiG-41s forty-two miles away the RWR gear indicated they were locked up. Fletcher locked on to the Foxbat with his own radar in preparation for firing when he got in range, but suddenly the RWR gear said a CW radar was on them. This meant a missile was on the way, coming head-on at something like Mach 4.

"Flight, missile launch, break left," Fletcher called, knowing with a right echelon formation the violent turn to the left was the safest. Inside five cockpits five fingers flipped five jamming pods on, Romano wincing at the thought of no jammers. They all punched out chaff.

The AA-6 missiles saw their targets and began homing. The AA-6 is a very large missile and can't pull the high Gs of the smaller AA-12 and AA-11. They began a leisurely turn to the right, homing on the fleeing MiGs. The third and fourth missiles sensed the chaff clouds and closed on them, their proximity fuses detonating in impressive fireballs well aft of the fleeing American pilots. The second missile apparently suffered a malfunction or was fooled by the jamming, because it detonated well short of its targets. The first missile launched, however, had the best shot at a hit. It was functioning perfectly and never noticed the spasms of chaff left in the MiGs wakes. The jamming caused it a bit of confusion, but it was able to stay locked onto the lead bandit. As the missile neared the MiG-41 piloted by Fletcher, he pulled hard, loading on the Gs and hit a small paddle on his stick engaging the thrust vectoring. The MiG pivoted in space for a moment and punched out chaff as he lit his burners and tried to outmaneuver the giant missile.

Had it been any missile other than the heavy, clumsy AA-6 Fletcher would have been a dead man, but in this case the missile fell about two hundred feet behind him and detonated, sending small, sharp slivers of metal against his MiG. He could hear the tiny projectiles hitting the right flank of his aircraft and he saw a small spider web crack on his canopy just behind his right ear. Still all the caution lights were out.

He tried to reacquire the now running MiG-25 and saw him on his scope at fifty miles running for home at better than Mach 1.5 and accelerating. They would never catch him, but it didn't matter now. He was obviously out of missiles and out of the fight.

"Flight, come back to heading 030," he called, turning them back toward Sandor. It was pretty damn obvious by the Foxbat attack that Kumari Mil had them on radar. Time to descend and head for the border.

"Flight, begin a descent back to TFR, single file, close it up," he called, pointing his nose down and descending. "Hawk, you want the lead back?"

"Negative, Fletch, you have the lead, no sense in changing now," Olmstead said.

They closed up the formation and dove back below Kumari radar coverage. Hugging the earth at a scant 200 feet they were in relative safety, however they were nowhere near out of the woods yet. The Sandori border was ahead. The big question mark now was what did Sandor know? They knew by their RWR gear they were being tracked by the Sandori SA-5 before they dove back to TFR, but would Sandor launch aircraft to intercept them? They were not being tracked at the moment and the odds of any Sandori interceptor being able to find them at 200 feet in the mountains was nil, even with their F-14s. Still they had to be on guard for anything. They didn't expect trouble, but they didn't expect to fly into a wall of flack attacking that convoy.

"Bear, how's what's your fuel state?" Fletch asked.

"It'll be close, Fletch," Romano answered grimly eyeing the offensive fuel gauge. "Since transferring the gas to the inboards I think the leak has stopped. Still, I'm a good 400 kilos below the curve."

"Roger," Fletch responded, not knowing what else to say. He would keep them relatively slow and try to cut a few more corners, but Bear might at best landing dead stick and at worse not be landing at all.

The Sandori border slipped under them at 500 miles per hour and Fletch aimed the formation for a long ridgeline out in front of them. The ridgeline ran to the north and he brought them up on the south side and paralleled the ridge to the west, racing north in the radar shadow of the small mountain. At the end of the ridgeline he saw a valley open up in front of them and he dove down into the long scar in the earth.

From terrain feature to terrain feature they flew always in the cover of some piece of dirt and only in the open for brief moments as they transitioned from valley to ridgeline, ridgeline to plateau, plateau to mountain saddle. They worked their way north, abeam the large lake in Sandor's northwest corner. Lakes always have a lot of people around and any aircraft would standout on radar as they flew over the glassy surface. It's always best to avoid lakes and rivers, those are the places the enemy always expects you to fly. That's why they set up cables and flak traps in river valleys.

The rest of the flight through Sandor went like clockwork. The RWR gear only showed intermittent hits by Sandori early warning radars and not one AI radar was detected. Even the long range SA-5 radar fell silent and never posed a threat to the rapidly retreating targets. They crossed over into Tangistan about ten minutes earlier than planned and Fletcher set a direct course for the base only fifty miles ahead. They climbed to 2000 feet.

With the base thirty miles off the nose Fletch told the flight Romano had landing priority.

"Negative, Fletch," Romano called back, his aircraft zooming skyward out of the formation. "I appreciate the thought, but I just ran out of gas about ten seconds ago," he said calmly. "I'll be on the nylon ILS shortly."

He was trading airspeed for altitude now in an attempt to both stretch his glide back to the base and to give him some altitude with which to bail out. He knew at thirty miles he had no chance of landing on the pavement, but he did want to get as close as possible to base before bailing out.

"Bear, don't wait too long to punch, buddy," Cowboy called.

"Rog, Cowboy, leveling at three thousand meters right now at 250 knots," he said. "I'll push it over, hold a 250 knot glide and punch when I get to 1000meters," he said, still as calmly as if he were pulling off the highway to grab a quick burger. "I oughta be coming down about 15 miles short right on runway heading. I'd appreciate a ride, guys."

"Roger, Bear, we'll have somebody there within the hour, even if I have to drive it myself," Olmstead said.

"Uh, that's okay, Hawk," Romano said. "I remember your last rescue. I'll wait for the real thing. Thanks, anyway."

"Razor Control, Bo Peep is twenty five out with four," Fletch called Tanner in the command post. "Need rescue for lost sheep at your 180 at 15 nautical miles, how copy?"

"Roger, Bo Peep," Tanner called back. "Understand lost sheep at 180 at

15. Rescue has been notified. Say remaining sheep status."

"Roger, two white, three gray and one black, how copy," Fletcher said, reporting two aircraft code one, three aircraft with minor battle damage and one aircraft lost.

"Razor Control, Bo Peep four, punching out at this time, position 185 at 14," Romano called, as his aircraft passed 1000 meters altitude, about 3000 feet. He reached down, grabbed the ejection ring, closed his eyes, braced himself with head back and back straight and pulled the ring to his chest. The canopy exploded off the MiG with a thud and a shower of sparks, the slipstream ripping it back and away from the dying MiG. A half a second later the automatic features of the seat took over, a rocket charge blasting Romano up the seat rails and clear of the cockpit, pulling about 9 Gs in the process. He felt the jolt of the Gs and the rush of air, hotter than he thought it would be, against his face. He somersaulted twice, still in his ejection seat when another charge blew him clear of the seat and he felt another heavy jolt, this one in his crotch as the parachute opened and he stabilized beneath it.

He looked up and saw the bright orange canopy even in the dark of night. It was by far the happiest sight he'd seen in his thirty-two years on this earth. Quickly he ran through his post ejection checklist. He couldn't see very well below him and he knew that coming down over the dark desert could give him the illusion he was higher than he really was. He knew bailing out at 2000 feet didn't give him much time to prepare for landing. He ripped off his oxygen mask, throwing it away and pushed up his visor. His canopy looked okay. He knew he was close to the ground and did his best to prepare for the impact that might come at any time. Ordinarily he'd want to try to steer into the wind, but he could barely make out the ground at all on this moonless night, much less which way he was drifting.

He bent his knees slightly, hands on the parachute risers, head looking straight ahead, eyes on the horizon. He hit, hard. He tried to roll into the impact and perform the PLF but could hear his left ankle pop as he hit and knew it was going to be bad. He'd touched down sideways in a ten-knot crosswind and broke his ankle at impact. He pain was sharp, but faded when the rest of his body hit with a hard thump, knocking the wind out of him and bruising his left arm and shoulder. He collapsed in a heap and just barely managed to pull his J-2 releases in time to avoid being dragged across the desert floor. He rolled over and surveyed the damage. He was sore all down the left side of his body, but thought it only bruises. His ankle was definitely injured, sprained, possibly broken. It was already starting to swell and he decided to gut out the pain and remove his boot now. The good news was there was no compound fracture. He was relieved at that. He hated the sight of blood, especially his own. He rolled over and pulled his survival radio from his survival kit. He flipped over to the beacon frequency and turned down the volume so he wouldn't have to hear the blaring sound. They had been briefed not to use voice messages if forced to bailout so close Sandor, so he turned on the beacon, set back and waited. All he had to do now was wait.

As he laid there, his head propped on the survival kit like a pillow, he looked up at the stars. This far from any city lights he could see them by the millions. Romano never knew there were so many stars. The pain in his ankle subsided to a dull ache and mesmerized by the heavens and coming down off an adrenaline high, he fell asleep. His last thoughts before giving in to sleep were of the stars, so many stars.

Twenty-five miles north of where Romano was laying Fletcher was having his own troubles. After the AA-6 blast fragments hit his aircraft it appeared as though all was well, but now things began to go sour. His primary hydraulic panel indicated a loss of both quantity and pressure in that system. *A fragment must have nicked a hydraulic line*, he thought grimly. He felt the stick go limp in his hand briefly then go rigid again as he flipped a switch engaging the standby hydraulic system. He performed a controllability check and determined the aircraft was flying nominally, but he still had a big problem...the brakes.

The MiG-41 brakes were run off the primary hydraulic system only. The standby system did not supply the brakes. It was a assumed by the designers that the MiG-41 would be landing on a normal sized runway, not the 4500-foot postage stamp he now was lined up on. The MiG did have a drag chute that would help the aircraft slow down, but this was only a supplement to the hydraulic disk brakes, and landing on 4500 feet of runway required both the chute and the brakes.

Another thought nagging at Fletcher's mind was his initial loss of hydraulic fluid. True his backup hydraulic system was functioning, but it might still be leaking. It all depended on where the leak was. If it was in the primary system reservoir or one of the nearby lines, the backup system might be bypassing the leak completely. Or, if the leak were out in the flight control hydraulic lines it was possible he was still pissing away the life giving hydraulic fluid and the backup system might only be buying him time, possibly a very short time. He needed to put the aircraft on the ground. Stopping was a problem, though.

He let the other four aircraft land first, while he went over his options with Tanner. General Kavinsky had one of his hydraulic troops there with him in the command post. The young technician was sweating profusely and hurriedly flipping the pages of a thick volume of MiG-41 technical schematics. He and Kavinsky exchanging excited words in what could best be described as rapid Russian.

Fletcher was now down to fumes, with only 200 kilograms of fuel remaining. Actually the gauge was not designed for accuracy below 300 kilograms. He was on a downwind leg setting up for a very slow approach, knowing full well he would go off the end of the runway no matter what he did. For the moment he concentrated on flying the slowest approach of his short MiG career. He had the airspeed down below 100 knots and was aiming for as far back on the overrun as he could get and still hit concrete.

He was sweating, his knuckles white on the control stick as he willed the wallowing aircraft around the pattern, descending in the darkness at the spot he thought was the overrun. He wasn't sure he'd have the elevator authority to arrest his sink rate at this low speed, but at least he'd be on the ground, maybe harder than he wanted, but as they say...any landing you can walk away from.

He was now on short final, the nose of the MiG dangerously high, showing an AOA of 26 degrees, something only the MiG-41 could do. His VVI was about 150 meters per minute, around 450 feet per minute. He danced on the rudder pedals to stay lined up on the runway and he was constantly pumping the stick left and right correcting the drift back and forth. Just as he approached the overrun his engines flamed out, due to fuel starvation. He heard the dying whine of his engines and his eyes grew wide. With an AOA of 26 degrees the MiG seemed to be standing on end in an attempt to fly the slowest possible approach. In this attitude there was enormous drag on the airframe, drag only offset by the thrust from the engines. With that thrust gone his airspeed bled down to 80 knots, the MiG's wings stalled and the nose began to fall.

It was fortunate he was in the flare when the engines died and not back at 400 feet. The nose came down and the aircraft slammed into the overrun in a nearly level attitude. The nose gear sheared off and the main gear struts were driven up into the belly of the wounded MiG by the impact. The Fulcrum slid along the runway for a thousand feet before coming to a stop, facing back the way it had come.

Fletcher was knocked unconscious by the impact. He awoke moments later when rescue crews pried off the bent and spider-webbed canopy. He was bruised and battered by the terrific impact, but otherwise unhurt, though his kidneys ached for days. It was fortunate that the fuel tanks were empty, because they ruptured in the impact and surely would have resulted in a fiery death for the battered and unconscious pilot.

It was really fortunate all around. Although Fletcher did not think of himself as lucky, his being alive at all was the product of many lucky factors. He ran out of fuel very close to the ground at a very high angle of attack. Which meant he basically crashed on the runway, sparing a high-speed departure off the far end. The fact that he was out of fuel meant there was no fire. If he had landed under normal power he would have surely ran off the far end and the fuel tanks would have ruptured and he would have died in the resulting fire. Sure the MiG was totaled, but it was going to be totaled anyway. Besides, any landing you can walk away from...of course he was more or less carried away.

STOVACORE AB, TANGISTAN
0415 LOCAL

The loss of the two aircraft threw another monkey wrench into the works. The original plan was to land, refuel and ferry the planes back into Russia as soon as possible, even before first light. Now with two aircraft down the evacuation was going to be a bit more complicated. Although the loss of the aircraft so close to the base was obviously not planned it was not totally unforeseen that one could go down in Tangistan. The whole idea of the bug-out was to erase their presence in the region as soon as possible so when Kumar looked around afterward for a potential foe the only possibility was Sandor. Now there were two wrecked MiG-41s to dispose of, one still sitting on the approach end of the airfield, the other fourteen miles south of the base.

Before bailout Romano pitched the nose forward so the MiG hit the ground in about a forty degree dive at about 300 knots, hard enough to break the MiG up and spread the parts out over an area a quarter mile long, but not so hard as to break up the larger parts, such as engines and landing gear. The wreck was obviously a downed aircraft to any casual observer and it was only about fifteen miles from the Sandori border. To make matters worse there was no all-consuming fire. You needed fuel for a fire.

The Russian rescue force that picked up Romano also brought with it a demolition team. While the medics were attending to Romano's ankle, the demolition team planted explosive charges in the remaining large aircraft parts, one wing segment, both engines, a horizontal stabilizer and the main landing gear. Before liftoff they detonated the explosive charges, turning the big pieces of MiG into little ones. They then went out and laid long camouflage netting across the impact crater itself. Since there was no fuel in the tanks and therefore no fire, there was no big scorch mark to hide. From the ground it was obvious, but from the air it covered up all signs of the MiG crash. They doubted the Kumaris or Sandoris would invade Tangistani airspace in search of clues; especially since they would not know what they were even suppose to be looking for. Still and all the camouflage added one more level of safety to the whole operation. It also helped that the crash site was basically in the middle of nowhere.

Fletcher's aircraft back on the runway was dealt with in a similar fashion, although it was more or less intact and therefore required less area to be camouflaged. The MiG was dragged off the runway and out onto the sandy plain that ran by a modest ridgeline. The charges were set and detonated and a squad of soldiers covered over the debris with sand. Since the airfield was essentially deserted it was possible no one would find the remaining debris. Even if someone found it they would assume it was part of a Russian aircraft that crashed long ago during the Cold War.

The other four MiGs were refueled and readied to fly back to the airfield in Southern Russia. Whether the pilots were ready was another question. The two Russians were obviously ready, but Olmstead and Cowboy came down out of the their cockpits mad as hell. They marched right pass the groundcrew and stormed into the command post in search of Tanner, oblivious to the flurry of activity as the troops were breaking down the base, packing the transport and helicopter for the return flight. The schedule said everyone should be off the base by sun up. They had two hours to sun up, but the two American pilots were going nowhere without an explanation. The two pilots found Tanner and Sutherland in the Command Post.

"General, just what the hell happened out there," Olmstead demanded as he entered the room.

Tanner looked up from the intel reports at the outburst.

"Gentlemen, welcome back," Tanner said holding out his hand to Olmstead. Olmstead glanced down at the outstretched hand and then looked hard at Tanner, ignoring the general's gesture. Cowboy stood behind him, his face taught, grim.

"Sir, what the hell is going on?" he demanded again. "We got our asses kicked out there. They knew we were coming, for God's sake! They had to have known we were coming. Now who fucked this operation up?"

Tanner withdrew his hand and put on a grim face of his own.

"Captain, you will calm down," he said in a level voice. "We are looking at the intelligence right now. I understand you are upset, but I assure you no one "fucked up" as you so eloquently put it."

"Then what would you call it, General?" Cowboy chimed in.

Tanner had to admit it was hard to argue that the operation wasn't "fucked up". All things considered the operation could have gone better. Two aircraft lost, two pilots injured, one out for over a month with a broken ankle.

"We believe we may have gotten some bad intel," Tanner said. "The planning and execution of this operation relied on intel from sensitive sources, sources that up until yesterday we thought were unquestionable. Since that informant was killed there were two ways to interpret what he told us. His information about Abdul's travel plans could have been true or it could have been planted to try and entrap Sandor into attacking. We thought we had good intel, but apparently it might have been a trap. Abdul Al Faisal as it turned out was not in the convoy," Tanner said. He gestured to Sutherland, "Lieutenant?"

"Sirs," he started, then cleared his throat. "We now believe this whole operation may have been a trap. Our informant in Kagned was either a double agent or he was intentionally fed bad intel in an attempt to provoke an attack and thereby blow his cover."

Olmstead frowned. "Lieutenant, the informant was executed prior to the attack. If he were a double working for Achmed they wouldn't have killed him. Everyone knows you leave double agents alone and you milk them for all they're worth."

"Well, sir, I believe they must have had proof before this that he was working for the Sandoris. They set the trap, killed the informant and waited for Sandor to fly into it. It may have been an attempt to get Sandor to attack and thereby generate sympathy from neighboring states."

"Of course they didn't know he was really working for us," Tanner mused. "Or do you think they did?"

"No, sir," Sutherland said. "The informant himself didn't even know he was working for us. Our contact with him was a Sandori agent working for us as a double."

"Yes, but is *he* trustworthy?" Olmstead asked.

"I read his dossier, Captain," Sutherland said. "His family was killed by Achmed in a chemical attack in 1987. He has no love of Achmed. He also blames Sandor for not defending the village his family lived in. They withdrew from the area to set a flanking trap for Achmed's army. They used that village as bait for the trap and the trap was never sprung. Achmed gassed them with mortar fire then never occupied the village. The Kumari army went around the valley. Thousands of civilians died. His motivation now is to get even with both countries, and of course retire early."

"Jesus, doesn't anyone just work for one side anymore?" Cowboy grumbled. "Too many double agents in this whole deal. It was bound to be a trap and we fell for it."

"The good news, " Sutherland said, "is that the Kumaris definitely think the Sandoris were the attackers. The reports they will have of MiG radar emissions and Russian munitions will only confirm their suspicions, especially since they believe the informant was working for Sandor. They may have even tortured him and he told them he was working for Sandor. Either way the effect's the same."

"Yeah, but we didn't get our bastard," Cowboy said dejectedly.

"It was a long shot anyway, sir," Sutherland said. "Besides, we took no losses."

"The hell we didn't, Lieutenant," Olmstead said brusquely. "We lost two aircraft and Romano will be down for a month. That puts a little crimp in our manning. Wouldn't you say, General?"

"What I'm more worried about right now is getting the hell out of here," Tanner said. "In case you didn't notice when you stormed over here the troops outside are tearing this place apart as we speak. Your aircraft is being refueled and I expect you off the ground within the hour. Gurevich will take the lead for the flight back to Russia. Let him do the leading, Dave, got it? You guys sit back and enjoy the ride. We'll have a real debrief tomorrow after you guys get some rest. We can tear the whole operation apart at that time. Now get going. I'll see you boys in Russia."

Olmstead and Cowboy shook hands with the General and turned to leave. As they got to the door Tanner called. "By the way, gentlemen, good job tonight."

Olmstead turned and shrugged his shoulders, "It wasn't much of a war, sir, but it was the only one we had." His lips formed a thin, tired smile.

Just outside the doorway Olmstead turned to Cowboy and spoke as they walked. “I can’t believe that coward didn’t even fire one fucking missile.”

“Maybe he had a problem,” Cowboy offered.

“Oh, he’s got a problem, alright,” Olmstead said.

Gurevich and Dobrinsky were outside the Command Post waiting for the two Americans and Gurevich’s eyes narrowed as he overheard the comments. He flicked his cigarette butt to the ground as Olmstead and Cowboy approached.

“You finished with your temper tantrum, Captain?” Gurevich, chided Olmstead. “You know we have to be off the ground within the hour.”

Cowboy reached out a massive set of arms to grab the Russian by the collar of his flight suit. Olmstead moved between them and ended the skirmish before it turned into an international incident. Not that Gurevich didn’t need a good beating, but prudence was the better part of valor.

Olmstead pulled Cowboy aside and said under his breath. “Easy, big guy, remember where we are. These Russian troops might not like to see an American beating the hell out of one of their officers. We are outnumbered here about five to one. Let me deal with Gurevich right now. You can have him later.”

Cowboy stepped back, his dark eyes still smoldering. Olmstead took a deep breath and turned to the Russian. “I understand you will be leading us back to Mother Russia,” he said.

“That is correct, Captain, I will be leading you,” he said with that smug smile.

“So I guess you will be landing first, correct?”

“Yes, that is correct,” Gurevich answered, confused by the question.

“That’s probably a good thing since you’ll obviously be short on gas when we get there.”

“What are you talking about? Why will I be short of fuel?” the confused Russian asked.

“You will have a fuel degrade due to the weapons still on your aircraft,” Olmstead explained patiently. “Since I actually fired on the enemy tonight my wings are clean. You better figure a ten percent degrade on those missiles, Major. I wouldn’t want anything unfortunate happening to you, like running out of gas. Perhaps next time if you actually fired on the enemy...” he said, his voice trailing off as he walked away toward his aircraft, leaving Gurevich red with anger.

Cowboy had been standing there listening to the exchange and now the Russian looked up at him anger in his gaze. Cowboy put his hand to his mouth and laughed aloud then turned and walked away. Dobrinsky turned away as well, trying to hide the smile as he walked to his aircraft.

Forty minutes later four MiG-41s left the runway, afterburners blazing and turned north toward Russia. The rest of the base soon followed in cargo aircraft. By sunrise the little Tangistani airfield was silent and empty, as it had been for several years before, the only sound that of the native birds and a gentle wind rustling the tall grasses in the fields around the strip of concrete.

KERESHNOV AIRBASE
SOUTHERN RUSSIA

"Evening, gentlemen," Tanner said as his pilots took their seats around the debriefing table, Romano struggling to stow his crutches under the table.

Fletcher had escaped with minor injuries, mostly scrapes, bumps and bruises, of which he had a particularly nasty looking one beneath his right eye, almost as if he'd been on the receiving end of a well-placed round house punch. He had a Band-Aid on the left cheek from an abrasion he received from his flailing oxygen mask during the ejection.

"I wanted to start the debrief without the Russians present," Tanner said. "They won't be in for another half hour. I want to hear your version uncorrupted by their presence. Also if any of you have some very nasty comments to make I am the final filter. I won't have any unnecessary feather ruffling of the Russians. But here and now you say what's on your mind."

Olmstead looked at Fletcher who nodded silently and knowingly.

"Lieutenant Sutherland will begin by giving you guys the low down on what's happened in the last 12 hours and the effects of our little jaunt into Kumar. Lieutenant?"

Sutherland cleared his throat and flipped a switch to darken the room then turned on the overhead projector. His first slide showed a chronological listing of events of the past 24 hours.

"Well, gentlemen, you definitely got the Kumaris' attention last night," he said. "Within ten minutes of your attack Kagned was notified through encrypted messages sent by HF radio. The coded message traffic continued to increase for the next three hours while Kumar brought their entire air defense force to full alert. Night patrols of Kumari MiG-23, MiG-29 and MiG-41 aircraft were launched and set up search patterns around the perimeter of Kagned, a first for the Kumari Air Force, by the way. How effective they would have been is a moot point now, but suffice it to say for Kumar this was a massive effort. Of course you were already egressing and there was no hope of catching you. They effectively closed the barn door after the cows came home.

"Early intel suggests they do believe the attack was Sandori. Aside from the patrols over Kagned they launched several roving patrols of MiG-23s and Mirage F-1s to cover the Sandori border. They also brought up numerous SAM acquisition radars along the border and the message traffic into the regional air defense headquarters was staggering. What was even more staggering was the lack of attention paid to their Northern, Southern and Western borders. They did not launch one patrol to cover those borders."

Olmstead raised his hand. "Todd, this is all wonderful, but do we know for sure what the hell happened out there?" he said impatiently.

"One of our contacts in Kagned, and yes we have contacts there, and no they are not double agents," he added, "indicates the whole thing was a mole operation to ferret out our informant. He was under suspicion by Achmed's internal police force and they fed him a phony travel schedule for Abdul to see if he would sell it to Sandor. They sent the convoy out anyway to lay in wait under full alert for anybody to fly into the trap. The convoy you hit was mostly empty vehicles. Most of the troops were sitting on a nearby ridgeline with IR SAMs and AAA waiting for you. Luckily they weren't real enthused about being set up as targets. More than likely most of them dug a hole and were hunkered down asleep when you came through."

"The bastards running those ZSU-23-4s were definitely awake," Cowboy exclaimed.

"Jesus, we were lucky!" Romano said, his palm on his forehead.

Fletcher was shaking his head. "You mean this whole thing was a trap and we walked right into it? For Christ sake, we didn't see this coming?"

"Hindsight is always 20-20, Captain," Tanner said. "At least we got both sides very nervous."

"General, are we trying to start a war between Sandor and Kumar?" Olmstead asked evenly. "I mean is that what we're looking at here?"

Tanner took a deep breath and let it out slowly. "Our goal here is to ensure that neither Sandor nor Kumar will pose a threat to the United States or her allies in the near and long term from weapons of mass destruction. We are also trying to break up an already shaky coalition of countries sponsoring terrorism against our country. If this leads to war between those two countries then they can take each other out. We need Sandor hating Kumar's ass again. We need the Shiites Muslims hating the Sunni Muslims. The missions we are flying are going to do just that. If they are fighting each other they won't be messing with us."

"We bomb that nuke, then Sandor bombs something else in Kumar and it won't take too many of those to start a full-blown war. Then what?" Fletcher asked.

"We get the hell out of Dodge is what," Romano said.

"General?" Fletcher insisted for an answer from Tanner.

"If that happens we get the hell out of Dodge, Captain," Tanner agreed.

"Is that the view of our Russian friends?" Fletcher asked.

Tanner fidgeted for a moment. The question of the Russians was a sticking point with him as well. Even though they had been completely cooperative in the operation so far, he felt he didn't have a good handle on their real objectives.

"Are the Russians trying to start a war between Sandor and Kumar?" Romano asked. "They supply military hardware to both countries and they pay cash. Russia needs hard cash right now."

"So far the Russians have been in complete agreement with us as far as how to proceed," Tanner said. "However, as you well know the Russians' real motives are never completely known to anybody but themselves. They claim to have concerns about weapons of mass destruction as well as Muslim unity on the terrorist front, but I'm sure that's a convenient way to get our cooperation. I don't know what they really want and it doesn't really matter as long as we benefit in the process."

Olmstead mulled this over for a moment then asked the question on everybody's minds.

"So what is the deal with Gurevich?" he asked simply. "I get the feeling if he slashed his wrists he'd bleed red…and I mean Red! Communist Party blood's still flowing through those veins. At least Dreschler seemed to think so."

"Yeah, and why'd he return with all his weapons?" Fletcher asked. "There was plenty to shoot at out there. I counted at least six separate radars he could have targeted. Dave took out two of them, but where was Gurevich?"

Tanner shook his head.

"Here's the real question," Cowboy said solemnly. "Is this guy a coward or somethin worse?"

"Is he working for someone else on the side?" Fletcher added.

"Either way he's a danger to us," Romano said.

Tanner put up both hands in protest. "Look we don't know the whole story yet," he said. "Let's see what he says during the debrief. I also had his ship checked out for weapons problems and I don't have that report yet. If he has no alibi, I'll see what I can do to dump him, okay?"

The pilots were in agreement. It was only fair to give the man his say, and maybe even the benefit of the doubt, but this was their lives at stake. If it had been Dobrinsky they would have given him the benefit of the doubt, but Gurevich didn't rate the same trust. He hadn't earned it yet.

The Russians came into the debriefing room fifteen minutes later and the real debriefing began. Sutherland had a map with the route of flight and missile threat rings laid out on the big central planning table. They would go over the entire mission from beginning to end, from planning to engine shutdown.

Air Force mission debriefings, even peacetime debriefings, can be harsh. The light of criticism is shone on all aspects of the mission and no topic is off-limits. The way a flight leader ran the radios or just the way he taxied or started engines might lead to hours of heated "discussion". Feelings get hurt and toes get stepped on, but real fighter pilots will never show that kind of weakness and when the debrief is over everything that was done was on that mission was in black and white, good and bad, nothing is ever gray. At least that is the idea. In fact leadership and reputations are forged in the debrief even more so than in flight. A man who can admit to error or defend his rationale successfully will walk away a better flyer. It was assumed the Russian Air Force debriefed the same way, but that was something they were about to find out.

Olmstead took his place at the front of the table. As flight lead he was responsible for leading the debriefing. He glanced down at the notes he had scrawled on a single sheet of computer paper. He cleared his throat and began the standard USAF debrief.

"Okay, gentlemen," he started. "This is the debrief for mission number 20041014. I want to start from the beginning which is mission planning. Due to time constraints Lieutenant Sutherland largely performed the mission planning. Are there any comments about the mission materials?"

There were none.

"Okay, engine start and taxi," Olmstead continued. "I called for start on time, and I thought it went pretty smoothly. We taxied soon after. Comments."

"Not on the engine start, but the taxi made me nervous as hell," Fletcher said.

"You mean when we doubled back and went beak to beak on the runway?"

Olmstead asked.

"Yeah, that was unnerving. On a wider runway it would have been fine, but man I swear I only had a couple feet of clearance from the guys on the take off roll," Fletcher said.

"It was about three feet actually," Tanner said. "I was your wing walker. But, yes, that is mighty close quarters, especially when one of the aircraft is on the take-off roll..."

"And it was at night," Romano chimed in.

"Next go around we'll take some time to look at that during the day," Tanner said.

"Okay, we're on the runway lined up for take-off," Olmstead said. "Any comments or questions?"

"Man, I sure would have liked to have had the IRST up and running for take-off," Cowboy said.

"No shit," Romano added. "It was black out there. I know you have to trust the book and the airplane, but man I would have liked to be able to see the end of the runway. As it was you reached rotation speed, pulled back and---wham---there's the overrun beneath you. That was scary."

Olmstead agreed. Those seconds of terror were almost as scary as the SAM launches.

"It would have improved safety on the rejoin and climb out if we had the IR working," Fletcher said.

"The system takes twenty minutes to cool down to operating temperature," Gurevich spoke up for the first time. "We cannot afford to sit with engines running and waste fuel while the IRST cools down."

"What if we start the IRST on external power and let it cool down while we're the chocks and running start up checklists?" Fletcher asked. "Is there a problem switching to internal power?"

"The system was not meant to operate that way..." Gurevich argued.

Dobrinsky was one of the systems experts having worked the IRST integration program in Russia. And he felt the time was ripe to jump in before a fight broke out.

"We can cool the seeker down on external power, but when we switch to internal the transition is not quick enough and it will trip a relay that will power down the unit and reset the timer..."

"There...I told you the system was not meant to operate this way," Gurevich interrupted with smug self-assurance. Self-assurance Dobrinsky was about to crush.

"It is true the system will power down when the current is interrupted during the switch over, however if you leave the IRST in BIT mode, you can restart it once internal power is on," Dobrinsky said. "It bypasses the internal timer and allows cooling to continue from where it left off. Just remember if you are going to switch from external to internal or internal to external power you must put the IRST in BIT mode, then you can return it to the previous mode after power transfer."

Gurevich glared at Dobrinsky, his face red with humiliation.

"Okay," Tanner said. "Problem solved."

Olmstead smiled a little, amused by the friction developing between Gurevich and Dobrinsky. He liked to see the squat spunky pilot put Gurevich in his place.

"Any other comments regarding the take-off?" Olmstead asked. There was only silence.

"Okay, let's talk rejoin. Any problems with the radar rejoin? I know we're not real used to flying a straight trail like that. Any problems?"

"Nah," Cowboy said. "It was the easiest formation I ever flew, at least until my radar went tits up. It was impossible to get visual cues that far in trail at night. Thank God for the IRST. Without that I wouldn't have seen you guys at all when we dimmed the lights."

Olmstead led the briefing through the mountains of Sandor just as he had in the aircraft the previous night. The comments were surprisingly few and far between. Realistically not very much happened on the mission until they entered the target area. It was no mean feat to fly undetected through a Third World country at treetop level in the black of night. The "mean feat" is when the target knows you're coming. With no terrain to hide behind you can't hide from a from a SAM radar that knows your coming.

"Okay, about twenty five miles out we started to get emissions from a couple SA-6 acquisition radars and at least one ZSU. That was the first clue this was not going to be a surprise," Olmstead said.

"Sir, were the radars sectoring on you or was it a general 360 degree scan?" Sutherland asked.

"They were sectoring on our quadrant, but they had no lock on us initially," Fletcher answered, Olmstead nodding in agreement.

"They were looking where they thought we'd be, Lieutenant," Cowboy said.

"That was when Gurevich and I became the bait. We separated, climbed and turned inbound," Olmstead said, talking through the maneuver with his hands, "about 90 degrees apart on inbound headings initially." The Russian nodded but said nothing. Olmstead paused for a moment and when he realized there would be no further comment he continued.

"I intended to swing up to the north east, but I got engaged and had to turn inbound on an almost westerly heading. I slowed in the turn inbound to give me more time on the run, but kept at my best cornering airspeed to be able to load on the Gs if I had to dodge a SAM."

"Sir, what locked you up?" Sutherland asked, taking notes.

"Initially a Straight Flush. The RWR gear put it in the Hotel band, and it acted like an SA-6."

"Did you actively jam the acquisition radar?"

"Yes, I had the jammers in auto, but I don't know how effective they were."

"Not very, if he locked you up, pard," Cowboy commented. Olmstead nodded.

"Anyway I fired off a HARM just about the time I got a TTR lock-on and missile launch indication," Olmstead said.

"So the RWR gear did detect the launch properly?" Sutherland asked.

"It seemed to work fine. Luckily the HARM was faster than the SAM. It took out the radar and the missile lost me in a high G turn."

"Did you punch out chaff, sir?" Sutherland asked.

"Yeah, I punched chaff all during the maneuver. I don't know whether it went for the chaff or just went stupid. I couldn't swear that chaff made any difference at all."

"What about your second HARM?" Tanner asked.

"Another SA-6. This one was textbook, blew up the bastard before it ever left the ground. The HARM homed on the Straight Flush before it ever locked me up," Olmstead said. "They never knew what hit'em. I also saw a few AAA radars up, but I was too far out to be engaged. They never locked me up."

Sutherland turned to Gurevich. It was time to ask the questions he had been dreading.

"Sir, were you engaged by any threats last night or see any threat signals?" he asked. The room held its collective breath.

Gurevich's eyes narrowed slightly and his Adam's Apple seemed to convulse once before he began speaking. Other than those slight visual cues, he was cool as a cucumber.

"As I turned inbound my RWR gear detected two SA-6 Straight Flush radars and some AAA" he said calmly. "The same two SA-6s and the AAA that Captain Olmstead saw, but I was not able to get a HARM solution. I received a transient missile interface unit master fault and was not able to get a lock-on tone."

"What do you mean 'transient'?" Romano asked.

"The fault cleared itself after we left the target area," Gurevich said calmly.

Tanner frowned inwardly. *A transient fault*, he thought. I wonder if that's true. It's hard to believe, equally hard to disprove.

"So what did you do?" Olmstead asked Gurevich directly.

"About the fault?" he asked, confused. "I checked my circuit breakers, and reset the MIU master power, but the warm up period is three minutes and we were out of the target area before it timed out."

"Okay," Olmstead said slowly. He paused for a moment, but there was no other comment. He sighed. No since beating this horse. Everyone in the room had their own idea about what really happened. "That puts us up to the bomb run. Fletch, you were in the lead. You have the brief."

Fletcher nodded and stood up to point at the chart on the table in front of them. "We came in from the south-south-west at 200 feet and about 440 knots. At about twenty-five miles out we started to get RWR indications of SA-6 and AAAs off the nose. We accelerated to 550 knots, mil power, and prayed Dave would get the Sixes before we got there. He got 'em and all we had left on the threat scopes were a Flapwheel and some Gun Dishes for the ZSU-23-4s. The big guns didn't bother us, because of our speed and altitude, but those pesky ZSUs can ruin your whole day at 6000 rounds per minute. We turned on the jammers and took down the gun director radars. I don't know about the other guys, but I blew probably 90 percent of my chaff on the bomb run. I still had a few bundles left, but it wasn't intentional. I just ran out of bomb run before I ran out of chaff."

"I didn't," Cowboy said. "I used every bundle I had on the run." Romano nodded in agreement.

"So we drove straight in, tightened up the formation until we were virtually wingtip to wingtip. We climbed to 400 meters just before release. Airspeed was 550 knots. Our track was 020 true," Fletcher said.

"You have trouble identifying the target in the dark?" Tanner asked. "Or did the IRST help out."

"What makes you think it was dark, sir?" Romano asked with a tight-lipped smile. "Hell, it was like daytime out there with all the AAA. The IRST wasn't all that useful due to the flashes from the AAA, but we had no problem seeing where the bad guys were."

"Amen to that," Cowboy agreed.

"What types of AAA did you see?" Sutherland asked.

Romano sighed and shrugged. "Hell, I don't know. It was moving pretty damn fast, Lieutenant. It had an ungodly rate of fire."

"Since there was at least on Gun Dish radiating most likely they were ZSU-23-4s," Fletcher said. "I think our chaff and jamming helped because it looked like barrage fire. I don't think they burned through the jamming."

"If they had you would be dead, Captain," Dobrinsky said in a somber tone. "If a ZSU locks you up for only a second he can hit you with over 100 shells."

"So we came off the target, turned northeast and climbed," Fletcher continued. "I buddy spiked Dave out front and Gurevich rejoined from behind. That's when we picked up the MiG-25."

"He'd been out there the whole time," Olmstead said. "I kept getting weak hits from his Foxfire radar. I kept expecting him to bingo home for gas, but he stuck with it. I guess after we hit the convoy he was ordered to stay and engage us. He probably ran out of fuel on the way home."

"He did run out of fuel, sir," Sutherland said. "Intel indicates a Kumari MiG-25 crashed just short of an airbase in Northern Kumar. The pilot bailed out and sustained no injuries."

"So how did that engagement develop?" Tanner asked.

"Well, the only guys with any AA-12s was Fletch and Cowboy," Olmstead started, "but Cowboy was gadget-bent by that time..."

"What did they find out about your radar, Cowboy?" Tanner interrupted with the question. He wanted the answer, but he also wanted to know if Cowboy was conscientious enough to go find out for himself. He wasn't disappointed.

"They said it was an antennae stabilization problem. They replaced the LRU and it works fine now."

"Okay, thanks. Please continue Captain," he said to Olmstead.

"Not much to tell from my end, sir. I let Fletch keep the lead since he was the only one capable of splashing the Foxbat. Cowboy's missiles were useless without the radar and the rest of us just had heaters, and a MiG-25 with Mach 3 speed won't let you get that close."

"Captain Fletcher..."

Fletcher took a deep breath. "Let me start out by saying it was poor planning to have only two AA-12 shooters in the package. One of us goes down we don't have enough missiles to protect us in a real battle. Turns out this guy was a loner and followed the strict MiG-25 tactical training manual to the letter. He locked us up and got off a shot with an AA-6 Acrid before we could get in AA-12 range. The RWR gear indicated missile in the air. A few seconds later he double-tapped us. Two AA-6s inbound. We jammed him in auto, punched out chaff and executed a high G turn away from the missiles. The second missile self-destructed well short of us, but the first kept homing straight and true. Just before impact I hit the thrust vectoring, turned ninety degrees and punched chaff. At least I think I did. Pulled like 10 Gs for a second. Damn near passed out. When it was over the chaff counter said zero. Anyway it detonated aft of my aircraft. I turned back to the north and locked up the Foxbat running for home. He was at fifty miles an accelerating past Mach 1 when I realized we weren't going to catch him. It didn't matter. He was out of the fight anyway. Thought I'd lucked out, but I guess he did get a piece of me."

Tanner nodded. He turned to Romano. "You were having some problems?"

"I caught some small arms fire or light AAA in the target area," he said. "I was leaking fuel pretty badly out my left outboard wing tank, so I set up the panel to burn from the outboards and transferred as much as I could in the process."

"When it became clear Bear didn't have the gas to get home we started cutting corners," Fletcher said. "We deviated to the northeast and crossed over into Sandor on a northeasterly heading."

"Yes, but the deception was successful, right?" Tanner asked cautiously.

Fletcher nodded. "Absolutely. They got a solid GCI radar lock on us and saw us heading back toward Sandor. As soon as we felt they had a good track we dove back to TFR and crossed over into Sandor. Before crossing the border I got some weak hits from a Sandori early warning radar, but we were so low and the signal so faint I'm sure they never got a lock on us. We crossed over the border well north of planned and basically turned due north to parallel the border on the Sandori side. We saw absolutely no threats and crossed over into Tangistan undetected. We thought we had it made, then it all hit the fan."

"I thought cutting those corners saved me enough gas, but I was wrong. Either I lost more gas from the outboards than I thought or the inboards had a slow leak I never detected. The nav computer said I was ten minutes from home and had five minutes of gas," Romano said. "You know the rest of the story. I took the nylon ILS. But I will say I'd like to buy stock in the company that built that ejection seat. Of course the PLF was my fault. It was more of a PFL," he said, referring to the Parachute Landing Fall versus the Poor Fucking Landing.

"That was just about when I realized I had a problem, too," Fletcher said. "I knew the shrapnel peppered me, because my canopy had a spider web crack at the right rear, but I didn't think it punctured the skin of the aircraft. I expected to find some dimples when I landed."

"Big dimples," Olmstead said dryly.

"Yeah," Fletch agreed. "I suddenly found myself with low hydraulic pressure in the primary system. I don't understand what happened. My last station check the pressure had been fine then suddenly it started to fall. The secondary system kicked in and gave me flight controls, but I didn't know how long they would last, because I couldn't be sure where the damage was. I didn't have time to give it much thought. I was low on gas. Hell, we all were. Without primary hydraulics I had no brakes and that postage stamp you call an airfield became the problem. If I landed normally I wouldn't be able to keep her on the runway. So I dirtied her up and slowed up, kept the Alpha just below the limit, and slammed that puppy on the end of the runway hard enough to break the main gear struts. I also flamed out on short final by the way, that's why my flare was a bit weak."

"Excuses, excuses," Olmstead said shaking his head in mock disgust.

"Flare to land, squat to pee, right," Fletch said, quoting the mantra of the naval aviator.

"You did a helluva job getting that plane back on the ground and saving yourself, Fletch," Tanner said. "I know you trashed the plane, but it was a goner anyway. I'm just glad we got you back. Good flying."

Fletch just nodded, clearly less impressed with his abilities than the general.

"Lessons learned, gentlemen?" Tanner asked the group.

Fletcher snorted. "It appears at least some of the Kumaris trained for night intercept," he said, directing his comment at Sutherland.

"You may be right, sir," Sutherland admitted. "but we had no intel that supported that. To be honest, sir, I think that guy was in the right place at the right time."

"You mean it was just luck, Lieutenant?" Olmstead asked.

"Dumb luck, sir."

"And I suppose it was dumb luck this guy was carrying two AA-6 Acrids on a routine night instrument proficiency flight?" Fletch asked, sarcastically.

"Well...maybe not, sir," Sutherland had to admit. "But intelligence still believes they don't train for night intercepts."

"What do you believe, Lieutenant?" Fletcher challenged him.

Sutherland conceded defeat. There was no sense playing a bad hand, especially one dealt by someone else.

"I believe current intelligence is wrong about that, sir," he said.

"Lesson learned," Fletch said.

Tanner chuckled. "Any other lessons?"

"With that last one fresh in the Lieutenant's mind, sir, I don't feel we should ever get caught again with only two BVR shooters, especially at night," Olmstead said.

"I agree," Tanner said. "The AA-11 is a fine missile, but for night ops you'd rather have fewer of them and more radar missiles, or maybe some extended range IR AA-10s, in case you are gadget bent. That's what your getting at, right?"

"Yes, sir," Olmstead said. "We can still carry wingtip AA-11s, but every one of us should have a pair of AA-10s or 12s. We can't sacrifice defense for offense, sir."

"Point taken. The reactor mission won't be as critical on the numbers of weapons. The strikers will be carrying two laser guided missiles, leaving you room for both BVR missiles and heaters," Tanner said. "Anything else?"

The men looked around the room at each other, each obviously dwelling on Gurevich a bit longer than the others. When it became obvious Gurevich wasn't biting Tanner spoke up.

"Okay, gentlemen, that is all. Get some rest. I'm not sure when we're going again, but my guess is the Sandori mission will come soon enough."

As the men got up to leave Tanner said, "Major Gurevich, please keep your seat. I'd like to speak with you in private."

Gurevich sat back down, his brow furrowed. The others had tight, thin smiles on their faces as the left the room, trying hard not to look too pleased and hoping Tanner let the bastard have it. After they left Tanner shut the door and sat back down, this time across from the Russian pilot.

"Okay, let's have it, Major," he said, his voice deadpan.

The Russian looked confused. "Have what, sir?"

"Cut the crap, Major," Tanner said. "What the hell really happened out there?"

"Sir, I told you my missile interface unit failed."

"Transient fault is what you said, Major."

"Yes, sir. Maintenance is looking at it even as we speak."

Tanner sat back in his chair, slouching now, his elbow on the table, his index finger resting against his left temple. He looked at the Russian for several uncomfortable seconds before speaking again.

"Major, I know you are a fine pilot, but I have to tell you," he said, looking into the man's blue eyes. "My boys are sick of you, your attitude, everything. Now you have a 'transient fault' on a mission and can't launch any missiles. Defensive missiles, Major. They are counting on you to protect them and they don't like that one bit. Then when you can't protect them in combat...well, what are they supposed to think?"

Gurevich nodded slightly, understanding. "General, I swear to you as an officer I had a transient MIU fault. If I could have targeted those missiles I would have fired them. I could not. That is what they are supposed to think."

"If they trusted you that is what they would think," Tanner said. "They don't. I'm not sure even Dobrinsky trusts you. Trust has to be earned. You haven't earned any yet, Major. Now I will see that maintenance report and if it turns out that MIU is okay you will have lost my trust as well. That is something you do not want to lose. You lose my trust---you are gone, understand? Is there anything else you want to say to me now?"

"No, sir. The MIU is bad. That fact will be born out."

"Perhaps...but even so, you're not a team player, at least not on this team. I'd better see some team play or you're out of the game, understand, Major?"

Gurevich sat back, deflated somewhat, his lips pursed. He looked at the general and nodded. *It was time*, he thought.

KERESHNOV AIRBASE
1030 LOCAL

It was late the next morning and the sun had been up for hours. The team was preparing to turn in for the "night" when there was a knock on the door. Romano opened it to find Dobrinsky's smiling face.

"Dobie, what's up?" Romano asked. The Russian appeared a little nervous, but as good-natured as ever.

"Uh, I need to borrow Captain Olmstead," he said.

Romano shrugged his shoulders and turned back into the room.

"Dave, Dobie needs to talk with you," he said with a yawn.

Olmstead came to the door. "What's up?" he asked.

"Dave, I have been asked to escort you to a meeting with someone," he said cryptically.

"Who wants to see me?"

"Major Gurevich wishes to speak to you alone," he explained. "He says it is very important, at least to you it will be, but he was too prideful to come here himself and face all of you."

"What does he want, really?"

"I really do not know," Dobrinsky insisted.

"Why me?" Olmstead said.

"He did tell me to give you one clue if you chose not to come with me."

"Alright, let's have it," Olmstead said.

"He simply said to say 'Korea'. I do not know what that means," Dobrinsky said, shrugging his own shoulders.

At the word 'Korea' Olmstead did a double take. He knew what that meant.

"Okay, where's he want to meet?"

"In his quarters. I am to take you there. It is on close by, on base."

Olmstead grabbed his jacket. He turned to Fletch who was lying on his cot reading a book.

"I'll be back in a little while. Got some business to finish," he said.

Dobrinsky drove him across base and walked him to Gurevich's quarters, a drab, single room apartment that field graders rated. Olmstead knocked and when Gurevich answered he waved at Dobrinsky, who nodded and left.

"Please, come in, Captain," the Russian said, ushering him through the door. "I want to thank you for coming. I really did not expect you to accept my invitation."

"What do you know about Korea," Olmstead said, staring Gurevich square in the eye.

"Please sit," Gurevich insisted, gesturing to the small couch. Olmstead did nothing for five seconds, then took a breath and sat as though he decided arguing over pleasantries was not worth it.

"Now...about Korea?" Olmstead prodded.

"Yes…Korea," Gurevich said walking over to the kitchenette. He reached into his small refrigerator and produced an ice tray. He produced two glasses and tossed in a couple ice cubes apiece. From under the counter he took a half full bottle of Russian vodka and poured three fingers each in the two glasses as he spoke. "Approximately six months ago you were in an air engagement against Korean MiG-29s. Your wingman was shot down by an AA-10E with IR and laser guidance. You shot down his attacker with an AIM-130 and you were yourself hit and disabled by an AA-11. You returned to base, your attacker returned to base."

"How do you know all this?" Olmstead demanded.

"Because I was there," he said simply, handing Olmstead a vodka as he took a long drink of his own.

Olmstead dropped the drink to the floor almost as soon as it touched his hand. He was flabbergasted. At first he didn't understand, then it dawned on him. Gurevich was in the number two MiG. He knew he looked familiar the first time he saw him and he also remembered that look of recognition in Gurevich's face as well. Of course all they saw of each other then was a few seconds of helmet and visor, but somehow he knew it had been Gurevich. His mouth fell open and he couldn't speak for a moment.

"You?" he finally blurted. "You were there? In the second MiG?"

Gurevich nodded. "Yes, I was in the second MiG. Let me pour you another drink," he said, retrieving the empty glass from the floor, adding two more ice cubes and pouring a fresh drink.

"You fired on me!" Olmstead said.

"Blew off your damn burner can. You still think me a coward? You blew my wingman out of the sky and you were locking me up. I had to fire on you or be killed myself," Gurevich explained matter-of-factly.

"I blew your wingman out of the sky because he blew my wingman out of the sky!" Olmstead shouted. "You attacked us with no provocation!"

"You are right, except I did not attack you, my idiot flight lead did," Gurevich said, handing Olmstead the fresh drink. "Try not to spill this one, please."

"What the hell happened then? Why were you even there?" Olmstead demanded, slamming the drink down on the small coffee table. He clearly had no intention of drinking with Gurevich.

Gurevich took a deep breath. "I was there demonstrating a retrofit of the long range IRST and laser guidance system on older MiG-29s. We were supposed to fly an intercept on another pair of MiGs, but there was an accident at their base and the runway was closed. The idea was to demonstrate our new long range IR targeting system on a fighter-sized non-cooperative target, the same system that is now in our MiG-41s. When the other flight failed to get airborne the flight lead went to his back up plan. He knew there were always ROK or US aircraft patrolling the DMZ. He also knew that if he drove down into the DMZ he would be intercepted. This was supposed to be an even better test of the system, since it would be against real enemy aircraft. The plan was to lock you up with the new IRST and laser. You would not even know you were targeted. Then we would break off before we got into AIM-130 range and fly back to the North. During the Cold War we always played these games.

"The flight lead either got nervous or overly ambitious and fired on you without orders. By the time the missile hit your wingman and you knew you were under attack, we were well inside AIM-130 range and we simply could not turn and run. You would have shot us in the back as we ran. You fired on him and took him out. I wanted to disengage, but you gave me no choice but to engage you. I fired an AA-8, which was way out of its envelope and intended to turn you defensive in hopes you would disengage, but no, you kept on coming. Finally I had to use the superior envelope of the AA-11 to stop you. I was very happy you were not injured. You are an excellent pilot, Captain, a worthy adversary. I am sorry about your wingman and I want you to know I had no idea my lead would fire on you."

Olmstead sat back heavily on the couch. He picked up the vodka and downed it in one gulp. He shook his head in wonder. *Do I actually believe this asshole*? he asked himself. Yes, he did, he decided. Why would Gurevich lie about this? He obviously was there and he could believe that a crazy North Korean would panic and fire on them. From what he could tell of his Russian colleagues so far, it did not seem in their character to panic like that in flight.

He looked up at the expectantly waiting Gurevich. "You know who my wingman was, don't you?" he asked.

"Da," he answered. "Captain Fletcher's brother."

"So why are you telling me this now?" Olmstead asked.

"Should I have told Captain Fletcher?" he asked.

"I would hope your instinct for self-preservation is greater than that," Olmstead said sarcastically, rolling his eyes.

"This is a secret I have been carrying around for three months," Gurevich explained, sighing heavily as he plopped down on the couch, throwing his feet up on the coffee table. "Not even my superiors knew they had inadvertently put me on the same team as you and Fletcher. As soon as I met you I felt you looked familiar. Then I overheard Lt Sutherland talking about the MiG you shot down in Korea and your problem with Fletcher and it all fell together. You must understand that even though it was not my fault, I still feel remorse about it.

"So I kept my distance. I decided it would be best if you just couldn't stand to be around me. So I was an arrogant bastard, not a real stretch for me in any event. I play these games with students all the time when I'm in "instructor-mode". If I were a 'son-of-a-bitch', you would hate me. The goal was to stay clear of you, keep my distance."

"And now your not 'keeping your distance'?" Olmstead asked. "Why tell me this now? You obviously have a problem with Fletcher and myself. Why not just leave the program?"

"You think me a coward," he said evenly. "I am not a coward, Captain. I do not run in the face of the enemy. Six months ago you were the enemy and I did not run. I blew your starboard engine to pieces. I could have finished you off, but chose not to. I let you live, Captain. You owe me."

"I owe you?" Olmstead said incredulously.

"You fired on me with the intent of killing me in an engagement I did not start. I wounded your aircraft and chose to let you live. You owe me your life."

"You think so?" Olmstead said. "Just what do you want?"

"An apology."

"For what?"

"For calling me a coward," Gurevich said, holding up a small postage stamp-sized, blackened circuit card. "Back in Tangistan I overheard you tell Cahill I was a coward as you came out of Ops."

"What's this?" Olmstead said taking the card from Gurevich.

"It is an input card from my Missile Interface Unit," he replied. "It overheated due to lack of cooling air as a result of a ducting obstruction in the cooling system. You can check with my crew chief if you like."

"Okay, so you really had a malfunction, so what? You're not a coward? Is that it?"

"Not quite, Captain," Gurevich said. "I do want your apology, but I owe one as well. I said in the debriefing that flying unarmed into an SA-6 threat ring was suicide. That is true, but it is equally true I could have taken that risk to take the heat off you and the others and it never occurred to me to do so. I admit this freely. When my MIU malfunctioned, my only thought was I was out of the game until I fixed the problem. It really never occurred to me to act as a target to try and draw off fire on the others. For that I apologize. I should have been thinking that way. It's not natural for me to be conservative or careful in the airplane. I'm usually a risk-taker, often to my own detriment. I think this time it did not occur to me to risk my life for you because subconsciously I knew you all hated me. I know I'm the cause of that hate, but I want to change all that. I cannot stay on this team under the present circumstances, so I have to change them."

"How?" Olmstead asked suspiciously.

"Part of that change is my calling you here tonight. I had to tell you my dark secret. I had to be honest with you. Captain, I do not wish to leave the team. I apologize for my behavior and I promise I will be an easier man to get along with."

"That will mean closer contact with Fletcher, you know," Olmstead said.

"Yes, I know. I will bear that burden," Gurevich said. "Can you accept my apology?"

Olmstead considered what he'd said. It was true. His wing leader had placed Gurevich in an awkward position and if Olmstead were in his place, he'd have defended himself just as vigorously. It was definitely out of character for him to be apologizing about anything. Maybe there was more to Gurevich than he'd originally thought.

"One more thing you need to promise: you have to be there when we need you," he said. "I'm willing to give you a chance, but this is life or death. You just be there when I need you and I'll be there for you. I'll remember you tried to kill me once. You screw me over out there again and I'll return the favor. Got it?" Gurevich nodded solemnly.

"I apologize for calling you a coward, Major," Olmstead said.

"Please, call me Sergei. Do you think I should tell Captain Fletcher what I told you?" he asked with enthusiasm, extending his hand.

Olmstead gripped his hand firmly and smiled. "Absolutely not."

CENTRAL INTELLIGENCE AGENCY
LANGLEY, VIRGINIA

"Sir, you have a minute?" Special Agent Scott Pritkin asked, poking his head in his boss's office.

"Sure. What you got?" Bill Smith asked, gesturing for the younger man to enter.

The junior agent shook his head. "Probably nothing, sir, but this did strike me as out of the ordinary," he said.

Pritkin was a liaison that worked daily with new intelligence gathered from foreign sources, agencies, etc. These sources covered a great deal of the world in nearly every theatre of interest. The tidbit that got his attention today was from Russia. Ten years ago that would have been a prized piece of intelligence, today it was akin to discovering the Japanese are building a new surface to air missile. So what. Still this nagged at him.

"Well, sir, I received this from MI-5 this morning," he said. "They have a agent in Turkey who got this from a source inside the Russian Army. It appears that Ivan is inoculating his Special Forces troops for Anthrax..."

"Nothing surprising there, Scotty," Smith interjected. "We've done the same thing."

"Yes, sir, but there is more to it," he continued. "They were also inoculating for Small Pox."

"Huh," the senior agent said, sitting back in his leather chair. He drummed a pencil on the tabletop as he thought. "I guess Ivan could just be nervous about bio-terrorism. Hell, he's nervous about everything else."

"I know we're gearing up production of Small Pox vaccine over here in case we get a bio-attack," the young man said, "but I always assumed the terrorist wouldn't risk unleashing the virus in their own back yard. I mean we can get the vaccine. Small Pox would wipe out most of that part of the world."

"Russia obviously thinks someone might let it loose over there," Smith mused. "Is it just his special forces getting the shots?"

"For now, but the source says it will extend to all military personnel eventually," he replied. "However, troops on the southern border will get the serum first. That tells me he might be expecting something to happen."

The older agent was concerned. *What if Russia knew something they didn't. We got a hell of a lot of troops stationed over there right now*, he thought.

"Is there any way to get this information through open channels?" he asked. "I want you to look into this, Scotty. I want you to find the same information in an open source. We don't want to blow anybody's cover, but we may need to confront Russia on this. If they are inoculating for small pox they must think someone over there's a hot threat. We need to know who that someone is."

"Yes, sir," the young agent said. "I'll get right on it, sir."

"Kid," Smith called as the young agent was leaving. "You were right to bring that to me. Now find out what Ivan is up to."

Pritkin smiled and nodded.

KERESHNOV AIRBASE

It was four in the afternoon on the Russian air base when the word came down. It was literally one word, with a reference time, and was sent directly to General Kavinsky's office. A sweaty and nervous looking young sergeant from the cryptography section consulted the decode document. It decoded to one word: Fallout.

Kavinsky grabbed the message from the out of breath sergeant, dismissed him and slammed the door behind him. He opened his wall safe and produced the document given to him by Victor Komiskov in the strictest confidence. He sat down behind his desk and pulled his gold-rimmed spectacles from their well-worn case. Perching the glasses on the end of his nose he opened the decode document. Working through a series of tables he was able to cross-reference the meaning of the word. It was the execution order he'd been waiting for. He sent for his aid who in turn was sent to roust Tanner out of bed. Five minutes later the American came rushing into his office.

"It's here?" he asked with excitement, as he slammed the door behind him.

"Da," Kavinsky said, handing Tanner the sheaf of paper. "It is confirmed. The code is Fallout."

Tanner read over the order quickly then went back and read it again, this time savoring the word he'd long to read. Then he noticed the reference time, upon which all mission timing was dictated. He did the math in his head.

"Whoa, this is for tonight," he gasped, looking down at his watch…4:00 PM. He converted the Zulu times from the orders to local time, did some quick mathematical gymnastics and derived a 10:00 PM local launch time.

"Holy shit, we launch in six hours!" he exclaimed. "The transport is due in four hours!"

"Da," Kavinsky said. "I had my aid wake up your young lieutenant. He should be on his way to mission planning."

"I better get over there," Tanner said.

Kavinsky handed Tanner the orders. "I'll send my aid over to help them pack up. I have contacted my maintenance officer and they should be starting the final pre-flights within the hour."

"Roger," Tanner said, turning for the door. The six aircraft had been configured with weapons and pre-flighted daily. They were kept in an obscure and abandoned hangar at the far end of the field.

"George," Kavinsky said as Tanner reached the door. "Does *your* Air Force do everything in such a chaotic manner?"

Tanner gave him a thumbs up. "As Irwin Rommel once said, 'War is chaos and the US military practices it on a daily basis'."

On his way to mission planning he stopped off at Olmstead's room. He pounded on the door. For a moment he heard nothing, then a thump and a loud curse as someone made their way to the door. The doorknob turned slowly then the door swung open to reveal a giant of a Texan staring down at him through bleary eyes. For a second there was no recognition, then it hit and his eyes grew wide.

"Sir," Cowboy stammered. "Yes, sir. Sorry to take so long, sir..."

"It's alright, Captain," Tanner said, "just shut the hell up and listen. We have a deployment order. Wake up your buds, get a quick shower, and pack your gear. I'll send a bus by to get you guys in an hour. You have that long to get ready..."

"Sir, I can be ready in fifteen minutes..."

"No, you'd just be in the way over there. Intel's not ready for you and it doesn't help if you're looking over his shoulder asking dumb ass questions. You have an hour and, oh, Cowboy, do shower, okay? That basement is smelly enough as it is. Now get moving. You launch in less than six hours. "

"Yes, sir," he said as smartly as a man can while standing in his underwear.

He woke Olmstead, threw on some sweat pants and ran around the corner to pound on Fletcher and Romano's door. An equally bleary-eyed Fletcher opened the door angrily.

"What the hell you want?" he demanded.

"Wake up, Pard, we got orders to deploy. We leave in less than six hours," Cowboy said.

"No shit?"

"Tanner himself came by. We got an hour to shit, shower and shave and pack our gear. He'll send a bus over to get us."

"Hot damn!" Fletcher said, closing the door. "Bear, get your ass up, man. The balloon is going up," he yelled into the next room. There was no answer.

"Bear! Romano! Get your ass up," he yelled again, jamming a toothbrush into his mouth.

There was no response from the next room. Oh, no. Please dear God let him be in there, he prayed as he crossed the floor. He turned the corner.

"Damn!" he yelled in rage.

Olmstead was just stepping into the shower when there came a beating on the door. Cowboy opened it and a panicked Fletcher stormed in. Cowboy knew he was panicked at first glance. Usually Fletcher remembers to put on some pants before going outside. He was standing there in his skivvies, eyes wide.

"He's gone," he said. "He's missing."

"Who is?" Cowboy asked.

"Romano. He's not in the room," Fletcher cried.

"Now just relax, pard. Maybe he just stepped out for a few minutes to get some air."

"In broad daylight? Even he's not that stupid," Fletcher insisted. "Unless..."

"Unless what."

Fletcher slammed his fist into his palm. "That son of a bitch! I told him to forget about it. Now he's gone and done it!"

"Who's done what?" Olmstead said, stepping out of the shower, a towel around his waist.

"Romano's missing."

"Missing?" Olmstead said, puzzled.

"The little bastard snuck out to get laid," Fletcher said.

"No way. He wouldn't be that stupid..."

"Well, maybe to get laid..." Cowboy said, with a wry expression. Olmstead and Fletcher both looked at him.

"You know something, Cowboy?" Fletcher said, moving closer to the taller Texan.

"Spill it."

The Texan looked sheepish. "I don't even know if this is what's happening, but Bear told me Dobie was going to fix him up with this babe over in the comm shop. I thought he was just bullshitting, you know. I didn't think he'd pull this. If anything I expected him to bring her here."

"He's out there in the middle of the fucking day," Olmstead said angrily. "That stupid son of a bitch. And we have a bus picking us up in fifty minutes!"

"We have to find him," Fletcher said. "Fast."

"Does the woman live on base?" Olmstead asked.

"I dunno, I think so," Cowboy said.

"We gotta find Dobie. That's our only chance," Fletch said.

They called his room and got no answer. There ensued a fervent debate about the wisdom of three Americans running around in broad daylight on a

Russian airbase looking for some woman's quarters, a woman whose name they didn't even know. They decided it would be equally bad form to just saunter into the Russian comm shop and ask. They were left with only one other option, a last resort.

"Gurevich?" Fletcher asked, with a raised eyebrow.

Olmstead cringed, closed his eyes and nodded. "Gurevich."

He picked up on the first ring. He was in the middle of packing himself. To say he was surprised to hear from the Americans was an understatement. He listened quietly while Fletcher laid out their problem. He said he didn't know where Dobie was but he would take care of the matter. He hung up. No smart-ass comments. No wry remarks about American fools. All he said was "I'll take care of the matter."

They really didn't know what else to do but continue packing and hope Gurevich would come through, or Bear would show up. All the while he was getting dressed, though, Olmstead was running the scenario through his mind. The scenario where he had to explain to Tanner that they had lost Romano, that Romano went off in broad daylight to get laid, against orders. Olmstead was pissed. He and Fletcher were essentially equals, but he took a lot of the team's problems on his own shoulders. If Tanner had an issue with the team he went to Olmstead. He really was the unofficial ops officer for the deployment. Now Tanner would hold him responsible for this. Damn that little shit!

About twenty minutes later there was a knock on the door. Olmstead opened it to find Romano standing there looking sheepish, Gurevich standing behind him. Olmstead looked past him and saw Dobrinsky sitting in Gurevich's staff car, looking equally as sheepish. It seems the Major took care of the matter, quickly and efficiently.

"I believe you lost a pilot?" Gurevich said with a smile.

Olmstead rolled his eyes and glared at Romano who cringed.

"Get to your room, clean up, and pack your gear. You have fifteen minutes. Move," he said, the statement clearly a command. Romano judged it a good career move to simply follow the order.

Olmstead reached out and shook Gurevich's hand. "Thank you, Sergei. You are certainly a man that can get things done. You've saved our butts on this one."

"As you say, no problem. Your friend does not show the best judgement, but he is a long way from home and only human, yes?"

"I guess. Dobrinsky too?" Olmstead asked.

"Da, but he should know better. Perhaps they could not help themselves."

"What do you mean?"

"Russian women," he said smiling broadly. "Who can resists Russian women?"

Olmstead raised an eyebrow. "Between me and you, Sergei," he said, leaning close. "They worth it?"

"Da," he said with a sly smile as he turned away.

The bus pulled up outside exactly on the hour. The flyers lugged their gear out of the rooms and stowed it at the back of the bus. The ride over to mission planning was quiet, each man deep in his own thoughts. They knew within a day or so they would be in combat. That was a sobering thought. The mission into Kumar had come up suddenly and there was no time to reflect on the dangers. Now they had plenty of time, the last month even, to contemplate what they were about to do.

Sutherland had mission packages laid out for each pilot and the route of flight displayed on an overhead projector. The men took their seats, the Russian pilots already sitting at the end of the row. Tanner came in and the room was called to attention.

"Seats," Tanner said as he stepped up behind the briefing lectern. Kavinsky took a seat at the back of the briefing room. "Gentlemen, we will be returning to Stovacore Air Base this very evening. Your scheduled take-off will be at 10:00 PM local time. The transport plane will carry your maintenance crews, General Kavinsky, the lieutenant, and myself. We will leave two hours before you and land about thirty minutes before you arrive. Mission timing calls for a launch 24 hours after you touch down in Tangistan. Tonight is just a ferry mission. Don't do anything stupid. If your aircraft has a problem get it fixed here. You stand a much better shot at a quick fix here than you do down there. We may even be able to swap aircraft. So don't take any problem you can't live with. Lieutenant Sutherland will brief you on the route, clearances and weather. I have nothing further. Good luck and see you in Tangistan."

Tanner finished speaking then left. He spent the next several hours personally checking the aircraft, weapons, air traffic control clearances and speaking with Michaels back in Washington. Kavinsky left with him and drove him around the base, clearing the way of any Russian problems in a loud, abrasive bark of commands.

Sutherland briefed them on the route and the weather they could expect. The route was the reverse of what they flew earlier and the weather was expected to be good for departure and arrival with scattered thunderstorms in route. The storms were scattered far enough apart that they would be easy to pick through and would cause no delay.

The only aspect of the mission that was a tad complex was the flight-plan itself. They would take off on a flight plan calling for a round robin flight back to the base. As they approached the turn back point they would tell ATC they were going "due regard" and leaving their flight plan open.

ATC facilities hate to hear the phrase "due regard". It means that the military assumes responsibility for clearing itself of all traffic conflicts. They would no longer be under ATC control and had to ensure they were separated from civilian traffic. The plan called for Gurevich to call in the "due regard" and Kavinsky to have their flight plans closed an hour later, meaning they have returned to base. Meanwhile they would continue on for a low level penetration into Tangistan, final destination Stovacore Air Base.

Sutherland gave them the latest intelligence briefing.

"The current situation is quiet throughout the region, unusually quiet even, which is probably why we are deploying now. Your route of flight to Tangistan has no significant threats you need to concern yourself with.

"As far as you target goes, there is no appreciable air activity in the North of Sandor. There was a flight of Tomcats in the region this morning, but we believe they were transiting the area and not really patrolling it. The signal intelligence for the target area shows both an SA-6 and an SA-10 were brought up yesterday afternoon for ten minutes each. We don't consider this unusual as those radars come up every week at that time. It is generally thought this is a regularly scheduled part of the missiles' preventative maintenance. They were also operating independent of any early warning systems. There was no coordination with other parts of the IAD. There has also been no missile radar activity at night for three months. They seem to be content on letting the early warning elements of the IAD warn them if anybody's coming.

"Aside from the missile threats, the AAA in the area is mostly optical. Satellite photos show a ZSU-23-4 parked nearby, but we've received no emissions from its radar at all. The radar may be inoperative and they may be relying on optics to aim it. More than likely they just don't consider it a priority to fix the radar with the SA-10 sitting nearby.

"There has been an increased amount of construction activity at the site in the last week, though. It has been observed only in the daytime, but there are nearly twice as many cars and trucks in the parking lot as there was a few weeks ago. We believe they are finishing up the work and are nearly ready to begin fuel loading."

"It's critical to take this plant out before they load the fuel," Tanner cut in. "Once the fuel is in place, the high pressure cooling systems will be activated and your gonna have tons of radioactive water flowing through the pipes and around the core. This thing gets its water from a nearby river and returns the secondary steam condensate back into that river. That water is not radioactive, but we put a few big holes in the reactor we'll not only cause a melt down, we'll probably irradiate that river for the next ten thousand years. That kind of fiasco would kill thousands, which is probably why we're being sent in right now. The timing is good because the US attention is on the Balkans, but it's also a matter of taking this thing out before they load the fuel and go online, which may be any day."

With the briefing complete the pilots ate a quick meal of sandwiches, gathered their mission materials and headed out to their jets, two of the MiGs recently flown in as replacements for the two lost in the first mission. It was dusk outside and the glow on the horizon still illuminated the flight line. The hangar doors were still closed, their warbirds still hidden from prying eyes. They ran the checklist, step by step. There were no surprises and each aircraft was deemed ready to fly. With the checklist held at "Engine Start" they climbed down from their aircraft and met near a corner door of the hangar. They still had thirty minutes until their engine start time.

They stepped out into the cool, crisp night air, the sun down for an hour by now. The Americans sat down on a row of benches along the wall. Dobie stretched out on the tarmac itself, while Gurevich leaned against the hangar wall. The two Russians each fired up a cigarette and Fletcher took one when offered.

"Beautiful night," Olmstead commented.

"This is my favorite time of year back home," Gurevich commented wistfully.

"Where is home?" Cowboy asked.

"St Petersburg," he said, smoke flowing out of his mouth as he said the word.

"Dobie, where you from?" Romano asked.

"I am from a village forty kilometers south of Omsk."

"Home," Fletcher said, the cigarette dangling from his lips. "Everybody loves home. Doesn't matter where home is. I knew a guy from some god-awful place in North Dakota, winds 50 miles an hour all the time, wind chills of a hundred below. Where did he want to go after the Air Force? Home."

"Yeah, I miss my Mamma somethin fierce," Cowboy admitted. "I'm all she's got in the world and she ain't seen or heard from me in months. I told her I'd be away for awhile, but I know this is hard on her."

"God, you need a woman," Romano sighed.

"That's the key, right there," Olmstead said, with a yawn. "Home is great if you have somebody back there to return to. If you don't, it's just a place, nothing more."

"Maybe a place full of memories," Romano said.

"Memories are just that," Olmstead snorted. "Images. You can't live in the past. The moment you start to live in the past the sooner you begin to die."

"That's profound," Fletcher said with sarcasm.

"It's true," Gurevich said quietly. "You have to adapt. Sometimes the past can kill you if you let it."

There was no reply to that.

At fifteen minutes until take-off the crew chiefs rolled open the huge hangar doors. The aircraft were parked six abreast. In an almost Thunderbird-like unison the pilots each climbed up into their cockpits and began strapping in. Soon the whine of turbines filled the hangar as they spooled up. Then came the roar of jet engines as fuel and fire were entered into the formula. Electronic systems came alive at their fingertips as each MiG-41 awoke from its long nap and began to warm up. Sensors opened their virtual eyes and power poured off each generator in proper voltages and frequency. Computers began crunching bytes and mission data was entered into the navigation system, where the small inertial navigators were spinning up to their operating speed of 100,000 RPMs. Across the hangar and across the boards there was not a warning light illuminated, nothing to indicate any problem real or potential. The MiGs and their operators were happy with each other and ready to meld into one synergistic entity, at least for the next few hours.

With flashlights fanning the air the crew chiefs directed each aircraft through the open hangar door and into line in trail formation, with Gurevich in the lead as planned. As they taxied by each crew chief popped to attention and rendered a salute to the pilot, who returned the age old custom and gave one of their own, a thumbs up.

The line of MiGs moved off into the night across the darkened ramp, Gurevich talking to Ground Control and getting their clearance. They taxied to the hammerhead at the far south end of the base and pulled to one side in echelon formation to run their final checks. They pulled over to allow other aircraft to taxi by them, but there were no other flights scheduled this late at night. Each man ran his last pre-take-off checklist. The IRST was up in each cockpit, turning the darkness outside to daytime. They had followed Dobie's procedure and it had worked as advertised.

Finally they were ready and Gurevich got clearance for the formation departure. They pulled out on the runway in line astern and one by one pushed the power up, about 6 seconds between aircraft. Gurevich's aircraft accelerated slowly at first then faster, diamond shock waves from his afterburner visible in the thirty feet of fire coming from his burner cans. Olmstead counted to six and released his own brakes, simultaneously pushing his throttles past MRT and into burner. One by one they took to the skies, each leaving their burners on slightly longer than the one before to assist in the join up.

They leveled at 8000 meters and slid out into a loose right echelon formation, Gurevich setting the formation speed at 480 knots true airspeed. Each wingman set his throttles accordingly to stay on his wing. The flight was uneventful. They dodged a thunderstorm that had the audacity to challenge them, but didn't deviate more than a few miles from course. When they reached their turn around point on the flight plan, Gurevich called up ATC with the due regard message.

"Razor 21 flight going due regard at this time. Please leave our flight plan open," he called.

They had just passed over the Russian border and were expected to turn back for base soon. The Russian controller was adamant about their turning back before they went due regard.

"Negative," Gurevich had said firmly. "We will be turning back shortly, but we are due regard at this time. Keep our flight plan open. Razor Flight push Gold." With that they switched radio frequencies and left the Russian controller behind, fuming.

"Razor Flight, Lead on Gold, begin descent, coming right," Gurevich said.

They descended and turned back to the right to perform a right 270-degree turn, rolling out to the south. The turn was slow and by the time they rolled past their return heading they were below Russian civil radar coverage. All the Russian controller saw was the formation turn back and descend, as they were expected to do. What he didn't see was the continued turn and the dive to TFR altitudes. The deception here had worked. They were now at low level, spaced 300 meters apart, 420 knots indicated airspeed at 300 feet terrain following. They had planned forty minutes on the deck before they entered the pattern at Stovacore and sure enough, forty minutes later a familiar shape appeared on the edge of the radar scope, the MiG-41 synthetic aperture radar outlining clearly the single short runway and base ops complex. As they got closer the complex began to come to luminescent life on the IRST as it detected the heat from the building and vehicles now scurrying about.

"Satan's Lair, Razor Flight inbound for the full stop," Gurevich said. It was generally agreed that Stovacore Air Base was a hellhole and they could think of no better call sign for the command post. Besides the Sandoris called America the Great Satan. Soon they would think hell was raining on them.

"Razor Flight, Satan's Lair, cleared to land, your discretion. Welcome to hell boys," Tanner said from the abandoned and crumbling base ops.

Sutherland had already begun working up the mission while winging across Southwest Russia on the transport plane. He laid charts out on the top of a power cart and worked up the basic route of flight. The known threats in Sandor were kept on a database in his laptop and updated regularly. He used a computer program that searched that database then utilizing a sophisticated algorithm would generate a route of flight that would minimize the risks of detection and engagement by enemy forces. He ran the program three times and it generated three different, but very close flight plans. Satisfied he picked the one he thought best and sent the data to a new mission file which, when he landed and set up their printer, would print out kneeboard size charts with threat rings, waypoints, headings, timing and speeds. The mission planning in the field was nearly automatic, and had to be as there were not vast resources available, nor a lot of time to develop options manually.

The pilots were told the scheduled briefing and take-off times and told to get some food and rest. Most particularly they were told to stay the hell out of Sutherland's hair until briefing time. He had a lot to do in the next twenty-four hours and didn't need a bunch of pilots hanging around asking dumb questions.

STOVACORE AIRBASE, TANGISTAN

Olmstead awoke an hour early. He lay there for a few minutes on his Russian Army issue cot and tried to go back to sleep, to will himself to sleep. He wanted to be as fresh as possible for the mission tonight, but he was too excited to sleep. Besides now that he was awake he could hear every little noise of the base around him gearing up to go to war. In the distance he could hear men yelling, a vehicle engine revving and what sounded like tools being dropped from waist high. They put the pilot's tent as far from the flightline as possible, but it was no use. Soon he heard the whine of a distant turbine spinning up as the maintainers started up an air cart. He could also hear a muffled pok-pok-pok sound of an electrical supply cart running. He got up, threw on his flight suit and stepped out of the tent, leaving his buddies to continue their slumber.

As he stepped outside he saw Fletcher was already up as well. He was sitting on the ground leaning back against the trunk of a tall tree, a cigarette dangling from his lips. Fletcher looked over and saw Olmstead and beckoned him over.

"Woke up about a half hour ago and couldn't get back to sleep," he said.

"Same here," Olmstead said, sitting down opposite him and leaning back against the scraggly tree. "You suppose we're getting old, Fletch. When I was younger I had no trouble sleeping 12 hours straight."

"I don't know about you, but I'm definitely getting older. This deployment has aged me about two years and it's not over yet."

The sun was just starting to set in the West, the golden-red orb slowly letting down, the shadows it casts growing long. It was beautiful, but somehow out of place here at this time and this place. Lovers somewhere were watching this same sunset. Little children were watching it go down and being called home for dinner. Old men were glancing up at the sunset and wondering if it would be their last. The world was moving along and the sun rose and fell over it. But here in this corner of the world, men were going to war. It was a beautiful sunset, but the only men to enjoy it were Olmstead and Fletcher, the rest of the scurrying men out on the tarmac glanced up and cursed that soon they would lose their light to work by.

Nightfall also meant a launch coming up they had to be ready for. They willed the sun to hold its position or slow its fall to give them more time, but the sun doesn't bow to the will of mortal men and it fell over the horizon as it has done everyday since the beginning of time. No one said it, but both Olmstead and Fletcher were wondering if it would be their last sunset.

"So what do think?" Olmstead asked.

Fletcher shrugged. "I just hope it's worth it. I mean that assassination attempt was a fiasco. I came out here to make a difference, not to just be another target in some raghead shooting gallery."

"Yeah," Olmstead agreed. "This is a big one, though. To be honest this is the one that made me want to come in the first place. The Sandori Ayatollahs getting their hands on nukes scares the shit out of me."

"They don't have the self-preservation instinct the Russians had."

"Exactly. Those bastards will believe Allah wants them to nuke the Great Satan even if it means their own destruction."

"Or they'll just resort to nuclear terrorism," Fletcher said. "Smuggle a nuke into the country and one day Los Angeles just disappears."

Olmstead nodded.

"You do know it's a losing battle, though. Right?" Fletcher asked.

"What do you mean?"

"I mean we can keep them from getting a nuke today, but not forever and we can't keep all the bad guys from getting them," Fletcher said grimly. "I mean for Christ's sake the A-bomb was invented before color TV. Thermonuclear technology is very complex, but your basic dirty little A-bomb isn't. That's what I fear the most, the little backpack 10 kiloton A-bomb, not the big mega-ton strategic warhead. And all it takes to make one is the uranium or plutonium that they can get from a commercial reactor, like our target. But the bottom line is you can't keep them all from getting the bomb."

Olmstead took a deep breath and let it out slowly. "I'm not trying to keep them all from getting the bomb. Today I'm dealing with Sandor. Tomorrow is another day."

"Take'em one at a time, then?" Fletcher asked with a smile.

"Set'em up and I'll knock'em down. One at a time, fuckin-ay."

Sutherland had been a blur of motion ever since they landed. Now he had a moment to relax. The mission briefing was not scheduled to start for another fifteen minutes and the mission materials, the charts, comm plan, threat briefing, were all complete. All that was left was to just go over the plan one last time then brief the pilots. Normally an intel/planning team wouldn't even have a minute to relax, but today he was following a plan that had been laid out for over a month. Tanner wandered in and began looking over the charts.

"Pretty much the way we figured it, sir," Sutherland commented to the general.

He nodded in agreement. "Yeah, everything's just like we figured except for the F-14 thing the other night."

"Yeah," Sutherland agreed. "That's got me a little worried."

The night before an Air Force RC-135 patrolling somewhere in the Sandori border detected an AWG-9 radar coming from Northern Sandor. The AWG-9 radar can be found in only one airplane: the Grumman F-14 Tomcat, the US Navy's front line fighter for nearly twenty-five years. The Sandoris bought twenty-four Tomcats back in the 70's when relations were warm with the US. Ever since the Islamic Fundamentalists came to power in 1979 the spare parts line was cut off for these aircraft. The Sandoris had to resort to cannibalizing half their aircraft in order to keep the other half flying. The bad news was the AWG-9 radar was a damn good radar with a very long range. The Sandoris had been using the F-14s not so much as a fighter but as a mini-AWACs, utilizing their superior radars. The other bad news was they still had about fifty AIM-54 Phoenix missiles purchased from the US when they bought the Tomcats.

The Phoenix was the first true fire and forget, active homing missile with an extremely long range, better than 80 nautical miles. Intelligence reports said the missiles were poorly maintained, well past their service life. If they were still in service they would probably malfunction. Probably. This was all based on the assumption that the Sandoris couldn't properly maintain or repair the missiles.

What really bothered Sutherland, though, was the fact the F-14s were patrolling at night. That in itself was cause for concern. The Sandoris did not usually operate at night but suddenly they launch a two-ship of Tomcats? The Tomcats had hung out for two hours and effectively covered the whole Northwestern half of the Sandor/Kumar border. If the MiGs had tried to penetrate Sandori airspace last night it would have been unlikely they would have escaped detection and possibly engagement. If they were up again tonight the MiGs would no doubt have to deal with them and maybe their Phoenix missiles.

"I think it was a fluke, Todd," Tanner said confidently. "The Sandoris do not have a history of night ops. They might be training to develop that capability, but I think it was just that, a training sortie. Besides, even if they are patrolling at night, they don't have the night intercept experience our boys have."

"You might be right, but remember it doesn't take a rocket scientist or a Chuck Yeager to lock up a target with the AWG-9 and punch off a missile from eighty miles," he said. "Maybe they are expecting a Kumari response to our little jaunt last week."

"Maybe," Tanner admitted. "You think the intel on the AIM-54s is wrong?"

"I don't know, sir, but we have to assume they are operational. We can't let our guys go in there blind. If they are operational, they are a real threat."

"You think the jamming packages on the MiG can take down the AWG-9?"

"Not a chance," he said. "It might beat the missile itself, but the AWG-9 is a very powerful radar. Noise jamming's gonna be useless, especially at 100 miles."

"False target jamming? Range gate pull-off?" he asked.

"Maybe," he said. "Maybe not. The Phoenix is an old missile. I just don't know how effective the MiG's jamming is going to be. Major Gurevich might know."

"Well I'm sure he'll be willing to share his opinion," Tanner said, smiling. "Todd, I have to run over to the comm shack. I'll be back in ten minutes. Don't start without me."

"Of course, sir," Sutherland said, thinking to himself how redundant that order was.

Ten minutes later the pilots filed into the briefing room and took their seats. Tanner and Kavinsky came in together behind them and Sutherland called the room to attention.

"Seats," Tanner said, as he and Kavinsky took their own seats. He motioned to Sutherland. "Go, Lieutenant."

Sutherland cleared his throat and began the briefing. As spoke he passed out the mission materials to each pilot, charts, target data, flight plan, comm card and the rest.

"The weather is expected to be clear and a million all the way to the target and back," he said, passing around a satellite photo of the region. "The route of flight is basically the same as we practiced in the sim, except for this little jog right here. I had to route you a little to the south here because of an Army unit deployed in this valley for a training exercise. You'll go up the next valley over. You'll have GPS link up, but make damn sure you don't go up that valley by mistake. That Army unit carries with it a couple ZSUs and lots of MANPADs, probably SA-7 and SA-14s."

Sutherland finished briefing the route of flight then began the target study. He passed around satellite imagery of the reactor complex taken a week earlier, showing several construction vehicles unloading heavy equipment. The target's defenses were the SA-10 covering the approach and the SA-6 and ZSU-23-4 in the point defense role. The ZSU's radar was confirmed to be inoperative, and the big rapid-fire gun could only be aimed optically. They had no plan to test that, though, the weapons consisting of standoff laser-guided missiles fired from over 6 miles away, well out of AAA range.

The weapon of the day was the AS-22 laser-guided missile with a 500 kg warhead. This missile was a precision-guided supersonic needle of high explosive. Fletcher, the primary striker, would carry of two of them. Their thousand pound warheads would make short work of the reactor complex. One lesson learned over Kumar was not to skimp on defense. This time Olmstead and Gurevich, in the primary SEAD mission, were carrying two HARMs apiece, with 2 AA-12's on the outboard pylons. Romano and Dobrinsky, acting as CAP, were carrying two AA-12s, two AA-10Fs and two AA-11s. Fletcher would carry two AS-22s and two AA-12s. He would be the primary strike aircraft. Cowboy would have a mixed load of two AA-12s, one ARM and one AS-22, as a backup for everyone. They would all be carrying AA-11s on their wingtips.

Finally it was time to break the bad news about the F-14s. Sutherland briefed them on the Tomcat flights the night before. They sat in silence, impassive, and listened. He had expected some kind of reaction, apprehension maybe.

"Lieutenant, is their any reason to believe these flights are part of a new Sandori doctrine for night operations or was this just happenstance?" Fletcher asked.

"No sir, we have no reason to believe the Sandoris have developed night intercept capability, however this could be the beginning of training for such a capability," he said.

"You mean those guys were just out training the other night?" Romano asked.

"Probably," Sutherland said. "The Sandoris do keep proficient at night instrument flying, but no actual night combat training. The thing that made these flights unusual was the patrol-like nature of them. The Tomcats took off from a base in Central Sandor, flew northwest a hundred miles, and set up a counter-rotating search pattern, similar to what we fly. We have documented reports from the Sandor/Kumar War that the Sandoris used the F-14s in a mini-AWACS role, but they never flew at night."

"So this isn't a trend?" Fletcher asked.

"Well, shit, if we run into them tonight, I'd call that a trend," Romano snorted.

They spent next ten minutes discussing their capabilities against the F-14. The plan was simple. If they detected the F-14s they'd either have to run or engage them. The problem was the Tomcats AIM-54 has a range about twice that of the AA-12. They'd have to evade or spoof a couple of Phoenix shots before they could put the Adders on them.

"More than likely the Tomcats will pickle off their Phoenix missiles at max range, then bolt for home. They won't want to risk those planes, especially against a MiG in close. They know and respect the AA-11. Their MiGs carry them and they know the Kumaris have them too. If a Sandori MiG detects you they might be willing to merge and take the risk. They won't risk the F-14s, though."

Romano shook his head. "It's the same damn thing as that Foxbat in Kumar. All these bastards have longer ranged missiles than us and they shoot and scoot," he complained.

"True, but their missiles aren't that good," Cowboy said.

"Ask Fletch how good they are," Romano said, jabbing a thumb in Fletcher's direction.

"Lucky shot," Fletcher grumbled.

"What about our jamming package?" Olmstead asked.

"Why don't we ask the Major," Tanner said indicating Gurevich, who like Dobrinsky had been listening intently, but remaining silent.

Gurevich cleared his throat. "The Gardenyia onboard jammer is programmed against the AWG-9 as well as the missile radar itself. We designed it to jam both radars, but we were only guessing as to how effective it would be. We knew we couldn't generate the power to take down the AWG-9, but we believed we could cause it and the missile both to lock onto false targets generated by the jammer. We can induce errors in both azimuth and range by an advanced algorithm that modulates our jamming. I believe your country has already developed electronic-counter-counter measures to defeat our false targets, but the Sandoris may not have. I believe we can at least pull the missile radars off onto false targets."

"Odds of beating the missiles?" Tanner asked, getting right to the point.

Gurevich cocked his head in thought as he considered the question. "Fifty-fifty?" he said with a shrug.

Tanner rolled his eyes.

"So what is the plan?" Olmstead asked impatiently. "We engage them and hope we can beat the missiles or bug out?"

"I say we engage them," Fletcher said. "We can beat the Phoenix, with or without the ECM."

"Did you hear what Sutherland said?" Romano asked tersely. "We won't get the chance. They'll never get within our missile range. They'll be running for home as soon as they pickle off their missiles and calling their buddies for help."

"For all the good it will do," Fletcher snapped.

"Look, I agree we don't run for home if they show up. I say we put'em on the beam, let'em take a low PK shot and beat the missiles. Then we press ahead and bomb the shit out of that reactor. No sweat," Romano said confidently.

"Yeah, but if they're taking a shot then everybody will know we're coming. We lose the element of surprise," Olmstead said.

"They might know we're coming, but they won't know what our target is," Fletch said.

"We'll be out in the middle of nowhere," Romano said sarcastically. "They'll take a good freakin guess."

Tanner realized the briefing was breaking down into a debate, a debate they couldn't afford at the moment. He decided it was time to step in and make some decisions.

"Alright, alright. Quiet down," he commanded. "Lieutenant, I have a couple questions for you."

"Shoot, sir," Sutherland said.

"Okay. To the best of our knowledge, can we beat the AIM-54?"

"Yes, sir. The missile might be deceived by our jamming, but even if it's not the missile is designed to hit a non-maneuvering bomber. If they maneuver hard, put it on the beam, punch out chaff and stay at TFR, they have a good chance of beating it."

"Okay. Second question. If the Tomcats are out there, will they be able to pick us out of the ground clutter?'

"Yes, sir. That won't be a problem for the AWG-9."

"Last question. Even if they detect us, how good is their IADS? Can they warn the ground defenses at the reactor or scramble more fighters in time to matter?"

"Probably not, sir. The Sandori IADS is very good at transmitting targeting information to other airborne assets, but are lousy at integrating the land-based forces into the engagement. They might be able to alert their home base to scramble more fighters, but given the location of the target and the distance to the base, they really won't be a factor, even if they are sitting on alert waiting to launch, which they aren't. I'd be surprised if they had two more Tomcats even flyable, much less fueled and ready."

"I hope you aren't surprised, Lieutenant," Fletcher said grimly.

Tanner thought for a moment then made his decision.

"Okay, gentlemen, it's a go. We penetrate as planned. If you encounter the F-14s, try to evade them, if not possible and you get close enough, splash'em. Let'em take their shots, beat the missiles, and press. Anybody takes any frag damage from the missiles---that plane turns back. If more than one of you has to turn back, it's a mission abort. We're not going in there with our ass hanging out anymore than it already is. Got it?"

"Yes, sir," they said in unison.

"Okay, you guys got about an hour to get your shit together here and then head out to the jets," Tanner said. "I'm heading out there right now, to check on them personally. Lieutenant?"

"Yes, sir," Sutherland answered.

"You give them whatever they need, got it?"

"Yes, sir. I'll take care of them," he said, understanding the General's meaning.

Tanner knew that there was a lot to be worried about on this mission and the more information a pilot has the more confidant he will fly. The biggest fear is the unknown and that's the real enemy of the intelligence world. Sutherland knew this as well.

After forty minutes of study Olmstead stepped outside to get some fresh air. Fletcher was already there, smoking a cigarette.

"Those things are gonna kill you," Olmstead said.

"Don't you read your aerospace physiology? Smoking helps constrict your arteries, giving you higher blood pressure and increasing G-tolerance," Fletcher said, blowing smoke as he spoke.

"Humph," Olmstead grunted, sitting down on the concrete and leaning back against the building.

"Besides, I stand a better chance of dying of lead poisoning tonight than of cancer or high blood pressure."

"That's an old joke, pal," Olmstead complained. "That joke went out when they introduced copper jacketed ammo."

"We gonna bag a Tomcat tonight?" Fletcher asked casually, the cigarette dangling from the corner of his mouth.

"Probably never get a shot."

"I got a buddy who's a Marine Hornet pilot. He claims the Phoenix is worthless against a fighter."

"Yeah, well if he's a jarhead you have to take that with a grain of salt. I mean those guys are programmed to charge machine gun nests with bayonets. Besides, Hornets can't carry the Phoenix."

"I know that," Fletcher said, irritated. "But he plays with Tomcats all the time."

"You worried?"

"I'm a fighter pilot," Fletcher said flipping his cigarette away.

Olmstead stood, looked into Fletcher's ice-cold eyes for a moment. That said it all.

"Fuckin-ay, brother," he said.

The jets were fueled and ready when they arrived on the flightline. The crewchiefs were pulling the covers off the missile seeker heads and wiping off the canopies. The six MiGs glistened in the artificial light of the makeshift flightline, their deadly cargo drooping beneath their sturdy wings. Olmstead began his walk around and immediately noticed the Kumari flag on the twin vertical stabilizers. He paused for a moment, took a deep breath, and continued the walk around. He shook his head and marveled at the amazing turn his life had taken. A year ago he would have never dreamt he'd be flying a MiG into combat, much less one with Kumari markings. He finished the walk around and found everything copacetic.

He climbed the ladder into the cockpit and found it aglow with light. The crew chief had already applied power and his internal lighting was glowing red. He settled into the bloody light and began strapping in. A second later a crew chief appeared at the top of the ladder. He assisted Olmstead in donning his harness, parachute and seatbelt. Once he was strapped in the crew chief reached down and pulled the last safety pin and showed the red streamer to Olmstead who nodded as he tightened the chinstrap of his helmet.

He reached down and turned on the radio. He dialed up the correct strike frequency and looked up and to his right, down the row of MiGs. Every man was strapped in and going through his pre-engine start checks. He looked down at his watch. Thirty more seconds. He jumped back to his checklist and flipped two more switches then checked two more circuit breakers. Now is time.

"Arson Flight, check," he said.

"Two."

"Three."

"Four."

"Five."

"Six."

They answered in sequence in crisp, professional voices. There would be no more communications between aircraft unless there was a problem. By checking in, each man said he was in the green, ready to start engines. From no on everything would be done on timing. Engine start, taxi and take-off.

No talk, no risk of anyone hearing.

They started engines on time and began the arduous taxi out of parking and down the narrow taxiways to the south end of the runway. Once again Tanner was out there at the end directing the MiGs through the dangerous turn around and line up.

The time for take-off arrived and a single red flare was fired into the night sky. That was the signal for take-off. Olmstead stood on the brakes and eased his throttles forward into burner. He released the brakes and Gurevich moved into position behind him as he moved away down the runway. One by one they lined up, blue diamond shockwaves would form in the deafening roar of power and they would accelerate slowly down the runway. Olmstead was off the ground as Fletcher in the last ship made the turn to line up.

Fletcher could see Olmstead climb away from the ground, the light from the twin burners disappearing as Olmstead pulled his power back for the rejoin.

At last they were all airborne and Olmstead was leading them into a long arcing turn to the south, allowing his wingmen to cut him off in the turn and take position. As he rolled out on the proper heading Fletcher swung into position. Fletcher clicked the microphone switch three times and Olmstead knew the formation was assembled.

Olmstead set his airspeed at 420 knots at 600 feet agl, each man about a hundred feet in trail. They engaged their TFR systems and autopilots. Using Global Positioning Satellite data the nav systems kept them on course and in perfect trail. The pilots only had to massage the throttles to keep the proper spacing, each man keeping the plane in front centered on the IRST and using the laser ranger for distance.

It was a short fifteen minutes from the take-off to the Sandori border and they barely had time to accomplish all their pre-combat checks, oxygen, hydraulics, electrics, fuel, weapon arming, lights off, IRST set, etc. Soon the Sandori border would pass beneath them. At thirty miles out Olmstead commanded his TFR to 100 feet agl. The MiG nosed over and leveled off a scant 100 feet above the desert floor, racing by at 7 miles a minute. Each man brought his plane down to that pulse pounding altitude and prepared himself for combat. This was it.

The border raced by with nothing but a change in the latitude readout to indicate they were now in Sandor. The RWR gear showed some long-range acquisition radars, but the signals were weak and it would be impossible to track them from long range at 100 feet in any case. The curve of the earth would protect them from most of the radars. Only the very closest radars or an airborne interceptor would be able to see them at this altitude.

They cut across the northwest corner of Sandor and down the mountain, which provided excellent terrain radar masking from both sides of the border. They followed these mountains south until they funneled the screaming MiGs into Northeast Kumar. The mountain range extended well down into Kumar providing excellent cover from probing Kumari radars.

They drove to the southwest for about thirty miles and began to parallel the border, waiting for the turn East that would lead them into the heart of Northern Sandor. The RWR gear picked an AI threat at their three o'clock, a Slotback radar, not unlike their own, possible MiG-29. The signal was in search, but very weak. Soon it fell off the scope completely. A few moments later the RWR gear indicated an SA-3 Goa missile at their 12 O'clock, also in search and very weak. The SA-3 was a real threat, even at 100 feet, and Olmstead's pulse quickened. Then he realized the turn to the east was coming up in three miles and he let out a sigh o relief. The turn would take them away from the SA-3 and it wouldn't be a factor after all.

At the turn point he let the autopilot make the turn and selected ten degrees of bank. This was rather leisurely for a fighter, but it was pre-planned that way to provide as small a radar profile as possible and to limit the detectability of his TFR emissions. If he'd banked it up to ninety degrees his radar profile would have increased by a factor of about four and his TFR radar altimeter would have lost lock and the radar beam itself would have swept out over Central Kumar and Southern and Central Sandor while in the turn, possibly to be detected by a passive detection outpost. Surprise was a key element in this operation and it would do no good to give any listening station a signal to worry about. Both Sandor and Kumar utilized Soviet built Ramona passive detection systems and incorporate them into their respective integrated Air Defense Systems (IADS).

They rolled out on an easterly heading, Sandor dead ahead. At the pre-planned time he pushed his throttles up an inch and as he felt the power surge the airspeed needle crept upwards to 550 knots, the planned penetration airspeed. He felt more comfortable at this airspeed. He had more energy and therefore he had more maneuverability. Unfortunately he also noticed the needle creep upwards on the fuel flow gauge in conjunction with the speed increase. That was the penalty for speed.

The sensation of speed was now much greater as the raced across the desert floor at better than 9 miles a minute. The border was just ahead, twenty miles to go. At the ten mile point he heard 5 audible clicks on his radio, about a second apart, a silent check in. His team was ready.

The radio silence was a good plan, but they also knew that at some point they would have to communicate. They were running secure encrypted on their radios so there was no danger of anyone listening in, but any transmission at all on comm frequencies would be detected by a passive detection site and the strobe on their scope would lead them straight back to the MiGs. Radio silence was planned up until about twenty miles from the target if all went well. At that point it was reasoned there was little anyone could do to stop them anyway. Unfortunately they would have to talk earlier.

They crossed over the border and ducked down a valley running east/west, flying well below the ridgeline in a perfect military crest. As they popped out of the valley on the far side their RWR gear went off. An AI radar was up in search dead ahead. It was identified as an AWG-9. The Tomcats were out tonight after all.

It was Romano that broke the silence. "Well, there's our trend."

"Rog," Olmstead called back. "Fletch, you and Cowboy work north ten miles, the Major and I will work to the south. Bear, they're all yours, pal. We'll see you guys at Waypoint Foxtrot."

"Rog, Hawkeye, I'm hot and hungry," called Romano. "Break high right, Dobie. I'll take the left. Combat spread, loose deuce."

"Rog, Bear, I'm hot and hungry," Dobrinsky called, jerking his stick right and pulling back, as he lit minimum burners, his MiG clawing for altitude.

When the two MiGs locked onto the F-14s the Tomcats RWR gear went absolutely wild. The F-14 crews were too stunned to act. It took about two minutes before they understood a pair of MiGs was locking them up. Two crucial minutes, the equivalent of about 40 miles of closure. The next question was whose MiGs were they? The RWR gear indicated a Slotback radar, but was it a friendly?

The lead Tomcat pilot radioed his Ground Controller, who was equally confused. Autonomous operations were not the hallmark of the Sandori Air Force pilot. Besides these F-14s were used exclusively as mini-AWACS, not as active combatants. The Tomcat pilot asked for permission to fire, but was told to hold fire until further notice. The Controller was not about to authorize anyone to shoot live AIM-54s on a training mission, especially when he might be shooting at friendlies. The RIO of the lead F-14 called out the range to the MiGs at 40 nautical miles, almost in range of the AA-12. Once again the Tomcat lead pilot begged permission to engage and once again he was denied.

At some point a survival instinct must have taken over. The lead Tomcat pilot considered his options. One, he could disobey orders, engage and possibly shoot down a friendly MiG. Two, he could drive straight ahead and if the MiGs turned out to be hostile he'd get waxed himself. Three, he could say fuck this, break away to the South and get the hell out of Dodge at Mach 2. He had about ten seconds to make up his mind and he had about eight seconds left over after he made it.

"Coming left to disengage---burners---now," he called to his wingman, who was happy to oblige.

On their scopes Romano and Dobrinsky saw the F-14s turn to the south and accelerate, making haste for home. Soon they were out of the fight and still accelerating. They'd managed to scare them off with no fight at all. That was something they hadn't counted on.

On the Guard frequency the Sandori Controllers were trying to determine just who had locked up the Tomcats.

"Unidentified aircraft, Sandori Mil on Guard, respond please," they called.

Romano ignored the call and turned the volume down on Guard.

"Okay, Dobie, let's close it up and get back down to TFR," he called to the Russian off his right wing. The buried the nose thirty degrees low and set their airspeed to rendezvous on time at point Foxtrot. Soon they were back at TFR and saw a couple of warm objects in the IRST at their one o'clock.

"Hawkeye, Bear, we're coming up on your left, looking for Foxtrot on time," he called.

"Rog," Olmstead answered. "Fletch, say status."

"Still six miles north of centerline, expecting Foxtrot on time," he answered. "I have IRST contact."

"Rog," Olmstead answered.

A couple of minutes later they were formed up again in trail, with the SEAD out front, followed by the Air-to-Air, and bringing up the tail end, the Strikers. Point Foxtrot came and went at 550 knots and now they were less than ten minutes from the target. The route led them down into the valley Sutherland had briefed them on. They were cruising along the valley floor, well masked from the prying eyes of any radar. They could breathe easy for a couple minutes and get ready for the main event. This canyon would drop them off a short ten miles from the target. Ten miles they would cover in a little over a minute, but ten very vulnerable miles, vulnerable to the SA-10 in the area and the SA-6 they knew would be nearby.

The plan was to come screaming out of the valley, and perform a starburst. Earp Flight would go high and wide to set up a patrol just out of SAM range, Budweiser Flight would split left and right as well as climb to 2000 meters to act as decoys, and Stick Flight would barrel straight ahead, launching their missiles at about six miles out and guide them in by laser coupled to their IRST display. Simple plan.

If the SA-10 or SA-6 were up and radiating the strikers and air to air package would pump and run, turn a 180 and dive back into the safety of the valley until Budweiser called clear.

As they cleared the canyon wall at the end of the valley, the RWR gear sounded an alarm. The SA-10 was up and radiating in search mode. Damn, cried Olmstead, slamming his fist on the glare shield. The Sandori Mil controllers must have put the whole sector on alert after the MiG scare with the Tomcats.

"Arson Flight, Flashlight is on, repeat Flashlight on. Pump and run," Olmstead called. "Budweiser, cleared high right, cleared hot on the flashlight." This told Gurevich he was cleared to take spacing and fire on the SA-10 radar.

Olmstead snatched the stick back and zoomed to 2000 meters to give his HARM targeting pod a clear view of the SA-10 radar and the HARM a solid beam to ride down. The SA-10 did not disappoint him. The Ten took about five seconds to lock him up. He got a solid tone in his helmet indicating the HARM seeker head had a valid lock and he squeezed the trigger. The big missile disappeared off into the night, just as he received a missile guidance warning from his RWR gear. He saw a flash off to his right, which would be Gurevich pickling off his own HARM. He rolled inverted and pulled for the deck, breaking hard to the left as he dove, the G forces pinning him back into his seat as the black earth rushed up at him.

The RWR gear still indicated a missile inbound and he began to pump out the chaff. A glance at his jammer told him it was actively jamming the missile radar, a comforting if not completely accurate situation. He rolled back up right and leveled off just a scant fifty feet off the deck, his engine exhaust blowing up twin rooster tails in the sand behind him and still the missile was closing. He knew the SA-10 followed an up and over profile, and that dodging the missile would be difficult as it hurtled down from above. Once the motor burned out it was nearly invisible, even though it was still homing at three thousand miles an hour.

He began jinking up down, left and right, loading up the Gs in an effort to get the missile to miss. His evasive action worked, at least partially. The designers of the SA-10 would have argued if what happened could be classified as defeating the missile. The warhead, still homing, screamed down from above and physically missed the wildly gyrating MiG, but it's proximity fuse sensed the closest approach and detonated, sending shards of ragged steel outward in all directions. The missile itself plowed into the ground and a over half of the warhead's deadly projectiles followed the missile into the ground, but a few found their mark.

Olmstead knew he was in trouble immediately. He saw the flash of the explosion, heard the blast and felt the impact of the shockwave and closed his eyes tight, involuntarily awaiting death. But death never came and a scant two seconds later he realized he was still alive, still flying and had better open his eyes if he was going to remain so. The good news was he was alive and flying, the bad news was his MiG might not be able to claim the same for much longer.

The RWR gear no longer indicated an SA-10 radar was up, but then again it wasn't indicating anything at all. The RWR panel was completely dark, as was most of the electronics in the MiG.

SA-10 BATTERY #2
HABRUK NUCLEAR PLANT, SANDOR

"Impact!" the young Sandori called with a wave of his fist.

The warning had been issued just a scant ten minutes before, but he had his missile radar up and searching in less than five minutes. Now he'd splashed his first bandit and he was sure promotion and reward would follow.

The contact fell off his scope just after missile detonation so he could only assume it was destroyed. Now he had to be sure there were not others out there. He turned back to his scope and began re-tuning the radar. There were jamming strobes streaking his display meaning at least one more plane out there, one with a big jammer. No matter. *The SA-10 will home on his jamming, he thought with elation. Yes, keep the jamming up, Kumari dog.*

"Battery #2, report!" he heard his commander bark over the radio.

His eyes did not leave the display as he switched pulse repetition frequencies and adjusted his frequency-hopping mode to maximum.

"You answer, Ibrahim," he said to his comrade sitting beside him at the console. "There's another one out there."

His friend keyed the microphone just as Gurevich's missile left the rail.

"Central, Battery #2 reports two bandits inbound, one splashed," he said, giving his final report.

The commander was elated at the news, but worried that another foe lurked in the darkness and his other SA-10 battery was not yet up and running. He was counting on Battery #2 and his life was now in their hands.

The young Sandori corporal flipped another switch and his picture cleared completely. *There! There is the bastard*, he said to himself as he enabled the computer-controlled launch sequence for the second time. It was at that moment that Gurevich's missile arrived in a hypersonic spray of cubed steel. The radar dish, the van, the fueling truck and missile launcher erupted in flame followed by an explosion that the commander back in the reactor complex could feel through the soles of his boots. He knew what that explosion meant and knew that his career was now over, maybe his life as well.

BUDWEISER FLIGHT

"Stick Flight, picture's clear," he heard Gurevich call over the radio. The SA-10 must have been taken out, Olmstead thought.

"Budweiser 2, lead is gadget bent," he called, informing Gurevich he had systems malfunctions and would not be able to fire any more weapons.

"Bud Lead, Two, how bent are you?" Gurevich called back.

"Bent, Two, very bent, but flying." Olmstead turned his MiG back toward the valley and began checking his systems.

Ten miles away and inbound to the target Fletcher was staring intently into his IRST, now bore-sighted to the MiGs ground-mapping synthetic-aperture radar. The radar cross-hairs were centered on the reactor complex, now he would rely on the IRST to aim his laser at specific structures. At about ten miles his IRST would begin to give resolution he could target with. Already he could see individual buildings in the display. He climbed to 500 meters, Cowboy in combat spacing off his right side. Cowboy carried a laser as well and his missiles were coded for a different laser frequency. That way the missiles Cowboy would launch wouldn't be distracted by Fletcher's laser.

As he pressed towards the target, Fletcher engaged his autopilot to hold heading and altitude while he diverted his attention to the task at hand, killing a nuke. He was peering intently into the IRST waiting for the resolution to improve. He was about thirty seconds out from launch. He moved the laser cross hairs over onto the reactor vessel itself.

Something didn't look right, though. Something was wrong here. He was sure of it. But what? *Something...the cooling tower!* The massive cooling tower just to the right of the reactor complex, almost off the IRST display…it was hot. There was hot water vapor venting off the top of that cooling tower. That reactor was online. They were too late to stop it. It was operational.

"Cowboy, abort, abort, abort," he called. "Rainout, I say again rainout."

"What the hell?" Cowboy yelled into his mask and pulled his MiG off the target heading and back toward the valley. *Fletcher'd better know what he's doing*, the big Texan thought.

Fletcher turned away as well and began to head back to the valley and the egress routing.

"What's going on, Fletch," Olmstead called.

"That reactor is operational," he called. "We blow the sucker we create another Chernobyl. It's a rain out, mission abort."

No, Olmstead cried. *Those bastards are gonna get the Bomb*, he thought, shaking with frustration.

"We gotta be able to do something," he complained.

"No way, Hawk," Fletcher said. "No way I'm gonna cause a meltdown. That's not what we're here for."

Olmstead thought hard. He reached back into the dark cobwebs of college physics and came up with an idea.

"Fletch, I've got an idea," he called. "Take out the cooling tower. It's the primary cooling system and the water is not radioactive. If they lose the cooling tower they'll have to SCRAM the reactor. You can also take out the turbines with no risk of radiation leak. "

"You sure about this?" Fletcher said, doubt in his voice.

"Look, man, I have a minor in physics," Olmstead assured him. "And my cousin works in a nuke plant. He once told me if they would lose the cooling water they would have to manually shut down the reactor completely. It can't function with the low pressure cooling system down."

"And you're sure about the radiation?"

"Only the high pressure system is hot. The water that goes through the cooling tower is low pressure and it's clean, I tell you. Trust me."

"Alright, what do the rest of you guys think?" Fletch asked.

"I say we go for it," Cowboy said. "You take out the cooling tower. I'll take out the generator. We'll trash the place and they'll have to spend years rebuilding it."

"Bear?"

"Blow it and let's get out of here before those Tomcats we scared off come back for us," he said.

"Alright, Cowboy, you're with me," he said. "The rest of you stay clear."

"Negative, I'll give you cover from the SA-6," Gurevich called. "I'm at your 3 o'clock, three miles."

"Alright, you're in," Fletch said. "Coming left back to target heading, Cowboy. Cleared hot."

"Rog, Pard," Cowboy said.

"Just make sure you don't hit the reactor, huh," Fletcher called. "In the left turn."

Gurevich and Cowboy turned with him and took spacing for the shots. Earp Flight executed an Immelman and set up a patrol overhead the valley, while Olmstead slowed to conserve fuel and evaluate his numerous malfunctions.

They rolled out on heading, the power plant off the nose at twenty miles.

"Climbing and accelerating, Fletch," Gurevich said. "Let me get out front a little."

"Rog, just stay high and wide. If that SA-6 comes up, take the shot. We aren't coming back this way again," he told him.

The power plant once again grew large in the IRST. Fletch selected Laser Lock and once again the targeting laser was slewed to the radar cross hairs. In the IRST he could make out the reactor clearly now and rolled the cross-hairs over onto the cooling tower, aiming at the fat of the base, about 50 feet up the tower.

In the MiG just a mile off his right wing Cowboy had the large generator building under his own cross hairs. At ten miles out they both activated their lasers and a narrow, invisible beam of infrared coherent light leaped out, touched the target and returned causing a bright dot on the IRST over the cross hairs. The range of the missile was six miles and they had only about twenty seconds to go.

Suddenly the RWR gear sounded its alarm once again. This time is was the SA-6 Gainful, the Three-Fingers of Death.. The SA-6's target tracking radar, the Straight Flush, was up and radiating in search mode. This time Gurevich was quick on the trigger. Three seconds after the RWR gear indicated the radar's presence, the AS-23 on the wing of Gurevich's plane gave him a solid tone and two seconds later it left the rail and began homing.

"Magnum, Magnum," Gurevich called, using the US lexicon for a HARM missile launch.

The HARM accelerated to two thousand miles an hour in only a matter of seconds and began following the invisible radar beam back to the origin. Just five seconds later the Straight Flush had Fletcher locked up and the PRF switched to the missile illuminator mode, indicating a launch in progress. The RWR gear in Fletch's plane signaled the new threat they suddenly went dark as the HARM found its mark. It sensed the missile radar below it and detonated just a scant 100 feet above the target, sending shards of hot steel cubes down in a sizzling, deadly shower. The incredibly fast, hot projectiles peppered the SA-6, destroying the Straight Flush, the three Gainful missiles and the two soldiers operating the system.

"Flashlight's down," Gurevich called. "Cleared hot."

At six miles to go, in a single practiced movement, Fletcher flipped up the little red guard and pushed the consent button on top of the stick and squeezed the trigger. Two seconds later, and what seemed an eternity, there was a flash of light off his left wing and a whoosh as the big missile left the rails. He counted to three and squeezed the trigger again. There was another flash, a whoosh, and a second missile streaking away into the dark Sandori night.

Onboard the first missile the laser seeker head woke up just two milliseconds into the flight. It didn't take but another two milliseconds for it to notice the hot spot out in front. The seeker evaluated the spot and sent steering cues to the fins at the back of the missile. The missile pitched up slightly and the hot laser spot moved to the center of the seeker head's field of view. Now it was happy. Any time the spot began to drift out of center, the little computer would send the steering commands, a fin would bite a bit more air, and the hot spot would return to center.

Now just ten seconds into the flight the missile had corrected itself thirty seven times and the hot spot was starting to get big in the seeker head. The magnitude of returning laser energy was getting larger and the missile began to compensate for it. The steering commands were coming quicker now, but the control surface deflections were lessening for each correction. There was less time to fix the trajectories and soon the flight would be over. Just as the onboard computer sent it's eighty second steering command the seeker head was completely blinded by the hot spot, which now covered the whole seeker head field of view.

The missile was now flying blind, but that didn't matter since it was only about fifty feet from the base of the cooling tower, traveling at over 2000 miles an hour. In order to miss the two hundred foot wide base the missile would have to pull over 200 Gs and that wasn't going to happen. What happened was impact. The missile guidance computer lost communication with the seeker head as the first three inches of the missile was crushed and vaporized by the kinetic energy of the collision. A few scant milliseconds later the computer itself followed its eyes into oblivion. Just before it died, though, it had time to send one last signal. It sensed the destruction of the seeker head and had but one last function to carry out. It didn't have long to send that last signal, not by human standards. But by computer standards it had an eternity. It could have sent thousands of such signals in the millisecond or so it had left to live, but it only had to send one.

The warhead detonator received that last signal, that last gasp from the guidance computer, and a simple high voltage electronic pulse was unleashed, which began the detonation sequence of the missile warhead still being pushed along by the rocket motor at the rear. The explosive train began in the detonator and spread through the rest of the explosive very quickly, at better than 20,000 feet per second. The internal pressure began to rise. The warhead casing, a solid cast steel casing some one-inch thick, swelled to one and a half times its original diameter. Just as it reached that critical size, the internal forces acting on the steel casing overcame the tensile strength of the steel itself and the casing fractured. The casing was scored and cast in such a way as to control the way it fractured. The fracture lines raced around the casing and the internal pressures built to the point it could no longer remain whole. The casing was transformed into an expanding shell of high speed, steel cubes, racing outward and expanding outward as it fulfilled its designer's purpose.

The second missile impacted a short three seconds after the first, the only indication in Fletcher's aircraft a small puff of light on his IRST screen as he banked hard away from the target. A second later Cowboy's missiles also hit their mark. Or it should be said one of the missiles hit what it was aimed at. The other missile malfunctioned twelve seconds into the flight and fell short of its target, taking out a substation at the periphery of the power plant and mercifully missing the reactor vessel just a scant 100 yards beyond.

The damage was tremendous. Up close the warheads caused a lot more than little puffs. The first missile that hit the cooling tower penetrated the outer wall and first set of piping before detonating, blowing huge holes all through the structure. The second missile detonated inside as well, only this time the much-weakened structure could no longer maintain its integrity and the whole top of the cooling tower collapsed in on itself.

Cowboy's missile that did function correctly penetrated the ceiling of the generator room, where the giant turbines converted the steam to electrical power. The missile detonated as it struck the huge turbine itself, punching through the turbine casing and playing hell with the internal shaft and blades. Even if the missile itself hadn't exploded the imbalance caused by the damaged turbine shaft would have destroyed the whole generator room. The blast of the missile and the damage to the turbine spinning at tens of thousands of RPMs caused the bearings to fail and the whole assembly let go, throwing turbine blades and shards of shattered steel throughout the complex. The huge shaft itself came off its bearings and took on a life of its own as it smashed through the generator and out the far wall of the building.

The damage was substantial. Almost immediately the whole electric grid of Northern Sandor failed and darkness swept across the northern half of the country. The power plant had been generating almost 500 megawatts at the time of the attack. The darkness would only be temporary, though. There was plenty of generating capacity out there. After all the plant had only been online for two days. Within an hour the switching would have occurred returning power to the grid and Northern Sandor.

Fletcher and Cowboy didn't wait to see the damage. They had banked up their aircraft and turned back toward the valley just after missile launch. The laser designator on the little chin turret under the nose of the aircraft swiveled in place and kept the laser stabilized on the target during the violent maneuver.

Gurevich had already turned back just after his HARM shot and he was ten miles in front of Fletcher and Cowboy who were at Mil power in their dash to safety. The aircraft accelerated easily now, with the weight and drag of the missiles gone, and they were seeing better than 580 knots without burner.

Meanwhile Romano and Dobie dove back to TFR for the egress. They hadn't detected any bandits out there while they were orbiting high, now they needed to get low again for the dash to the Kumari border.

The Sandori GCI radars had locked onto the two MiGs while they were up high, as did the SA-5 Ganef, the extremely long-ranged SAM covering most of Northern Sandor. The SA-5 had them locked up briefly, but failed to launch. Again there was probably a foul up in the Command Control of the SAM. Probably a poor SAM operator asking permission to fire and his captain calling his major who called his colonel and so forth to get permission to fire. Finally the President of Sandor or some Ayatollah was awakened and asked permission. By the time the affirmative got back to the poor SAM operator the MiGs were off his screens. The last thing they saw was what appeared to be two aircraft with Slotback radars descending and racing at high speed for the Kumari border. That was just what they were supposed to see.

Fletch and Cowboy dove into the valley and kept the speed up above 550 to catch up with Olmstead and Earp Flight now back at TFR and 25 miles in front of them.

Olmstead was having his own problems. The SA-10 had done serious damage to his aircraft electronics. *The shrapnel must have punched holes through one of the main avionics boxes just behind the cockpit,* he thought. His radar was out, and therefore the TFR was out. The IRST, the RWR gear and nearly every other display in the cockpit was dark. The engines, generators and hydraulics all looked good, at least for the moment.

Olmstead strained to see through the blackness, but it was a dark night and the horizon kept fading in and out. His radar altimeter was out and he was flying by eyesight alone, a dangerous way to fly at night at better almost 600 miles an hour through a river valley.

"Okay, this is bullshit," he said to no one in particular. He knew he had to climb, get away from the ground before it got him. He nudged the stick back the MiG climbed fifty meters. He leveled off and strained his eyes, willing them to cut through the blackness of night. No good. He was still in the dark. Just how high could he go without that SA-5 locking him up and firing on him? He didn't know the answer. It didn't really matter, though, because with his RWR gear down he'd never even know they were taking a shot at him until the missile blasted through his cockpit. He needed help and he needed it now. Fletch and Cowboy were too far behind him and Gurevich was probably too far as well. That left Romano and Dobie. He prayed they were nearby.

"Earp Lead, Budweiser Lead, Bear, you out there?" he called.

"Affirmative, go ahead," Romano called back.

"Man, I need to some help here. I am so gadget bent I can't even see where I'm going," he explained. "I know I'm flying higher than I should, but I can't see the ground. You close by?"

"Standby, taking a look," Romano replied, as he switched his radar from TFR to Range While Search. There at the edge of his ten mile scope was a target, heading 270, speed 480 knots, altitude 400 meters. It was Olmstead.

"Okay, Dude, I got you locked up at ten miles at my twelve o'clock," he said. "Pull your throttles back to 250, and hold altitude. I'll be up with you in a few minutes. I'll come in on your right, Dobie will be to my right. I'll switch the nav lights on dim as I pass you. You fill in left echelon, and keep me visual. Let me know when I can kill the lights again, got it?"

"Oh, yeah," Olmstead said with a sigh of relief. If he could get a visual on Bear's nav lights he could get into formation and ride his wing out of here, ride it all the way home.

A few minutes later Olmstead looked over to his right and saw the familiar bulging shape of a MiG-41 slide pass him, nav lights twinkling on the wingtips. He pushed his throttles up and fell into formation.

"Budweiser is in," he called. Immediately Romano's nav lights dimmed and went black.

"Roger, Hawk, airspeed 540, power coming in," he called, giving Olmstead warning of the airspeed change. Normally this would not be necessary, but since visual contact was all Olmstead had going for him, Romano gave him the courtesy call.

They left the radar masking cover of the valleys and canyons behind. They were now a short fifty miles from the Kumari border. Fletch and Cowboy were now ten miles in trail and falling below the fuel curve with the higher than planned airspeeds required to play catch up. They decided to pull the power back and save the gas. They would wait until the turn northbound then catch up by cutting the turn short and just falling into close trail with the others.

The formation was flying a rock steady 540 knots at 100 feet above the desert when once again the RWR gear signaled impending peril. Simultaneously the RWR gear in all the MiGs, save Olmstead's, registered the powerful emissions of the AWG-9 radar, in search at their six o'clock.

"Shit," Romano said to himself before keying the mic. "You guys see what I see?"

"Roger, Earp," Fletch called back. "What do you think, Bear? Turn to fight or let it go?"

"What the hell is going on?" Olmstead asked.

"Tomcat at six o'clock in search," Cowboy answered.

"We'll cover you, Fletch," Bear said. "Your call."

"No, you guys are too far out front," he said. "I don't want you turning back when we can do the job back here. Besides, you've got a wounded bird with you. We've got four Adders between us."

"Guys, we're only about forty miles to the border," Cowboy reminded them. "We don't even know how far back there they are. I say we press ahead and wait til they take a Phoenix shot. Then we turn to fight. Hell, that AWG-9 is a powerful radar and they might be a lot farther away than we think. They don't have a lock on us yet. "

"Cowboy's got a point, Fletch," Olmstead agreed. "I think we can beat them to the border."

"Shit!" somebody said over the radio.

"What is it!" Olmstead cried. "We've have more problems, gentlemen," Gurevich said. "Check your RWR."

Gurevich said "shit"? Olmstead thought in wonder.

The RWR gear showed another threat had popped up. This time it was off the nose, and it was obviously two aircraft with Slotback radars. The radars were in search mode, but the signals were gaining in strength. It would only be a matter of time before they locked on. Two Slotback radars coming from that direction meant only one thing. Kumari MiGs! Possibly MiG-29s or even MiG-41s closing on them.

"Son of a bitch," Romano said. "We're screwed six ways to Sunday."

"Okay, Earp, you'll take out the MiGs, we'll take out the Tomcats," Fletch called.

"Roger," Romano replied. "Sorry, Hawk, but we're gonna have to leave ya. You might as well start heading back and stay the hell out of this fight."

Something was nagging at Olmstead's mind. Something was right there at the front of the brain, an idea waiting to be born. Suddenly it occurred to him.

"Negative, negative," Olmstead said with enthusiasm. "We all turn north, right now!"

"What the hell you talking about, man? Those Tomcats will overtake us and get in firing range," Fletch argued, thinking his friend had gone mad.

"Maybe, but they won't take the shot," Olmstead said confidently. "Now turn right now. We don't have time to argue. Turn heading 360 right now! Trust me!"

"Okay, man," Romano said with a sigh. Fletcher angrily jerked his stick to the right his eyes bouncing from his HUD to the RWR display and back again.

They rolled out on heading 360, due north, Fletcher and Cowboy cutting them off in the turn and falling into trail. That put the Kumaris at their nine o'clock and the Sandoris at their three o'clock and them right in the middle.

"This is suicide, man" Romano said nervously. "I hope you know what you're doing, Hawk."

"He does," Dobie said, speaking up for the first time. "Maintain heading."

"Okay, Hawkeye," Fletch called. "They are closing on us from both sides.

Why won't they take the shot?"

Olmstead laughed. "Oh, they'll take a shot alright, but not at us."

"I don't get it," Cowboy said.

"They are both using pulse Doppler radars. We have them both on the beam and we've dropped off their scope, at least for a few minutes. During that time they'll lock each other up and the Sandoris will fire on the Kumaris. Simple." Realization dawned on every man in the formation.

"Oh, that's beautiful," Romano cried. "They'll shoot down the Kumaris MiGs, whom they will believe is us turning back to fight. Meanwhile we scoot off to the north and slink our way back to Tangistan. We don't even have to go back into Kumar. When they shoot down those hostile Kumari planes that will be proof to the Sandoris that Kumar was responsible for the reactor attack."

"They don't even have to shoot them down," Olmstead said. "Just seeing them run back into Kumar will be all the evidence they need."

At that moment the RWR gear went off again, this time indicating a missile launch from the F-14s. The F-14 radar was in track while scan mode, but the RWR display showed they were obviously locked onto somebody else, the two Kumari MiGs. Shortly after the launch the missile's onboard radar signal appeared on the RWR display. The RWR gear was showing what appeared to be a radar side-lobe, which meant the missile radar was pointed away from them. Thirty seconds later the signal went down as did one of the Kumari Slotback radars.

As it turned out the other MiG escaped back into Kumar, but the diversion was just long enough for the team to escape the two F-14s attention. By the time the F-14s were finished dealing with the Kumaris they were low on gas and were recalled to base. In fact they assumed the attackers had been dealt with and weren't even looking for anyone else. In fact a celebration was underway in the Regional Air Defense Headquarters for repelling the Kumari threat. It was under this cover of confidence that the team sneaked back across the border and returned to their tiny base.

As the last plane touched down Tanner breathed a sigh of relief. It was then that the phone rang. Reports that something big was happening inside Sandor were all over the cable news channels. Michaels was calling and Tanner listened in silence. The phone went dead with a click as Michaels hung up. Tanner's arm dropped to his side still clutching the phone receiver. He pulled his handkerchief out of his back pocket and wiped his brow.

"Shit," was all he said.

STOVACORE AIRBASE, TANGISTAN
0400 LOCAL

Tanner had the team report immediately to the briefing room in Base Ops upon landing. There the doors were closed, the window shades pulled and Tanner was preparing the grief he intended to dish out. They were suppose to take out the reactor, but only if it wasn't operational. The goal was never to irradiate the Northern half of Sandor. The consequences of the attack weren't quite clear as of yet and no one was sure how much if any radiation was leaking. Tanner was furious.

"Well, gentlemen, you had a hell of a night, huh?" Tanner said rhetorically. "About an hour ago I got off the phone with Dr. Michaels. You may remember his little role in our being here? Well apparently the media is reporting some big happenings in Sandor. It seems Kumari MiGs attacked and heavily damaged a nuclear power plant in Northern Sandor. That in itself is not the bad news. The bad news is that they seemed to have attacked an *operational* nuclear reactor, of which I'm absolutely sure they didn't have authorization to attack. And now the Sandoris are really pissed and the whole region is on the brink of war. If the "Kumaris" had hit a reactor under construction the Sandoris would probably have tried to cover it up to save face. But since they hit an operational reactor the Sandoris are using it for propaganda to whip up anti-Kumari sentiment and calling it a crime against humanity, of which Achmed isn't exactly unfamiliar with that term. Now I'd like you to explain why those 'Kumaris' attacked an operational reactor," he said, his voice rising through out the sentence, finishing just short of a yell.

"Sir, we can explain," Olmstead assured him.

"You shut the hell up, Olmstead," Tanner barked. "I don't remember you leaving here with AS-22s strapped to your wing." He turned to Fletcher. "You tell me what happened and why," he said, pointing a finger at Fletcher.

"Well, sir, we were inbound on the target the first time and we..."

"The first time? You mean there was a second time?" Tanner gasped, rolling his eyes.

"Yes, sir," Fletch said nervously. "On the first run inbound I noticed the cooling tower appeared to be in operation. I immediately called an abort, a rain out. It was pretty obvious the reactor was in operation."

"That was the right call," Tanner agreed. "Now why didn't you just come home?"

"Sir, that's where I come in," Olmstead confessed.

"Well, Captain, you seem bound and determined to take credit for this fiasco. Please proceed," Tanner said with a sigh.

"Well, sir, I figured we couldn't hit the reactor without releasing radiation and causing a meltdown, so I suggested we go for the cooling towers and generators," Olmstead said.

"So you didn't hit the reactor itself?" Tanner asked, uncertainty in his voice.

"No, sir," Fletch cut in. "I laid my missiles on the cooling tower and Cowboy took out the generator building."

"Why take out the cooling tower?" Tanner asked. "If you were worried about a reactor meltdown, I mean?"

Olmstead cleared his throat. "Well, sir, if we took out the cooling tower, they would lose their low pressure cooling loop. The high-pressure loop, which contains the radioactive water, is in the reactor building itself and we left it intact. But without the low-pressure loop, which runs the steam turbines and is cooled in the cooling tower, the reactor would overheat in a matter of minutes. I knew the operators would have to SCRAM the reactor, perform an emergency shutdown, where they insert all the controls rods and effectively shut down the chain reaction."

"How did you know the Sandoris could shutdown that reactor before it melted?"

"Well, sir, I didn't," Olmstead said. "But I knew the French technicians they got to replace the Russians when they left would be able to shut it down."

"Where'd you get all this information about nuclear plants, Captain?" Tanner asked.

"His cousin works at one, sir," Fletcher said. "And Dave has a minor in physics."

Olmstead just shrugged his shoulders.

"I see," Tanner said. "So you figured if you can't destroy the reactor, then destroy its supporting equipment so it can't be put into operation and breed weapons grade plutonium. That about the size of it, Captain?"

Olmstead nodded. "Yes, sir. That about sums it up, but stopping the plutonium production was the idea from the get go, right, sir?"

Tanner nodded and sighed. Then he turned to Fletcher and Cowboy.

"You guys did hit what you were aiming at, didn't you?" he asked.

"Both my missiles hit dead on the cooling tower, sir," Fletcher said confidently.

"I had a missile fall way short, malfunctioned. The other hit the generator shed," Cowboy said.

Tanner's expression changed to worry when Cowboy mentioned the malfunctioning missile.

"You sure it fell short?" he asked.

"Definitely, sir. Well short of the reactor."

Tanner sighed again. "Well, maybe we got lucky. We'll have satellite over the region in the next few hours looking at radiation levels. A WC-135 is being dispatched from USAFE to monitor radiation as well. Hopefully the Sandoris are just using this as propaganda. Either way, gentlemen, my guess is we're finished here."

"You mean here in Tangistan?" Olmstead asked.

"No, I mean finished period," Tanner said. "You will be taking off for Russia within the hour and then I expect we'll get a recall to Nellis. As the Lone Ranger used to say, 'our work here is finished, Tonto'."

"Sir, what about my plane?" Olmstead asked.

"Maintenance is replacing a bunch of black boxes right now. Hopefully you'll have most of your systems back by take-off. I told them to forget about the weapons and targeting systems for the time being. After all we're just leasing," he said with a smile. "I say we pay the deductible and be done with it."

The men laughed.

"Anyway, you should be okay to fly," he went on. "The major systems are okay, engines, fuel, flight controls. If all else fails you just stay on Fletch's wing all the way back."

"Yes, sir," Olmstead said, hoping it wouldn't come to that. He hoped to at least have his radar back.

"Okay, guys," Tanner said. "There are sandwiches in the next tent over. Grab a bite to eat and get back out to the jets. We're outa here."

As they left the tent Romano pulled Olmstead aside. "You don't have no fucking physics minor, do you?" he asked with a smirk.

"Shit no," he said with a laugh. "My minor was geography."

Romano shook his head with wonder, the proverbial shit-eating grin on his face.

"And your cousin doesn't work at a nuclear plant, does he?" he asked, with a sly smile.

"Oh, that part is true," Olmstead assured him. "He's the best damn cafeteria fry chef in the whole electrical power industry." He slapped Romano on the back as he passed. Romano's mouth fell open and he shook his head, smiling.

KERESHKOV AIR BASE COMMONWEALTH OF INDEPENDENT STATES

"Well, gentlemen, you seem to be living a charmed life," Tanner told the assembled pilots the next evening. "Both Russian and US intelligence sources have had Sandor under a microscope for the last twelve hours and we don't detect any 'Chernobyl' going on there. You wouldn't know that by the propaganda the Sandoris are putting out, though. They are claiming it's a tragedy of epic proportions, but of course they have refused assistance from Western nations, as well as from Russia. Lieutenant Sutherland has some intelligence on their 'statements'. Lieutenant?" Sutherland stood up and moved to the front of the room.

"We believe the Sandoris are raising all this fuss as a unifying measure for their population. The Fundamental Islamics and their elected, moderate President have been at odds with each other ever since he came into power. Now the President is trying to use the attack as a rallying point, common ground if you will. He is using the threat from Kumar as a unifying force, and it is working. The old Islamic hard-liners hate Achmed as much as we do. They may take the issue and run with it, pushing Sandor into war. They wield a lot of power in that country and I'm not sure who the military would side with if it came right down to it."

"So what's the current status of Sandor's military?" Olmstead asked.

Sutherland took the remote in hand and flipped up the first slide, showing massive mobilization of troops, increased air patrols and a posture heading toward war.

"As you can see the Sandori Armored Forces are mobilizing," he said, pointing to several icons on the screen. "They are coming out of their garrisons near Fashren and moving to the northwest. The Division that was camped out in that valley we told you to avoid was suppose to be re-deploying to their home base in the South. At last report they are moving west, to a position near the border. It looks like the whole Sandori Army is moving to the border with Kumar. The air patrols have increased in number and there is a pair of F-14s aloft twenty four hours a day for early warning in the North and a couple of SU-AWACs operating in the South and West parts of the country."

Romano let out a low whistle. "Wow."

"What are the Kumaris doing?" Olmstead asked.

Sutherland shrugged his shoulders. "They aren't doing anything. They still claim they didn't attack the reactor and that they were intercepting aircraft about to enter their airspace."

"Well they can claim all they want," Fletch snorted. "If Achmed's lips are moving everyone assumes he's lying."

"Kinda ironic, ain't it?" Cowboy said.

"Yeah, well Achmed's a shrewd character," Fletcher said. "You can bet he has some kind of plan to deal with the Sandoris."

"He's gonna sit perfectly still," Olmstead said. "He won't do anything resembling preparing for war. He won't do anything to initiate hostilities. He knows how to play the game. He also knows what the Sandori president is thinking. It's just tough talk and Achmed has lived through plenty of that in recent years."

"Damn, one more sortie and we could start a war, you know?" Romano said.

All eyes turned to look at him. He shrugged. "Isn't that the point?"

Tanner stood back up. "The objective was to destabilize the relationship between Kumar and Sandor, while taking out their WMD programs and knocking off as many terrorists as we could find. I'm supposed to speak with Michaels later tonight. My guess is that they'll pull us out of here soon enough. In the mean time you guys keep a low profile and stay out of trouble. And that means you, Romano," he said with a smile as he walked out.

A bewildered Romano held up his palms and shrugged. "How'd he know?"

THE KREMLIN

"The operation progresses as planned, Victor?" Kamorova asked over morning tea.

"Da. We have managed to bring Sandor and Kumar to the brink of hostilities and maintain our deception," Komiskov answered, between mouthfuls of a sweet Russian pastry.

"The reactor strike had us worried, my friend," Kamorova confided.

"Only because your friends knew it went online," Komiskov said with disdain. "Why did you not tell me this?"

Kamorova appeared hurt. "My friend, I did not know this prior to the attack. I swear it."

Komiskov grunted and mulled that over. His friend was probably lying, but it did not matter now. The point was moot.

"You liked their solution?" he asked. "Ingenious, no?"

The KGB man nodded his approval. "Da, very well done. Very resourceful, these Americans."

"Indeed."

There was silence for a moment while the two sipped their tea. Finally Kamorova spoke.

"Achmed is not mobilizing, you know."

The older man nodded. "Yes, he is no fool. He knows it is not to his advantage to go to war with Sandor."

"And he knows he is being set up. Sandor probably knows as well, yes?" Kamorova asked.

"Yes, but they more than likely think Achmed is setting them up," Komiskov answered.

"One more mission to light the fuse?"

The older man nodded and wiped his mouth with a napkin. "They must be pushed over the line. It will take at least one more."

"I can't see the Americans supporting more, Victor," he said. "Their goal was only to bring them to this point. How do you change this?"

Komiskov smiled. "Just as Sandor and Kumar need a little push now, I foresaw our American friends needing a push as well."

"And how do you "push" them?"

"The Americans have a soft spot for human tragedy and who better to provide human tragedy than Achmed the Butcher," Komiskov said. "I think it is time for phase two, Yuri."

The ex-KGB man nodded casually, but Komiskov noted the perspiration across his brow. This option had been in the works for months and they were mostly in agreement, but Kamorova still seemed hesitant.

"This move makes you nervous, Yuri?"

"It would make any sane man nervous, Victor," he said evenly. "Do you feel nervous?"

It was a loaded question and Komiskov knew it. He laughed and slapped his old friend on the shoulder.

"Of course I'm nervous, my friend," he assured him. "Still great things come to those that dare. This is a great opportunity, Yuri. True, it is dangerous.

But we are prepared."

"But to release this on the world after so long?"

"Yuri!" the elder man said sternly. "Are our inoculation programs complete?"

Kamorova nodded. "Mostly. All Southern Tier and Spetnatz Troops have received the vaccine. The rest of the Army will be complete within the month."

"And the general population?"

"We have enough vaccine for 250 million," Kamorova said. "Not enough for everyone, but there are remote areas that may need no protection at all. Are you sure we cannot begin inoculating the general public?"

"Nyet," Komiskov said with a jab of his hand. "Inoculating our troops is not so unusual given today's terrorist climate, but if we begin to distribute it to the general populace there will be too may questions. Why now? Where is the threat coming from? Our friends the Americans will be interested. No, we must wait until there is an outbreak and then begin mass inoculations. You will see that we are ready for this without raising suspicions?"

"Da. I will make sure we are ready," Kamorova said. Komiskov knew he would do just that. His fear of this thing would make him efficient in his task.

The two say and sipped their tea in silence for a few minutes, both men contemplating the future.

"Is this not needlessly risky, my friend?" Kamorova asked with apprehension. "To deliver by aircraft? Why not release it on the ground. We have operatives that could infiltrate Sandor easily."

Komiskov shook his head. "You forget---we must make this look like a Kumari attack. The strike by aircraft will leave just the right amount of evidence. Remember---we do not want the release of our "little friend"" to be a mystery. It must be traceable to Achmed."

"Dah. I understand," he said wiping the perspiration from his brow. "When?"

"Soon," Komiskov said, pouring another cup of the steaming tea from the silver urn.

CIA HEADQUARTERS
LANGLEY, VIRGINIA

"Son of a bitch," muttered Stu Gurney as he clicked the mouse and printed out the screen display. He picked up a phone and dialed. "Scotty, get your ass over here. Yeah, I found something."

Gurney and Pritkin had been working night and day for three weeks trying to find unclassified Russian sources that would explain the "secret inoculations" the Russians were giving to their military. Now here was the answer, dumped right into their laps.

"What ya got," Pritkin said, slamming the office door behind him.

Gurney held up the print out.

"USA Today?" he said incredulously.

"The fucking Russians had a press conference last Thursday," Gurney said. "Guess this ain't so secret after all."

Pritkin shook his head in wonder. What were the Russians up to?

"Press conference? What'd they say the reasons for the inoculations were?"

Gurney read from the sheet, "Intelligence sources indicate with increasing hostilities between Sandor and Kumar, both confirmed terrorists states, the likelihood of bio-attack is not insignificant. Russian troops are being inoculated to safeguard their military should intervention become necessary."

"Intervention? What does that mean? They would try to stop a war between Sandor and Kumar?" Pritkin asked.

Gurney scanned the article further. "It says that due to the allegiance with the United States in its war against terrorism they felt they might get drawn into a conflict within the region. They add a bunch more bullshit about doing all they can to protect their brave young men who defend the Rodina and all that."

"They mention Smallpox directly?"

"Ummm, no," Gurney said scanning the document again. "They mentioned Anthrax and Yellow Fever by name, but added that there were also inoculations for a host of other diseases."

"A host of other diseases," Pritkin repeated with a frown. "They actually mentioned the United States and the war on terrorism in the statement?"

"Yep."

"That's both amazing and shrewd," he said.

"How so?"

"Well, their story is they have to be ready to assist us in the region. It's amazing they ally themselves so closely with us. Virtually guaranteeing support for whatever we do. How can we argue with that? It's also very shrewd if they are using it to hide their real intentions."

"Which are?"

Pritkin shook his head. "I just have this gut feeling they are up to something."

"You mean preparing for something, don't you?" Gurney said.

Pritkin nodded absently. That afternoon his boss met behind closed doors with the National Security Council. The news raised eyebrows, especially Dr. Charles Michaels', who read the decoded message traffic over breakfast the next morning. *What was Victor up to, he wondered?*

OFFICE OF DEPUTY DEFENSE MINISTER THE KREMLIN, MOSCOW

"Victor, what is this about inoculations?" Michaels demanded. "Why all of the sudden are you immunizing your forces?"

Komiskov feigned surprise at the question. "Charles, surely you see the threat, yes? We know Kumar has stooped to germ warfare in the past. We are simply preparing for that contingency. You have inoculated your own troops years ago."

"Yes, we did," Michaels admitted, "but why the big press release?"

Komiskov smiled broadly.

"Two reasons, my friend," Komiskov started. "First to let Kumar know our troops will have some level of immunity, second to show our solidarity with the United States should war come to the region."

Michaels kept a poker face, but inside his brow was furrowed. "Victor, do you have any intelligence that indicates Kumar is preparing for germ warfare in the near future?"

Komiskov shook his head. "Charles, as much as we trust each other, I cannot go into our sources of intelligence," he said with as much sincerity as he could muster.

As much as we *trust* each other? Michaels thought with exasperation. Who does he think he's kidding?

"Our source within Kumar is very close to the leadership and extremely valuable. I cannot share his name or even his report with you, Charles. I'm telling you too much just letting you know we have a source in position who can make this call," Komiskov confided. "You know how these sources have to be protected. The smallest leak and he could be compromised."

"Yes, I do understand sources, Victor," Michaels said with disdain at the Espionage 101 lecture he was getting. "So your man believes Kumar may resort to germ warfare?"

Komiskov shrugged. "He believes it is possible given their past history and given the tensions between the Shiites and Sunnis."

"You will let us know of any immediate threat, right?" he asked.

"Of course, my friend," Komiskov assured him.

After Michaels left the room Kamorova entered from another doorway.

"A dangerous game you play, Victor," he said, lighting a cigarette.

Komiskov smiled. "Nyet."

"You think he believed you have a source in Kumar?"

"Da, he believed," Komiskov assured him. "He will still have his doubts as to our motives, but he will believe."

"Tomorrow?"

"Da. Stop him as he leaves the hotel tomorrow morning," the old Russian said. "Bring him straight here."

"What is the bait?" Kamorova asked, blowing smoke.

"Something he cannot resist."

OFFICE OF THE DEPUTY DEFENSE MINISTER
THE KREMLIN, MOSCOW
THE NEXT MORNING

"Charles, I'm so glad we caught you before your plane left," Komiskov said, extending his hand to shake the American's. He gestured to a couch along the wall. "Please sit," he said. "Tea will be here momentarily."

"What is this about, Victor," Michaels said, plopping onto the couch and not caring that tea was on the way. He wanted to get the hell out of Russia before anyone noticed his hanging around the Kremlin. He was not happy about meeting here yesterday and he was not any happier about having to come back again.

"My friend, there has been a development in Sandor," he said most seriously. "Last night a source we have in a small town south of Hanrah brought us some disturbing photos." He handed a packet of photographs across the coffee table to Michaels.

"Who is this source," Michaels asked as he opened the packet. "Can you tell me?" he said with a wry smile.

The humor was not lost on Komiskov. "He is an ex-soldier of the Red Army from Turkmenistan, now living south of Hanrah. He's very smart for a country peasant, very observant and loyal to Russia. We consider him a very good source. The GRU recruited him long ago and he "defected" to Sandor for religious reasons."

"What the hell is this?" Michaels asked, pointing to a photo. It showed a truck backed up to what appeared to be a cave. A hole in the face of the cave was nearly big enough to swallow the truck. The truck ramp was down and a white cylindrical object was halfway out of the trailer.

"That, my friend, is the warhead of an SS-20 Intercontinental Ballistic Missile," he said matter-of-factly.

Michaels' eyes went wide as golf balls.

"What did you just say?" he asked, not believing his ears.

Komiskov leaned back in his chair as a steward brought in a tray of tea. He sat it down on the coffee table, bowed slightly and left. As soon as the door was closed Komiskov spoke.

"You heard me," was all he said, pouring a cup of tea from the silver urn.

"Holy shit."

"You are glad I called you now?" Komiskov asked.

Michaels nodded. "How did they get an SS-20 warhead? How big is it?"

"We don't know how they got it," Komiskov said. "And it is 2 megatons."

A strategic thermonuclear bomb one hundred times the size of the Nagasaki bomb. A real crowd-pleaser.

"What do you mean you don't know how they got it? You had to notice one missing, right?"

Komiskov sipped his tea and did not respond to the question.

"Tea?" he asked Michaels, politely, still evading the question.

"You did notice it missing, right?" Michaels asked again. "Victor?"

The old man finally sighed gruffly and sat down his tea, splashing it onto the tabletop.

"Yes, of course we noticed it missing," he said grumpily.

"And you didn't tell us?" Michaels asked.

Komiskov snorted with laughter. "You must be joking, Charles. Admit to the United States we lost a fusion bomb…right."

"So you did nothing?"

"Don't be ridiculous," Komiskov said, clearly offended. "We have been looking for it."

"Looking for it?" Michaels said, his mouth open in disbelief.

"Well we found it didn't we?" Komiskov said with finality. "Now we must act."

"Steal it back?"

"Nyet," Komiskov said. "Destroy it."

"With the MiGs? Is that it?" Michaels asked in disbelief.

"Why do you act surprised, Charles," Komiskov asked. "This is the perfect mission for a covert strike team designed to stop terrorists from acquiring weapons of mass destruction."

Michaels was nonplussed. "I would expect the Russian military would take more positive measures than this when they find one of their stolen nukes, Victor."

"I am sure my President would indeed take such steps, Charles, but he does not have to. We have the tools and talent in place here and now to deal with this," he said with assurance.

"You're talking about launching a strike in the next 24 hours, right?" Michaels asked. "I mean if we are going to send the MiG team in we have to go now, before they move the damn thing."

"Of course we will move quickly," Komiskov assured him. "That is the beauty of our little operation."

Michaels considered this. It was probably true that the regular Russian forces could never mount anything like this on a moment's notice. The target will have escaped by the time that sleeping giant awoke.

"Okay…okay," Michaels said finally. "When?"

"This very evening if possible," Komiskov said.

"Deployment to Tangistan? By the time they turn around the jets and the team gets rested the target may have moved on."

Komiskov was ready with the answer to this. "That is why we do not deploy this time," he said with a dismissive wave. "We have an air refueling tanker drag them down over Tangistan, top them off for the mission then pick them up for the drag home after the strike. Round trip from Russia with love, yes?"

Michaels liked the idea immediately. It definitely shortened their reaction time to a crisis by eliminating the need to deploy to a forward base. The tanker compensates for the short range of the MiG. It also meant they wouldn't touch Tangistani soil again which meant less of a physical presence that could bite them later.

"Okay, that sounds like a plan," he admitted. Then he added, "but I've got to get out of here right now. I can't be in Moscow during this. You understand?"

"Of course, Charles," Komiskov said. He knew Michaels would leave as soon as possible. If the team were shot down or captured they would disavow them, but Michaels being in Moscow if that were to happen would be too hard to explain. "I do need you to inform General Tanner of this mission. I am sure he will want to speak to you personally. I can provide a secure communication channel from here if you like. Better to get this moving as soon as possible. "

"Yes, of course," Michaels said absently.

"Tonight, then?" Komiskov asked holding out his hand.

"Tonight," Michaels said, standing up to take the Russian's hand in what would be their last handshake.

After Michaels was led from the room Kamorova entered from a small office off Komiskov's where he had been listening.

"Very well done, my friend," he said with admiration. "That was brilliant. A stolen nuclear warhead. That is bait they cannot pass up."

"Dah," Komiskov said, spinning his high-backed leather chair around to face Kamorova. "Is the weapon ready?"

"Of course," he said with confidence. "Not two megatons, but just as deadly."

"It is a good deception?"

"The weaponeers did a fantastic job of disguising the bomb. From the outside it looks just like an external fuel tank," he said.

"It operates like a cluster bomb, yes?" Komiskov asked. "Dobrinsky can employ it as if it were a cluster bomb?"

"Indeed. It is designed to open and dispense the bomblets over a wide area. The bomblets themselves are a very brittle plastic with a small charge designed to shatter upon detonation, not explode. The air stream will aerosolize the virus-rich media will be spread over a wide area." he said with a knowing smile. "He should have no trouble, but are you sure of the target?"

"Dah," Komiskov assured him. "The truck stop we have chosen is a major node for commercial and military trucking to all points inside Sandor. This target will have the greatest impact, the best possible distribution of our little friend." Kamorova shivered at the reference of the virus as "our little friend".

"We are standing by with the vaccine as needed along the southern tier," he said.

"Good. Hopefully that won't be necessary, but better to be safe," the old Russian said with a grim smile.

Safe! thought Kamorova. God help us.

"What of Dobrinsky?" Kamorova asked. "He is a very reliable agent. He has served well."

"I agree. It is a pity," Komiskov added, "but he knows too much."

"And the others?"

"They have outlived their usefulness," he said. "Once our "little friend" is out and about we won't have to do any more of this covert nonsense."

"How do you dispose of the pilots?" Kamorova asked out of curiosity.

Komiskov smiled grimly. "Each plane has an explosive charge and a barometric fuse. As they descend to low level the self-destruct charge is armed. When they climb above 7000 meters to rendezvous with the tanker it detonates. Simple…but unfortunate."

"And Tanner?"

"He will be on the AN-124 tanker. Unfortunately it will have a mechanical problem and also blow up in mid-air, something about a fuel pump overheating or some such technical malfunction," Komiskov said, "at least that is what the investigation will report. It is a shame, wasting one of our precious few tankers."

"As well as the pilots," Kamorova said.

"Da," Komiskov said as if that were obvious. The Motherland had a history of sacrificing good men. He would see to it the pilots would get their names on the Wall of Honor in Red Square.

"What about Michaels?"

"He is contacting Tanner as we speak," Komiskov said. "I know Tanner will need his 'authorization' on this one."

"Yes, but what of him…after?"

Komiskov shook his head. "Terrorism, my friend, is a horrible thing. I'm afraid Dr. Michaels will not make it to his plane. Intelligence says the terrorists were Muslim extremist from Chechnya, protesting the United States' presence in the Persian Gulf."

"When did this happen?" a stunned Kamorova asked.

Komiskov looked at his watch. "Twenty five minutes from now."

"Oh," Kamorova said simply.

KERESHKOV AIR BASE
1900 HOURS LOCAL

Kavinsky had been called to Moscow for a conference, so Tanner had the reigns of command all to himself. Tanner briefed the team personally, who only got word of the mission himself a half-hour before. Sutherland passed out the strike packages, which consisted of little more than a comm plan, a strip chart and target coordinates. There was no time for anything else. They didn't even have the latest weather reports form the target area. It didn't matter if it were raining or not...they were going.

"Gentlemen, I expect you will feel this mission is rushed and that we are not ready," he started. "If you feel that way, you are absolutely correct. However, this is one where we cannot drop the ball." He passed out a single black and white photograph to each man.

"We'll start with the photo," he said. "This is why we're going tonight. This is your target, the white cylinder being lowered down the ramp of that truck."

"What is it, sir?" Romano asked.

"That is a two megaton strategic nuclear warhead from an SS-20 ICBM," Tanner said.

"Wow," Cowboy said.

"How'd they get it, sir?" Fletcher asked.

"Captain, I don't know and I don't care," he said firmly. "I want it in a million pieces by morning, gentlemen. I hope you understand the urgency of this mission. We know an ICBM warhead is missing from the Russian Strategic Rocket Forces. A spy inside Sandor has tracked it down and we have to destroy it before they move it again. If it seems that we are taking extreme risks on this mission, you are right. This is important enough to warrant those risks.

"Your planes are being fueled and armed as we speak," he continued. "We will not deploy to Tangistan for this mission. We don't have the time. A Russian AN-124 tanker will drag you down to Tangistan where you will drop low before crossing into Sandor, you will penetrate, strike the target and get the hell out. The tanker will pick you back up over Tangistan for the flight home. I will be onboard the tanker and in contact with you over a satellite com system. The lead aircraft will be the only aircraft with this system so you will have to relay the mission changes to your wingman," he said pointing to Olmstead. "We have to use satellite communications since you'll be out of UHF range for most of the strike routing. If you receive my message you can just hit the acknowledge button and it will send an acknowledgment message back to me. If you need to talk you can do that as well. It's gonna be a long night, gentlemen. I hope you slept well last night."

The preflight went smoothly and each MiG was pulled out of its hangar. The sun was just below the horizon and the cockpit canopies were glowing cherry red in the twilight. The weapons were loaded and armed, all pins pulled and streamers accounted for. The fuel tanks read full and there was a small puddle below each aircraft where the tanks had overflowed momentarily, ensuring every last ounce of gas possible was squeezed within the swollen airframe of the MiG-41, as well as the external drop tanks they now carried. No one noticed that one of the drop tanks on Dobrinsky's aircraft had no puddle beneath.

The pilots climbed into their cockpits and began their internal power-on checklists. Hands danced over switches and knobs. MFDs came to life with eerie green glows that flickered across the pilots' clear Plexiglas visors. They checked every circuit and hydraulic actuator possible. The navigation system was programmed with the waypoints and target coordinates.

Olmstead and Fletcher programmed their AS-23 anti-radiation missiles for the SA-10's radar frequencies, which they knew to be a threat according to the ferret-like, Russian intelligence officer. They received good data transfer indications between their HARM targeting system and the missiles on the wings. They checked their missile interface systems for their AA-11s and AA-12s. The radar computer was talking and the missiles were listening. Keeping the computers happy and talkative is half the battle in modern air combat maintenance. They checked their Gardenyia active jammers and confirmed all electronic countermeasures were operating through all bands in automatic mode. The passive detection system was functioning and linked to the active jammers, more computers talking to each other. They had a full load of expendables, chaff in the left ejector and flares in the right.

Finally the time came and the canopies came down and the scramble checklist was started. Each man selected Auto-Engine Start on their MFD and advanced the throttle to flight idle while the computer began the engine start sequence. The computer controlled digital engine management system activated the compressed air start system and fired the igniters when the RPM reached 15%. The left engine was started first and once it was running at idle, the pilots began to taxi to the end of the runway while the computer started the right engine.

By the time they reached the end of the runway both engines were started, generators were online, all hydraulic, avionics and flight control systems were checked. Olmstead pulled out onto the wide concrete expanse and pointed the nose down the runway. He tapped the brakes to stop and ran through one last check of the flight control surfaces. He performed the standard "stir the pot" where he moved the stick around in a circle and watched his flight control surfaces move. All looked well, fuel, oil pressure, electrics, hydraulics, radar on, ready to go.

He clicked his microphone three times and received five sets of three clicks in reply. His flight was in formation, in the green and ready for take-off. Here we go, he said to himself as he advanced the twin throttles to full military power. This long, wide runway in front of him seemed like the plains of Kansas compared to the postage stamp they last took off from. He held the toe brakes for a full ten seconds to let the two screaming RD-333 turbofans stabilize. He nodded his head, released the brakes and began to roll; Fletcher sitting in echelon off his right wing released his brakes at the same time. Cowboy and Romano counted to three and released their brakes followed by Gurevich and Dobrinsky three seconds later. All aircraft were rolling, and the airbase was rocked with the blatting roar of twelve jet engines.

The six MiGs leveled off in close formation a thousand feet below the tanker's altitude and soon had the big ship on radar. Their tanker, a modified AN-124, had taken off thirty minutes prior. They moved into one-mile trail from the big refueling tanker as it turned toward the southwest, the last of the reddish sunset glinting off its shiny aluminum skin. With full tanks they did not immediately refuel. But stayed in close trail of the big tanker. About thirty minutes out from the drop off point the tanker extended its two refueling hoses, one from each wing tip, each having a basket drogue at the end. Two at a time the pilots slowly, but smoothly brought their ships up behind the basket, held formation for a moment to set up the fuel switches and extend their refueling probes. Finally they eased their warplanes forward, flying the probes into the baskets. Once they got a solid contact the fuel began to flow. It only took ten minutes to top off a pair of MiGs and by the time they reached the drop off point they were all carrying maximum fuel loads. At least they thought everyone had full fuel loads.

KERESHKOV AIRBASE
COMMONWEALTH OF INDEPENDENT STATES

Earlier Sutherland had watched as the MiGs rocketed off into the evening sky. Tanner was onboard the tanker so he was the lone American in a sea of Russians. His role in the strike was manning the Command Center and relaying any new intelligence forward to Tanner as it develops. He had a vast array of American and Russian surveillance assets available for this task. Although the adventurous part of him envied the pilots, his practical side knew he was in the right place doing the right job.

Intelligence was a very diverse and interesting field in its own right. The data analysis part of the job was concerned with war-fighting and how to best make use of your assets and the enemy's weaknesses. Although the strategy of warfare intrigued him, he was also interested in the data acquisition side, the intelligence gathering services. He sat in the end zone of the intelligence football game. Spies, spy planes and satellites were the players, risking their necks to hand him the ball in the end zone. Of course what he did with that ball really determined who won or loss.

Back in the dark Command Center, lit only with the screens of several terminals and computers, was a large electronic map of the Eastern Hemisphere, the Big Board. Here a thin string of red light showed the planned track of the mission as well as the known threats, written directly onto the Plexiglas face with fluorescent markers. As a new threat was identified, by several sources available, the position and threat information was written on the screen. Satellites circling overhead could tell if threat radars were up near the target and Sutherland would plot its position on the board. So far nothing too exotic was happening, of course the team was still forty minutes from dropping off its tanker.

Sutherland sat down behind a Russian computer terminal he'd been instructed how to use. They were allowing him to use a threat categorization program similar to one he used back in Nevada, but it was linked to the Russian assets around the world. A young Russian captain, whom normally occupied this Command Post, had hesitantly shown him how to use the system several weeks before and now he was a veteran. He freely roamed the Russian database of known threats in Sandor. Russia had outstanding intelligence regarding the weapons Sandor was employing, since they had in fact sold them most of the systems.

Sutherland was typing a command into the computer when he accidentally hit a key combination that exited the program. "Damn," he said to himself. He looked around the room for his Russian counterpart, a Russian lieutenant that had helped him put the strike packages together, but he was nowhere to be found. *Probably stepped out for a smoke*, he thought.

I know computers, Sutherland said to himself. It's a damn 486 machine for Christ's sake. I ought to be able to boot up the program again. He called up a directory, unfortunately all of which was in Cyrillic. There were several programs to choose from and with another glance around the room he clicked on one of them.

The screen went blank and a map of Sandor came up immediately. *Okay,* he thought. *No problem.* There was a triangle located just south of Hanrah, just where their target was supposed to be. There were words at the top and sides of the screen but again they were all in Cyrillic. Although he'd had a few semesters of Russian in college and spoke it in a very basic fashion he could not read Cyrillic. There was a single button highlighted at the bottom of the screen and the mouse cursor sat right on the button, as if tempting him to push it. *What the hell*, he thought as he left clicked.

The triangle symbol in the target area brightened briefly then a series of dots began to surround the target. Every few seconds the dots would multiply and it looked like a time code of some kind was being displayed that updated itself every time the area of dots grew. The program continued and the dots grew in a widening circle about the triangle until eventually the whole map was filled with the dots and the time code stopped advancing. The final number was 45:12:00, whatever that meant.

Sutherland frowned. Something about this looked familiar, but it wasn't coming to him, at least not quickly. He ran the program again and the dots swept the screen once again. Again. All of a sudden a terrible realization came upon him. He had seen screens like this before. He had to know what this one said. He quickly scribbled down the few words written on the screen. He then exited the program and moved away from the terminal just as the young lieutenant entered the Command Center.

"Vasily, I accidentally aborted the program on that terminal and I don't read Cyrillic," he explained matter-of-factly. "Could you reboot the program?"

"Da, no problem," the lieutenant said, sliding behind the keyboard.

"While you do that I'm gonna hit the can," Sutherland said.

The Russian gave him a questioning look.

"Restroom," he added. "Gonna use the restroom."

"Dah," the Russian said absently as he turned his attention back to the computer.

Sutherland entered the stall in the far corner and sat down. He slipped a little Russian-English translation book from his shirt pocket. It had come in handy so far. He thumbed back to the Cyrillic to English section and decoded the top line: Operation Virulent Winds. The second line said: Progress of Contagion. The third line bore a single word: Smallpox. The numbers decoded to 45 days. The little triangle was marked with: Weapon Impact area. One series of words at the bottom left hand said: Mode of delivery. The next said: MiG-41 and finally the word: Dobrinsky.

"Oh my God," he said to himself.

THE SKIES OVER TANGISTAN

Once over Tangistan and just seventy-five miles from Sandor the six planes dropped back off the tanker and dove for the deck and the cover of terrain. This time they had a flying gas station waiting for them so they didn't have to fly slowly to save gas. They had the throttles up and were cooking along at better than 560 knots. They flew in a loose diamond formation with Olmstead in the lead.

Olmstead actually had it the easiest flying lead position. He set his TFR to 100 meters and engaged the autopilot. His wingmen had to concentrate on staying in position within the formation and not hitting anyone. They had to trust their leader, and his TFR set, completely as far as altitude was concerned. At these close quarters you couldn't afford a glance at the radar altimeter. Their eyes were outside the cockpit, their eyes straining to make out leads dimmed wingtip lights, their hands and feet making minute adjustments to throttle, pitch, roll and yaw constantly. This flying was much more demanding than on the previous missions, but they had flown countless training sorties back home that involved close-in formation so each man was proficient.

They flew down the west side of the big lake, just as they had in the past and skirted along the ridgelines into the mountains of Northern Sandor, invisible radar beams reaching out, searching the skies constantly for intruders. Olmstead glanced at his RWR gear. There were several early warning radars out there and the ever-present SA-5 radar, but he knew that the weak signal strength coupled with their nape of the earth profile would prevent the bad guys from tracking them. Of course as they approached Hanrah it would be more difficult to remain hidden.

They raced across the foothills and valleys deeper into the heart of Sandor. All aircraft reported in the green. There was only one little potential stumbling block tonight. The Russian intelligence officer said the Sandoris were keeping two F-14s on strip alert 24 hours a day due to the possibility of Kumari attack. I guess when they shot down those MiG-29s on the last mission they finally figured out they can use these things at night, Olmstead thought. It was a sure bet that when the weapons storage site is attacked the Sandoris will launch those F-14s. They could either deal with the Tomcats now proactively or wait until the trip back to the tanker and deal with them in the air. The airbase was a scant fifty miles from the target area so taking out the

F-14s beforehand seemed the prudent answer. Better to knock them off now rather than run the risk they pop off a few Phoenix's during the attack on the weapons storage site.

As they approached Olmstead alone climbed to 700 meters to take the shot. Only one would be needed so there was no sense in exposing the whole formation to enemy radar, stealthy airframes or not. Off the nose he could see the runway lights starting to appear, just ten miles away. Olmstead thumbed the weapons selector switch on his throttles and selected an AS-22 missile. The HUD indicated it was armed and ready. He thumbed another switch and slewed the IRST to the preprogrammed coordinates, the coordinates of the alert pad at the military airfield. He selected maximum magnification on the IRST and switched the laser designator to standby.

They were now eight miles out and his ECM receivers indicated a new India Band radar looking his way, not locking on yet, but getting stronger. *Better get this shot off and get back low*, he thought.

He peered hard into his IRST display and before his eyes the image came into focus. He saw the alert pad and the two F-14s parked wingtip-to-wingtip, power carts behind them, no other people or vehicles to be seen. Perfect. He switched the laser on. He thumbed a switch on the throttle and slewed the cross hairs to lie just between the two Tomcats.

"Arson, Magnum," he called to the flight as he closed his eyes and thumbed the button.

Through his closed eyelids he saw the flash and heard a whoosh as the missile lit and screamed away from the MiG. Approximately two seconds into the flight the missile seeker head found the laser reflection it was looking for and terminal guidance began. The rocket engine on the missile burned out in about six seconds, but not before accelerating the missile to about 1800 miles an hour. The time of flight would not be long, Olmstead knew. A few seconds later the IRST display went white with static as the missile detonated. The IRST camera was momentarily overloaded by the intensity of thermal energy it detected and the screen went dark. A couple of seconds later the image came back into focus and the damage was evident. There was no longer two distinct shapes on the alert pad, just one fiery mass of burning jet fuel and a hot spot where the missile detonated. The rocket motor had burned out well short of the airfield and it was the middle of the night. No one on the field even saw the missile before it detonated.

ONBOARD THE AN-124

Tanner was sipping a tepid cup of stale coffee and trying to stay busy. He'd watched the refueling through the observation ports and was impressed to see his boys get their gas so expertly, having never refueled behind an AN-124 before. Now they were penetrating Northern Sandor and soon the shit would hit the fan. He was given the flight engineer's workstation as a worktable where he had maps of Sandor, satellite imagery of the target and the MiG-41 flight manual laid out for emergency use. He also could run the SatCom system from this seat and he was monitoring it constantly, listening for both voice as well as text messages printed out on a small thermal printer next to the keyboard.

He was nervous. He could not smoke, although the Russian pilot told him it was okay. Thirty years in the USAF didn't allow him to even think about smoking a cigarette on a military airplane. He paced instead. The rear cockpit bulkhead behind the flight engineer's station was mostly open to the cargo area so he paced back and forth, dragging his comm cord with him, which connected his headset to the ships comm system. The Russian flight crew found it amusing the American general was so fidgety, however, in keeping with Russian military procedures, they had not been briefed on what the MiGs were attacking this night. As far as they knew it was all a joint exercise. They might have been a little nervous themselves had they known, the truth, which was even far scarier than the lie Tanner believed.

On one of his circuits pass his station he noticed a strip of shiny metallic paper sticking out of the thermal printer for the SATCOM. *That wasn't there a moment ago*, he thought, grabbing the strip. It contained a message in plain text from Sutherland. He read the message and as he did his mouth fell open in disbelief.

LOW LEVEL
CENTRAL SANDOR

Now came the real reason for being here, the bomb run was coming up fast. In their cockpits each man got ready for the attack, setting up weapons panels and removing safeties. Although each plane had a slightly different weapons load, each would put at least one weapon of the WSA ensuring the structure and it's content's destruction. The target area was seventy miles off the nose, a short seven minutes flight. Just as they rolled out onto the bomb run a voice came over Olmstead's satellite radio, a familiar voice.

"Arson, this is Maddog on Satellite Channel One. Abort mission, repeat abort mission, this is a rain out, repeat a rainout," the voice called.

What the hell? Olmstead said into his mask.

"Say again, Maddog," Olmstead called, this time selecting Satellite One and keying the mic.

"This is Maddog. I repeat target is not valid," the voice said. "Arson Lead, listen carefully. This whole mission is a set up. Dobrinsky has gone rogue. Repeat he is off the reservation. He is carrying a biological weapon, probably disguised as a fuel tank---a Smallpox weapon, Hawk. His orders are to dump it in the target area. It'll spread smallpox virus all through Sandor within a month. You have to stop Dobrinsky from delivering that weapon. "

Son of a bitch! Olmstead thought. "Any ideas about just how to do that, Maddog? If I shoot him down won't that release the virus?"

That was a problem. Knowing there was a bio-weapon on Dobrinsky's aircraft was one thing. Keeping the weapon from deploying either intentionally or accidentally was something else entirely.

"The fire from the internal fuel tanks might kill the virus if it impacts the ground in one piece," Maddog radioed, sounding unsure.

"What if he blows apart in mid-air and there is no fire on the ground?"

"Your call, Hawkeye," Maddog conceded. "I don't have any answers. You can't recover back in Russia. I'm working a deal with the Navy right now. Plan to head south into the Gulf for egress. Take care of your little problem and get back with me. Pronto."

"You're sure about this, Maddog?" Olmstead asked hesitantly.

"That's affirm, Hawk."

"Roger," was all Olmstead could think to say.

There was a long pause. This is a hell of a lot to think about in five minutes, Olmstead thought. That was how long they had until they'd fly right over that target area. Dobie a traitor? A rogue agent? Or just a tool of the Russian government who has not given up its expansionist aims? Who cared at this point? There was no way he'd allow anyone to commit genocide, even against the Sandoris. Now how to do it?

Olmstead glanced back over his shoulder. There was Dobrinsky's plane, in tight high left echelon. *I'm not even going to be able to give him a chance*, Olmstead thought. If he suspects anything he'll just drop the weapon. It might spread the virus or might not. It all depended on whether any hosts were passing by. Of course that's the same gamble he would be taking if he shot him down. I have to kill him with extreme prejudice, no warning. It would be murder, but justified…wasn't it? Olmstead didn't have time to think about it. Now how to do it? I gotta isolate him from the rest of the team and take a point blank shot. The problem was there was no way to let anyone else in on it without giving Dobrinsky warning. Five minutes to go.

"Arson Flight, take spacing between elements," he said. "Let's spread it out just a bit for the bomb run. Forty nine miles to go."

This made sense tactically; in case a plane had to maneuver for a threat it gave them a little room to play with. He watched as the lights of the two other elements dimmed as they moved away, Fletch still on his right echelon, in close. He selected AA-11 on his weapons panel and flipped the targeting mode to HMS. He turned to look at Dobrinsky and Gurevich's element in the dim starlight. In his HMS he could see them in bright Infrared, their heat standing out brilliantly against the coolness of the desert night. The targeting-cue was hopping between aircraft, Dobrinsky to Gurevich and back again, the heat signature of each plane fighting for dominance in the HMS.

"Damn," Olmstead said to himself. *I need them farther apart.* He could not get a solid lock. If he fired now it was a toss up as to who would get the missile.

"Arson, let's loosen up the element's a tad, guys," he said nonchalantly, as if simply critiquing their technique and trying to ease off on the tension. Off his right wing he saw space open between himself and Fletcher. He glanced back over his other shoulder. The distance between Dobrinsky and Gurevich opened a bit, but was still too damn close. He was running out of time.

Just a short three minutes to target and Olmstead could see the lights of civilization ahead. Once we get over a populated area it won't matter where the damn bomb comes down. People'll be climbing all over it by morning. It was now or never. The missile lock was still sporadic, but he had no choice. He'd pickle all four of his AA-11s off and hope something hit Dobrinsky.

He glanced over his shoulder again and took a last look. He keyed the mic, "Gurevich, break left, now!!" he screamed into the mic as he squeezed off all four AA-11s.

The Archers came off the rails like hungry wolves looking prey, facing the wrong way, but knowing which way to go for the easy meal. The missiles pivoted in space and came back over the shoulder, bracketing the element that was Dobrinsky and Gurevich. Gurevich had loaded the Gs within a half second of hearing the warning. He opened an additional fifty feet of spacing from his wingman and the IR ambiguity was gone. All four missiles impacted Dobrinsky's plane, rupturing fuel tanks and producing a blinding fireball which followed the debris to the ground below, leaving a blazing trail of jet fuel a quarter mile long on the desert floor. That's the best I can do, thought Olmstead.

Gurevich's plane tumbled in the expanding shock wave of the explosion, the sides of his aircraft peppered with fragments from the missile warhead as well as Dobrinsky's MiG. Blinded by the flash of the explosion and with every warning sound the aircraft made filling his helmet, Gurevich blindly kept the backpressure on the stick. He knew where the ground was and flying away from that until his vision recovered seemed the best bet. His MiG, already at 550 knots for the bomb run, had a lot of energy and it rocketed upwards after the explosion. As he passed 3000 meters above sea level the barometric fuse gave an audible click, just as it sent the required electrical pulse out to the six demolition charges attached to the airframe in strategic area. These charges lived up to their name as Gurevich's plane exploded in a fireball even larger than the GRU man before him.

"Holy shit," cried Fletcher, close enough to have seen the missiles streaking off the wings. "Are you insane, Hawkeye!"

"Easy, guys," Olmstead said. "I can't explain now, but Dobrinsky was on the wrong team. It was a double-cross. I just got off the SatCom with Maddog."

"Gurevich too?" Romano asked, not believing his ears.

"I don't know," he said. "He just blew up, might have caught some frag. The target is a rain out, I say again target is a rain out."

"Not another screw up," Cahill moaned.

"You have no idea," Olmstead said. "Okay, form up on me tight. We're heading south to the Gulf. I'm waiting for words right now."

The remaining MiGs closed in tight and streaked toward the south. Olmstead tried reaching Tanner, but there was no answer. Soon behind them the RWR gear indicated another pair of F-14s up and hunting. The signals were faint, but that would soon change, Olmstead thought.

"Check your RWR gear, guys," Romano said.

"Yeah, got it," Fletch replied.

"Can we push it up?" Cahill asked. "If they are up at 25,000 feet they'll be running up our ass at Mach 2 while we're sitting down here subsonic. Ain't gonna take long to get within Phoenix range."

"If they got anymore Phoenixes," Fletcher said.

"We go to burners, Zone 1, we might get Mach 1.2," Olmstead said. "and we'll be out of gas in twenty minutes."

"We'll be over the Gulf in twenty minutes," Fletcher said optimistically.

"What's Maddog planning? Don't tell me we have to put these bitches on a carrier deck?"

"He didn't say," Olmstead said. "Hold off on the burners, guys."

Just then a crackle of static came across the SatCom in Olmstead's cockpit.

"Arson, Maddog, how copy?"

"Copy you Maddog," Olmstead answered. "Do you have words?"

"Roger, squids agree to play," he said. "Here's the plan."

Maddog relayed the plan to a skeptical Olmstead who passed it along to his equally skeptical wingmen. The plan was simple, easy and nearly foolproof. It could also kill you.

"Maddog, Arson, no questions," Olmstead said. "See you after the game. Good luck."

There was only static now.

"Maddog, Arson." No reply. That's not a good omen, Olmstead thought.

"Okay, boys, we've lost contact with Maddog," he said. "Any last questions?"

At that moment his RWR gear lit up. The two F-14s were locked on to them at their seven o'clock. He checked his jammers and saw they were already transmitting, trying to break their radar lock.

"Bear, you and Cowboy make for the waves," he said. "Fletch and I will keep the Tomcats off you for a while. We'll talk on Winchester secure."

"Roger, good luck, Hawk," Romano called, as he and Cahill broke formation.

"Go to Winchester, secure," Romano instructed Cahill to go to frequency 303.0, which was nicknamed Winchester for the legendary Winchester 30-30.

"We're too fucking heavy, Fletch," Olmstead called. " We need some speed."

"Jettison your HARMs, Hawkeye," Fletcher called, as he flipped a switch and sent his two AS-23 missiles crashing to the earth below. Olmstead did the same and the loss of drag did help the acceleration slightly. They had full burners selected and slid past Mach One smoothly. The F-14s were still at their 6 o'clock, their radars still locked onto the retreating MiGs.

"What do you think, Fletch?" Olmstead asked. "Your jammers active?"

"Roger, but I think we're pissing into the wind against the AWG-9," he said wryly. "We can't keep showing them our asses at this altitude."

Fletch looked down at his RWR panel and checked the F-14's PRF, or pulse repetition frequency. A high PRF meant they were very close and that is what the digital readout showed.

"Dave, check out their PRF. They're close, man," he said. "Too close for AIM-54s. They gotta have Sparrows or Sidewinders. We're gonna have to fight."

Olmstead confirmed what Fletch was saying. He agreed the F-14s would have shot already had they carried Phoenix missiles, but they were probably very close to Sparrow range. Since it was a tail shot with a fleeing high-speed target, the F-14s would have to get close to their targets, lest the missile run out of energy before it overtook them.

"I agree," Olmstead said. "We're too low to get much better than Mach 1 and those guys might be ten thousand feet higher and doing Mach 2. We have to fight."

Twelve miles behind them and fifteen thousand feet above them the pilot of the lead F-14 was concentrating on his HUD display. A small box in the bottom left of his HUD displayed the range to the enemy and showed it decreasing steadily. The closure on the target was a good 200 knots. He glanced at the "In Range" indicator for his missiles on the left side of the HUD, not yet, but any second now. It was inevitable the cowardly Kumaris would mount a sneak attack in their inferior Russian hardware and now rather than turn and fight. They were running away. It was obvious they were inexperienced and frightened. They were running straight out into the Persian Gulf. Nowhere for them to go. At these speeds they wouldn't have enough fuel to reach any safe base.

The GCI controller said they were probable MiG-29s, due to the passive detection of their Slotback radars. *Not quite as helpless as a MiG 21 or 23, but a juicy target nevertheless*, the pilot thought. Once again they would show the Kumari dog that Sandor would not be trifled with.

Olmstead weighed their options. The warrior in him took over. "Roger," he said. "I'll break right, you go low left. I'll take the northernmost target. Stay low, got it?"

"Roger," was all Fletch said as he sat up straighter I the cockpit and tightened his grip on the stick and throttles. He had AA-12 selected and armed on his HUD. He had his IRST slewed to his radar, which was now in Track While Scan mode.

"Three, two, one, break!" Olmstead called, deploying his speedbrakes and slamming the stick hard to the right. The instant he dropped below Mach 1 he thumbed a little paddle on his throttle and hit maximum deflection on his thrust vectoring system for to assist the turn. In his cockpit, Fletch did the same.

The two MiGs didn't execute a normal, smooth high G turn. They performed a maneuver outside the normal envelope of comparable Western Fighters and once again demonstrated the phenomenal ability of the MiG to point the nose wherever the pilot wants it. They nearly pivoted in space, their forward airspeed bleeding to near zero as they hit their afterburners to regain the lost energy. They had both pulled instantaneous 11 G turns and would have black out had the turn not been over in a mere six seconds, their G suits crushingly tight against their abdomen and lower extremities.

In the Sandori F-14s, the pilots were stunned by the information their HUDs were giving them. The radar momentarily lost lock. When it did reacquire a few seconds later they couldn't believe their eyes. It seemed impossible for their quarry to have changed speed and aspect angle so rapidly. The MiGs had been heading directly away from them, a 180 degree-aspect angle with a closure of only 200 knots. Now they had split up and were heading directly toward them with a better than a 1000 knots of closure, and the range was only 10 miles!

Olmstead and Fletcher rolled out and each got a radar lock on his target in less than five seconds. The IRST, slewed to the radar lock, showed the white-hot dot of the closing Tomcat. Olmstead and Fletcher both selected AA-11, got solid tones and fired.

"Arson Lead, Fox 2," Olmstead called.

"Arson Two, Fox 2," Fletcher said, two seconds later.

The two MiGs didn't even know the Archers were inbound. Lacking an infrared targeting system they had to rely on their radar missiles for shots BVR. The lead F-14 was hit first. The pilot saw a flash of light as the Archer streaked past his port side and into his number one engine. He felt the impact at once and did not hesitate. Some voice in the back of his head told him it was a fatal blow and he initiated ejection immediately. He was lucky. The voice was right. The missile impacted inside the first stage compressor in the port engine intake. The blast blew turbine blades off their shafts and the fragments of hot metal, projectiles now, sliced through hydraulic lines, fuel lines and a center fuel tank, causing the tank to rupture and explode, blowing the stricken F-14 apart. The ejection seat managed to escape the fireball and the pilot survived with bruises and minor shrapnel in his left knee.

The other F-14 was not hit directly. A jink at the last second caused the missile to near miss down the right side. The proximity fuse of the AA-11saw the Doppler shift it was looking for and detonated, spraying hot cubes of steel shrapnel down the length of the fuselage of the lone Tomcat. This shrapnel ripped open the right side engine and started a fire. Crimson fire warning lights lit up the front panel of the now wounded F-14. The pilot pulled his right engine fuel cutoff T-handle and brought the throttle back over its detent to shutdown. He then rolled inverted and performed a Split S as if to disengage.

Fletcher saw the F-14 apparently retreating and he decided not to press home for the kill. He lit his burners and yanked back on the stick, performing a perfect Immelman and rolling right side up and running back out to sea.

"Lead, Arson Two is disengaging," he said. "Heading 180, at Base plus 5."

"Rog, I've got a Judy on you," Olmstead called back, indicating he had Fletcher on his radar. He turned to an intercept course to rejoin his wingman, who was about ten miles south of his location.

One of the basic rules of aerial combat, since the days of biplanes dog fighting over France, was a simple one: Always press home the attack, never break off the attack and run. This was a surefire way to allow the enemy a chance to re-engage. When Fletcher saw the flash of the missile detonation and the F-14 performing a Split S he assumed it was badly damaged and the pilot was trying to disengage. To a certain extent he was right. The Sandori was hurt, but not fatally, at least not yet. His radar still operating, the stricken F-14 pilot decided to pop off all of his remaining missiles at his fleeing attacker. He turned back into the fight and with a good tone in his helmet, pressed his trigger five times. A few seconds later his fire spread along the wing and he and his RIO punched out, leaving one old Tomcat in a plunge to its death and four heat seeking Sidewinder missiles screaming toward the fleeing MiGs.

The infrared warning gear in both MiGs screamed a warning. Oh, shit, Fletcher thought.

"Fletcher, break hard right," he shouted. "Inbound missiles, six o'clock."

Fletcher saw and heard the beeping of the IR gear even before he heard Olmstead's warning. He flipped the MiG over on its back and performed a Split S coupled with a hard turn to the right, punching out flares all the way. He kicked in the thrust vector system and the nose skidded around hard.

If there were only three missiles inbound he might have had a chance, but the salvo of four AIM-9s had him bracketed, no way to avoid all four. It was computer versus man, gyro versus inner ear, microchip versus brain. In these modern days of aerial combat, the flesh and blood usually come up the loser.

All four AIM-9s sensed their nearest approach and the IR Doppler shift signaled each warhead to explode in a shower of shrapnel, bracketing Fletcher's MiG which exploded in a ball of flame, three seconds later.

Olmstead stared in horror at the fireball that had been Fletch's MiG. Then he heard it, faint at first, but it as there. He heard the beeping of an ELT on Guard frequency. He listened carefully and could only hear one ELT, but whose was it? Fletcher's or the F-14 pilot's?

He didn't have time to figure it out. As he reconfigured his radar to a long range scan he counted three more aircraft to the north heading his way, MiGs this time. This confused him until he realized they were Sandori MiG-41s. It was time to get out of here. He turned southbound, out to sea, and lit his burners. He was lighter now and he accelerated nicely, stabilizing at Mach 1.5. A glance at his fuel gauge gave him a sudden sense of urgency. He had maybe fifteen minutes of gas left and that was if he killed the burners right now. He selected UHF radio and keyed the mic.

Now it was up to Tanner's plan, he thought. He flipped his radar range setting out to maximum and could see four aircraft, two formations of two headed towards each other. Olmstead surmised the far group must be US Navy F-14s and the near Romano and Cahill. They were closing beak to beak at better than a thousand knots. *I hope Tanner knows what he's doing*, he thought.

On his RWR gear he saw the AWG-9s of the two US Tomcats locking up his colleagues. Now the timing had to be just right. They were fifty miles apart when Olmstead got the first indication of a missile launch, two Phoenix missiles to be more precise, now rocketing toward his friends. A minute later both MiGs disappeared from his radarscope. In the distance he thought he saw the flashes of missile detonation.

The silky female voice of the automated warning system suddenly broke the silence in his cockpit. "Warning, low fuel, ten minutes flight time remaining." The voice messages were recorded at the MiG factory and Olmstead, like most of the pilots in the Russian Air Force, wished he could meet the woman behind that voice.

Olmstead switched his radar range again and peered intently at the scope, ignoring the fuel warning. The two F-14s were 93 miles off his nose and closing fast. For the first time he also noticed two more contacts, very low, at 50 miles, moving slowly towards him at 110 knots. The slow contacts were probable helicopters. One check of the RWR panel indicated a now familiar site. Two AWG-9 radars were locked onto him. He reached down and flipped the MiG onto autopilot. It was almost time. In his mind he remembered Tanner's instructions.

"Drive right into their carrier defensive zone. Do not reply to their radio calls. F-14 Tomcats will lock you up and fire Phoenix missiles at you. As soon as your RWR gear gives you a launch indication you will eject. They will blow your MiG into a million pieces and we will report to the Sandoris there were no survivors. The rescue helicopter will pick you up within minutes. Have your ELT off for the ejection, but be ready to use it once in your life raft. Listen up and whatever you do, do not answer their transmissions. We have to make this look real."

"Roger," Olmstead had said, uncomfortable with the thought of a big missile like the AIM-54 heading at him at Mach 3.

The radio crackled to life. The Tomcats were transmitting on Guard frequency 243.0.

"Aircraft at Flight Level 180, heading 330, this is Rambo 21, you are approaching a United States warship in international waters. You will break off your approach, decrease velocity and reverse course immediately. How copy?"

Olmstead remained silent, but tightened up his parachute straps, disconnected his automatic ELT lanyard and performed one last safety check of the cockpit. *The plane had performed flawlessly and it was a shame to send it to Davy Jones' locker*, he thought. On the other hand he was glad to be getting the hell out of these MiGs and this program. He looked forward to climbing back into his F-15 and being a real Air Force Officer again.

"Aircraft we are tracking, reverse course immediately or you will be fired upon. You are in violation of a United States warship's defensive zone. Repeat, decrease velocity and reverse course. This is your last warning," the Tomcat pilot said.

On his radar the two F-14s were at 35 miles and he could see them open the gap between aircraft slightly in clearing each other to loose their big AIM 54s. Olmstead knew it was all going to happen very soon. He pulled his throttles back to 90 percent and engaged the speed brakes momentarily to slow to 450 knots, well below Mach 1.Well, I may as well make this look good, Olmstead thought. He reached down and killed his active jammers, to make sure the AIM-54 didn't bite off on a false target. Then he thumbed a switch on his throttles and locked his radar onto the lead F-14. In the F-14s cockpit the tone of a radar lock began sounding in the pilots' ears. *That would be the expected aggressive move*, he thought.

Olmstead's RWR gear lit up with the AIM-54 missile guidance radar. He pulled the cord of his emergency parachute oxygen bottle and felt a blast of cool air in his mask. He checked the auto-pilot to be sure it was engaged, took one last look around, took a deep breath and reached overhead for the ejection handle. As he pulled it downward the last thing he saw in the cockpit was the RWR gear going wild indicating an AIM-54 inbound. Then he heard the explosive bolts blow the canopy away, felt a tremendous kick in the ass as the rocket motor ignited. He pulled an instantaneous 14 Gs and was finally hit by the blast of 500 mile an hour wind, knocking the breath out of him just as the G forces caused him to black out.

The AIM-54 guided straight and true. It would have had a hard time against a maneuvering MiG, but not tonight. *This MiG was behaving just like a fighter-bomber carrying an Exocet missile,* the Tomcat pilot thought. . *Obviously the "Kumari" flying this jet was on a suicide mission. First an attack on Sandor, now attacking a US warship?* And the fact that he didn't even maneuver meant he must have been so intent on pressing in and getting that missile off he didn't care about the missiles coming inbound on him. In any case the big Phoenix hit with a tremendous impact and the warhead, designed for taking down bombers, literally blew the MiG into metallic dust that rained down over the ocean for the next hour.

Olmstead awoke with the jerk of his chute opening just in time to see the fireball in the distance.

The term distance is a relative one. The explosion was more than five miles away, but Olmstead swore he could feel the heat of the blast through his Nomex flying suit.

As he floated down he ran through the post-ejection checklist every aviator was made to memorize in survival school: Canopy…visor…mask…seat kit…LPUs…four line…steer…. Prepare…splash…release J2s. First thing he did was look up to make sure his chute was okay and didn't have any malfunctions. It looked just fine. Then he raised his visor, disconnected and threw away his oxygen mask and deployed his seat kit, the small one man rubber life raft inflating in a mere ten seconds. His LPUs, life preserver units, were contained in a horse collar arrangement on his parachute harness and would automatically inflate when they hit the seawater. They could also be manually triggered which he decided would be the prudent thing to do, since his life depended on these things. He decided it would be best to know if something was wrong with them now at fifteen thousand feet, rather than when he hit the water. If he had to he could pull them out by hand and blow them up through a small tube. His fears were for naught, however, as they fully inflated in three seconds.

The Four Line modification was a way to steer the parachute by pulling to sets of cords on the rear risers. These would disconnect four of the rear parachute lines and cause air to spill out the back of the chute, giving the chute some forward momentum. This allowed the pilot to steer the parachute into the wind and hit the water with the least amount of forward travel possible. With out the four-line modification the pilot would hit the water with whatever velocity the wind was blowing and it could cause injury. The danger of using the four line at night, though, was if you couldn't tell which way the wind was blowing you could land with the wind and hit even harder. Olmstead looked at the inky blackness below and decided he wouldn't take the chance tonight.

The black of night play tricks on the eyes and it can be hard to judge your height above the water. The solution to that problem was to just bend the knees slightly, back straight, eyes on the horizon, thumbs on the parachute releases and wait for the impact. Splash! Olmstead hit the water hard and went under. As soon as he felt the impact he pulled the J2 releases on his harness and released his chute.

He kicked to the surface as the parachute separated and settled over him like a sheet thrown over a bed on a hot humid night. He broke the surface directly beneath the nylon chute. He felt the wet nylon tight against his face and immediately stopped his flailing. He knew the danger of this. The parachute was now a giant fish net that could ensnare him and drown him if he got tangled in it. It was hard enough to do this in broad daylight, but in the black of night he couldn't even see the chute, only feel its wet tightness against him. Slowly he began feeling for a panel cord. He found one and began to slowly pull the chute over his face hand over hand following that cord. After a minute he felt the center opening go over his head and he knew he was only halfway home. Damn, the bad luck, he cursed. If he'd pulled the other direction he'd have been out by now. He was lying on his back in the water, his face breaking the surface beneath the wet nylon, water lapping at his eyes and mouth. He kept on his methodical pulling, hand over hand until at last the edge of the chute fell away and he was clear of it. He opened his eyes and thought he'd gone blind at first, it was that dark. He looked up and knew his eyes were okay. The sky was alive with millions of crystal clear twinkling stars.

He reached down to his waist and grabbed the lanyard that was attached to the life raft. He pulled it hand over hand and eventually the life raft came out from under the chute and floated over to him. He closed the covers of his harness releases so he wouldn't puncture the little raft, and climbed into it. The little rubber raft was black with a spray shield that was colored bright orange inside. It could be closed and the raft effectively camouflaged in the sea or it could be spread wide open and used to signal for help. Tonight no one would care what color it was. The only way they were going to find him was by lighting a flare, of which he had two in his seat kit. He quickly retrieved the flares and his survival radio from the kit and waited in the darkness of the night, the only sound the gentle slapping of the water against his small craft. He waited the thirty minutes as instructed then keyed the radio mic.

"Rescue, Rescue, Arson Lead, how copy?" he said. Silence.

He keyed the mic again. "Rescue, Rescue, Arson Lead, how copy?"

The radio crackled. "Arson, key your mic for ten seconds then standby," the voice on the radio said.

He did as requested and waited. Soon he could hear the wop-wopping sound of a helicopter approaching.

"Arson, pop flare," he was commanded.

The flare had two ends, one for day, which produced a cloud of red smoke, the other for night, which produced a bright red flame. He uncapped the night end of the flare, extended the little bar and pushed it down with his thumb. The flare lit up bright, so bright it blinded his night-adjusted eyes and he threw his free hand over his face while he waved the flare back and forth. He was careful not to hold the flare over his raft as burning liquid dripping from the flare would melt a hole through his raft.

A minute later the helicopter was directly overhead and Olmstead struggled to keep the little raft upright in the rotor wash. A Navy diver entered the water and was soon at his side, helping him aboard the extraction device that had been lowered. Two minutes later he was safely inside and on his way to the carrier. It was the first time he felt relaxed in a long time. The cool night air and the vibration of the copter soon put him right to sleep, exhausted from the mission and emotionally drained. The last thing that went through his mind as he drifted to sleep was Fletch giving him that last thumbs up just before they took off back in Russia.

He awoke as the helicopter touched down with a bump on the deck of the carrier. He was met by a young Marine private cradling an M-16 in his arms.

"Sir, I'm Private First Class Gomez, and I'm to escort you below," the Marine said, saluting.

Olmstead returned the salute. It was a good sign. The salute meant that at least the young Marine's first thoughts weren't about killing him.

"Lead, the way, Private," he said, hopping down out of the helicopter.

He was led to a conference room deep in the bowels of the ship.

"Sir, you are to go right in," the Marine said. "I'll be waiting outside the door, sir." Olmstead nodded.

He opened the door and stepped inside. Romano and Cowboy were sitting at a central table. They stood when he came in.

"Dave, you okay?" Romano asked, shaking his hand.

"Yeah, you hurt?" Cowboy asked, slapping him on the back.

Olmstead shook his head wearily. "No, I'm alright," he said.

"Fletch?" Romano asked.

Olmstead shook his head sadly.

"How'd he buy it?" Romano asked.

"Does it matter?" Olmstead asked.

"No, I guess not," Romano said. "Any word from Tanner."

"No. He was still in the tanker when I lost contact with him," Olmstead said. "I don't have a good feeling about that."

The three men sat down at the table.

"So what the fuck did Tanner tell you about Dobie?" Romano asked.

"That he was carrying a bio-weapon disguised as a fuel tank and he was going to unleash Smallpox on Sandor," Olmstead said.

"Smallpox? Isn't there a vaccine for that?" Cahill asked.

"Yeah, in some parts of the world," he admitted. "We have a vaccine."

"And so does Russia, right?" Romano asked, his eyes gleaming with sudden understanding.

"I guess so."

"They were going to kill off the population of Sandor and take over the oil and port facilities," Romano surmised. "Makes sense. They tried it with Afghanistan. Make it look like Achmed launched a Bio-war and they'd even get us on the band wagon with them."

"Could be," Olmstead admitted.

"So there was no nuclear warhead?" Cahill asked.

"Who knows," Romano muttered. "I don't even give a fuck anymore."

Olmstead nodded. "I'm out of this business."

"Ditto," Cahill agreed.

At that moment the door opened and an admiral entered. The pilots came to attention when they saw the braids on his sleeves.

"Gentlemen, my name is Admiral Reeves," he said, sitting down at the head of the table. "I'm senior commander of this task force and we need to have a talk. This whole 'rescue' is the result of an HF communication with a General Tanner. He dropped the right authentication codes and call signs, some very high profile call signs by the way, so we had no choice but to assist. Now I want some answers. I don't give a shit what your security clearance is, let's just assume I'm higher, okay?"

The three pilots looked at each other and all three shrugged. What the hell, Olmstead thought.

"Does what we tell you stay in this room, sir?" he asked. The Admiral nodded.

"Good enough for me," Olmstead said. They spilled their guts.

EPILOGUE

A month later Olmstead was standing alone in Arlington National Cemetery over a small, modest headstone. On it was the name: Michael David Fletcher, Captain, USAF. Olmstead laid a wreath of yellow tulips on the headstone and stepped back. There was a drizzling rain in the air that was threatening snow, the skies cottony white with the coming winter. Water droplets fell off the bill of Olmstead's service wheel cap and down the front of the issue raincoat. He didn't seem to notice the rain. In his mind he was ten thousand miles away, in the middle of the desert, sitting beside a tent, smoking a cigarette with Fletch as the mechanics hurriedly prepared their MiGs for flight.

Of course they never recovered the body and the Sandoris were closed-lipped about the whole incident. The plane had exploded so there would have been very little left to put in a casket in any event. Like many of the graves marked here in Arlington, this grave was a mere monument, no body lie in rest beneath. Just a simple head stone and a white stone cross, among thousands who went before him. The same was true of Tanner who died in the explosion of the AN-124. The Russian investigation said malfunction, but Olmstead didn't buy it. Likewise Michaels dying in a terrorist attack the same day? *What do the Russians take us for*, he wondered? Still nearly everyone in the United States who knew about the team was dead and even after being debriefed by the CIA and DIA there was no US policy change with Russia. This was something Uncle Sam wanted to forget about or just didn't know.

Sutherland turned up in Germany a few weeks after the mission. He'd just walked away from the Russian Air Base and kept on going. No one really missed him. The one man who might have missed him, Komiskov, was dead. The plan to infect Sandor had failed and with failure came certain traditional punishments in Russia, Communist or Capitalist. The Bio-bomb did not get a good dispersion of bomblets when it impacted the ground still attached to the dying aircraft. As Tanner hoped the several thousand pounds of burning jet fuel incinerated the gelatinous, virus-laden substance, and an entire country was saved, a very lucky country.

"I'm so sorry, Fletch," he said, staring down at the grave. "You were a strong man, strong where it counted, in your soul, your convictions. You were a great officer and you should have never let yourself get dragged into this mess. I don't know what your motivations were for joining the team. We compromised our honor and our integrity for a little vengeance. They destroyed a good man when they brought you into this. They destroyed us all and we let them. We jumped at the chance. In the end it killed all of us all, one way or another. Rest in peace, friend."

Olmstead glanced at his watch. He'd have just enough time to make his flight back to Nellis. As he walked back to his car and man approached him, wearing a black coat and dark sunglasses. There was no doubt it was a spook and for a moment Olmstead thought, "Well, Fletch, I guess I'll be seeing you sooner than I thought." He expected the man to produce a silenced 9 mm at any moment.

"Captain, my name is Special Agent Collins," the young man said. "We need to speak. It's a bit of an emergency, I'm afraid."

"What now?" Olmstead said gruffly, annoyed by the intrusion on such a private affair. "I'm on leave for thirty days and as far as I'm concerned there are no emergencies."

Collins stopped and just looked at him with impatience. He folded his arms across his chest and waited. Olmstead made a move around him and he stepped into his path. Olmstead tried again and met the same response. It was clear he was going to be heard.

"Alright, alright," Olmstead said with annoyance, glancing again at his watch. "You have two minutes. What is your goddamned emergency?"

Collins began. "Pakistan and India have broken off diplomatic relations and are beginning to deploy tactical nuclear forces throughout their countries. We need a reconnaissance capability that can map out the deployments of both side's weapons."

"So use a satellite," Olmstead broke in.

"We need a system more flexible than satellites. It takes too long and costs too much to change orbits and if there's any high cloud cover they're virtually useless. It's the rainy season and the satellites are nearly useless. The closest U-2 is based in Japan," Collins insisted. "and even if they could reach India or Pakistan we can't just invade their airspace to spy on them."

"So what do you want with me?"

Collins paused for a moment, a sly smile forming at the corner of his lips.

"You ever flown a MiG-25?" he asked.